The Secrets of
Nicholas Flamel

BOOK 4

ᚯ ☉ ♏ ⊕ ⚸ ♏ THE ▽ ᚯ ☉ ♏ ⊕

NECROMANCER

www.thealchemyst.co.uk
www.randomhousechildrens.co.uk

Josh Newman

Josh Newman was born on December 21st 1991, just seconds after his twin sister, Sophie, with whom he has a very strong bond, as is often the case with twins. Tall, athletic, with blond hair and blue eyes, Josh is quite impulsive, hates snakes, rats, spiders and scorpions and sometimes suffers from claustrophobia. He is not at all sure that he trusts Nicholas Flamel. His aura is gold, with a scent of orange.

Sophie Newman

Also blonde, with blue eyes, Sophie Newman tends to be more trusting and less quick to judge than her twin brother, Josh. She is still learning how to control her new powers of the Magic of the Air and the Magic of Fire. Sophie is aware that Josh seems strangely jealous of her magical powers. Her magical aura is silver, with a scent of vanilla.

Nicholas Flamel

Nicholas Flamel was born in France in 1330 and is a powerful alchemyst. With his wife, Perenelle, he discovered the secret of immortality contained within the Book of Abraham, the Codex, which also contains the spell which would allow the Dark Elders to regain control of our world. The Flamels have spent centuries protecting the Codex while searching for the twins of prophecy, whose magical powers, once fully awakened, could banish the Dark Elders forever. Severely weakened in the battle at Stonehenge, Nicholas has transported the twins to San Francisco. His magical aura is green with a scent of peppermint.

Perenelle Flamel

Tall, elegant, with black hair and green eyes, the seventh daughter
of a seventh daughter and over 600 years old, Perenelle Flamel is a
powerful alchemyst and sorceress. Like her husband, Perry uses the
spells in the Codex to become immortal. Without the book, which
was stolen by Dr. John Dee, neither of the Flamels can renew their
immortality and will soon begin to age rapidly. Perry can see
ghosts and her aura is white, without a specific scent.

Dr. John Dee

Originally magician and advisor to the Tudor queen, Elizabeth
I, Dr. John Dee is an immortal, bound to serve the Dark Elders.
Having once served as an apprentice to Nicholas Flamel, from
whom he learned alchemy and other arcane secrets, Dee now has
an abiding hatred for his former teacher. His Dark Elder master is
getting increasingly impatient with his failure to recapture the final
two pages of the Codex. Dee's magical aura is yellow with a scent
of brimstone.

Scathach

Also known as Scatty, this slight, athletic girl with spiky red hair
appears to be about 17 years old but has been in this world for
millennia. She is both a Next Generation Elder and a vampire.
She is an implacable foe while being capable of strong love and
friendship. She and Joan of Arc are currently trapped in what
appears to be the Pleistocene era. Her magical aura is grey of
unknown scent.

Joan of Arc

The history books will tell you that the heroine of France, Joan of Arc, was burned at the stake in 1431 at the age of nineteen. In fact, she was rescued in the last seconds by her close friend, Scathach, (see *The Death of Joan of Arc* ebook) and became an immortal. Joan is very thin, about Sophie's height, with auburn hair and grey eyes. Like Sophie, her aura is silver but with a scent of lavender.

Francis, Comte de Saint-Germain

The chart topping techno-music star, known to his legions of fans as "Germain", is in fact the immortal Francis, Comte de Saint-Germain. A performer since his time in the salons and theatres of 18th century London, Germain also spent time with Nicholas Flamel studying alchemy. He has long, curly black hair, blue eyes and tattoos of butterflies around his wrists. He uses the Magic of Fire and is married to Joan of Arc. His aura is red, with the scent of burnt leaves.

Niccolò Machiavelli

Methodical and calculating, the immortal Niccolò Machiavelli, once the most influential philosopher and politician in the 16th century, is now the head of the DGSE (*Direction Générale de la Sécurité Extérieure*), the French external intelligence agency. Following Perenelle's clever escape from Alcatraz, Machiavelli is stranded on the island. Machiavelli's aura is grey with the scent of snakes.

More information about the characters in
these books can be found at
http://j.mp/flamelcharacters

The Secrets of the Immortal
Nicholas Flamel

BOOK 4

THE
NECROMANCER

MICHAEL SCOTT

CORGI

THE NECROMANCER

A CORGI BOOK 978 0552 57843 1

Published in the US by Delacorte Press,
an imprint of Random House Children's Publishers UK
a division of Random House, Inc

First published in Great Britain by Doubleday,
an imprint of Random House Children's Publishers UK

Corgi edition published 2011

3 5 7 9 10 8 6 4

Set in Galliard

Corgi Books are published by Random House Children's Publishers UK,
61–63 Uxbridge Road, London W5 5SA

www.**randomhousechildrens**.co.uk
www.**randomhouse**.co.uk

Addresses for companies within The Random House Group Limited
can be found at: www.randomhouse.co.uk/offices.htm

THE RANDOM HOUSE GROUP Limited Reg. No. 954009
A CIP catalogue record for this book is available from the British Library.

Penguin Random House is committed to a sustainable future for
our business, our readers and our planet. This book is made from
Forest Stewardship Council® certified paper.

Printed and bound in Great Britain by Clays Ltd, Elcograf S.p.A.

For Piers,

Cura te ipsum

I am frightened.

Not for myself, but for those I will leave behind: Perenelle and the twins. I am resigned that we will not recover the Codex in time to save my wife. I have perhaps a week left, certainly no more than two, before old age claims me; Perenelle has no more than two weeks.

I do not want to die. I have lived upon this earth for six hundred and seventy-six years, and there is still so much that I have never done, so much that I wish I still had time to do.

I am grateful, though, that I have lived long enough to discover the twins of legend, and proud that I began their training in the elemental magics. Sophie has mastered three, Josh just one, but he has demonstrated other skills, and his courage is extraordinary.

We have returned to San Francisco, having left Dee for dead in London. I am hoping we have seen the last of him. I am disturbed, however, that Machiavelli is here in the city. Perenelle trapped him and his companion on Alcatraz along with the other monsters, but I am unsure how long the Rock can hold someone like the Italian immortal.

And both Perenelle and I are agreed that Alcatraz is a threat we will have to deal with while we still can. Just knowing that the cells are full of monsters is chilling.

More disturbing, however, is the news that Scathach and Joan of Arc have gone missing. The Notre Dame leygate should have brought them to Mount Tamalpais, but they never turned up. Saint-Germain is frantic with worry, but I reminded him that Scathach is over two and a half thousand years old, and she is the ultimate warrior.

My real concern lies with the twins. I am no longer sure how they view me. I always knew Josh harbored reservations about me, but now I am sensing that they are both fearful and mistrustful. It is true that they discovered portions of my history I would have preferred left uncovered. I am not proud of some of the things I did, but I regret nothing. I did what I had to do to ensure the survival of the entire human race, and I would do it all again.

The twins have gone back to their aunt's house in Pacific Heights. I will give them a day or two to rest and recuperate. Then we will begin again. Their training needs to be completed; they need to be ready when the Dark Elders return.

Because that day is almost upon us.

From the Day Booke of Nicholas Flamel, Alchemyst
Writ this day, Tuesday, 5th June, in
San Francisco, my adopted city

TUESDAY,
5th June

CHAPTER ONE

"Never thought we'd ever see this place again." Sophie Newman grinned and looked at her brother.

"Never thought I'd be so happy to see it," Josh said. "It looks . . . I don't know. Different."

"It looks the same," his twin answered. "We're the ones who've changed."

Sophie and Josh were walking down Scott Street in Pacific Heights, heading for their aunt Agnes's house on the corner of Sacramento Street. They had last seen the house six days earlier—Thursday, May 31—when they had left for work, Sophie at the coffee shop, Josh in the bookstore. It had started as just another ordinary day, but it had turned out to be the last ordinary day they would ever experience.

That day their world had changed forever; they too had changed, both physically and mentally.

"What do we tell her?" Josh asked nervously. Aunt Agnes

was eighty-four, and although they called her aunt, she was not actually related to them by blood. Sophie thought she might have been their grandmother's sister . . . or cousin, or maybe just a friend, but she had never been quite sure. Aunt Agnes was a sweet but grumpy old lady who fussed and worried if they were even five minutes late. She drove both Sophie and Josh crazy and reported back to their parents about every single thing they did.

"We keep it simple," Sophie said. "We stick to the story we told Mom and Dad—first the bookshop closed because Perenelle wasn't feeling well, and then the Flamels . . ."

"The *Flemings*," Josh corrected her.

"The Flemings invited us to stay with them in their house in the desert."

"And why did the bookshop close?"

"Gas leak."

Josh nodded. "Gas leak. And where's the house in the desert?"

"Joshua Tree."

"OK, I got it."

"Are you sure? You're a terrible liar."

Josh shrugged. "I'll try. You know we're going to get grilled."

"I know. And that's even before we have to talk to Mom and Dad."

Josh nodded. He glanced over at Sophie. He'd been mulling something over for the past few days, and figured this would be the perfect time to bring it up. "I've been thinking," he said slowly. "Maybe we should just tell them the truth."

"The truth?" Sophie's expression remained unchanged and the twins continued walking, crossing Jackson Street. They could see their aunt's white wooden Victorian house three blocks away.

"What do you think?" Josh asked, when his sister said nothing more.

Finally Sophie nodded. "Sure, we could." She brushed a few strands of blond hair out of her eyes and looked at her brother. "But just let me get this straight first. We're going to tell Mom and Dad that their entire life's work has been for nothing. That everything they have ever studied—history, archaeology and paleontology—is wrong." Her eyes sparkled. "I think it's a great idea. But I'll let you go ahead and do it, and I'll watch."

Josh shrugged uncomfortably. "OK, OK, so we don't tell them."

"Not yet, in any case."

"Agreed, but it'll come out sooner or later. You know how impossible it is to keep secrets from them. They always know everything."

"That's because Aunt Agnes tells them," Sophie muttered.

A sleek black stretch limousine with tinted windows drove slowly past them, the driver leaning forward, checking addresses on the tree-lined street. The car signaled and pulled in farther down the block.

Josh indicated the limo with a jerk of his chin. "That's weird. It looks like it's stopping outside Aunt Agnes's."

Sophie looked up disinterestedly. "I just wish there was

someone we could talk to," she murmured. "Someone like Gilgamesh." Her blue eyes magnified with sudden tears. "I hope he's OK." The last time she had seen the immortal, he'd just been wounded by an arrow fired by the Horned God. She looked at her brother, irritated. "You're not even listening to me."

"That car *is* stopping outside Agnes's house," Josh said slowly. A vague warning tingled at the back of his skull. "Soph?"

"What is it?"

"When was the last time Aunt Agnes had a visitor?"

"She never has visitors."

The twins watched a slender black-suited driver get out of the car and climb the steps, his black-gloved hand trailing lightly on the metal rail. Their Awakened hearing clearly heard the knock on the door, and unconsciously they increased their pace. They saw their aunt Agnes open the door. She was a slight, bony woman, all angles and planes, with knobby knees and swollen arthritic fingers. Josh knew that in her youth she had been considered a great beauty—but her youth had been a long time ago. She had never married, and there was a family story that the love of her life had been killed in the war. Josh wasn't sure which one.

"Josh?" Sophie asked.

"Something's not right," Josh muttered. He broke into a jog; Sophie fell into step beside him, easily keeping up.

The twins saw the driver's hand move and Aunt Agnes take something from him. She leaned forward, squinting at what looked like a photograph. But when she bent closer to get a better look, the driver immediately slipped around behind her and darted into the house.

Josh took off at a sprint. "Don't let the car leave!" he shouted at Sophie. He raced across the street and up the steps into the house. "Hi, Aunt Agnes, we're home," he called as he ran past her.

The old woman turned in a complete circle, the photograph fluttering from her fingertips.

Sophie followed her brother across the street but stopped behind the car. She stooped and pressed her fingertips against the rear passenger tire. Her thumb brushed the circle on the back of her wrist and her fingers glowed white-hot. She pushed; there was the stink of burning rubber, and then, with five distinct popping sounds, the rubber tire was punctured. Air hissed out and the tire quickly settled onto its metal rim.

"Sophie!" the old woman shrieked as the girl ran up the steps and grabbed her confused aunt. "What's going on? Where have you been? Who was that nice young man? Was that Josh I just saw?"

"Aunt Agnes, come with me." Sophie drew her aunt away from the door, just in case Josh or the driver came rushing out and the old woman was accidentally knocked down. She knelt and picked up the picture her aunt had dropped, then helped the older woman a safe distance away from the house. Sophie looked at the photograph: it was a sepia image of a young woman dressed in what looked like a nurse's uniform.

The word *Ypres* and the date 1914 had been written in white ink in the bottom right-hand corner. Sophie caught her breath—there was no doubt who the person was. The woman in the photograph was Scathach.

Josh stepped into the darkened hallway and pressed flat against the wall, waiting until his eyes had adjusted to the gloom. Last week he wouldn't have known to do that, but then, last week he wouldn't have run into a house after an intruder. He would have done the sensible thing and dialed 911. He reached into the umbrella stand behind the door and lifted out one of his aunt's thick walking sticks. It wasn't Clarent, but it would have to do.

Josh remained still, head tilted to one side, listening. Where was the stranger?

There was a creak on the landing and a young-looking man in a simple black suit, white shirt and narrow black tie came hurrying down the stairs. He slowed when he spotted Josh, but didn't stop. He smiled, yet it seemed more of a reflex than a voluntary gesture—it didn't move past his lips. Now that the man was closer, Josh saw that he was Asian; Japanese, maybe?

Josh stepped forward, the walking stick stretched out in front of him like a sword. "Where do you think you're going?"

"Past you or through you, makes no difference to me," the man said in English tinged with a strong Japanese accent.

"What are you doing here?" Josh demanded.

"Looking for someone," the man answered simply.

The intruder came off the bottom step into the hall and moved to walk out the front door, but Josh barred his route with the stick. "Not so fast. You owe me an answer."

The black-suited man grabbed the stick, yanked it from Josh's grip and snapped it across his knee. Josh grimaced; that had to hurt. The man tossed the two pieces on the floor. "I owe you nothing, but you should be thankful that I am in a good mood today."

There was something in the man's voice that made Josh step back. Something cold and calculating that made him suddenly wonder if the man was entirely human. Josh stood in the doorway and watched the man move lightly down the steps. He was reaching for the car door when he spotted the back tire.

Sophie smiled and waggled her fingers at him. "Looks like you have a puncture."

Josh hurried down the steps and joined his sister and their aunt. "Josh," Agnes said querulously, "what is going on?" Her gray eyes were huge behind thick glasses.

The rear passenger window eased down a fraction and the Japanese man spoke urgently into it, gesturing toward the tire.

Abruptly the door opened and a young woman climbed out. She was dressed in a beautifully tailored black suit over a white silk shirt. There were black leather gloves on her hands and a pair of tiny round black sunglasses perched on her nose. But it was her spiky red hair and pale freckled skin that gave her away.

"Scathach!" both Sophie and Josh cried in delight.

The woman smiled, revealing a mouthful of vampire teeth. She pushed down the glasses to reveal brilliant green eyes. "Hardly," she snapped. "I am Aoife of the Shadows. And I want to know what has happened to my twin sister."

CHAPTER TWO

"Never thought I'd see this place again," Nicholas Flamel said, pushing open the rear door to the Small Bookshop.

"Nor I," Perenelle agreed.

The bottom of the door stuck and Nicholas pressed his shoulder against it and shoved hard. The door scraped on the stone floor and the stench hit them immediately: the slightly sweet stink of rotten wood and moldering paper mixed with the cloying rancid odor of decay. Perenelle coughed and pressed her hand to her mouth, blinking sudden tears from her eyes. "That's foul!"

Nicholas inhaled cautiously. He could still smell traces of Dee's brimstone odor on the dry air, the rotten-egg smell of sulfur. The couple moved down a dark corridor piled high on both sides with boxes of secondhand books. The cardboard boxes were streaked with black rot and the tops had started to curl. Some had burst apart, spilling their contents onto the floor.

Perenelle brushed a fingertip against one and it came away black with mold. She held it up for her husband to see and said, "Tell me?"

"The doctor and I fought," he said softly.

"I can see that," Perenelle said with a smile. "And you won."

"Well, winning is a relative term. . . ." Nicholas opened the door at the end of the corridor and stepped into the bookshop. "I'm afraid the shop did not fare too well." Reaching back, he took his wife's hand and led her into the large book-filled room.

"Oh, Nicholas . . . ," Perenelle breathed.

The bookshop was ruined.

A thick layer of furry green-black mold covered everything, and the smell of sulfur was overwhelming. Books lay everywhere—pages torn, covers shredded, spines broken— among the crushed and splintered tables and shelves that had held them. A huge swath of the ceiling was missing, the plaster hanging like tattered cloth, revealing wooden joists and trailing wires, and where the entrance to the cellar had been was now a gaping hole, the wood around it rotted to a foul black mess speckled with mushrooms. Tiny wriggling white maggots crawled through the muck. The brightly colored rug that had once covered the center of the floor had shriveled to an ugly gray threadbare cloth.

"Destruction and decay," Perenelle murmured, "Dee's

calling card." The tall elegant woman picked her way carefully into the room. Everything she touched either crumbled to dust or dissolved into a powder that gave off spores. The floorboards were spongy and sticky and creaked ominously with each step, threatening to send her into the basement below. Standing in the middle of the room, she put her hands on her hips and turned slowly. Her huge green eyes filled with tears. She had loved this bookshop; it had been their home and their life for a decade. They had worked at many careers through the centuries, but this bookshop more than any other reminded her of her early life with Nicholas, when he had been a scrivener and bookseller in Paris in the fourteenth century. Then, they had been simple, ordinary people, living unremarkable lives, until that fateful day when Nicholas had bought the Codex, the Book of Abraham the Mage, from the hooded man with astonishingly blue eyes. That was the day their mundane lives ended and they entered the world of the extraordinary, where nothing was as it seemed and no one could be trusted.

She turned to look at her husband. He hadn't moved from the door and was staring around the shop with a stricken expression on his face. "Nicholas," she said softly, and when he looked up, she realized just how much the last week had aged him. For centuries, his appearance had changed very little. With his close-cropped hair, unlined face and pale eyes, he'd always looked around fifty years old, which was the age he'd been when they started to make the immortality potion. Today, he looked at least seventy.

Much of his hair was gone, and there were deep wrinkles on his forehead; more lines were etched into the corners of his sunken eyes, and there were dark spots on the back of his hands.

The Alchemyst caught her looking at him and smiled ruefully. "I know. I look old—but still, not too bad for someone who's lived for six hundred and seventy-seven years."

"Seventy-six," Perenelle corrected him gently. "You're not seventy-seven for another three months."

Nicholas stepped forward and gathered Perenelle into his arms, hugging her close. "I don't think that's a birthday I'll be celebrating," he said very softly, his mouth close to her ear. "I've used more of my aura in the past week than I've done in the last two decades. And without the Codex . . ." His voice trailed away. He didn't need to finish the sentence. Without the immortality spell that appeared once a month on page seven in the Codex, he and Perenelle would both begin to age, and death would follow quickly afterward as their accumulated years caught up with them.

Perenelle suddenly pushed her husband away from her. "We're not dead yet!" she snapped, anger making her revert to the provincial French of her youth. "We've been in bad situations before—we survived." The merest suggestion of her aura crackled around her, icy tendrils smoking off her flesh.

Nicholas stepped back and folded his arms across his narrow chest. "We've always had the Codex," he reminded her in the same language.

"I am not talking about immortality now," Perenelle said, her Breton accent thickening. "We have lived centuries,

Nicholas, *centuries*. I am not afraid to die because I know that when we go, we will go together. It is living without you that would be unbearable."

The Alchemyst nodded, not trusting himself to speak. He could not imagine a life without Perenelle.

"We need to do what we have always done," she insisted, "fight for the survival of the human race." Perenelle reached out and caught her husband's arms, her fingers biting painfully into his flesh. "For six hundred years we have protected the Codex and kept the Dark Elders off the earth. We will not stop." Her face turned hard. "But now, Nicholas, we have nothing to lose. Instead of running and hiding to protect the book, we should attack," she said fiercely. "We should take the fight to the Dark Elders."

The Alchemyst nodded uncomfortably. It was at times like these that Perenelle frightened him. Although they had been married for centuries, there was still so much he didn't know about his wife and the extraordinary gift that allowed her to see the shades of the dead. "You're right, we have nothing to lose," Nicholas said softly. "We have lost so much already."

"This time we have the advantage of the twins," Perenelle reminded him.

"I am not sure they will entirely trust us," the Alchemyst said. He took a deep breath. "In London, they learned about the existence of the previous twins."

"Ah," Perenelle said. "From Gilgamesh?"

The Alchemyst nodded. "From the King. Now I'm not sure they will believe anything we tell them."

15

"Well then," Perenelle said with a grim smile. "We tell them the truth. The whole truth," she added, looking hard at her husband.

Nicholas Flamel held her eyes for a moment and then nodded and looked away. "And nothing but the truth." He sighed. He waited until she had left the room and then added softly, "But the truth is a double-edged sword; it is a dangerous thing."

"I heard that," she called.

CHAPTER THREE

"You phone your parents right now." Aunt Agnes glared nearsightedly at Sophie and then turned to Josh, who was closer. "They've been worried sick about you. Phoning me every day, twice, three times a day. Only this morning they said if you weren't home today they were going to contact the police and report you as missing." She paused and then added dramatically, "They were going to say you'd been kidnapped."

"We weren't kidnapped. We talked to Mom and Dad a couple of days ago," Josh muttered. He was desperately trying to remember just when he'd talked to his parents. Was it Friday . . . or was it Saturday? He glanced sideways at his sister, looking for help, but she was still staring at the woman in black who looked so astonishingly like Scathach. He turned back to face his aunt. He knew he'd gotten an e-mail from their parents on . . . was it Saturday when they were all in

17

Paris? Now that he was back in San Francisco, the last few days were beginning to blur together. "We just got back," he said finally, settling on the truth. He kissed his aunt quickly on both cheeks. "How have you been? We missed you."

"You could have called," the tiny woman snapped. "You *should* have called." Flint-gray eyes magnified behind enormous spectacles glared up at the twins. "Worried sick, I've been. I phoned the bookshop a dozen times looking for you, and you never answered your cell. Not much point in having a cell if you don't answer it."

"We had no reception most of the time," Josh said, sticking to the truth, "and then I *lost* my phone," he added, which was also the truth. His phone and most of his belongings had disappeared when Dee had destroyed the Yggdrasill.

"You lost your good phone?" The old woman shook her head in disgust. "That's the third phone this year."

"Second," he muttered.

Aunt Agnes turned and climbed slowly up the steps. She waved away Josh's offer of help. "Just leave me be; I'm not helpless," she said, and then reached out to grip his arm. "You could help me, young man." When they reached the door, she turned and looked down to where Sophie was still standing in front of the red-haired woman. "Sophie, are you coming?"

"In a minute, Aunty." Sophie looked at her brother, then her eyes drifted toward the open door. "I'll be there in a minute, Josh. Why don't you take Aunt Agnes inside and make her a cup of tea?"

18

Josh started to shake his head, but the old woman's fingers bit into his arm with surprising strength. "And while the kettle is boiling, you can phone your parents." She squinted at Sophie again. "Don't be long."

Sophie Newman shook her head. "I won't be."

As soon as Josh and Aunt Agnes had disappeared inside the house, Sophie turned to the stranger. "Who are you?" she demanded.

"Aoife," the woman said, pronouncing the name "E-fa." She bent and ran black-gloved hands over the limo's punctured tire, then spoke in a language Sophie recognized as Japanese. The young-looking man Josh had encountered in the house took off his jacket, flung it onto the front seat and then popped the trunk and pulled out a brace and jack. Fitting the jack under the heavy car, he levered it up with ease and started to change the tire.

Aoife brushed her gloved hands together, then folded her arms across her chest and tilted her head to look at Sophie. "There was no need to do that." There was a hint of a lilting foreign accent in her voice.

"We thought you were kidnapping our aunt," Sophie said quietly. The name Aoife had sent a dozen strange thoughts and images whirling through her brain, but Sophie was finding it hard to distinguish between memories of Scathach and those of Aoife. "We wanted to stop you."

Aoife smiled without showing her teeth. "If I had wanted to kidnap your aunt, would I have turned up here in the middle of the day?"

19

"I don't know," Sophie said, "would you?"

Aoife pushed her small dark glasses up her nose, covering her green eyes, and considered for a moment. "Perhaps. Perhaps not. But," she added with a smile that exposed her vampire teeth, "if I had wanted your aunt, I would have taken her."

"You are Aoife of the Shadows," Sophie said.

"I am Scathach's sister. We are twins. I am the elder."

Sophie took a step back, the Witch's memories of Aoife finally falling into place. "Scathach told me about her family, but she didn't say anything about a sister," she said, unwilling to reveal to the woman that she knew about her.

"No, she wouldn't. We had a falling-out," Aoife muttered.

"A falling-out?" Sophie asked although she already knew they had fought over a boy, and even knew his name.

"Over a boy," Aoife said, with just a hint of sadness in her voice. She looked up and down the street before turning back to Sophie. "We've not spoken in a very long time." She shrugged, a quick roll of her shoulders. "She disowned me. And I her. But I've always kept an eye out for her." She smiled again. "I'm sure you know what it is like to look out for your sibling."

Sophie nodded. She knew exactly what Aoife was talking about. Even though Josh was bigger and stronger than she was, she still thought of him as her baby brother.

"He's my twin."

"I did not know that," Aoife said slowly. Dipping her head slightly, she looked at Sophie over the top of her dark glasses. "And you are both Awakened, too," she added.

"What brought you here?" Sophie asked.

"I felt Scathach . . . *go*."

"Go?" Sophie didn't understand.

"Vanish. Leave this particular Shadowrealm. We are connected, my twin and I, by bonds similar to those which undoubtedly exist between you and your brother. I have always known when she was in pain, when she was hurt or hungry or frightened. . . ."

Sophie found herself nodding. She had felt her brother's pain at times: when he had broken his ribs playing football, she'd felt the sting in her side, and when he'd nearly drowned in Hawaii, she'd woken up breathless and gasping. When she'd dislocated her shoulder in tae kwan do, her brother's shoulder had swelled up and discolored with a bruise that matched hers precisely.

Aoife barked a question in rapid-fire Japanese, and the driver answered with a single syllable. Then she turned to Sophie. "We can stand here and talk in the street," she said, smiling, flashing the tips of her canines, "or you can invite me inside and we can talk in comfort."

A tiny alarm bell went off at the back of Sophie's head. Vampires could not cross a threshold unless they'd been invited to do so, and she instantly knew she was not going to invite this vampire into her aunt's house. There was something about her. . . . Slowly and deliberately, Sophie allowed the remainder of the memories that had been crowding at the back of her head to come surging forward. Suddenly—shockingly—she knew everything the Witch of Endor knew about Aoife of the Shadows. The images and memories were terrifying. Eyes wide with horror, Sophie took a step back, away from the creature, realizing just in time that the driver was behind her. Immediately, she reached for the trigger tattoo on her wrist, but the man caught her arms, holding them to her sides, before she could make the connection. Aoife stepped forward, caught Sophie's wrists and twisted them to expose the design Saint-Germain had burned into her flesh. Sophie tried to struggle, but the driver held her tightly, squeezing her arms so hard that she could feel her fingers begin to tingle. "Let me go! Josh will—"

"Your twin is powerless." Aoife pulled off one leather glove and took the girl's hand in her cold fingers. Filthy gray smoke coiled off the vampire's pale skin. She rubbed her thumb across the ornate Celtic-looking band that wrapped around Sophie's wrist, and stopped on the underside at the gold circle with a red dot in the center. "Ah, the sign of *tine*. The Mark of Fire," Aoife said softly. "So you would have tried to burn me?"

"Let me go!" Sophie tried to kick out at the man holding her, but his grip on her arms tightened and she suddenly grew frightened. Even the Witch of Endor was wary of Aoife of the Shadows. The vampire turned Sophie's wrist painfully and bent forward to examine the tattoo. "This is the work of a master. Who gave you this . . . gift?" Her lips curled in disgust as she said the word.

Sophie pressed her lips together. She wasn't telling this woman anything.

Aoife's glasses slipped down her nose, revealing eyes that were like chips of green glass. "Maui . . . Prometheus . . .

Xolotl . . . Pele . . . Agni . . ." Aoife shook her head quickly. "No, none of those. You have just returned from Paris, so it is someone in that city. . . ." Her voice trailed away. She looked over Sophie's shoulder at the black-suited driver. "Is there a Master of Fire in the French capital?"

"Your old adversary, the count, lives there," the man said softly in English.

"Saint-Germain," Aoife snapped. She saw Sophie's eyes widen and she smiled savagely. "Saint-Germain the liar. Saint-Germain the thief. I should have killed him when I had the chance." She looked at the driver. "Take her. We will continue this conversation in private."

Sophie opened her mouth to scream, but Aoife pressed her forefinger to the bridge of the girl's nose. The vampire's gray aura leaked from her fingers, the smoke curling around the girl's head, seeping into her nostrils and mouth.

Sophie tried to bring her own aura alight. It crackled faintly about her body for a single heartbeat before she slumped unconscious.

CHAPTER FOUR

*A*gnes hit a speed-dial number on the phone and handed it to Josh. "You speak to your parents, right now," she ordered. "And where is Sophie? Who is that girl she's talking to outside?"

"The sister of someone we know," Josh said, pressing the phone to the side of his face. The line rang only once before it was answered.

"Agnes?"

"Dad! It's Josh."

"Josh!"

The boy found himself smiling—the relief in his father's voice was clearly audible—and then a wave of embarrassment washed over him and he felt guilty for not getting in touch with his parents sooner.

"Is everything all right?" Richard Newman's voice was almost lost in a crackle of burbling static.

Josh pressed his finger to his ear and concentrated hard on the sounds. "Everything is fine, Dad. We're OK. We just got back to San Francisco."

"Your mother and I were starting to get worried about you. Seriously worried."

"We were with the Fla—Flemings," Josh quickly corrected himself. "There was no cell-phone reception," he added truthfully, "though we did manage to get your e-mail on Sunday night. I got the jpeg of the shark teeth. I didn't recognize the type, but from the size, I'm guessing a freshwater shark?" he asked quickly, deliberately changing the subject.

"Well done, son. It's a Lissodus from the Upper Cretaceous period. It's in very nice condition too."

"Is everything OK with you?" Josh pressed on, trying to keep his father talking. He glanced at the door, wishing his sister would come in. He could distract his father with questions, but the same trick wouldn't work with his mother, and he guessed that she was hovering at his father's shoulder and would pluck the phone from his fingers at any moment. "How's the dig going?"

"It's been great." Wind howled at the other end of the line, and dust and grit crackled against the phone. "We discovered what we think is a new ceratopsid."

Josh frowned. The name was familiar. When he'd been younger, he used to know the names of hundreds of dinosaurs. "Is that a horned dinosaur?" he asked.

"Yes, from the Cretaceous, about seventy-five million years old. We also found a small and possibly untouched

25

Anasazi site in one of the canyons, and some extraordinary Fremont-culture petroglyphs outside of the Range Creek Canyon site."

Smiling at his father's bubbling enthusiasm, Josh walked toward the window. "Which race are called the Ancient Ones in Navajo?" he asked, although he already knew the answer. "Fremont or Anasazi?" He wanted to keep his father talking, to give Sophie more time.

"Anasazi," Richard Newman said. "And actually, the proper translation is 'Enemy Ancestors.'"

The two words shocked Josh to a standstill. A couple of days ago, the name would have meant nothing to him, but that was before he'd learned of the existence of the Elders, the race who had ruled the world in the distant past. He had come to realize that there was more than a grain of truth to every myth and legend. "Enemy Ancestors," he repeated, trying to keep his voice steady. "What does that mean?"

"I don't know," Richard Newman said, "but I prefer the term Ancient or Ancestral Pueblo or Hisatsinom."

"But it's such a strange name," Josh persisted. "Who do you think used it? They wouldn't have referred to themselves that way."

"Probably another tribe. Strangers, outsiders."

"And who came before them, Dad?" Josh said quickly. "Who came before the Anasazi and the Fremont?"

"We don't know," his father admitted. "That's known as the Archaic period. Why the sudden interest in ancient America? I thought archaeology bored you."

"I guess I've started to be more interested in history and

the ancient world," Josh said truthfully. He headed toward the window again . . . and was just in time to see Scatty's sister press her hand to Sophie's forehead and his twin slump into the black-suited driver's arms. He watched in horror as the vampire's head snapped around to look at him and she bared her fangs in what might have been a grin. Then she jerked open the rear door of the car and held it as the driver dropped Sophie onto the backseat. Standing by the open door, Aoife waved a mocking salute at Josh.

Josh felt as if he'd been punched in the stomach. He could not draw breath and his heart was pounding. "Dad— I'll be back in a sec . . . ," he whispered hoarsely. He dropped the phone on the floor, then raced out of the room and down the hallway. Snatching up the two pieces of the walking stick the limo driver had broken, Josh jerked open the door and almost fell down the steps. He'd half expected to see the car driving away, but Aoife was waiting patiently for him. "Give me back my sister!" he shouted.

"No," Aoife said lightly.

Josh ran toward the car, trying to remember everything Joan of Arc had taught him about sword fighting. He wished he had Clarent with him now. Even Scatty—who was frightened of nothing—had been terrified of the stone blade. But all he had were the two halves of the walking stick.

The vampire tilted her head to one side, watching the boy run toward her, and smiled.

As Josh raced across the street, terror alighted his aura and the faintest of golden glows surrounded his body. He could see his sister lying unmoving on the backseat of the car, and his fear turned to a raging anger. Abruptly, his aura blazed, steaming gold threads smoking off his skin, his eyes turning to molten coins. His aura hardened around his hands, sheathing them in metallic gloves, and then it flowed down the wooden sticks, turning them into golden rods. He tried to speak, but his throat was tight, and the voice that came from his mouth was deep and gravelly, more beast than human. *"Give . . . me . . . back . . . my . . . sister. . . ."*

Aoife's arrogant smile faded. She shouted a single word in Japanese, turned and flung herself into the limousine, slamming the door behind her. The engine immediately roared to life, the rear tires spinning and smoking on the street.

"No!" Josh reached the car just as it took off. Lashing out with one golden rod, he shattered the rear window nearest him, the glass exploding into white powder, the stick leaving a long gouge in the shining black metal. Another blow left a deep impression in the trunk and cracked a rear light. The car squealed down the street, and in desperation Josh flung the two golden sticks after it, but the moment he released them, they returned to plain wood and bounced harmlessly off the fender.

Josh raced after the car. He could feel his aura surging through him, lending him speed and strength as he pounded down the road. He was conscious that he was moving faster than he ever had before, but the limo kept accelerating. It shot through an intersection, then rounded a corner with a squeal of protesting tires and disappeared.

And just as quickly as it had come, Josh's strength left him. He collapsed on his hands and knees at the bottom of

Scott Street, lungs heaving, heart thundering, every muscle in his body stressed and burning. Black spots danced before his eyes and he thought he was going to throw up. He watched the golden glow fade from his hands, his aura drifting off his flesh like yellow vapor, leaving him aching and exhausted. He started to tremble and a sudden cramp caught his calf muscle behind his knees. The pain was excruciating, and he quickly rolled over and dug his heel into the ground, pushing down hard, trying to ease it. Climbing to his feet, feeling sick and miserable, he started to hobble back to his aunt's house. Sophie was gone. Kidnapped by Aoife. He had to find his twin.

But that meant returning to Nicholas and Perenelle Flamel.

CHAPTER FIVE

$\mathcal{J}$he Shadowrealm was called Xibalba.

Even among the countless ancient Shadowrealms, it was old, and unlike so many of the others, which were beautiful and complex, it was crudely simple.

Xibalba was a single cave, impossibly vast, unimaginably high, speckled with slowly bubbling pits of black-crusted lava. Occasionally, one of these would rupture, spitting thick globules of liquid rock high into the air, sending shadows dancing red and black on the walls. The air stank of sulfur, and the only illumination came from a gelatinous yellow-white fungus that coated the walls and the massive stalactites hanging from the distant and barely visible ceiling.

Every Shadowrealm opened onto at least one other realm. Some connected with two. Xibalba was unique: it touched nine other Shadowrealms and was sometimes referred to as the Crossroads. Arranged at regular intervals around the cave were nine separate openings in the walls. The entrances to each of the cave mouths were carved and etched with crude and blocky glyphs, and although the sticky glowing fungus covered most of the dark walls, none of it even came close to any of the symbols. They were the gates to the Shadowrealms.

Usually, nothing moved in Xibalba except the bubbling lava, but now a steady stream of messengers was flitting and scrabbling from one cave mouth to the other. Some were leathery and resembled bats, others were furred and looked like rats, but they were neither, and none were truly alive. They had been created for one purpose: to carry a message from the heart of the Dark Elders' Shadowrealm out into every connected world. Once the messengers' task was complete, they would melt back into mud, sticks and scraps of hair and skin.

The messengers were carrying news of Dr. John Dee's death sentence.

And none of those who heard it—Elder, Next Generation or immortal human—were surprised. There was only one price for failure, and Dr. John Dee had failed spectacularly.

CHAPTER SIX

"*There* have been worse days," Dr. John Dee said, though he couldn't remember when.

Following the disaster at Stonehenge and the twins' escape through the leygate, the Magician had spent the remainder of the night and the early part of the following day in the tumbled ruins of the barn where, only a few hours previously, Flamel and the twins had been hiding out. Helicopters buzzed overhead and police and ambulance sirens howled along the nearby A344. When all the police activity had finally died away in the early afternoon, Dee had left the barn and started walking toward London, keeping to the back roads. Beneath his coat, wrapped in a ragged cloth, he carried the single stone sword that had once been two, Clarent and Excalibur. It throbbed and pulsed against his skin like a beating heart.

There was little or no traffic on the narrow country lanes, and he was just beginning to think that he would have to steal a car in the next town or village he came to, when an elderly vicar in an equally ancient Morris Minor stopped and offered him a lift.

"You're lucky I came along," the old man said in a crackling Welsh accent. "Not many people use these side roads now, with the motorway so close."

"My car broke down, and I need to get back into London for a meeting," Dee said. "I got a bit lost," he added, consciously shifting his accent to match the vicar's.

"I can take you. I'm glad of the company," the white-haired man admitted. "I've been listening to the radio—and all this talk about the security scare was making me nervous."

"What's happened?" Dee asked, keeping his voice light and casual. "I thought there was a lot of police activity."

"Where have you been for the past twelve hours?" the vicar asked with a grin that shifted the false teeth in his mouth.

"Busy," Dee said. "Met up with some old friends; we'd a lot of catching up to do."

"Then you missed all the excitement. . . ."

Dee kept his face expressionless.

"A major security operation closed down the city yesterday. The BBC were reporting that the same terrorist cell that had been operating in Paris were now in London." Gripping the big steering wheel tightly, he glanced at his passenger. "You *did* hear about what happened in Paris?"

"I read all about it," the Magician murmured, unconsciously shaking his head. Machiavelli controlled Paris—how could he have let Flamel and the twins slip through the net?

"These are dangerous times."

"They are indeed," Dee said. "But you would not want to believe everything you read in the press," he added.

There were roadblocks in place on all the major roads leading into the capital, but the police barely glanced at the battered car carrying the two older men before waving it through.

The vicar dropped Dee in Mayfair in the heart of the city, and the doctor walked down to Green Park Station. He caught the tube on the Jubilee Line, and took it right into the heart of Canary Wharf, where Enoch Enterprises had its UK headquarters. The doctor was taking a calculated gamble. His Dark Elder master might have the building under observation, but Dee was hoping everyone would think he had run away and wouldn't be so foolish as to return to his own head-quarters.

Entering unseen through the underground parking garage, he made his way up to his offices at the top of the building, where he took a long luxurious shower in his private bathroom, washing away the grime and filth of the past few hours. The hot water eased the pain in his right shoulder, which he rotated carefully. Josh had flung Clarent at him during the battle at the barn, and although Dee had managed to turn his aura into a shield before the stone sword hit him, the force of the blow had driven him to the ground. He'd been sure he had dislocated it; only later had he realized that his shoulder was badly bruised but not broken, and for that he was grateful. A break wasn't serious—his enhanced metabolism would work quickly to repair any damage, or he could use a little of his aura to repair it instantly, but that would draw the Dark Elders and their minions to him.

The Magician changed into fresh clothes, a nondescript dark blue two-piece suit, a dark blue shirt and a tie with the discreet gold pattern of the fleur-de-lis of St. John's College, Cambridge. While the kettle in the tiny kitchen boiled water for tea, Dee emptied his safe, stuffing wads of sterling, euros and dollars into a money belt he wore around his waist, hidden under his shirt. There were a dozen passports in as many names at the back of the safe. Dee shoved them into his suit coat pockets. He had been collecting these passports for years and wasn't about to abandon them now.

The kettle boiled and the Magician made himself a cup of Earl Gray. Sipping the perfumed tea, he finally turned to look at the rag-wrapped bundle on his desk. A rare smile curled his lips. He might have lost the battle, but he had certainly come away with the greatest prize.

Clarent and Excalibur. *Together*. Yesterday, he had held them in his hands and watched as the two swords had fused together to create a single stone sword.

Even from across the room, Dee could feel the power radiating from the object in long slow waves. If he lowered his guard, he caught the vaguest hints of whispered thoughts in countless languages, only some of which he recognized.

He suddenly realized—almost with surprise—that finally, after a lifetime of searching, he finally had the four ancient Swords of Power. Two—Durendal and Joyeuse—were hidden in his private apartments in San Francisco, and the remaining two were here on the table before him . . . or was it now one? And what would happen, he wondered, if he brought this sword in contact with the other two stone swords? And why had *they* never fused together? They'd been side by side for centuries.

The doctor took his time finishing the tea, calming his thoughts and putting protective barriers in place before he approached the bundle and unwrapped it. Some magicians used combinations of words—spells and cantrips—to shield their thoughts, but Dee used the oldest of all magical sounds: music. Staring at the desk, he started to hum "Greensleeves," Queen Elizabeth I's favorite song. The Queen believed that it had been written by her father, Henry VIII, for her mother, Anne Boleyn. It was a tale Dee knew wasn't true, but he'd never had the heart to tell her. Regardless, its simple tune and ancient rhythm created a perfect protective spell. Murmuring the words aloud, he approached the desk.

"Alas, my love, ye do me wrong to cast me off discourteously . . ."

There was a definite tremble in his fingers as he carefully peeled away the filthy gray cloth he'd found in the ruined barn, revealing the object it concealed.

"And I have loved you so long, delighting in your companie . . ."

Lying on the polished black marble desk was one of the oldest objects on the planet. It looked like a simple stone sword, but it was more, much, much more. These twin weapons melded together were said to predate the Elders and even the Archons, belonging to the mythical Time Before Time. Famously, Arthur had carried Excalibur, and Mordred, his son, had slain him with Clarent, but the King and the Coward had been merely two of the generations of heroes and villains who had wielded these blades, which had been present, either individually or collectively, at every major event in the history of the earth.

"Greensleeves was all my joy, Greensleeves was my delight, Greensleeves was my heart of gold . . ."

It was hard to believe that he had finally found Excalibur's match. Half a millennium ago, when Henry VIII had ruled England, Dee had begun his quest to find the legendary Sword of Fire.

"I have been readie at your hand, to grant what ever you would crave . . ."

Taking a deep breath, the doctor lifted the sword. Although it was little more than twenty inches in length, it was remarkably heavy. The blade and the plain hilt looked like they had been carved from a single piece of sparkling granite. The moment his fingers touched the warm stone, the power from the sword washed over him. . . .

Voices raised in anger.

Shouts of terror.

Cries of pain.

Dee shuddered as sounds filled his head, threatening to overwhelm him. His singing faltered. *"I . . . I have waged life and . . . and land, your love and . . . and good will for to have . . ."*

The sword was powerful, incredibly powerful, wrapped in mystery and legend. Yesterday, when Gilgamesh had seen the sword, he had used the words of the ancient prophecy—*the*

37

two that are one, the one that is all—to describe it. Dee had always thought that the prophecy referred to the twins, but now he was not so sure.

"Greensleeves, now farewell adieu . . ."

In fact, he was sure of nothing anymore. In the last few days, his entire way of life, his whole world, had shifted. And it was all because of Flamel and the twins. They had made him look a fool and put him in terrible danger. Dee's short fingers brushed the length of the flesh-warm stone.

Whispered secrets . . .

Vague promises . . .

Hints of ancient knowledge, of hidden lore . . .

Dee jerked his hand away and the voices faded from his consciousness. His thin lips curled in a cruel smile: this sword might well prove his salvation. The Dark Elders would pay dearly for a weapon like this. He wondered if it might even be worth his immortal life.

The doctor's phone suddenly buzzed and vibrated in his pocket, startling him. Stepping away from the sword lying on the table, he slipped the phone out of his pocket and looked at the fingerprint-smudged screen. He'd been expecting to see his Elder master's impossibly long number on the screen, but it read *Restricted*. For a single instant he thought about not answering it, but then curiosity—always both his greatest strength and his worst failing—got the better of him and he pressed Answer.

"You recognize my voice?"

Dr. John Dee blinked in surprise. The voice on the other

end of the phone belonged to Niccolò Machiavelli, who had gone to San Francisco. "Yes," he said cautiously.

"This is supposed to be a secure line, but you know my motto . . . trust no one."

"A good motto," Dee murmured.

"I understand you survived."

"Barely." The doctor hurried over to the security monitor and turned it on, quickly flipping through the channels. His suspicious mind wondered if this was a trap: was Machiavelli talking to him, distracting him, while the building was being surrounded? But the offices and its corridors were empty and the parking lot deserted. "Why are you calling me?" he asked.

"To warn you."

"Warn me!" Even though he had centuries of practice, he was still unable to keep the note of surprise from his voice.

"A few minutes ago, messengers flowed through Xibalba and out into the Shadowrealms. You know what that means?"

Almost unconsciously, Dee nodded. "Xibalba?" he asked aloud.

On the other side of the world, a note of impatience crept into Machiavelli's voice. "Yes, the Crossroads, the Place of Fright. It's one of the ancient Shadowrealms."

"I know it," Dee said tersely. "The Morrigan took me there during the last Great Conclave."

"You've been there?" Machiavelli sounded impressed.

"I have."

Xibalba was a neutral ground, used when Elders and Dark Elders from various Shadowrealms needed to meet. Dee was one of only a handful of humans who had ever been there. He had even chosen his distinctive aura smell to match the Shadowrealms sulfurous stench. If the Dark Elders were sending messengers through Xibalba, it meant that they wanted to ensure that every Shadowrealm, even the most distant, was aware of their commands. "I have been judged?" the Magician asked. In the aftermath of his failure, he had no doubts that his sentence had been handed down and that his Dark Elder masters were making sure he would not be able to hide in even the most distant Shadowrealm. He was stuck on earth. Stepping back from the monitor, he stared at his reflection in a mirror: he realized he was looking at a dead man.

"Judged and found guilty."

Dee nodded but said nothing. He had given the Dark Elders a lifetime of service, and now they had condemned him to death.

"Did you hear me?" Machiavelli snapped.

"I heard you," Dee said softly. A wave of exhaustion washed over him and he reached out to steady himself against the wall.

The transatlantic line crackled. "All of the Next Generation or immortal humans you called to London to hunt for Nicholas Flamel and the twins will now turn on you . . . especially when they discover that the reward for you is double the reward you offered for the Alchemyst."

"I'm not sure whether I should be flattered or not."

"There's one difference." The line crackled again and Machiavelli's voice faded in and out. "Our masters will take Flamel dead or alive, but you they want alive. They have been very clear about that: anyone who kills you will suffer an appalling fate."

Dee shuddered. He knew his masters wanted him alive so they could remove his immortality, watch him age before their eyes, and then make him immortal again. He would be cursed to endure an eternity of suffering as a very ancient humani. "How do you know this?" he wondered.

Machiavelli's voice lowered to a whisper. "My American companion was contacted by his master."

"And why are you telling me?"

"Because, like you, I too have failed in my appointed task," Machiavelli said urgently. "Perenelle escaped the island. In fact, I am trapped on Alcatraz."

Dee could not keep a smile from spreading across his face, but he bit down hard on the inside of his cheek to prevent himself from speaking.

"There may come a time when you and I need one another, Doctor," Machiavelli continued.

"The enemy of my enemy is my friend," Dee answered, using the ancient saying.

"Exactly. Doctor, it is time for you to run, to hide. Your masters have declared you *utlaga*."

The line suddenly went dead. Dee slowly slipped his cell phone into his pocket and looked in the mirror one last time. He was *utlaga*, a wolf's head, an outlaw. And then he laughed aloud: the last being the Elders had declared *utlaga* was the Elder Mars Ultor.

CHAPTER SEVEN

When Josh limped back to the house, Aunt Agnes was standing in the doorway, waiting for him. Her narrow face was fixed in a scowl and her thin lips had vanished completely. "You flung the phone on the floor and then stormed out of the house," she snapped as he started up the steps. "I want an explanation, young man."

"I don't have one. Sophie was . . ." He hesitated. "Sophie was calling me."

"You didn't have to throw the phone on the floor."

"I'm sorry." Josh took a deep breath, determined not to say anymore. He was worried about his sister; the last thing he needed was his aunt nagging him.

"Phones cost money. . . ."

Josh slipped past his aunt. "I'm going to finish talking to Dad."

"He's gone. It was a bad line—and a lot worse after you

dropped the phone," she added. "He said to tell you he'll call back later. Your mother said neither of you is to leave the house until she talks to you. She is very unhappy with the pair of you," Aunt Agnes added ominously.

"I'm sure she is," Josh muttered. He crossed the hall, making his way toward the stairs.

"And where's your sister?" Aunt Agnes demanded.

"I don't know," Josh said truthfully.

The old woman folded her arms and squinted up at him. "You mean she just left without even stopping in to say hello?"

"Something important must have come up," Josh said, plastering a smile on his face, even though he felt sick inside.

"I don't know what's gotten into the pair of you," Aunt Agnes was muttering. "Staying away from home for days . . . not even bothering to call. . . . The young people of today have no respect. . . ."

Josh started to climb the stairs.

"And where do you think you're going?"

"To my room," Josh said. He knew he needed to walk away from his aunt before he said something he was going to regret.

"Well, you can just stay there, young man. I've got a feeling you're both going to be grounded for quite some time! You need to learn some respect for your elders."

Josh tried to ignore his aunt as he continued up to his bedroom and closed the door behind him. He leaned back against the cool wood, then closed his eyes and took a deep breath, trying to calm the queasy feeling in his stomach.

43

Sophie was gone. She was in danger.

Aoife had his sister and he had no idea why—though he knew it couldn't be good. Was Aoife working for the Dark Elders? Why had she taken Sophie—and then why had she run from him? Even though he was scared and exhausted, Josh couldn't prevent a wry smile from forming on his lips. When he'd run out of the house, Aoife hadn't appeared scared, she had looked arrogant, and when he'd asked her to return his sister, she had been quick to say no. But then something had frightened the vampire. Maybe it was the way his aura had started to form a golden armor around his body. Josh lifted his hands and looked at them. They were flesh and blood now, the skin on his palms scraped and bruised where he'd fallen, his fingernails chipped and dirty. But only a short while ago they had been encased in golden gloves. He remembered how the gold had flowed down his hands to cover the two halves of the broken walking stick, turning them to bars of metal. When he'd struck the car, they had ripped through the glass and steel with ease. But the moment he'd thrown the stick after the car, the instant it had left his hand, it had returned to wood. Josh suddenly remembered the story of the Greek king Midas. Everything he touched turned to gold. Maybe the ancient king had possessed a gold aura.

And then Josh's smile faded. He had failed his sister. He should have kept running; he might have caught up with the car. Maybe if he'd somehow managed to focus his aura, he would have been able to do something . . . though he wasn't really sure what.

He would find her, he vowed.

Dropping to his hands and knees, he pulled his backpack out from under his bed. He then stood and began opening drawers, dragging out clothes and shoving them into the bag: socks and underwear, a spare pair of jeans, a couple of T-shirts. He stripped off the grimy clothes he'd been wearing since Paris, dumped them into the wicker basket at the end of the bed and pulled out clean clothes. Before he tugged on his red *49ers Faithful* T-shirt, he removed the cloth bag hanging around his neck and sat down on the edge of his bed. He opened the bag and peered inside. It held the two pages he'd torn from the Codex last week. According to the Alchemyst, they contained the Final Summoning, which Dee needed to bring back the Dark Elders.

Josh shook the pages out onto the bed beside him. Then he lined them up side by side. They were about six inches across by nine inches tall and looked as if they had been made out of pressed bark and leaf fibers.

The last time he'd really looked at the pages they had been on the floor of the ruined bookshop and both he and his sister had been dazed and confused by everything they'd just witnessed. When he'd looked at the pages then, he could have sworn that the words were moving, but now they weren't.

Both pages were covered front and back with jagged writing. He'd seen similar carvings on ancient artifacts in his father's office, and he believed that the writing looked a lot like Sumerian. One letter—which he thought might be the initial letter—was beautifully colored in vivid golds and reds, while the rest was in black ink that was still crisp even after countless centuries. Picking up a page, he held it to the light.

And blinked in astonishment.

The words *were* moving. They slowly crawled, shifted and rearranged themselves on the page, forming words, sentences, paragraphs in countless languages. Some of the letters were almost recognizable—he saw pictographs and runes and he was able to pick out individual Greek letters, but most were completely alien.

A phrase in Latin caught his eye: *magnum opus*. He knew it meant "great work." He traced the words with his index finger . . . and the moment his flesh touched the page, heat blossomed deep in his stomach and his finger started to smoke with a warm orange glow. He then noticed that while all the other letters around the simple phrase changed into a score of other scripts and languages, the ten letters beneath his fingertip remained fixed. The moment he lifted his hand away, the letters disappeared. Running his fingertips lightly over the pages, he watched in awe as whole sentences shifted and formed beneath his flesh. He wished his mother or father were here: they would be able to translate some of the ancient languages. There were hints of Latin and Greek scattered in the text, and he recognized a few Egyptian hieroglyphs and one of the square Mayan glyphs.

Mindful of the Flamels' warning about using his aura, Josh carefully lifted his hand and the text flowed in chaos again. He slipped the pages back into the hand-sewn cloth bag and draped it around his neck. It felt warm against his skin. He wasn't entirely sure what he'd just discovered, but he recalled that when Flamel had touched the page the previous week, the words hadn't stopped moving for him. Josh flexed his fingers: it was obviously something to do with his aura. He kicked his ruined sneakers under the bed, then opened the wardrobe and pulled out the walking boots he used when he went hiking with his father, and pulled them on. Then he slung the backpack over his shoulder and pressed his ear against the bedroom door, listening intently.

He could hear his aunt in the kitchen . . . could hear water boiling in the kettle . . . the fridge door opening . . . the clink of a spoon against the side of a china cup . . . the radio tuned to NPR.

Josh jerked his head back. The kitchen was at the very rear of the house; there was no way he should be able to hear those things. And then he realized that the faintest wisp of golden smoke had gathered in his palm. Bringing his hand to his face, he wondered at the physical evidence of his aura. It looked like the dry ice he'd seen in chemistry class, except that it was a faint golden color and smelled strongly of oranges. As he watched, the foglike vapor sank back into his palm and disappeared. Josh closed his hand into a fist, squeezing hard. He'd watched his sister create a silver glove around her hand, and in the street, only a few minutes earlier, he'd seen a similar gauntlet appear over his own without even thinking about it. But what would happen if he deliberately *focused* on seeing his left hand encased in a gauntlet? Immediately, his skin sparked, glittering with speckles. The faintest impression of a golden glove surrounded his hand. As he watched, a studded metal gauntlet formed around his flesh, the fingers tipped with pointed golden nails. Josh made a fist again. The glove closed with the sound of metal rasping on metal.

"Josh Newman!"

Aunt Agnes's voice on the other side of the door made him jump. He'd been concentrating so hard on creating the glove that he hadn't heard her come up the stairs. His aura dissipated, the glove drifting away in curls of golden smoke.

Agnes pounded on the door. "Didn't you hear me calling you?"

Josh sighed. "No," he said truthfully.

"Well, I've made some tea. Come down now before it gets cold." She paused and added, "I made some fresh muffins this morning also."

"Great." Josh felt his stomach rumble; Aunt Agnes made the best muffins. "I'm just getting changed. I'll be right down." He waited until he heard his aunt shuffle away, her flat-soled shoes rubbing the carpet. Then he looked at his hand again and smiled broadly at a sudden thought. If he was able to mold his aura without training, then that meant he had to be more powerful than his sister.

Settling his backpack over both shoulders, he inched open the door and listened with his enhanced senses. He could actually hear his aunt pouring tea from the pot into a cup, could smell the tannin of fresh black tea and the richer odor of warm pastry. His stomach rumbled again and he felt his mouth fill with saliva: he could almost taste the buttery cake. He wondered if he could stop for just one . . . but that would mean sitting down with Aunt Agnes, and she'd want to know all the details of the past few days. He'd be there for an hour—and he couldn't afford to waste the time.

He padded silently down the stairs, cracked open the front door and slipped out into the cool San Francisco morning. "Sorry, Aunty," he muttered, pulling the door silently closed behind him. She was going to be furious when she discovered he'd left. She'd probably call his parents, and he had no idea what explanation he was going to give them.

What he *did* know was that he was not returning to the house in Pacific Heights without his sister.

CHAPTER EIGHT

Agnes heard the hall door close and padded out of the kitchen. She blinked at the door and then tilted her head to one side, listening. "Josh?" she called.

The house was silent.

"Josh?" she called again, her voice cracking with the effort. "Where is that boy?" she muttered. "Josh Newman, you come down here right this minute!" she shouted.

There was no response.

Shaking her head, the old woman prepared to climb the stairs again when something crunched under her slippers. She bent painfully to lift it off the carpet. It was a chunk of dried and hardened mud. Agnes squinted at the stairs. They'd been spotless when she'd walked down them only a few moments earlier, but now, all the way up to the second floor, they were covered in fragments of mud. Someone had followed her down, wearing old muddy boots. Turning her head sharply, she spotted the telltale traces of mud on the floor leading straight to the door.

"Josh Newman," she whispered, very softly, "what have you done?"

Moving as quickly as her arthritic hips would allow, she hurried upstairs and pushed open the door to Josh's room without knocking. She immediately spotted the dirty clothes tossed in the basket and the filthy sneakers shoved under the bed. She opened the wardrobe and found the space where the walking boots had been.

Standing in the center of the room, she turned slowly, conscious that there was something odd in the atmosphere. Her senses were no longer as sharp as they had once been; age had robbed her sight and hearing of their acuity . . . but her sense of smell remained strong. The still, dry air of the room was touched with the sweet odor of oranges.

The old woman sighed and fished her cell phone out of her pocket. She wasn't looking forward to telling Richard and Sara Newman that their children had vanished. Again.

Some guardian she'd turned out to be!

CHAPTER NINE

"J can smell Dee's stink on everything," Perenelle complained. She had showered and changed into fresh clothes: stonewashed blue jeans, a beautifully embroidered Egyptian cotton shirt and a pair of boots that had been handmade for her in New York in 1901. Her still-damp hair was pulled back off her face and tied into a thick ponytail. Lifting a heavy woolen sweater from a carved chest of drawers, she pressed it to her face and breathed deeply. "Ugh! Rotten eggs."

Nicholas nodded. He too had showered and changed into one of his almost identical combinations of black jeans and T-shirts. This shirt had the iconic *Dark Side of the Moon* design on the front. "Everything organic is starting to rot," he said. He held up a hideously tie-dyed T-shirt. It was dusted with mold spores, and much of the bottom half of the shirt had decayed to curling threads. Even as he held it up for inspection, one of the arms tore away. "I got that at Woodstock," he complained.

"No, you didn't," Perenelle corrected him. "You bought it in a vintage store on Ventura Boulevard about ten years ago."

"Oh." Nicholas held the destroyed shirt up again. "Are you sure?"

"Positive. You didn't go to Woodstock."

"I didn't?" Nicholas sounded surprised.

"You didn't go when Jethro Tull decided not to attend and Joni Mitchell pulled out. You said it would be a waste of time." Perenelle smiled. She was busy with the lock on a heavy steamer trunk at the foot of the bed. "In fact, you said that several times."

"Something else I was wrong about, then." He looked around the bedroom and then pressed his foot against the floorboards. "I don't think we should hang around here. I've a feeling the floor could give way at any moment."

"I just need a minute." The fist-sized lock clicked open and the woman heaved the lid back. The faint odor of roses and exotic spices filled the air. Nicholas joined his wife and watched as she carefully brushed dried rose petals off the leather-wrapped bundle within. "Do you remember when we last packed up this box?" she asked softly, unconsciously slipping back into French.

"New Mexico, 1945," he said immediately.

Perenelle nodded. Peeling back the leather covering, she revealed an ancient-looking carved wooden box. "You wanted to bury it at the Trinity Site so that the first atomic bomb would destroy it."

"And you would not let me," he said reminding her.

Perenelle looked up at her husband and a shadow moved

53

behind her eyes. "I am the seventh daughter of a seventh daughter. I know . . ." She paused, and a look of terrible sadness touched her face. "I know certain things."

Nicholas rested his hand lightly on her shoulder and squeezed. "And you knew we would need these items?"

Perenelle looked back at the box without answering and then lifted the lid. Inside lay a thick coiled silver and black leather whip. She wrapped her long fingers around the dark handle and lifted it, the leather rasping and creaking softly together. "Now, here's an old friend," she murmured.

Nicholas shuddered. "It is detestable."

"Ah, but it saved our lives on more than one occasion," Pernelle said, winding it around her waist, threading it through the loops on her jeans like a belt. The handle hung down by her right leg.

"It is woven from snakes you pulled from the Medusa's hair," Nicholas reminded her. "Do you know how close we came to dying that day?"

"Well, technically, we would not have died," Perenelle said. "She would have solidified our auras . . ."

". . . turning us to stone," Nicholas finished.

"Besides," Perenelle added with a grin, patting the wooden box, "we got what we wanted, and it was worth it to see the expression on the Gorgon's face when we escaped." Reaching into the chest, she pulled out another box. "And this is yours," she said.

Nicholas rubbed suddenly damp palms on the legs of his trousers, but made no move to take the box from his wife. "Perry," he said quietly, "are you sure about this?"

The Sorceress's green eyes turned hard and brittle. "Sure about what?" she snapped. She came gracefully to her feet, the wooden box cradled in her arms. "Sure about what?" she asked again, anger clearly audible in her voice. "What are we waiting for, Nicholas? We have waited so long now that we have run out of time. You have weeks to live. . . ."

"Don't say that," he said quickly.

"Why not? It's true. If I survive a week or ten days after you, then I'll be lucky. But do you know something: we are both going to live long enough to see the end of the world as we know it. The Dark Elders have most of the Codex, and Litha is fast approaching. There are Dark Elders moving freely through the world, and you told me that there was an Archon in London." She pointed in the direction of the bay. "And Alcatraz is full of monsters ready to be loosed on the city. There are creatures there I have not seen in centuries."

Nicholas held up his hands in surrender, but Perenelle was not finished.

"What will happen, do you think, if San Francisco is overrun by nightmares from the dark edges of human mythology? Tell me," she demanded. "You've studied history and human nature, tell me what would happen." Anger sent static crackles running along her hair. "Tell me!"

"There would be chaos," he admitted.

"How long before the city fell?" The elastic band holding her ponytail in place snapped and her mane of silver-streaked dark hair rose in a crackling sheet around her head. "Weeks, days or hours? And once this city is a smoking ruin, you know the creatures will spread out across America like a disease.

How long do you think the humani—even with all their weapons and sophisticated technology—would be able to survive against the monsters?"

The Alchemyst shook his head and shrugged.

"They have brought down civilizations before," Perenelle said. "The last time the Dark Elders released monsters onto this world, the Elders were forced to destroy Pompeii."

Nicholas reached out and silently took the wooden box from his wife's arms.

"The last thing we do, Nicholas, before old age and death claim us, is to destroy the army on Alcatraz. And for that, we need allies." She tapped the lid of the box with the palm of her hand. "We need this."

The Alchemyst turned and placed the box on the bed. Its sides had been etched with a triple spiral, and he allowed his fingers to trace the curls. He'd bought the box in a backstreet in Delhi in India, just over three hundred years ago, and then sketched the spiral design on it with a stick of charcoal. A local craftsman had cut the shape into the four sides of the box, and then on the lid and the base. "In my country, this is an ancient powerful symbol of protection," the tiny wizened man had muttered in Hindi, not expecting the foreigner to understand him. He had been shocked when the Westerner had lifted the box from his hands and replied in the same language, "In mine too."

There was neither lock nor clasp on the box, and Nicholas carefully lifted off the carved lid and placed it on the bed. A hint of jasmine and exotic spices touched the air: the unmistakable odor of India. He was reaching into the cloth-packed interior, when Perenelle suddenly grabbed his arm, her fingers biting into his flesh. He watched as she carefully lifted her hair and tilted her head to one side. She was listening.

And then Nicholas heard it: someone was moving stealthily through the shop below.

CHAPTER TEN

*N*one of the late-evening tourists crowding noisily into Covent Garden in London paid any attention to the tall slender woman with the cascade of jet-black hair. She had taken up a position between two of the pillars in front of the Punch & Judy Pub and placed a square of soft leather painted with red curling spirals on the cobbles at her feet. Finally, she unwrapped a carved wooden flute from a leather cover, put the flute to her lips, closed her eyes, and blew gently.

The sound was extraordinary.

Magnified by the stone pillars, the haunting, ethereal music drifted out across Covent Garden, washing over the cobbles stopping everyone in their tracks. Within minutes a crowd had gathered in a half circle around the woman.

Standing perfectly still, she played with her eyes closed. It was a tune none of the listeners recognized, though many found it vaguely familiar and discovered that their fingers or toes were tapping along with the beat. A few were even moved to tears.

Then, finally, the ancient-sounding wordless music ended with a single high-pitched note that sounded like distant birds flying overhead. There was a long moment of silence and the musician opened her eyes and bowed slightly. The crowd applauded and cheered, and most immediately started to drift away toward the Apple Market. A few dropped money—British sterling, American coins and euros—onto the leather cloth and two people asked if the musician had a CD of her music for sale, but she shook her head and explained that every performance was different and unique. She thanked them for their interest in a soft whispering voice that had just the hint of an American East Coast accent.

Finally, only one listener remained: an older man who watched her intently, gray eyes following her every movement as she wiped down the flute and slid it back into what was obviously a handmade leather case. He waited until she had stooped to gather up the red leather cloth with its scattering of coins and then stepped forward and dropped a fifty-pound note onto the ground. The woman picked it up and looked at the man, but he had positioned himself so that the light was behind his head, leaving his face in shadow. "There is another fifty if you'll spare me a few minutes of your time."

The woman straightened. "Now, there's a voice from my past." She was taller than the man, and while her elegant fine-boned face remained expressionless, her slate-gray eyes danced with amusement. "Dr. John Dee," she murmured in an accent that had not been heard in England since the time of Queen Elizabeth in the sixteenth century.

"Miss Virginia Dare," Dee replied, slipping easily into the same accent. He moved his head and the evening light ran across his face. "It is good to see you again."

"I cannot say the same." The woman glanced quickly left and right, nostrils flaring. Her tongue flickered, like a snake's, almost as if she was tasting the air. "I'm not sure I want to be seen with you. You have been marked for death, Doctor. The same mercenaries who only yesterday hunted the Alchemyst are now looking for you." There was nothing friendly about the smile that curled her lips. "How do you know I will not kill you and claim the reward?"

"Well, two reasons, really. First, I know my masters want me alive, and second, because there is little our Dark Elder masters could offer you that you do not already have," Dee said, smiling easily. "You are already immortal, and you have no one to call master."

"There is a very big reward on your head," Virginia Dare said, shoving the money into the pockets of her long denim maxi coat. She pushed the leather cloth into another pocket and slung the flute over her shoulder, carrying it like a rifle.

"I can offer you more," Dee said confidently. "Much more."

"John," Virginia said almost affectionately, "you always were a terrible braggart."

"But I never lied to you."

Virginia seemed surprised by the statement. She took a

moment before answering. "No, you did not," she finally admitted.

"Are you not in the least bit curious?" he asked.

"John, you know I have been curious all my life."

Dee smiled. "What do you want most in the world?"

A look of terrible loss flickered across Virginia Dare's face and her eyes clouded. "Even you cannot give me what I most desire."

The Magician bowed slightly. He had known Virginia Dare for over four hundred years. There had been a time when they had talked seriously of marriage, but even he admitted that he knew little about this mysterious immortal human.

"Can you offer me a Shadowrealm?" she asked lightly.

"I think I can do one better than that. I might be able to offer you the world."

Virginia Dare stopped in the middle of Covent Garden. "Which world?"

"This one."

The young-looking woman slipped her arm through Dee's and maneuvered him toward a café on the opposite side of the square. "Come and buy me a cup of tea, and we can talk about this. I've always rather liked this world."

But Dee froze, eyes fixed to the left.

Virginia slowly turned, nostrils flaring again. A trio of shaven-headed young men had entered the square. They were dressed in a uniform of faded, dirty T-shirts, jeans and heavy work boots. Their arms and shoulders were heavily tattooed, and one, the shortest of the three, had an intricate red and black spiral tattoo curling up around his throat and across the top of his head.

"Cucubuths," the Magician murmured. "We just might be able to slip away without them noticing. . . ." Dee paused as one of the three men turned to look at the couple. "Or then again, we might not," he added with a sigh.

Virginia Dare took one step backward and then another, leaving him standing alone. "You're on your own, Doctor."

"I see you haven't changed, Virginia," he muttered.

"That's how I've survived for so long. I never get involved. I never take sides."

"Maybe you should."

CHAPTER ELEVEN

*T*he two huge ravens, Huginn and Muninn, arrived over London. Although they looked like birds, these were creatures almost as old as the race of humani and were neither living nor dead, but something caught in between. Practically immortal, they possessed the power of human speech and had been created by the three-faced goddess, Hekate, as a gift to the one-eyed Elder, Odin.

But now Hekate was no more—for the first time in generations an Elder had been slain—and her Shadowrealm and the adjoining realms of Asgard and Niflheim destroyed.

And Dee was to blame.

Many Elders had called for the Magician's death, but in the days immediately following the destruction of the Yggdrasill and the Shadowrealms, Dee's powerful Elder masters had protected him. Following the carnage in Paris and the escape of the Alchemyst and the twins from England, however, that protection had been revoked. When Dee was declared *utlaga*, he became fair game for all.

Odin had sworn to wreak terrible vengeance on Dee, whom he blamed for the death of Hekate, the woman he had once loved. The one-eyed Elder knew that his foul rival Hel had escaped the destruction of her own Shadowrealm, Niflheim, and was also now chasing Dee, but Odin was determined to find and deal with the Magician first. So he sent his messengers into the humani Shadowrealm.

The birds scoured the city with eyes that saw beyond the physical, alert for any unusual activity. They noted and reported back to the Elder the myriad creatures that now moved through the city's busy streets. Floating over the smoldering ruins of a used car yard in London, drifting in the oily wind, they felt the gossamer traces of extraordinary and ancient powers. Soaring across Salisbury Plain, they circled the ancient site of Stonehenge, where the air was heavy with orange and vanilla and the ground churned to mud by a host of hooves and claws.

Then they flapped back into the city and floated lazily on currents and eddies in the air, almost too high to be seen, looping in huge circles, waiting, waiting, waiting. . . .

And because they did not know the meaning of time, they were endlessly patient.

CHAPTER TWELVE

$\mathcal{T}$he three shaven-headed men closed in on Dee.

"There's a reward for you," the figure with the tattooed skull announced, walking right up to the doctor. Although the Magician was not tall, this man was at least an inch shorter, but broad and muscular. His lips moved, trying to mimic how the humani smiled, yet his mouth merely twisted into a savage snarl that revealed short pointed yellowed teeth. "A big reward."

"Alive," another added. He had taken up a position to Dee's right.

"Though not necessarily unharmed," the third said from the left. He was the biggest of the three, and wore a dirty green camouflage T-shirt that strained across a heavily muscled chest.

"Funny how the world turns," the leader said. His accent

was a curious mixture of North London and Eastern European. "Yesterday we were working for you, hunting the Alchemyst. Today we are hunting you." He rubbed his hands briskly together. "For double the money, too. I think you might have been underpaying us for Flamel and the children." The short man smiled again. "You always were cheap, Dr. Dee."

"I prefer the term *frugal*," Dee said calmly.

"*Frugal*. That's a good word. I bet it means 'cheap.' " He looked at his companions, and they both nodded.

"Cheap," one repeated.

"Miserly," the largest added.

"Frugal does not buy loyalty. Maybe if you'd paid us a little extra, we might have been encouraged to look the other way just now."

"If I had paid you more, would you?" Dee wondered out loud, curiously.

"Probably not," the creature said. "We are hunters. We usually catch what we hunt."

The Magician's thin lips twisted in a nasty smile. "But you failed to capture Flamel and the children yesterday," he said.

The small man shrugged uncomfortably. "Well, yes . . ."

"Failed," Dee reminded him.

The tattooed man stepped closer, lowering his voice as he glanced quickly left and right. "We tracked their scent as far as St. Marylebone Church. Then the Dearg Due turned up," he added, a touch of horror in his voice.

Dee nodded, careful to keep his face impassive. The stink

coming off the creatures was appalling—a mixture of old meat, stale clothes and unwashed bodies. The cucubuths were hunters, the children of a vampire and a Torc Madra, more beast than man, and he was guessing that at least one of the figures standing around him had a tail tucked in the back of its pants. But even the savage mercenaries were terrified of the Dearg Due, the Red Blood Suckers. "How many were there?" he asked.

"Two," the cucubuth leader whispered. "Female," he added with a grim nod.

Dee nodded again; the females were far deadlier than the males. "But they didn't catch Flamel or the twins either," he said.

"No." The creature grinned again, showing his appalling teeth. "They were too busy chasing us. We lost them in Regent's Park. It was a little embarrassing to be chased through the park by what looked like two schoolgirls," he admitted. "But capturing you will more than make up for it," he said.

"You haven't captured me yet," Dee murmured.

The cucubuth stepped back and spread his arms wide. "What are you going to do, Doctor? You dare not use your powers. Your aura will bring everything—and I do mean *everything*—that is now in London down on you. And if you do use it and manage to escape, the sulfurous stink will linger about you for hours. You'll be easily tracked to your lair."

The cucubuth was correct, Dee knew. If he used his aura, then every Elder, Dark Elder and immortal human in London would know his whereabouts.

"So you can come quietly with us . . . ," the cucubuth suggested.

"Or we can carry you out of here," the larger creature added.

Dr. John Dee sighed and glanced at his watch. He was running out of time.

"In a hurry, Doctor?" the cucubuth asked with a toothy grin.

Dee's right hand moved. It started low on his hip, palm up, rising at an angle, twisting in midair, so that the palm caught the creature under the chin. The tattooed cucubuth's teeth snapped together, and the force of the blow lifted him off his feet and sent him sprawling across the cobblestones. Dee's right leg shot out, catching the biggest creature high on the inside of the thigh, numbing his entire leg, dropping him to the ground into a puddle of dirty water, a look of shocked surprise on his broad brutish face.

The third cucubuth darted away from Dee. "Mistake, Doctor," he snarled, "big mistake."

"I'm not the one who made the mistake," Dee whispered. He took a step closer, hands loose at his sides. The Magician had survived for centuries because people always underestimated him. They looked and saw a slight gray-haired man. Even those who knew his reputation imagined him to be nothing more than a scholar. But Dee was more—much, much more. He had been a warrior. When he had still been fully human, and later when he had become immortal, Dee had traveled across Europe. It was a lawless time, when brigands and outlaws roamed the roads, and even the cities themselves were not safe. If a man was to survive, he had to be able to protect himself. Many people had made the mistake of underestimating the English doctor. It was a mistake he never allowed them to repeat. "I don't need to use my aura to hurt you," the Magician said softly.

"I am cucubuth," the creature said arrogantly. "You may have surprised my brothers, but you will not be able to use the same trick on me."

The Magician heard groaning behind him and glanced over his shoulder to find the cucubuth leader scrambling to his feet. He was holding his jaw in both hands and his eyes looked unfocused.

"You have injured my little brother."

"I'm sure he'll make a full recovery," Dee said. Cucubuths were almost impossible to kill, and even possessed the vampire ability to regenerate injured limbs.

The largest of the three came slowly and painfully to his feet. He stood awkwardly balanced on his left leg, rubbing his right furiously, trying to bring feeling back into it. "And you've ruined my jeans," he growled. The seat and legs of his jeans were black with water.

"What are you going to do now, Doctor?" the unharmed skinhead asked.

"Come a little closer and I'll show you." Dee's smile was as ugly and inhuman as the cucubuth's.

The creature suddenly threw back his head and his mouth formed a sound that could never have come from a human throat. It was a cross between a bark and a howl. All the pigeons gathered on the Covent Garden roofs took to the air in an explosion of flapping wings. From somewhere nearby, what sounded like a wolf howl echoed across London's rooftops. It was joined by another, and then another until the air trembled with the terrifying primeval sounds. All traces of humanity left the cucubuth's face as he laughed. "This is our city, Doctor. We have ruled Trinovantum since before the Romans claimed it as their own. Have you any idea how many of us are here now?"

"I'm guessing it's more than a few."

"Many, many more," the creature snarled. "And they're coming. All of them."

From the corner of his eye, Dee saw movement. Glancing up, he saw a shape move on the triangular roof of St. Paul's Church opposite. A skinhead appeared, silhouetted against the evening sky, then another, and another. There was a commotion on the other side of the square as six skinheads appeared, and then, at the opposite entrance, another three appeared.

The human tourists, seeing the sudden influx of skinheads and fearing a brawl, began to scatter. Shops hastily closed. Within moments, only the ugly shaven-headed cucubuths were left in Covent Garden's cobbled square.

"So what are you going to do now, Dr. Dee?"

CHAPTER THIRTEEN

*T*he noise echoing across the London rooftops and up into the skies alerted the ravens: the primeval howling of cucubuths that had once terrified primitive humani huddling in caves.

Huginn and Muninn dipped toward the sounds.

Blackbirds and crows streamed past them, the simple creatures radiating raw fear. Doves whirled in the air almost directly below; frightened, but incapable of doing anything about their fear, they settled back onto the rooftops around a broad cobbled square, only to immediately rise into the air again as another howl broke through the night.

The ravens flew low across the Thames River, over Victoria Embankment and the Royal Opera House. They spotted the first of the cucubuths in the streets below, seeing through its almost-human guise to reveal the beast-man beneath, with its tusks and ragged claws. Each cucubuth was swathed in a dark aura. And there were hundreds of them, running, loping, jogging, singly and in pairs, converging on the enclosed space of Covent Garden.

Instantly, the ravens knew that they must have found the English Magician. As one, their beaks worked to form a single word: "Dee."

And in a place beyond time, in an isolated Shadowrealm, Odin awoke.

The Elder's huge gray eye opened, but he did not see the bitter snowfields and towering ice crystals that surrounded him. He found he was looking down on a scene in shifting monochrome and without sound: a single human surrounded by three cucubuths. More and more of the creatures swarmed closer. And even though there was no sign of Dee's distinctive aura, Odin knew the human was the English Magician.

The Elder bared his teeth in a ferocious grin: those to whom Dee owed allegiance wanted him brought before them for sentencing and punishment, but Odin had other plans. The huge figure pushed away from the only living thing in his world—a puny and twisted version of the Yggdrasill—and prepared to cross the Shadowrealms.

CHAPTER FOURTEEN

*H*e'd found the rear door to the bookstore open.

Josh Newman shrugged off his backpack as he stepped into the gloomy hallway and then waited, allowing his eyes to adjust. The stink was incredible—a mixture of rot and mildew, a sickly mustiness overlain with the noxious stench of bad eggs. He tried to breathe only through his mouth. Closing his eyes, he concentrated on his hearing. Since Mars Ultor had Awakened him, he'd become extremely conscious of just how important the senses of hearing, taste and smell were. Modern humans tended to rely heavily on sight; Josh had come to realize that his Awakened senses were really the same heightened senses that primitive man had possessed and needed to survive.

But there were no sounds in the building: it even *felt* deserted.

Less than a week ago, he'd run up and down this corridor

unloading a delivery of books from the back of a van. Now all the boxes he had so carefully piled on top of each other were black with mildew, the sides burst open, the books swollen like rotten fruit, almost unrecognizable.

Less than a week ago.

The realization suddenly brought home to Josh how much had changed in the past few days, how much he had discovered and how little he—and the rest of the world—knew about the truth.

Taking a deep breath, the fetid air catching at the back of his throat, Josh then opened his eyes and crept down the corridor, pushed open the door and stepped out into the bookshop.

And stopped in shock.

The shop was an unrecognizable ruin, lost beneath a thick layer of dust and furry mold—it was decaying right before his eyes. The sunlight shafting through the filthy streaked windows showed that the air was thick with drifting spores. Josh clamped his lips shut; he didn't want to risk getting any of them in his mouth. He took a step forward and felt the creaking floorboards shift beneath his weight. A bubble of foul black liquid formed on the wood, and his foot began to sink. Jerking back, he pressed himself against the wall, only to discover that it too was slimy with decay. The plaster was so soft his fingers sank into it.

Looking around, Josh realized with horror that the shop was being eaten: this fungus was feeding off everything—wood, paper, carpet. What was the place going to look like in a couple of hours?

He'd come to the bookshop because Nicholas and Perenelle lived in the apartments above it, and he was hoping that they had returned there. Glancing upward, he noticed the gaping hole in the ceiling, the trailing wires and rotten joists. He suddenly wondered how long it would be before the supports gave way and the upper floors collapsed and then the rest of the building crashed into the cellar.

He edged his way along the wall toward the stairs. It stood to reason that the Flamels would have more than one address in the city. They must have set up places they could escape to if danger threatened. Josh hoped that he'd be able to find an address upstairs—a bill, a letter, something, *anything* to give him a hint of where they were. The banister shifted as he grabbed it—the wood had the consistency of jelly. He pulled his hand back in disgust and was about to rub it against his jeans when he stopped. If the filthy black mold was able to eat through wood, what would it do to his pants? The last thing he needed now was for his pants to rot off his legs. Could this eat through his flesh? he suddenly wondered with a shudder. The desire to turn and run was almost overwhelming, but he knew that his only chance of finding his sister lay with the Flamels, so he started up the stairs.

Each step moved beneath his weight. He was halfway up when his foot went all the way through a stair with a dull snap. He felt the entire staircase sway, and he realized that it was going to collapse. He launched himself up the rest of the way just as the staircase shuddered and collapsed, crashing into the shop below. Josh's chest slammed onto the landing; his legs dangled in midair as his fingers scrambled to grab hold of the thick carpet covering the upper floor, but it ripped and shredded to threads in his grip. He attempted to scream but the sound got caught at the back of his throat. A chunk of carpet ripped away in his hand and he jerked backward. . . .

Iron-hard fingers caught his wrists.

Josh was hauled up and found himself looking into Perenelle Flamel's bright green eyes. "Josh Newman," she murmured as she set him down gently on the landing. "We were not expecting you."

Nicholas appeared out of a doorway and stopped beside his wife. "We were expecting . . . trouble," he said quietly. "It's good to see you."

Josh rubbed his numb wrists. Perenelle's strength was astonishing, and she'd almost wrenched his shoulders out of their sockets when she'd lifted him straight up in the air. He pressed his hands against his chest where it had hit the landing and took a deep breath. He was bruised, but he didn't think he'd broken any ribs.

"What brings you here, Josh?" Perenelle said softly, her eyes searching his face. She answered her own question: "Sophie."

"Sophie's missing," Josh said breathlessly. "She was kidnapped by a girl calling herself Aoife. She said she was Scathach's sister," he added. "She sure looked like her." He saw their expressions change slightly, watched what he recognized as fear flicker in the Alchemyst's eyes. "That's not good, is it?"

Perenelle shook her head. "Not good at all."

CHAPTER FIFTEEN

"*Vingt* . . . *vingt-et-un* . . . twenty-two." Joan of Arc slid down the grassy incline and rejoined her companion on the banks of the narrow stream. "What do you call twenty-two saber-toothed tigers?" the slender, gray-eyed woman asked breathlessly. "A pack, a pride?"

"I call them trouble," Scathach said shortly. She straightened and looked back up the incline. "And you're about to tell me they're heading this way."

Joan nodded. "They are heading this way," she said with a grin.

Scathach tapped her foot at the edge of the stream. It fit into a huge splayed footprint sunk in the mud. "This is their watering hole." Closing her eyes, she breathed deeply and then pointed with one of her matched short swords. "More are approaching from the south."

"And from the east," Joan added.

Scatty opened her eyes and looked at her friend. The late-afternoon sunshine turned Joan's pale skin golden. "How do you know?"

The Frenchwoman caught the red-haired warrior's shoulder and turned her. Three enormous saber-toothed tigers had appeared out of the tall grass. They stood still, savage jaws gaping, eyes wide and unblinking, only their tails twitching slightly. "Fight or run?" Joan asked.

"If we run, they'll chase us," Scatty said matter-of-factly.

"If we fight, they'll overpower us. There are too many of them. Maybe thirty in total."

The largest of the saber-toothed tigers moved almost in slow motion and took a tentative step forward. Enormous slit-pupiled golden eyes fixed on Scathach.

"I think he likes you," Joan murmured. She touched the sword strapped to her shoulder and realized that if all the creatures attacked at once, her weapon would be useless.

"I've always preferred dogs," Scathach said, watching the creature carefully. "You know where you are with dogs." She slid her matched swords into their sheaths on her back and pulled her nunchaku from their pouch on her hip. "Stay here," she commanded, and then, before Joan could reply, she raced toward the tiger.

The huge creature froze.

A dozen steps carried the warrior across the ground, the nunchaku buzzing and spinning in her right hand.

The tiger hunched, tail swishing wildly, ropy threads of saliva on its enormous teeth . . . and then it jumped, thick claws extended.

"Scatty!" Joan managed to gasp, even as the red-haired warrior launched herself into the air, like a swimmer diving into the sea. Her leap carried her straight over the tiger, and her nunchaku snapped out, the blunt end of the twelve-inch length of carved wood catching the creature on the back of the skull. Scatty spun in midair and landed lightly on her feet. The tiger, stunned by the blow, crashed to the ground in a tangle of limbs. The beast immediately clambered shakily to its feet, wobbled and then fell over again.

Scatty turned to face its two companions, tapping the nunchaku in the palm of her left hand. The creatures looked at her, looked at their companion, then stepped back, melting into the long grasses.

When Joan spun around, she discovered that the other tigers had disappeared too. "Very impressive," she said.

"You just have to show them who's boss," Scatty answered, kneeling beside the huge saber-toothed tiger. She ran her hand over the back of its head, then raised its eyelid to look at it. The beast rumbled but made no attempt to get up.

Joan crouched beside her friend. She looked at the tiger's teeth. The incisors were the length of her hand and tapered to points that could probably pierce armor.

"The trick," Scatty said, "is to hit them just where the base of the skull touches the spine. The blow stuns them."

"And if you miss?"

"Then you just make them mad." Scatty's smile revealed her own savage teeth. "But I don't miss." She patted the huge beast. "It'll wake up with a headache."

Joan of Arc straightened and tapped her friend's shoulder. "What?" Scatty looked up.

Joan nodded toward the hill. The twenty-two saber-toothed tigers had gathered on the brow. They were joined by two more, and then another four appeared. They all looked to be fully grown adults, and their rumbling growls actually vibrated through the ground.

"Do you think this one might have been the leader of the pack?" Joan asked.

The animals parted and another saber-toothed tiger appeared. It was huge, towering head and shoulders over the others and at least half as long again. Its dun coat was white with the lines of ancient scars, one of its bottom teeth had broken off into a ragged spur, and its left eye was only a white glassy globe.

"*This* one is the leader of the pack," Scatty said, taking a step backward.

The creature's single good eye moved from the tiger on the ground to Scatty and back to the tiger again. And then it opened its maw and growled. The sound was incredible, a bone-shaking rumble that sent birds wheeling into the air for miles around. Then, slowly, almost delicately, it started to pick its way down the incline.

Scatty took a step toward the creature, but Joan caught her arm. "Do you remember something you taught me when I was fighting the English?" she asked urgently.

Scatty looked at her blankly.

"You told me that it was a mistake to fight the scarred warriors. They were the survivors." The Frenchwoman nodded toward the beast approaching them. "Look at this creature. It has survived many battles."

Scathach looked at the huge scarred saber-toothed tiger. "I am the Shadow," she said simply. "I can defeat her."

Joan's fingers tightened on her friend's arm. "You also told me never to engage in a battle unless it was completely unavoidable. You don't have to do this."

"You're right, I suppose." Scatty sighed, then asked, almost regretfully, "So what do we do?"

"We run!"

CHAPTER SIXTEEN

*N*iccolò Machiavelli took a deep breath of the salty sea air and pressed his hands against his aching stomach. Before he'd become immortal he'd been troubled with ulcers, and although his Elder master had cured him of all human ills, at times of great stress his stomach still cramped. Now, standing on the quay on Alcatraz, staring out toward San Francisco, his stomach felt as if it were on fire.

"We're going to be fine, just fine," the young man in the stained jeans and battered cowboy boots standing beside him said for the tenth time. "We're going to be fine."

"William," Machiavelli said carefully, keeping his voice low, "how long have you been immortal?"

"One hundred and twenty-six years," Billy the Kid said proudly.

"I became immortal in the year 1527," the Italian said,

glancing at the American. "I was alive when Columbus claimed discovery of this country. I am not the oldest immortal— I am older than Dee, but the Alchemyst Flamel is older than I, Duns Scotus is even older still, and Mo-Tzu older still. Gilgamesh is older than all of us. But I have had more contact with the Elders than these others. And let me tell you that our Elder masters do not countenance failure. They demand complete obedience. They expect results. And we have failed," he added. He held up his closed fist and extended his little finger. "We were sent here to kill the Sorceress Perenelle"—he stuck a second finger up—"and release the creatures in the cells into the city." Another finger. "Perenelle escaped, in our boat," he added, extending a fourth finger, "leaving us trapped on the island with the monsters still in their cells. We failed. We are most definitely *not* going to be fine."

Both men turned as the sound of an engine drew nearer. Machiavelli shaded his stone-gray eyes and saw a boat approaching, leaving a wide white wake across the bay.

Billy held up his cell phone. "I called for help," he said, almost apologetically. "What do you reckon will happen?"

Machiavelli sighed. "We will be summoned before our masters and our immortality will be removed. We will die. Quickly, if we are lucky, but our masters are often cruel. . . ."

Billy shuddered. "Not sure I like the thought of that. I've sort of grown used to being immortal." Then he shook his head quickly. "My master is . . ." He paused, trying to find the proper word. "He's different from some of these other

83

Elders. I can explain all this to him." He waved his hand vaguely in the direction of the prison buildings behind him. "We'll be fine."

"Please stop saying that."

A bright red speedboat pulled up to the dock and a tall, striking-looking Native American with copper skin and hatchet-sharp features grinned up at Billy the Kid. "Our master wants to see you—you too," he said, looking at Machiavelli. "You are both in so much trouble."

CHAPTER SEVENTEEN

$\mathcal{T}$he cucubuths closed in on Dee.

Dozens had crowded into Covent Garden; scores more lined the roofs of the surrounding buildings, and their bestial howls still echoed across the city. The shaven-headed leader spread his arms wide, exposing the black tattoos that snaked along the underside of his arms. "What are you going to do now, Doctor?"

Dee reached under his coat and touched the hilt of the stone blade that hung beneath his arm. He had fashioned a sheath for it out of two leather belts. He had no idea what would happen if he actually used the sword. He had carried Excalibur for centuries and still had only the vaguest understanding of its powers. His limited experience with Clarent suggested that it was even more powerful than its twin blade. Though now that they had fused, they had to be even more powerful . . . or did the two cancel each other out?

The Magician quickly considered his options. If he did wield the sword, he was sure it would light up the London skies for miles around, and probably blaze into the nearby Shadowrealms. But if he didn't use the sword or his powers, then the cucubuths would capture him and bring him before his Dark Elder masters. And he most certainly did not want to do that: he hadn't reached his five hundredth birthday yet. He was far too young to die.

"Come quietly, Doctor," the cucubuth said in the ancient Wendish language of east Europe.

Dee's hand tightened on the hilt of the sword. He felt its chill numb his fingers, and instantly, strange and bizarre thoughts flickered at the very edges of his consciousness.

Cucubuths in leather and hide armor . . . vampires wearing chain mail and metal . . . wading ashore from narrow metal boats, fighting on a beach, battling hairy, primitive one-eyed beasts . . .

The sound that sliced through the night was so high-pitched it was almost beyond the range of human hearing: a single drawn-out wavering note.

The cucubuths fell as if they had been struck. Those closest to Dee dropped first, and then in a long rippling wave the creatures toppled to the ground, hands pressed to their ears, writhing in agony.

Virginia Dare stepped out of the shadows, her flute pressed to her lips, and smiled at Dee.

"I am indebted to you." The doctor bowed deeply, an old-fashioned gesture last used in the court of the first Queen Elizabeth.

Virginia drew in a breath. "Consider this repayment for the time you saved my life in Boston."

One of the cucubuths reached for Dee's ankle and he kicked the hand aside. "We should go," he said. A few of the creatures were already staggering to their feet, but another series of piercing notes from Dare's flute dropped them to the ground again.

Stepping lightly over the mass of squirming bodies, Dare and Dee made their way out of Covent Garden. Dee paused at the King Street entrance and turned to look back. The cobbled square was a mass of twisting, shifting bodies. Some of the creatures were already beginning to lose their human appearance as their hands and faces reverted back to their beast forms. "That's a neat trick," he said, hurrying to catch up with Dare, who had continued on down the street, still playing the flute. "How long will the spell last?" Dee asked.

"Not long. The more intelligent the creature, the longer the spell endures. On primitive beasts like these: ten, twenty minutes."

The street was littered with cucubuths squirming in pain, their hands pressed to their ears. Two fell off the roof of a building directly in front of Dee and Dare, hitting the ground hard enough to crack the paving slabs. Without breaking stride, Virginia stepped over their twitching bodies. Dee walked around them; he knew a simple fall would not harm the creatures, only slow them down.

"I learned the tune from a German," she said between breaths. "He used to be a rat catcher."

"What made you choose my side?" Dee asked.

"You promised me a world," Virginia Dare said seriously. "You better keep that promise," she added. "I learned some other tunes from the rat catcher, and believe me, you do not want me to play them."

The Magician attempted a laugh. "Why, that sounds almost like a threat . . . ," he began.

"It was," she said, then grinned. "Actually, it was more than a threat. It's a promise."

CHAPTER EIGHTEEN

The ravens watched the slender female figure step out of the shadows, a long wooden flute pressed to her lips.

Vaguely—more a sensation in their bones than a vibration in the air—they experienced the ghost of a sound. Ancient instincts sent them soaring upward, higher and higher, away from the deathly noise.

From their great height, they watched the cucubuths fall like grass flattened by a wind. And they saw Dee and the woman move through the bodies, strolling unhurriedly away from the chaos.

In his Shadowrealm, Odin watched the couple through the raven's eyes. Who was this woman and how had she rendered the cucubuths unconscious?

The Elder frowned, trying to focus on the female humani. There was something about her, something almost familiar.

She was obviously an ally of Dee's, and she possessed what looked like one of the ancient artifacts of power.

And suddenly, the name came to him in a flood of bitter memories, and he threw back his head and howled in delight. Virginia Dare: one of the few immortals who had slain their master and survived. He had known her master and counted him a friend. Now he could avenge the death of his love *and* his friend.

"Bring Dee to me," he instructed the ravens. "Kill the female."

High above the city, the ravens followed the immortal humani and the Elder watched through their eyes.

CHAPTER NINETEEN

"*W*hen we first saw her, we thought it was Scatty," Josh said.

"Aoife of the Shadows," Perenelle said, "Scathach's twin sister."

"Younger or older?" Josh asked. He was twenty-eight seconds younger than his sister, and although he was a head taller, he still felt like the little brother. Perenelle and Josh had climbed down the metal fire escape and were standing in the alleyway behind the shop, waiting for Nicholas to join them.

"Well that depends on whom you talk to," Perenelle said with a smile. "Scathach says she is the elder, but Aoife claims that she was born first."

Nicholas appeared at the top of the stairs and started to climb down. He was moving slowly and awkwardly because of the wooden box strapped to his back.

"Scatty never said anything about having a sister," Josh

said. He found the concept hard to believe. He couldn't imagine ever not acknowledging his sister, his twin.

"Yes, well, they had a terrible argument a long time ago. There was a boy they both loved. Cuchulain, the Hound of Ulster. And despite his name, he was completely human."

"What happened?" Josh asked.

"He died," Perenelle said shortly, then she sighed. "Scatty will not speak of it, but Cuchulain died a hero's death. The sisters blamed one another for it, though as far I can see, neither was entirely to blame. Cuchulain was young and headstrong. No one could control him. He was also one of the finest warriors who ever lived, and the last to be trained by both Aoife and Scathach. The sisters have not spoken in a very long time. In the early days, Scatty remained in Europe and the Americas while Aoife traveled south into Africa, where she was worshipped as a goddess. Then Aoife went east into the Orient, where she now spends most of her time. I doubt they have met in the last four or five centuries."

"Was Aoife responsible for Cu . . . Coo . . ."

"Cuchulain."

"For his death?" Josh asked.

"As responsible as Scathach. If they had fought by his side, he would not have died."

Nicholas reached the end of the ladder and Perenelle and Josh helped him down the last steps. He stood leaning against the wall, his breath coming in great heaving gasps, and Josh suddenly realized that the Alchemyst was now an old man. He looked at Flamel closely, and as he did it became clear just how much the events of the past week had aged the man—his close-cropped hair was now almost bone white, and wrinkles were etched deeply into his forehead and cheeks. The veins on the back of his hands were prominent, and the skin speckled with age spots. Josh turned to look at the Sorceress. She too had aged, though not quite so dramatically as her husband. Perenelle caught him staring at her and her smile turned wistful. Reaching out, she pressed her forefinger to Josh's chest. Paper crinkled under his T-shirt. "Unless we get the Codex and renew the immortality spell, we will be dead of old age within a matter of days." Abruptly, her green eyes grew huge with tears. "Nicholas first, then me."

Josh felt his breath catch in his throat. Although he didn't trust Nicholas and was unsure how he felt about Perenelle, the thought of them dying filled him with terror. He and Sophie needed the Flamels.

"We must get the Book of Abraham the Mage," Perenelle repeated.

"Dee has the Codex," Josh said. "He's probably passed it on to his masters by now."

Nicholas shook his head. "I doubt he's had time to do that. Everything has happened so fast." He handed Josh the carved wooden box. "Carry that for me, would you?" Josh grunted with the weight of the box; it was surprisingly heavy. "Think—the Magician has been close behind us from the moment he got the Codex last week. I don't think he would have had time to give it to his Elder masters. And I think it unlikely he would carry it to England with him in his luggage. Logic says it's probably still here in San Francisco."

"Where?" Josh asked quickly. "Maybe we could steal it

back. . . ." He stopped. Both Perenelle and Nicholas were shaking their heads.

"Even if we could," the Sorceress said, "I'll wager it is protected by more than human guards. Also"—she tapped the box in Josh's arms—"we have more important things to do."

"We have to find your sister," Nicholas said.

"And destroy the creatures on Alcatraz," Perenelle added.

Josh looked at them both in alarm. "But how are you going to do that? Won't that use all your powers and age you? And kill you?" He added in a whisper.

"Yes," Nicholas and Perenelle Flamel said in unison.

"And it is a price we are willing to pay," Perenelle declared.

CHAPTER TWENTY

$\mathcal{S}$ophie regained consciousness, but she remained still, her eyes closed. Concentrating on her Awakened senses, she tried to create a mental picture of her surroundings from the sounds, smells and sensations that engulfed her. There was salt in the air, which wasn't unusual in San Francisco, but this was a bitter, slightly sour odor, as if she was very close to the sea. The salt smell was touched with the tang of diesel fuel, which suggested that she might be in a port. Oddly, there was also the crisp smell of wood and the hint of spices in the warm, close air. Even before she felt the slight shifting movements beneath her and heard the faint slap of water against wood, she knew she was on a boat. She was lying down, not on a bed, but on something soft that held her tightly and raised her head and feet.

"I know you're awake."

The voice brought Sophie's eyes open. Scathach! The

shock of red hair was the only point of color in the dark room, and for a single instant, Sophie thought the woman was floating in midair. She struggled to sit up—she'd been lying in a hammock, she realized—and discovered that the woman was sitting cross-legged on a wooden box, her black clothing helping her to blend in with the darkened room. But as Sophie straightened, memories flooded back and she knew that this was not the Shadow. This was Aoife of the Shadows.

Sophie looked around, noting the heavy curtains covering the windows. One of the windows had been boarded up, and the rest were crisscrossed with thick metal bars.

"How did you know I was awake?" she asked, struggling upright in the hammock.

"I heard the change in your breathing," Aoife answered simply.

Sophie maneuvered herself to the edge of her swinging perch. Dangling her legs, she looked at the figure sitting on the box. The resemblance to Scathach was startling—the same bright red hair, the same brilliant green eyes and pale skin—but there was something about the jut of her jaw that set her apart from her sister. And while Scatty had tiny laugh lines around her eyes and at the corners of her mouth, Aoife's face was smooth.

"You are not frightened?" Aoife asked, tilting her head slightly to one side.

"No," Sophie said with sudden realization. "Should I be?"

"Perhaps if you knew me . . ."

Sophie was about to say that she knew all about Aoife, but

96

that would mean revealing that the Witch of Endor had passed on her memories, and she still didn't want Aoife to know that. "I know your sister," she said instead.

"I am not my sister," Aoife said, her accent changing, revealing hints of her Celtic background.

"Who do you serve?" Sophie asked.

"Myself."

"Elders or Dark Elders?" Sophie persisted.

Aoife's hands moved in a dismissive gesture. "The terms are meaningless. Good or bad is a matter of perspective. I met an immortal humani once, a man called William Shakespeare, who wrote that there is nothing either good or bad, but thinking makes it so."

Sophie bit the inside of her cheek to keep a straight face. She wasn't about to tell Aoife that she'd actually met the famous bard only the day before yesterday. "Why did you kidnap me?"

"Kidnap you?" Aoife's eyes widened in surprise and then her lips curled. "I suppose I did. I just needed to talk to you without interruption."

"We could have talked on the street."

"I wanted to talk in private. You could have invited me in."

Sophie shook her head. "No, I wasn't going to do that. My brother will find you," she added.

Aoife laughed dismissively. "I doubt that. I had a brief encounter with him—he is powerful, but unskilled." Then, with a touch of what might have been awe in her voice, she asked, "He is Gold?"

"And I'm Silver," Sophie said proudly.

"The twins of legend." Aoife sneered disbelievingly.

"You don't believe that?"

"Do you know how many twins of legend there have been?"

"I know that there've been others . . . ," Sophie said cautiously.

"Many others. And do you know where they are now?"

Sophie started to shake her head, though she knew the answer.

"These gold and silver auras are not gifts. They are a curse," Aoife snapped. "They will destroy you and everyone around you. I have seen entire cities laid to waste to kill just one twin."

"The Alchemyst said that the Dark Elders—"

"I have told you: there are no Dark Elders," Aoife snapped. "There are just Elders, neither good nor bad. Just a race of beings we now call Elders. Some encourage the humani, others despise them: that is the only difference between them. And even those guardians of humanity often change their allegiances. Do you think my sister was always the champion of the new humani race?"

The question shocked Sophie into silence. She wanted to refute the suggestion, but the Witch's insidious memories trickled into her consciousness and she caught hints and glimpses of the truth—the *real* truth—about Scathach and why she was called the Shadow.

"I need you to tell me . . . ," Aoife began.

"Are you going to hurt me?" Sophie asked suddenly.

The question caught Aoife by surprise. "Of course not."

"Good." Sophie slipped out of the hammock and dropped to the floor. She swayed slightly. "I need something to eat," she interrupted. "I'm starving. Do you have any crackers or fruit?"

Aoife blinked. She flowed to her feet and stood in front of the girl. "Well, no, actually. I don't eat. Not food . . . not as you would recognize it, anyway."

"I need some food. Real food. No meat," she added quickly, her stomach rebelling even at the thought. "And no onions either."

"What's wrong with onions?" Aoife asked.

"I don't like the taste."

The houseboat was moored in the bay at Sausalito. It was a long rectangular wooden box—like the upper story of a house set directly onto the water. It had been painted and repainted green—each time with a different shade of the color—but the sea air and time had stripped the surface and the paint now hung in long peeling sheets, revealing the mottled wood beneath. There was no engine, and it was clear that the houseboat hadn't moved from its moorings in years.

Sophie and Aoife sat on the deck in two white plastic chairs. Sophie had already eaten two bananas, an orange and a pear and was now slowly munching her way through a pound of grapes, flicking the seeds into the water.

"I am not your enemy," Aoife began. "Nor am I your

friend," she added hastily. "I just want to know what has happened to my sister."

"Why do you care?" Sophie asked curiously, glancing sidelong at the red-haired woman. Although Aoife's eyes were hidden behind dark glasses, the girl could feel them drill into her. "I thought you haven't spoken in centuries."

"She is still my sister. She is . . . family. She is my responsibility."

Sophie nodded. She understood that. She'd always felt she had a responsibility to look after her brother—even though he was perfectly capable of looking after himself. "How much do you know about what's happened in the past few days?" she asked.

"Nothing," Aoife said, surprising her. "I felt Scathach *go* and I came here immediately."

"Where were you?"

"In the Gobi Desert."

Sophie squeezed a seed between her fingers and watched it arc into the water. "But that's in Mongolia, isn't it?"

"Yes."

"Scatty only disappeared yesterday. You must have used leygates to get here."

Aoife nodded. "I used a little trick your friend Saint-Germain taught me a long time ago: he showed me how to see the gold and silver leygate spires. I used the gates to leap from Mongolia to the Ise Shine in Japan, to Uluru in Australia, then Easter Island and finally on to Mount Tamalpais." She leaned forward and tapped Sophie on the knee. "I hate leygates."

"Scatty said they make her seasick."

Aoife sat back and nodded. "Aye, that's just how they make me feel."

Sophie twisted around to where the Japanese man who had driven the limo was scraping paint from the wall of the houseboat. "Did he come with you from Japan?"

"Who? Niten? No, he lives here in San Francisco. He is an immortal human and we are old friends," she added with a hint of a genuine smile. "This is his houseboat."

"Looks like he hasn't been here for a while."

"Niten travels," Aoife said simply. "He wanders the Shadow-realms."

Sophie looked again at the Asian man. She had initially assumed he was in his late teens or early twenties, but now she could make out the faint lines around his eyes, and she noticed that his wrists and knuckles were thick: the sure signs of a martial artist. He was stripping old paint from the wood with smooth, fluid movements.

"Tell me what happened to my sister."

Sophie turned back to Aoife and put down the grapes. "All I can tell you is what Nicholas told me and Josh yesterday, and he heard it from Saint-Germain. Scathach and Joan of Arc were preparing to jump from Paris to Mount Tamalpais to attempt to rescue Perenelle, who was trapped on Alcatraz . . ."

Aoife held up her hand. "What has Joan of Arc got to do with this?"

"She's married to Saint-Germain." Sophie grinned at the look of surprise on Aoife's face. "You didn't know? I think they got married recently."

"Joan of Arc and Saint-Germain," Aoife murmured, shaking her head. "Did you hear that?" she said, without raising her voice.

"I thought you knew," Niten said, and although his voice was barely above a whisper, it carried clearly. He continued to peel long strips of flaking paint off the side of the houseboat.

"How would I know?" Aoife snapped. "No one tells me anything." She twisted in her seat to look at Niten. "Why didn't you tell me?"

"You never liked the Frenchman, and I knew you would dislike the Frenchwoman even more because your sister made her immortal with her blood."

"She did?" Aoife looked horrified. "Joan carries my sister's blood within her?"

"You didn't know about this?" Sophie asked, surprised.

The red-haired woman shook her head. "I did not. What happened?"

"Joan was condemned to be burned at the stake. Scathach single-handedly rode into the city and rescued her, but Joan was injured in the escape. The only way to save her life was to give her a blood transfusion," Sophie explained.

Aoife leaned forward, elbows on her knees, long pale fingers locked together. "Tell me about my sister. What happened to her?"

"I don't know much more," Sophie said. "Apparently, they were going to use the leygate at Notre Dame, but it was sabotaged. Saint-Germain found traces of mammoth dust around the spot. Nicholas thinks Machiavelli was responsible.

Instead of landing on Mount Tamalpais today, it looks as if they've been dropped sometime in the past."

"How far in the past?"

"Nicholas and Saint-Germain think the mammoth bones mean the Pleistocene era. So that could be anywhere from one point eight million years ago to just over eleven thousand years ago."

Sophie watched in astonishment as Aoife visibly relaxed. "Oh, that's not too bad, then. If that's all that's happened, we can go back and rescue them."

"How?" Sophie demanded.

"There are ways." Aoife looked over at Niten. "Perhaps it's time we talked to the Alchemyst and his wife, to see if they have any further information. Do you know where they are?"

"Yes," Niten said simply as he scraped away the paint.

"Would you like to tell me?" Sophie could clearly hear the annoyance in her voice.

The slender man raised his chin toward the shore, and Sophie and Aoife turned to see a bright red Thunderbird pull up to the dock in a cloud of dust. "Right here."

CHAPTER TWENTY-ONE

With his long hair tied back in a tight ponytail, head covered in a stained Dodgers baseball cap, eyes huge behind thick glasses, and wearing clothes at least two sizes too large for him, the Comte de Saint-Germain shuffled unnoticed through the Arrivals Hall at London's Heathrow airport. Stepping out into the cool damp evening air, he pulled his cell phone from his pocket and checked his messages.

There was one message. Number withheld. It said simply: *Level 3, space 243.*

He turned and headed into the parking structure, taking the stairs up to level three. He was moving quickly, checking the numbers, when a dark shape detached itself from the shadows and fell into step alongside him. "Looking for a taxi, sir?"

"Palamedes," Saint-Germain whispered, "don't do that. You could have given me a heart attack."

"Hardly. You knew I was there, didn't you?

Saint-Germain nodded. "I smelled you."

"So you're saying I smell?"

"You smell of cloves. Ah, but it is good to see you, old friend," the Frenchman said, using a Persian dialect that had gone extinct a century earlier.

"I wish it were in happier circumstances," the huge shaven-headed man said. He eased Saint-Germain's carry-on bag from his hands. The Frenchman tried to protest, but the Saracen Knight ignored him. "I sent a message to my master," the knight continued in the same ancient language. Both immortals were too experienced to allow anyone to come close enough to eavesdrop on them, but they were equally conscious that there were more security cameras in London than any other city on earth. Anyone looking at them now would just see a London taxi driver picking up a fare.

"And how is your master?" Saint-Germain asked cautiously.

"Still angry at you. You seem to have a gift for upsetting people," Palamedes added with a broad grin.

"Will he help me?" Saint-Germain asked nervously.

"I don't know. I will speak for you. Shakespeare will, too, and you know what a great talker he is." They stopped at a black cab and Palamedes pulled open the door to allow the Frenchman inside. "There will be a cost," the knight said seriously.

Saint-Germain gripped his friend's arm. "Anything. I will pay anything to get my wife back."

"Even your immortality?"

"Even that. What is the point in living forever, if it is not with the woman I love?"

A flicker of immeasurable sadness crossed the knight's face. "I understand that," he said softly.

CHAPTER TWENTY-TWO

"*T*his is my friend Ma-ka-tai-me-she-kia-kiak," Billy the Kid said as the small powerboat bounced across San Francisco Bay.

The sharp-featured man nodded to Machiavelli. "You'll find it more convenient to call me Black Hawk," he drawled. He was dressed, like Billy, in faded jeans, old cowboy boots and a T-shirt. Unlike Billy, though, who was thin to the point of scrawniness, Black Hawk was a solid mass of muscle. He handled the bucking powerboat with ease.

Billy tapped him on the shoulder. "Over there; my car is at Pier—"

"I checked. Your car is gone," Black Hawk said, and then laughed aloud at the stricken look on Billy's face.

"Stolen! Someone stole my car!" He turned to the Italian. "That's . . . that's criminal!"

Machiavelli kept his face expressionless. "I'll wager the Sorceress took it."

Billy nodded eagerly. "I bet you're right. She'll look after it, though, won't she? I mean, she'll know it's a classic car and treat it with respect?"

Machiavelli caught Black Hawk's eye and then had to look away quickly before he laughed. "I do believe I read in my files somewhere that Perenelle Flamel only learned how to drive recently," he said innocently.

Billy sank down to the side of the boat as if he'd been struck. "She'll ruin it. She'll wreck the transmission and she'll probably scrape the tires against the curb. Do you know how hard it is to find those whitewall tires?"

"If it's any consolation," Black Hawk said with a grin, "in about an hour, you'll never need a car again. The last time I saw our master this angry was in April 1906 . . . and you know what happened then."

Billy's face set in a petulant snarl. "Well, I don't know what you're so happy about. I was going to leave you that car in my will."

"Thanks." Black Hawk shrugged. "But I'm not a Thunderbird person; I prefer Mustangs."

CHAPTER TWENTY-THREE

Sophie leapt out of her chair as Josh pushed open the driver's door and climbed out of the red Thunderbird. Aoife's hand fell on her shoulder, squeezing gently, but the warning was clear: she was not to move. Perenelle climbed out of the back of the car and Nicholas slowly pushed open the passenger door. It took some seconds before he straightened.

Niten appeared by Aoife's side, two Japanese swords, one longer than the other, held lightly in his hands. "Be calm," he said quietly, and Sophie wasn't sure if he was talking to her or to Aoife.

"Sophie, are you all right?" Josh went to step forward, but Nicholas stretched out his arm, stopping him.

"I'm fine," she called, her voice echoing flatly across the water. The dock was slightly higher than the houseboat, and Sophie's face was at the same level as her twin, but they were less than ten feet apart. Without turning her head, she said, "I told you he'd find me."

"He is full of surprises," Aoife murmured, then raised her voice. "How did you find me?" she called out, addressing the question to Josh, but it was Perenelle who answered, stepping around her husband and walking right up to the edge of the dock.

"You have few friends in the Americas, Aoife," the Sorceress said, "and fewer still in this city. You had nowhere to go . . . except to the Swordsman, of course." She bowed slightly to the Japanese man, hands pressed flat against her thighs.

"Sorceress," he acknowledged. "I have heard much about you, and your husband, too." He matched her bow, dipping his head, though his eyes never left hers.

"We called your dojo earlier and discovered that you had not attended morning lessons. Then we drove past your home: the moment I saw that the newspaper was still in your driveway, I knew you were not there."

"You have my home address?" he said cautiously.

"I know all there is to know about you, Swordsman."

"How did you know I was here?" he said.

"You come here most weekends to work on the boat."

"How did you know that?" he asked.

Perenelle smiled but did not answer.

"I did not realize I had become a creature of habit and routine." Niten bowed again. "There is nothing more dangerous to the warrior. Nor did I realize I was being watched," he added.

"Not all of my spies were humani," the Sorceress said.

"Even so; I should have spotted them. I must have become lazy in my old age."

"And we know how dangerous that is, don't we?" Perenelle asked. "Laziness will kill even the strongest warrior."

"You will not be able to follow me again," the Swordsman said, head tilted to one side, the faintest smile on his thin lips.

"I know that."

"Why have you told me this?" he wondered aloud.

"Nicholas and I were content to monitor your movements, and once we were sure you meant us no harm, we left you alone. But what we did, others can do also . . . and you and your legendary swords would be quite a prize."

"Well, this is all very civilized," Aoife interrupted rudely, "but what—exactly—do you want?"

"We've come for the girl . . . and to talk," Nicholas answered.

"And if I refuse?" Aoife demanded.

Nicholas sighed. "I am having a really bad day, and Perenelle is not in a good humor. Now, you really do not want to make us angry, do you?"

"You do not frighten me, Alchemyst," Aoife snarled.

"I should," Nicholas whispered. "And Perenelle should terrify you."

"We should listen to what they have to say," Niten said suddenly. "Only moments ago, you wanted to talk to them," he reminded Aoife.

"Yes, but not here and not now."

"Talk to them," Sophie said.

"Be quiet."

Sophie rounded on the woman. "Don't you ever speak to me like that again," she said, suddenly angry. She hated—absolutely hated—when adults dismissed her.

Aoife looked at her in surprise, but before she could reply, Niten stepped up to the edge of the houseboat and looked from the Alchemyst to the Sorceress. "Give me your word that this is not a trick."

"I give you my word," Nicholas said.

"And I," Perenelle added.

Niten's arms moved and the swords disappeared into matched sheaths he wore strapped to his hip. "Come aboard," he said. "Enter freely and of your own will."

"Hey . . . ," Aoife began.

"This is my boat," Niten reminded her, "and the Flamels may be many things, but I believe that they have always kept their word."

"Tell that to the generations of people they betrayed and destroyed," Aoife muttered, but she stepped back and allowed Nicholas, Perenelle and Josh onto the boat.

"You need to learn how to trust a little more," the Swordsman said to Aoife.

"And you need to learn to trust the right people," she snapped. "And these are not the right people."

"Your sister likes and trusts them."

Aoife sneered. "I am not my sister."

CHAPTER TWENTY-FOUR

"*N*one of these things are of any concern to me," Aoife said finally. Nicholas and Perenelle had just spent thirty minutes explaining the events of the past few days, adding details that Sophie had forgotten or skipped over.

Niten had set up a wooden crate on the center of the deck and arranged an assortment of mismatched chairs around it. He'd placed a delicately beautiful, almost transparent white china teapot and matching cups on the crate and poured fragrant olive green tea. The Swordsman had not sat, however; he had stood behind Aoife, arms hanging loosely at his sides as Nicholas and Perenelle told their story, starting with the theft of the Codex from the bookshop the previous Thursday.

Aoife shook her head. "I just want my sister back safely."

"We all want that," Nicholas said firmly. "Scathach is precious to us, too." He reached for his wife's hand. "She is the daughter we never had." He drew in a deep shuddering

113

breath. "But Scathach's return—Joan's, too—is not our immediate priority. The Dark Elders have gathered together an army in the cells on Alcatraz. They plan to release them on the city."

"So?" Aoife asked.

Perenelle leaned forward and a static charge rippled down the length of her silver-streaked hair, raising it off her back. When she spoke, her words were as brittle as the look in her eyes. "Are you so divorced from humanity that you would condemn them to annihilation? You know what will happen to civilization if these monsters are allowed to prowl the city."

"It has happened before," Aoife snapped. Tendrils of faint gray smoke leaked from her nostrils. "On at least four previous occasions that I know of, the humani were almost wiped out, but they rose to repopulate the earth. You are old, Sorceress, but you have experienced only a fraction of what I have endured upon this earth. I have watched civilizations rise and fall and rise again. Sometimes it is necessary to wipe the slate clean and start fresh." She spread her arms wide. "Look at what this present batch of humani have done to the earth. Look at what their greed has wrought. They have brought this planet to the very brink of destruction. The polar caps are melting, sea levels are rising, weather patterns are changing, seasons altering, farmlands turning to desert . . ."

"You sound like Dee," Josh said suddenly.

"Don't you dare compare me to the English Magician," Aoife spat. "He is despicable."

"He said the Dark Elders could repair all this damage. Could they?" Josh asked curiously.

114

"Yes," Aoife answered simply. "Yes, they could. Tell him," she said to the Alchemyst.

Josh turned to look at Nicholas. "Is it true?"

"Yes," the Alchemyst sighed. "Yes, they undoubtedly could."

Sophie leaned forward, her forehead creasing in a frown. "So that means the Elders, the ones whose side you're on, could also do the same thing?"

This time there was a longer pause, and when Nicholas finally spoke, his voice was barely above a whisper. "I'm sure they could."

"So why don't they?" Sophie demanded.

Nicholas looked at Perenelle, and it was the Sorceress who finally answered. "Because sooner or later every parent must let their children go to live their lives and make their mistakes. That is the only way they can grow. In generations past, the Elders moved among the humani, living with them, working side by side—all those legends about the ancient gods interacting with humans have some truth in them. There really were gods on the earth in those days. But humankind did not progress. It was only when most of the Elders retreated to the Shadowrealms and left the humani to their own devices that the race started to grow."

"Think of all that mankind has achieved in the last two thousand years," Nicholas continued. "Think of the inventions, the accomplishments, the discoveries—atomic power, flight, instant worldwide communications, even space travel— and then remember that the civilization of Egypt lasted more than three thousand years. Babylon was established over four

115

thousand years ago, the first cities in the Indus appeared over five thousand years ago and Sumer is six thousand years old. Why did those great civilizations not achieve what this civilization has accomplished in a much shorter time?"

Josh shook his head, but Sophie was nodding. She knew the answer.

"Because the Elders—what the humani called the gods—lived with them," Perenelle said. "They provided everything. The Elders needed to retreat so that mankind could grow."

"But some stayed," Sophie protested. "The Witch, Prometheus . . ."

"Mars . . . ," Josh added.

"Gilgamesh," Sophie said. "And Scathach. She stayed."

"Yes, a few remained to guide and teach the new race, to nudge them along the road to greatness. But not to interfere, not to influence and definitely not to rule," Perenelle clarified.

Aoife grunted a bitter laugh.

"It is true that some Dark Elders tried to rule the humani, and the Elders fought with them, blocking their efforts. But everyone who remained had a reason to stay . . . except you," Perenelle said suddenly, looking at Aoife. "Why did you choose to remain in this humani Shadowrealm?"

There was a long pause while Aoife's eyes grew lost and distant. "Because Scathach stayed," she said eventually.

A series of terrible images swirled through Sophie's mind and a name popped into her head. "Because of Cuchulain," she said aloud.

"Cuchulain," Aoife agreed. "The boy who came between us. The boy we fought over."

A young man, mortally wounded, tying himself to a pillar so that his very presence could hold a terrifying army at bay . . .

Scathach and Aoife together, racing across a battlefield, trying to reach him before three enormous crowlike figures swooped down on his body . . .

The crows carrying the young man's limp body high into the air . . .

And then Scathach and Aoife fighting one another with swords and spears, their almost identical gray auras coiling around them, twisting and shifting into a score of beastlike shapes.

"We should never have fought," Aoife said. "We parted with angry bitter words. We said things that should have been left unsaid."

"You could have left for a Shadowrealm of your own creation," Perenelle said.

Aoife shook her head. "I stayed because I had been told that one day I would get a chance to redeem myself with my sister."

Even as Aoife was speaking, Sophie caught a flickering image: *Scathach—or was it Aoife?—clinging to the back of a monster that stood on human legs but had two coiling snakes' heads. It wore a robe of living serpents, and these struck out, again and again, at the red-haired warrior.* "Who told you that?" she asked in a hoarse whisper.

"My grandmother: the Witch of Endor." The vampire's

face was grim. "And she is rarely wrong. I cannot go with you, I cannot help you. I have to find my sister. I will go back through time if need be."

Nicholas looked over at her. "Even now Saint-Germain is going to see if he can travel back into the past to rescue Joan and Scathach."

Aoife grunted. "There are less than a handful of Elders in this realm with that power. And none of them are pleasant."

"The Saracen Knight is taking him to his master, Tammuz, the Green Man," Nicholas said shortly. "Like Chronos, he has the power to travel along the strands of time."

"And you expect him to help Saint-Germain?" Aoife's laughter, dark and ugly, rang out across the water. "Tammuz will tear him limb from limb."

CHAPTER TWENTY-FIVE

"We could just fly to San Francisco," Virginia Dare said quietly. "I quite like flying. Especially if it's first-class, and particularly if you are paying."

"I hate flying," Dee muttered. "Besides, there are two problems with that: booking a ticket will leave a trail that anyone can follow, and the first flight is not until tomorrow morning. Then it's an eleven-hour flight to the West Coast. We'd lose too much time, and it would allow the Elders to organize a welcoming committee for me when I land."

"What about a private jet? You're rich enough to do that."

"Yes, I'm rich enough, but the paperwork would take hours and leave a huge trail also. No, this is a much better idea."

"When you say better, does that mean dangerous?" Virginia asked softly.

"That has never bothered you before."

"I am immortal, not invulnerable. I can be killed . . . and so can you," she reminded him. "As I get older, I appreciate my long life. I have no desire to end it."

The couple, looking like any other pair of tourists, were standing beneath the shade of a tree admiring the brightly lit facade of the Tower of London, the pale cream stone turned the color of butter in the warm lights. A recent shower had swept across the city and created puddles that reflected the lights. Even at this late hour there were still plenty of sightseers enjoying the cool air, admiring the London landmark on the Thames River. Occasionally cameras flashed.

"All my life seems to have been spent in and around the Tower," Dee said wistfully. "I visited Walter Raleigh here just before his execution," he added. "And when I was a boy my father took me to see the lions here, when it housed the Royal Menagerie."

"Very touching," Dare muttered. "Do you want to tell me now why we're here?"

Dee nodded, a tiny jerk of his head. "There is an entrance to a Shadowrealm inside."

"The Traitor's Gate Shadowrealm." Dare nodded. "I've heard of it." She shuddered, her shoulders rolling beneath her coat. "Rumor has it that it is an evil place."

Dee ignored her. "Together, I believe we're powerful enough to activate and enter it. Once we're in the Shadowrealm, we can hop from realm to realm and then drop out in America." He grinned with genuine good humor.

"Once you activate the gate, you will have betrayed our position," Virginia said.

"True. But once we're in the Shadowrealm, no one will know where we're going."

Virginia Dare shook her head, her long hair flowing down her back. "Can I point out one or two very minor flaws in this plan?"

"Such as?"

"Let us assume we can overpower the guards in the Tower . . ."

"Easily done. You can spell them to sleep with your music."

"And then let us assume we can leap into the Traitor's Gate Shadowrealm."

"We can do that," Dee said confidently.

"Do we know whose Shadowrealm it is?"

The doctor shook his head. "No one knows. Some minor Elder, perhaps—but you know that many of the Shadowrealms that border the earth are empty."

"I also know that the Dark Elders have been calling their brethren who live in the outer Shadowrealms to draw closer as Litha approaches. Something might have taken up residence there."

Dee opened his mouth to comment, but Virginia pressed on.

"But let us assume that we find it empty. We then have to move through it to cross into one or two or three more Shadowrealms before we end up in a realm that touches the Americas."

"Yes."

"And it could be anywhere in the Americas from Alaska to Florida?"

"Yes. At worst we'll be a couple of hours away from San Francisco."

"So tell me why we are going back to San Francisco? I thought that city was about to be overrun by your Elder's nightmare army?"

"The Book of Abraham the Mage is in San Francisco. I need it."

"You finally got it!" Virginia sounded genuinely delighted. "Took you long enough," she added sarcastically. Then she stopped as a sudden thought struck her. "The Book is still in your possession—have you not surrendered it to your Elders?"

"No. I've decided to keep it."

"Keep it!" Virginia's raised voice made some of the late-night tourists turn to look. She lowered her voice to a hoarse whisper. "What for?"

Dee grinned. "I am going to use it to take control of this earth myself."

Virginia blinked in surprise, and then she suddenly laughed delightedly. "Doctor, you are mad . . . which must make me even madder, for associating with you. Do you think your Elders will allow you to take over this, their favorite Shadowrealm?"

"I'm not going to give them any choice," Dee said simply. "I gave them a lifetime—several lifetimes—of service. And yet, because of a few petty failures, they are prepared to

122

sentence me to an eternity of suffering. They declared me *ut-laga*. Now my loyalty is to myself—and to you too," he added hastily, catching a glimpse of the expression on his companion's face. "I am going to wrest control of this planet from the Elders, kill all the immortal humans, Elders and Next Generation who still live here. I will then seal the entrances to the Shadowrealms and cut this world off from all the others. I will make this planet mine. *Ours*, if you are with me. We can rule together."

Virginia Dare took a step away from Dee and slowly and deliberately looked him up and down.

"What are you looking at?" he demanded.

"A fool," she snapped. "How do you hope to achieve all this?"

"Yesterday I saw an Archon."

Virginia blinked in surprise. "I've never seen one. I thought they were myth."

"I saw Cernunnos, the Horned God. I stood as close to it as I am standing to you. And then later, it came to me: it sent a thoughtform, a being created, controlled and held together entirely by the power of its imagination. Its power was incredible . . . and yet Cernunnos is one of the *minor* Archons."

Virginia started to shake her head. "And what has this got to do with you taking control of this Shadowrealm?"

"I have the four Swords of Power. I intend to raise Coatlicue, the greatest of all the Archons. She will serve me."

Virginia Dare drew in her breath in a quick gasp. "John, this is insanity," she said urgently. "And even if you could raise the Archon, why should she serve you? What have you got to trade that would even remotely interest her?"

"Coatlicue despises and loathes the Elders. Millennia ago, they sentenced her to an eternity of suffering—I would imagine she will want her revenge."

"Revenge drives us all," Virginia murmured. "But I still don't see how . . ."

The doctor's smile was terrifying. "I know the entrance to Xibalba here on earth. If she serves me, I will give her that location."

"And once she is in Xibalba . . . ," Virginia whispered.

Dee nodded. "She will have access to the countless Shadowrealms. She can ravage her way through them, feasting off everything she finds."

The woman's laughter was shaky. "I have always admired your ruthless streak, John, but this is breathtaking. Even you, as powerful as you are, will not be able to raise an Archon. Especially the Mother of All the Gods. As soon as she steps into this world, she'll feed off the first things she sees."

Dee shrugged. "It is true I am going to need something extraordinary, something powerful, to draw her and then distract her while I bind her in spells." He touched the swords under his coat. The answer flowed through his fingers and the air was suddenly filled with the sharp citrus scent of orange. His smile turned savage. "I will offer her a pure golden aura."

CHAPTER TWENTY-SIX

Sophie and Josh walked side by side on the quay in Sausalito, past the gently rocking houseboats. Each one was different, some small and squat, others tall and long. Most had small dinghies tied to the side, and one even had a seaplane moored off one end.

The twins had left Nicholas and Perenelle arguing with Aoife back on Niten's houseboat. The Swordsman remained silent, only occasionally stepping in to place his hands on the vampire's shoulder when her temper grew heated.

"What do we do now?" Josh asked.

Sophie looked at him. "Do? About what?"

"I mean, do we go home?"

"And then what? What are we going home to?"

Josh dug his hands in the back pockets of his jeans and walked on. He had no answer to that. "You know, it was only when I was leaving the house earlier to look for the Flamels that I realized how much we've lost," he said.

"What do you mean *lost*?" Sophie was confused.

"These last few days we've spent with the Flamels has cost us everything," Josh continued. "Everything we thought we knew—all the history, the mythology, even the archaeology—it all turns out to be a lie. Even our futures have been wiped out."

Sophie nodded. She'd already had the same thoughts, but wasn't surprised that it had taken her brother a little longer to come to them.

"So where do we go?" Josh stopped to look back toward Niten's houseboat. Although it was over a hundred yards away, he lowered his voice to little more than a whisper. "What do we do, sis? I don't trust Flamel."

"Neither do I," she admitted.

"But we're sort of stuck with him."

Sophie nodded. "And I think we need to see this out to the end."

"What does that mean?" her brother asked desperately. "You've heard them—they're talking about attacking Alcatraz. That's just crazy!"

"But if they don't, then the creatures on the island will attack San Francisco." Sophie reached out to touch her brother and the air was suddenly filled with the sweet smell of vanilla. Her bright blue eyes flickered silver. "Have you ever thought that this is exactly where we're supposed to be? This is what we're supposed to be doing."

Josh took a step back, suddenly frightened of the intensity in his sister's voice. "What are you talking about?" he asked.

"Josh, ten thousand years ago, Abraham wrote about us. . . ."

Josh shook his head quickly. "No. He wrote about twins . . . and there have been lots of twins."

"None like us."

"Lots like us," he insisted. "Remember? The Flamels have been collecting gold and silver twins for generations. And none of them survived their Awakening."

"We did," she reminded him.

"Barely."

"Josh, I've been trained in Air, Fire and Water magics and you've been Awakened and trained in Water magic. We can't just ignore those skills. We have an opportunity now to use them, to protect the city."

"Have you ever wondered," Josh asked suddenly, "if we're fighting for the right side? If maybe Flamel is the enemy and Dee is the good guy?"

They both caught the flicker of movement at the same time and whirled around to face Niten. Even though the early afternoon was still and quiet, they hadn't heard the Swordsman approach. He bowed slightly. "They are calling for you," he said, glancing back at the boat. He turned and walked away, then stopped to glance over his shoulder, and the light washed over his face, turning his brown eyes into mirrors. "I could not help overhearing your last question. I am immortal, and though I have not lived as long as Nicholas or

Perenelle, I am now, and have always been, a warrior. And if that life has taught me anything, it is that in every war, both sides believe they are in the right."

"And what about us, Niten?" Josh asked. "Are we on the right side?"

"You are on a side, and that is important. You don't have to stay on that side. Often the greatest act of courage is admitting that one has made a mistake." He paused, then added, "Follow your hearts. Protect one another, trust one another, because, at the end of the day, all of these people want something from you, or want you to do something for them, or be something that you are not. Your only responsibility is to one another." Then he turned and walked away.

Nicholas and Perenelle were waiting on the dock. Sophie felt Perenelle's eyes searching their faces, almost as if she were reading their thoughts. The Sorceress stepped forward and Sophie realized with a sudden clarity that Perenelle—and not Nicholas—was in charge. It dawned on her that the woman had probably always been the boss.

"It is decision time," Flamel said with a wry smile.

"Well, we've been talking about—" Josh began.

"The time for talking is over," Perenelle said abruptly. "This is the time for action. Are you with us?" she asked.

"Do we have a choice?" Josh replied.

Perenelle opened her mouth to answer, but Nicholas tugged at her sleeve and shook his head slightly. Looking at the twins, he said, "There are always choices." He held up three bony fingers. "You can fight with us, you can side with Dee, or you can do nothing." The expression on his face turned cruel. "If you side with Dee, then this city and ultimately this world are doomed. If you do nothing, then this city and this world are still doomed. But if you fight with us, then there is a chance—a small chance, but a chance nonetheless—for humankind."

"But—" Josh began.

Sophie reached out and caught her brother's arm, pinching hard enough to silence his response. "We're with you," Sophie said. She looked at her brother and he nodded once. "We're *both* with you." She looked from Nicholas to Perenelle. "Now, what do we do?"

The Sorceress bowed her head slightly, but not before Sophie caught the hint of a smile. "Josh needs to learn at least one more Elemental Magic," Perenelle said. "If we had time we could find someone to train him in Earth, Air and Fire, but we don't. I think he will be able to learn one more magic in the time left for us."

"But which one?" Josh asked.

Perenelle swiveled around to look at the Alchemyst, her fine eyebrows raised in a silent question. No words passed between them, but the Sorceress nodded and turned back with a smile on her face. "We will train Josh in the Magic of Fire," she said.

Josh looked at Sophie and grinned. "Fire. I like that." He turned back to Perenelle. "But who's going to train me?"

Sophie knew the answer even before the Sorceress spoke. "We will go and see Prometheus, the Master of Fire."

CHAPTER TWENTY-SEVEN

*N*iccolò Machiavelli sat in the passenger seat of the stripped-down army surplus jeep, clutching the bar welded onto the dashboard in a white-knuckled grip. Billy sat in the back and whooped delightedly with each bump and dip on the unpaved road. Black Hawk drove the narrow country lanes at high speed, foot pushed hard to the floor, a ferocious grin on his face.

"I think," Machiavelli said, shouting to be heard over the noise of the engine, "I think that your master would probably prefer us alive so he can kill us himself. He might be irritated if you do the job for him. Slow down."

"This isn't fast," Black Hawk said. The jeep lurched forward, engine howling as all four wheels left the ground. "Now, this is fast."

"I'll be sick," Machiavelli promised, "and when I am, I'm

going to be sick in your direction. Yours too," he added, looking back over his shoulder at Billy the Kid.

Black Hawk reluctantly eased his foot off the accelerator.

"I've not lived through more than five hundred years of Europe's most turbulent history only to die in a car crash."

"Black Hawk could drive these roads wearing a blind-fold," Billy said.

"I'm sure he could, though why he would want to do something like that is beyond me."

"Have you never done something purely for the thrill of it?" Black Hawk asked.

"No," Machiavelli said. "Not for a long time."

Black Hawk looked shocked. "But that seems like such a waste of immortality. I pity you," he added.

"You pity me?"

"You are not living, you are surviving."

Niccolò Machiavelli stared at the Native American im-mortal for a long time before he finally nodded and looked away. "You may be right," he murmured.

The house was set back off the road.

At first glance it looked like a small, ordinary timber cot-tage, similar to so many others scattered across the United States. It was only when one approached closer that the truth was revealed: the house was enormous, much of it built into the side of the hill behind it.

Machiavelli felt his skin prickle and crawl the moment the car turned off the rough track onto a narrow rutted drive: the

131

telltale signs of warding spells. There was old magic here, ancient eldritch power. He caught glimpses of arcane symbols cut into trees, spirals daubed on rocks, stick figures carved into fence posts. The track cut straight across a field of grass that grew as high as the car doors. The blades rasped and hissed against the metal, sounding like a thousand warning whispers. The Italian caught flickers of movement all around him, and glimpses of snakes, toads, and quick, scurrying lizards. A gangling misshapen scarecrow dominated the field on the left-hand side of the track. Its head was a huge gnarled dried pumpkin that had been carved in a round-eyed face with a protruding tongue.

The grassy field stopped abruptly, as if a line had been drawn in the earth, and the rest of the approach to the house was across perfectly flat land. Machiavelli nodded his approval: nothing could get through the field without setting off countless alarms or being attacked by a poisonous lurking guardian. Getting close to the house undetected would be impossible. An enormous lynx, bigger than any he had ever seen before, lay on the ground before the open front door, regarding the car impassively, only the tiny movements of its black-tufted ears betraying that it was real and not a carving.

Black Hawk pulled the jeep up in front of the house, but kept the engine running and made no move to climb out. "End of the road," he said without a trace of a smile.

Niccolò climbed out gratefully and started to brush the dirt and grit off his expensive handmade suit, then gave up. The suit was ruined. He had a closetful of identical suits in his home in Paris, but he doubted he'd ever get a chance to wear them again.

Looking around, he breathed in the warm grassy air. Whenever he thought about dying—which he did with remarkable regularity—he imagined it would take place in a European city, Paris perhaps, maybe even Rome or his beloved Florence. He'd never thought he was going to end his days in California. However, he wasn't dead yet, and he wasn't going down without a fight.

As soon as Billy leapt out of the jeep, Black Hawk put it in gear and skidded away, showering him and Machiavelli in stones and grit, enveloping them in a cloud of dust. Billy grinned. "I knew he was going to do that."

"You seem remarkably cheerful for someone who may be about to die," Machiavelli said.

"I've seen men go to their deaths laughing, I've seen others wail and cry. They all died in the end, but those who were laughing seemed to have an easier time of it."

"Do you expect to die here today?"

Billy laughed. "Dying's not something I ever think about," Billy said. "But no, I don't think it's going to happen today. We haven't done anything wrong."

The Italian immortal nodded but said nothing.

"Mr. Machiavelli doesn't think I have the authority to remove his immortality. He's incorrect." The man who stepped out of the house was short and slender, his skin the color of brightly polished copper, his face bisected by an enormous hawklike nose and dominated by a full white beard that reached to his chest. His eyes were solid black with no whites showing. He was dressed simply in white linen trousers and shirt and his feet were bare. He smiled, revealing that every one of his teeth had been filed to razor-sharp points. "I am Quetzalcoatl the Feathered Serpent."

"It is an honor to meet you, Lord Quez . . . Quet . . . Quaza . . . ," Machiavelli began.

"Oh, call me Kukulkan, everyone else does," the Elder said, and headed back into the house. Machiavelli blinked in surprise: a long serpent's tail, bright with multicolored feathers, trailed behind the Elder.

Billy caught Machiavelli by the arm. "Whatever you do," he whispered urgently, "don't mention the tail."

CHAPTER TWENTY-EIGHT

The ghost of Juan Manuel de Ayala floated silently through the ruins of Alcatraz. The Spanish lieutenant had been the first European to discover the small island in 1775 and had named it after the vast number of pelicans that claimed the rock as their own: La Isla de los Alcatraces. By the time it was sold to the American government in 1854, it was called Alcatraz.

When de Ayala had died, his shade had returned to the island, and he had haunted and protected it ever since.

He'd seen the nature of the island change and change again over the centuries: it was the site of the first lighthouse on the coast of California; then it held a military garrison that soon became a prison, which from 1861 to 1963 was home to some of America's most violent and dangerous criminals.

More recently it had been a popular tourist attraction, and de Ayala had delighted in drifting unseen through the crowds of visitors, listening to their excited comments. He particularly loved to follow those who spoke his native tongue, Spanish.

In the last couple of months, however, the nature of Alcatraz had changed yet again. The island had been sold to a private company, Enoch Enterprises, which had immediately stopped all tours of the island. And quite soon afterward, new prisoners had arrived. None of which were human. There were creatures de Ayala vaguely recognized from sailors' tales—werewolves and dragons, wyverns and worms—and some he knew from myth, like the minotaur and the sphinx, but most were completely alien to him.

And then Perenelle Flamel had been incarcerated on the island.

De Ayala had helped her escape her cell and was more delighted when she managed to flee the island altogether, leaving the two dangerous newcomers, Machiavelli and Billy the Kid, stranded with the monsters. He had hoped that they would remain overnight so he and the island's other ghosts might have a little fun with them. But the two men had been rescued by a Native American, and as de Ayala watched their boat head toward the city, he wondered what would become of his beloved Isla de los Alcatraces. The sphinx still walked the prison's corridors, the hideous spider Areop-Enap was wrapped in an enormous cocoon in the ruins of the Warden's House and the Old Man of the Sea and his foul daughters patrolled the waters.

The ghost drifted to the top of the watchtower and turned to look toward the city he could never visit. What was

136

it like, he wondered, this huge city on the edge of the continent? He could see its towers rising into the skies, and the fabulous orange bridge spanning the bay. He watched the boats cruise the waters, saw the metal birds in the skies and could just make out the metallic glitter of cars moving on the shore. When he had discovered Alcatraz, Philadelphia had been the largest city in the United States, with a population of thirty-four thousand. Now, over eight hundred thousand people lived in San Francisco—an inconceivable figure—and more than thirty-six million lived in the state of California. What would happen to them when the monsters were loosed into the city's streets and sewers?

Unconsciously, de Ayala drifted out over the water toward the city, and then the invisible ties that bound him to Alcatraz drew him back. He protected the island—but for how much longer? he wondered. The forces of the humani and the Elders were gathering, and no matter how it ended, de Ayala did not think his beloved Alcatraz would survive the coming war.

And with no Rock to watch over, he too would finally cease to exist.

CHAPTER TWENTY-NINE

"Sophie, I am going to ask you to do something, something you might find a little . . . odd," Perenelle said softly. She had caught Sophie's arm and drawn her to one side while Josh and Niten were carrying the plastic chairs into the houseboat. Aoife had disappeared belowdecks, and Nicholas sat on the edge of the craft, eyes closed, lined face turned toward the sun.

"What?" Sophie asked cautiously, turning to look at the Sorceress. The late-afternoon sun highlighted the tracery of lines that were beginning to appear on the woman's face, around her eyes and at the corners of her mouth. Sophie wasn't sure how she felt about Perenelle. She still liked her— she still *wanted* to like her—but there was something about the woman that was beginning to trouble her, and she wasn't sure what it was.

"It would be better if you did not tell Josh what you know—what the Witch knows—about Prometheus."

At the mention of the Elder's name, the girl's eyes blinked—blue, then silver—and the faintest hint of her vanilla odor touched the salty air. "I try not to think about the Witch's memories," she said carefully.

"Why not?" Perenelle sounded genuinely surprised.

"Nicholas told me that there is a possibility that her memories could overwhelm mine, that I could become the Witch"—Sophie frowned—"or that she could become me. If I remember all that the Witch knew . . . would that make me the Witch?"

Perenelle laughed gently. "I have never heard anything more ridiculous in my life."

"But Nicholas said—"

"Nicholas told you what he believed to be true," Perenelle said. "He was mistaken."

Sophie pressed the heels of her hands against her eyes and shook her head, trying to make sense of what she was hearing. "But if the Witch's memories become stronger than mine . . ."

"But it is *you* who are remembering, Sophie. It will always be you. I have lived on this earth for centuries; I can remember the smell of my grandmother's hair, and she died more than six hundred and sixty years ago. I can recall the address of every house and apartment, hovel, tenement and palace I've lived in over the centuries. One memory does not crowd out another. The Witch's memories have only been added to yours. Nothing more. True, our memories and experiences help make us unique. But if the Witch had wanted to take over your memories, she could have done so immediately, instantaneously, when you were with her in Ojai."

The Sorceress paused and then added softly, "When Nicholas was imprisoned in the Bastille, I spent the time apprenticed to the Witch of Endor. She lived in the South of France then, and I studied with her for more than a decade. She can be cruel and capricious, and she is dangerous beyond belief, but she is extraordinarily disorganized. She was never able to plan ahead. I've often wondered about that. She sacrificed her eyes for the ability to observe the shifting strands of time. She can see years, decades, centuries, even millennia into the future, and can track the curling threads to their possible outcomes. But she is so scattered that she is unable to plan her own day. She often forgets even the simplest things. Yet she is cunning, and if she had wanted to control you, she would have done so when she was Awakening you."

Sophie felt as if a huge weight had been lifted off her shoulders. "So her memories and my memories will stay separate."

"They *are* separate," Perenelle assured her. "You know when you are experiencing the Witch's memories, don't you?"

Sophie nodded. "But Nicholas said—"

"Nicholas is often wrong," Perenelle interrupted, a touch of ice in her voice. "I love him, I have loved him for centuries, and while he is extraordinary and brilliant, he is still human, with all the faults and foibles of a human. He makes mistakes," she added. "We both do." Shaking her head, she smiled, and a warmth returned to her voice. "So, no, I do not think the Witch's memories will overcome yours. You are too strong-willed—you must be, to have survived the Awakening and learned Air, Fire and Water magic so quickly. And to be truthful," she added with a smile, "I do not think the Witch would have been able to plan something quite so sophisticated. She was never subtle."

Niten and Josh appeared from belowdecks. There was a broad grin stretched across Josh's face. "We will return in a few moments," Niten called. "We're going to get the car. We need something slightly less conspicuous than that red monstrosity you arrived in."

Sophie and Pernelle stood in silence and watched as Josh and the Japanese man climbed onto the dock and disappeared through the tangle of houseboats.

"Nicholas and I are going to ask Prometheus to gift Josh with the Magic of Fire," Perenelle continued. "But the experience must be new to your brother; he cannot be warned about the Master of Fire."

Sophie was about to ask why, when the memories suddenly popped into her head. She bit the inside of her cheek to keep a straight face: Josh definitely wanted the Magic of Fire, but he was *not* going to be happy with the process of acquiring it. She nodded. "I won't tell him anything."

"Good."

"Who is Niten?" Sophie asked. The name was unfamiliar to the Witch, and Sophie had been waiting for the opportunity to find out about the Japanese man.

The Sorceress's green eyes clouded and she raised them to follow the man's progress. "He is undoubtedly the greatest swordsman in the world—the only humani ever to defeat Scathach in single combat. But if you ask him what he is, he will tell you that he is an artist. And that also is true: his skill with the brush is legendary. Nicholas and I had one of his original bird paintings in our apartment in New York, before Dee burned it to the ground. Niten has traveled this world and the nearby Shadowrealms in search of opponents to fight simply to hone his skills. He was supposed to have been made immortal sometime in the seventeenth century by Benzaiten, who many—including the Witch—believe may even be one of the ancient Great Elders. Niten was also known as Miyamoto Musashi."

Sophie caught her breath. The names Miyamoto Musashi and now Benzaiten sent dozens of images flickering through her head. She stared at the gently lapping water, and the ripples dissolved into . . .

Niten, dressed in the exotic armor of a samurai, racing through a dense bamboo forest. Hundreds of snarling beast-faced monsters chased him. Most of the creatures were pink- and blue-skinned, though some were bright red. They were all horned and three-eyed, their mouths filled with savage teeth, their hands tipped with claws. The samurai broke out of the forest and stopped, swaying, on the edge of a sheer cliff that fell away to a raging sea and jagged rocks far below. He whirled to face the monsters, a sword in either hand. Howling savagely, hungrily, the beasts appeared and closed in on the human. . . .

And then Benzaiten appeared.

She rose from the sea behind Niten: tiny, ethereal and beautiful, riding on the back of an enormous pink-scaled dragon. She tapped the dragon on the back of its head with an ornate fan and the creature spread gossamer wings, opened its mouth to reveal hundreds of ragged teeth and a long black forked tongue . . . and the horned monsters turned and fled into the bamboo.

One remained. A huge blue-skinned creature with downward-curling tusks. Lifting a bow as tall as itself, it fired a long black-tipped arrow directly toward the tiny Elder.

Niten's swords flashed, impossibly fast . . . and sliced the arrow out of the air.

Sophie shuddered and drew in a great ragged breath. "Yes, Benzaiten made him immortal. . . ."

"What did the Witch think of Benzaiten?" Perenelle asked curiously.

Sophie nodded. "The Witch believes she is one of the Great Elders."

"See?" Perenelle smiled delightedly. "You can draw upon selective memories when you need them. You are controlling the memories, they are not controlling you."

"Names seem to make me remember. When we were in Paris, Joan did something to help me while I slept. When the Witch first gave me her memories, I felt as if my skull were about to explode. The noises in my head were incredible. I kept hearing voices speaking a hundred different languages, snatches of songs and sounds that were so alien they were terrifying. After a couple of days, I discovered that I'd started to understand what they were saying," she added, a note of awe in her voice. "When Joan was finished, the voices were still there, but they were like distant whispers. Now, if I concentrate, I can focus on a name and the memories appear. But I've been trying to ignore them."

"Do not. The memories are knowledge, and knowledge is power. It is an extraordinary gift the Witch gave you." Perenelle's expression grew distant. "I just wish I knew *why* she gave it to you."

"Why?" Sophie didn't understand.

"She must have seen something in your future that suggested that you would need that knowledge," Perenelle said. "She could easily have taught you the Magic of Air without gifting you her memories."

Something about this revelation disturbed Sophie, but she wasn't sure how or why. She'd talk to Josh about it later; maybe he'd be able to help. "So the memories aren't going to control me?"

"No." Perenelle smiled kindly. "You have no idea just how strong you are. You survived a terrible Awakening, and you have been trained in three of the Elemental Magics in a matter of days." Perenelle's voice was soft, touched with what Sophie recognized as sadness, and she wondered if the woman was thinking about the other twins who had not survived. "You should know that what you have achieved has never been done before. Never." She reached out to place her hand on Sophie's shoulder. "You have no idea how proud I am of you. I knew you and your brother were the ones."

The long black limousine appeared on the dock and came to a halt in a cloud of dust. Josh climbed out of the driver's seat, grinning delightedly. Niten emerged from the passenger side; he'd obviously allowed Josh to drive.

Sophie raised her hand and waved to her twin. Without looking at the Sorceress, she said, "You planned all this, didn't you?"

Perenelle did not reply.

Still not looking at the woman, Sophie continued. "That day when Josh went for the job in the bookshop and you met me in the Coffee Cup. The moment you learned that we were twins . . . you knew then, didn't you, that we were . . ."

". . . the twins of legend? I am the seventh daughter of a seventh daughter. I have the gift of foresight. The instant I saw you I knew you were *special*; the minute you stepped in the door I caught the faintest glimmer of your aura, just the hint of silver. When I discovered you were a twin, my suspicions were heightened, and when I saw Josh and saw the glimmer of gold on his skin, I knew for certain. I told Nicholas to employ Josh—he was just about to reject him," she added with a wry smile. "Your brother did not have a good interview! I don't think he really wanted the job."

"He didn't." Sophie glanced at her quickly. "And you made Bernice hire me at the Coffee Cup." It was a statement, not a question, but she wanted to hear the Sorceress admit the truth.

Perenelle's head moved in the tiniest of nods. "I suggested that she needed you, that is true."

"Suggested?"

"I can be very forceful."

"When were you and Nicholas planning on telling us?" Sophie asked, a note of anger in her voice. The idea that she and her brother had been manipulated by the Flamels for months was chilling.

"Actually, we were going to break the news to you in a couple of weeks' time: at the summer solstice."

"Litha." The name popped into Sophie's head.

"Yes, the ancients called it Litha. And it is the time of year when your auras—the gold and silver—will be at their strongest. We thought that would be the best time to Awaken you with the least danger to yourselves."

"But there *would* be dangers. . . ."

"There are always dangers."

Sophie looked into Perenelle's cold green eyes. "And you would still have gone through with it?"

"Yes."

Sophie felt sick. This woman, whom she had liked, admired, even respected, had just admitted that she'd been prepared to put her and Josh in terrible danger. Sophie saw the Sorceress in a new light. Perenelle's cool beauty suddenly took on an almost threatening aspect.

"Do you smell that?" Perenelle asked suddenly.

"What?" Sophie said, drawing in a deep lungful of air. "Vanilla," she answered. "It smells sour."

"Your anger has tainted your aura. You must learn to control that. And before you rush to judgment," the Sorceress continued with an icy smile, "ask yourself what you would have done if you and Josh were in our position. Nicholas and

I have spent centuries looking for the two people who can save this world from total destruction. And yes, we have made mistakes, terrible mistakes," she added sadly, "and we will live with those mistakes for the rest of our lives. But I ask you, what other option had we? Would it have been better if we had *not* looked for those two people? We were given a terrible responsibility: we accepted it."

"Gilgamesh said those other twins didn't survive the Awakening. You Awakened them knowing that they would most likely die."

"Some survived," Perenelle said coldly. "But we never forced anyone to go through the Awakening. We explained the risks. All of those twins accepted those risks—accepted them gladly, too," she added.

"Well, I wasn't warned," Sophie said angrily.

"Was there time?" Perenelle asked. "From the moment Dee burst into the shop last Thursday, events have moved at such a pace."

"I should have been warned," Sophie persisted.

"And if you had been warned about the risks, how would you have decided? What would you have done?" Perenelle took a step closer, looking into Sophie's eyes. "You are a good person, Sophie Newman. You are Silver—just like Joan. Like her, you are caring and considerate, and like her, you would have wanted to do what was right. If Nicholas and I had waited until Litha and explained the situation to you, as we'd planned, I believe you would have gone ahead with the Awakening."

Sophie opened her mouth to reply, then closed it again.

Perenelle was right; even if she had known the risks, she would have gone through with it.

"Would Josh?" Perenelle asked, her voice so soft that Sophie had to strain to hear it.

Sophie turned to look at her brother. She didn't have to think about an answer: if he had known the risks, Josh would not have even attempted the Awakening. Despite his bluster and bravado, he wasn't brave. But then she thought about him in Paris and London: he had shown extraordinary courage in both cities. This was a new Josh, a Josh she'd never really seen before. The old Josh, her brother of last week, would never have been able to do those things. He wouldn't even have tried.

"So I think it best that you not tell him about Prometheus," Perenelle finished. "Let's not scare him."

CHAPTER THIRTY

$\mathcal{T}$he security guards fell at the almost inaudible sounds from Virginia Dare's wooden flute. She kept one awake, mesmerizing him with an ancient Native American lullaby, and he obediently turned off the security cameras, disarmed the alarms and opened the gates to allow her and Dee inside. The soothing lullaby ended with a single piercing note, which dropped the guard unconscious to the floor, face twisted in agony.

The Magician stepped over the crumpled body, looked around at the sleeping guards and nodded in approval. He turned to regard the flute, tilting his head to one side to look at the hints of a spiral design running the length of the instrument. "I've always been fascinated by your flute," he said. "You never told me where you got it."

"No, I didn't," Dare said firmly, and turned away, forestalling the discussion.

Dee followed the woman through the empty Tower of London. "A gift from your master, perhaps?" he persisted.

"I don't have a master," she said slowly; then she glanced over her shoulder, eyes cold and angry. "But you know that, of course."

"Oh, that's right: you killed him."

"Only a fool kills an Elder," she snapped. "And I'm not a fool . . . unlike you!"

Dee shrugged. "You're referring to Hekate? What's done is done and cannot be undone. And technically, I did not kill her—the Yggdrasill fell on her."

"You always were a master of weasel words, John," Virginia said softly. "Even Shakespeare said you should have been a playwright. I heard you had an encounter with him and the Saracen Knight, and that you didn't come off too well," she added with a sly smile.

Dee fell into step beside the immortal. "You knew they were in the city?"

"I make it my business to know whom I'm sharing the city with." They were back outside under the night sky, and directly ahead of them was a red-and-black-paneled Tudor building. The sound of water slapping against stone was clearly audible, and the air smelled damp. "Shakespeare has been here since the sixteenth century; Palamedes comes and goes." Dare walked across the flagstones, completely silent in flat leather moccasins. She leaned on the metal rail and looked down into a pool of black water; then she pointed over to where an arched opening in the opposite wall had been sealed with a heavy-looking metal gate. The two halves of the gate sagged in the middle, and through the struts a second black pool rippled like oil. "And you are now about to tell me that the entrance to the Shadowrealm is in the pool behind that gate?"

"It is. You've never been here?" Dee asked, surprised.

"I have never had your dangerous curiosity," she said.

The Magician smiled. "We learn through curiosity." Leaning his elbows on the metal rail, he looked at the barred entrance to the pool. "If I could use my powers, I could—"

"If you even think about using your powers, you will draw everything in this city right here," Dare reminded him, "and this time, I won't rescue you."

Dee looked at her quickly. "You? Rescued me? Is that what you think you did?"

Virginia twirled the flute like a baton in her fingers. "I rescued you. You might have been able to fight one or two of them—but there were hundreds of the creatures closing in on you. Every cucubuth clan in Europe must be in the city. I even saw some rogue Torc Madra in there, and you know how dangerous the dogmen are. You would have been captured, and most of you would have been delivered to your masters."

"Most of me?" Dee swallowed hard at the sudden image.

Virginia's smile was savage. "I'm sure they'd have taken a few bites out of you on the way. Just a little taste."

Dee shuddered. "I hate cucubuths."

"And you can be assured that at this moment, they hate you too. Your enemies are multiplying by the hour."

"You're their enemy too," Dee said.

"Not I." Virginia twirled the flute again. "They never even saw me. They'll blame you."

Dee shook his head in admiration. "I had forgotten what a ruthless foe you are. We should have joined forces generations ago; together we could have ruled the world."

"We still can," Dare agreed, "but right now you need to work out a way to open the gates. We're being watched."

Dee didn't move; only the sudden tightening of his shoulders betrayed his tension. "Where? Who?"

The woman nodded into the reflective black water in front of them.

Dee looked, staring hard, before finally saying, "Two birds, flying high . . . and yet birds don't fly at night, and certainly not in perfect circles."

"Too high to see what they are," Virginia said, "but I'll wager they're ravens."

"Ravens?" Dee licked his lips nervously. "Well, there are ravens in the Tower of London . . ."

"Whose wings are clipped so they cannot fly," Virginia reminded him. "These birds are not natural. Which means . . ."

"Odin's birds," Dee whispered.

"Which also means that Odin's wolves, Geri and Freki, are probably not far behind." Virginia smiled sweetly. "What are they called, again? Oh, yes: Ravenous and Greedy. I'm *so* glad they're not hunting me."

Abruptly, the English Magician's aura blazed bright yellow around him, painting the walls in amber light and black shadow; the stench of sulfur polluted the night air.

"What are you doing?" Virginia Dare cried in alarm.

"You've betrayed our location!" Even as she was speaking, the sound of distant howls and triumphant screaming filled the sky. The cucubuths had awakened.

"I killed Hekate and destroyed the World Tree," Dee snapped. "Odin loved her. He won't want to capture me for the Elders, he'll want to destroy me, and he'll take a long time doing it. The time for subtlety and subterfuge is past: we need to get out of here now!" Dee's yellow aura rolled off his body and onto the dark water, instantly freezing it to foul yellow ice. The Magician leapt over the edge of the rail and landed surefootedly on the frozen surface. It creaked, and a tiny network of cracks appeared beneath his feet, but it held. The Magician looked up at the woman. "Last chance to make up your mind."

"Have I a choice now?" Dare's pretty face twisted into an ugly mask of rage. "I'm tainted with your stink." She sailed lightly over the edge of the rail and landed beside the Magician. Stepping close, she pressed the end of the flute against Dee's throat, pushing hard against his Adam's apple, driving his chin up and his head back. The Magician tried to swallow, but failed. "Do not betray me, John Dee," Virginia Dare whispered. "Do not make the mistake of adding me to your list of enemies."

"I made you promises," Dee gasped out.

"Make sure you keep those promises: I want to rule this world."

Dee started to nod . . . but suddenly became aware of the two huge ravens plummeting silently out of the night sky, pointed beaks and razor claws extended.

CHAPTER THIRTY-ONE

Josh sat beside Niten, who steered the black town car with his left hand. His right hand cradled a long dagger in a black-lacquered case that rested on his lap. In the seats behind, Nicholas was slumped beside Perenelle; Sophie and Aoife sat facing them. The Alchemyst's eyes were closed and his head was resting on Perenelle's shoulder, his fingers lightly touching the back of her hand.

"How long has he left?" Aoife asked bluntly.

Flamel's pale eyes opened and he straightened. "Long enough," he answered, his voice cracking. He coughed and tried again, his voice stronger. "And he's not dead yet, and certainly not deaf."

Aoife bared her teeth in a quick smile and, in that instant, was the image of her sister.

"Why are you here?" Perenelle snapped.

"I want my sister back," Aoife said, her voice as icy as the Sorceress's.

"It seems she may be trapped in the past," Nicholas said.

"My uncle Prometheus will take me to Chronos; I'll have him pull Scathach—"

"And Joan," Perenelle said quickly.

"And Joan," Aoife added reluctantly. "I'll have him pull them both from the past and bring them back here."

Sophie pushed up against the door and turned in her seat to look at the warrior. The name Chronos had filled her head with the Witch's thoughts. The Witch of Endor knew the Elder Chronos, knew what he was and what he was capable of doing. She had bargained with him before and paid a terrible price. "Will Chronos not want some sort of payment?" she asked carefully, struggling to keep her voice level.

"He will." Aoife shrugged and pushed her dark glasses up onto her nose again. "My uncle will take care of it. He is one of the most powerful of all the Elders," she added proudly.

"And you expect Chronos to bring your sister and Joan through time because Prometheus asks him?" Flamel coughed a laugh. He tried to smile, but failed. "And if he refuses?"

Aoife exposed her savage vampire teeth. "Then I will speak with him myself. No one has ever refused me anything."

"Except Scathach," Sophie said very softly.

The red-haired warrior turned to look at the girl, and for a long time the only sound in the car was the humming of the tires on the road. "Except Scathach," she acknowledged finally, a note of terrible loss in her voice.

"What happened?" Sophie asked.

Aoife blinked, and for an instant, her green eyes winked bloodred. Then she swiveled in her seat to look at Josh. "He is your twin," she said. "What would you do if you lost him?"

"Lost him?" Sophie shook her head, not understanding. "What do you mean, lost him?"

"If he turned against you, hated you . . ."

Josh started to laugh, until he realized that the vampire wasn't joking. "I would never . . . ," he began.

"That's what Scathach said," Aoife interrupted. She fixed her eyes on Sophie. "You did not answer my question: what would you do if you lost your brother, if he suddenly hated you? Would you give up on him?"

"Never," Sophie whispered. The very thought was chilling and made her feel sick to her stomach.

Aoife nodded slowly, then sat back and closed her eyes, the palms of her hands resting flat on her thighs. "I lost Scathach, but I never gave up on her. I have spent ten thousand years in this Shadowrealm waiting for that single moment to tell her, to show her, that I never stopped loving her."

The car turned onto the 101 heading north and picked up speed, the only sound the thrumming of the wheels on the road. Then Perenelle leaned forward and touched the vampire's knee. The air crackled with static.

"You love your sister?"

"Yes."

"She does not love you," the Sorceress said quietly.

"It does not matter."

They continued in silence and then Perenelle spoke very softly, her voice barely above a whisper, her eyes shining wetly. "Perhaps we have misjudged you, and if we have, then I apologize."

Aoife grunted a laugh. "No, you did not misjudge me, Sorceress. I *am* as bad as I'm made out to be."

Josh turned in the front seat. "Hey, did you just say you've spent ten thousand years on this earth?"

Sophie nodded. She knew exactly what he was about to ask, and knew the answer.

"But you're Scatty's twin, and she said she was two thousand five hundred and seventeen years old. How can you be ten thousand?"

"Scathach lies," Aoife said simply. She shook her head. "She's a terrible liar. You wouldn't want to believe a single word she tells you."

CHAPTER THIRTY-TWO

"*I* suppose Billy told you not to mention the tail?" Kukulkan said, sitting on a curved stone stool carved with hideous grinning faces. The brightly colored feathered tail coiled around his feet, the tip beating silently against the floor.

Niccolò Machiavelli sat back into an ornate hand-carved wooden throne, rested his elbows on its arms and brought the fingertips of both hands together before his face. A sense of calm settled over him, and the fact that they had not been killed immediately gave him reason to hope. Taking a slow deep breath, he composed himself before answering.

The Italian had been in situations like this before, when all that kept him from certain death were his wits and his skill with words. He had been an ambassador to the glittering courts of France and Spain, where a single wrong word or misplaced look could get a man killed. Later still, he had survived the deathly Papal court and the even more ruthless and dangerous world of the Borgias, where assassination and poisoning were commonplace. The Elder sitting opposite him, looking human in every respect—except for the tail and the solid black eyes—might be ten thousand and more years old, but Machiavelli had discovered that just about every being he had come across either in this world or in the nearby Shadowrealms, was driven by nearly the same needs and desires. Humani's earliest myths were full of tales that revealed just how petty the gods could be. It was said that the gods had made man in their image. If so, then the humani had inherited all the faults and frailties of those same gods.

Kukulkan's tail twitched as he waited for an answer.

Finally, Machiavelli smiled and said, "Billy may have suggested that I avoid the subject of the tail." From the corner of his eye, he saw the American immortal close his eyes in dismay. "Though I have to say," he added, "it is one of the finest tails I have ever seen."

Billy the Kid's eyes and mouth snapped open in horror. He had been standing behind the Italian's right shoulder, facing the Elder, but now he slowly and carefully stepped aside. He'd been in enough shoot-outs to know that it was not a good idea to stand behind a target.

"And you have seen many tails?" the small man with the white beard said. His almost lipless mouth was a horizontal slash, and his solid black eyes fixed on Machiavelli's face.

"Many, in both this world and the Shadowrealms. I have always had a fondness for beautiful things," the Italian added. "I collected antiques for centuries, and for years one of my most prized possessions was an Abelam Yam Mask from

Papua New Guinea. It was adorned with the most magnificent bird-of-paradise plumes."

"A beautiful bird," Kukulkan agreed.

"Though I do believe yours is the finer plumage," Machiavelli added.

"If I thought you were attempting to flatter me, I would strike you dead on the spot." The old man's face shifted subtly.

Billy took another step away.

"You want to know whether I am lying?" Machiavelli asked.

Kukulkan tilted his head to one side, listening.

"Are your feathers more beautiful than the plumage of the bird-of-paradise?" Machiavelli asked.

"Why, of course," the Elder agreed.

"So I was merely stating a fact. I have found that the truth is usually the simplest way," the immortal said. "Fools lie, clever men stick to the truth."

"Your master said you were . . . complex," Kukulkan said after a long pause.

"I was unaware that you knew my master," Machiavelli said. "Though I should not be surprised; I suppose most of the Elders know one another."

"Not all," Kukulkan answered. "I am still occasionally shocked when someone I have not heard of in millennia reappears in this Shadowrealm." He turned his head to look out the enormous window that took up one wall. From this angle, with his strong chin and hooked nose, he resembled

160

the faces on the stone statues Machiavelli had seen carved into temples across South America. "Your master and I are related," Kukulkan said softly, glancing over at the Italian, "not by blood or family, but by bonds forged in struggle and adversity. I am honored to call him brother."

"Can I ask how you know my master?"

"In the terrible days after the sundering of Danu Talis, the survivors took to the remnants of our once-great fleet of metal boats. For many days, we floated adrift on seas boiling with lava, the air foul and stinking with brimstone while the heavens rained burning coals and boiling water. When my ship struck a newly created lava reef and sank, I was the sole survivor. Against his crew's wishes, your master turned his boat around just to rescue me, even though I was a different clan and caste. He shared his food and water with me, and when I despaired, he regaled with me tales of the World That Was and the World to Come. He taught me that out of the destruction of Danu Talis a new world would form—a world neither better nor worse than the one which had been destroyed. Your master changed me, made me realize the potential in this new humani race. We needed them, he said, in order to survive. I believed him." Kukulkan rose to his feet and wandered around the room, the tail rasping along on the ground behind him. "I still do."

Now that his eyes had adjusted to the gloom, Machiavelli could see that the huge room was filled with countless artifacts from the Aztec, Maya and Olmec cultures: stone carvings, etched squares of gold, elaborate jade masks and bejeweled black obsidian knives. Scattered among the antiques were pieces that were obviously Egyptian, some of them astonishingly similar to their Mayan counterparts.

The Elder's fingers trailed over an Aztec sword—a length of jade inset with black volcanic glass. "I went west to the Land of Jungle and Mountain, while your master, Aten, continued on to the east and the Lands of the Middle Sea." Kukulkan picked up a tiny carved scarab beetle and looked at it closely before returning it to its shelf. "We trained the humani, nudged them toward civilization. In time the humani came to worship us, though in different ways. And I was never happier." Something must have shown on Machiavelli's usually impassive face, because the Elder's lips curved into a smile. "You are surprised that we are capable of happiness?" Kukulkan asked.

The immortal shook his head. "The Elders I have dealt with over the centuries showed rage, anger, jealousy. I never considered that they might enjoy some of the other emotions," he admitted.

"Why?"

Machiavelli shrugged. "Because you are not human," he suggested.

"There are some emotions that are common to all living creatures—from Elder to humani and even the beasts," Kukulkan said. "Have you never watched a dog mourning its master, nor a herd of elephants honoring their dead? Surely you have seen the excitement a hound exhibits when its master returns?"

Machiavelli nodded.

"But it is true that as a race, the Elders are not entirely comfortable with some of the lighter emotions. Centuries of power and authority stripped us of much of our joy in life. We had everything and we wanted more. In those last years before the island sank, there was not much laughter. The Elders were cruel to their servants and to one another. We fought because we could; we waged wars for no reason other than we were bored." Kukulkan looked quickly at Machiavelli. "I was as guilty as all the others. Aten changed that. He was the fiercest, bravest warrior I have ever encountered, and yet he was also the gentlest and kindest." He saw the look of surprise on the Italian's face. "You did not know this about your own master?"

"I met him twice face to face," Machiavelli said, "and then only briefly. The second time he made me immortal. Although we've spoken often over the centuries, we've not met again." He smiled. "And while I think I could call him many things, I would never describe him as gentle and kind. He single-handedly destroyed an entire way of life in Egypt. He was so hated that almost every instance of his name was removed from the historical records."

Kukulkan waved his hand dismissively. "I was there. He did—*we* did—what was necessary. We made Egypt great." The Elder returned to his stone seat and silently faced Machiavelli. He was completely still, only the feathers on his tail shifting slightly in the warm breeze that wafted through the open door.

Machiavelli sat back in his chair and waited. He had infinite patience—he considered it one of his greatest

163

strengths—so he knew he could outwait Kukulkan. Hasty words and hasty actions had destroyed many a plan. He wasn't sure he entirely believed the Elder. Machiavelli had done his own research: when his master, Aten—who was also known as Akhenaten—had ruled Egypt, he had been such a tyrant that later generations would refer to him simply as the Enemy. Machiavelli also knew that Akhenaten's son, Tutankhamen, had possessed a rare gold aura.

"What do I do with you, Italian?" the Elder said suddenly.

"Do with me?"

"Do you always answer a question with a question?"

"Do I?"

Kukulkan's feathered tail twitched and tapped impatiently on the floor.

"Mac," Billy whispered in alarm.

"Don't call me Mac. I hate that."

"Then don't irritate the all-powerful Elder," Billy muttered.

Kukulkan's face and coal black eyes betrayed no expression, nor was there any emotion in his voice when he spoke. "I am unsure whether you are arrogant, stupid or very clever."

"I am arrogant," Machiavelli said with a smile. "I have always known that. But I am very clever, too. I am also valuable"—he waved his hand to include all the rare treasures in the room—"and I can see that you appreciate valuable things."

Kukulkan's head dipped in acknowledgment. "I do. And a valuable tool should not be hastily put aside."

"I've been called a valuable tool before," Machiavelli said.

"By your master?"

"Aten has called me that on several occasions," Machiavelli agreed.

The Elder nodded in agreement. "Aten gave me many tools and many gifts," Kukulkan continued. "He taught me how to live, how to respect and how to love. There is much that I owe my brother; I have always been in his debt. And although he has not asked that your life be spared, I believe I will spare it, as a gift to him. A debt must always be honored."

Machiavelli bowed slightly. He swallowed a quick rush of anger. He knew he should be grateful that he was still alive, but something about the creature's reasoning bothered him. It was something he'd put aside and think about later; he had a rule never to allow anger to cloud his judgment. "I am grateful," he said simply.

"Me too," said Billy.

"Who said anything about sparing you!" Kukulkan snapped.

CHAPTER THIRTY-THREE

"*O*ld friend," Palamedes said carefully, "are you sure you want to go through with this?"

Saint-Germain nodded, his face the only lightness in the gloomy cab. "Of course I do." They had been driving north for more than two hours. They'd left the M1 and the M25 far behind and were now driving down a series of twisting country lanes.

The Saracen Knight shifted uncomfortably in the front seat. The occasional streetlight washed across his face, turning his eyes to liquid orange. "My master is unpredictable," he said eventually. "Dangerously so. His contempt for humani is absolute. He despises what they have done to the world he helped create."

"He liked you well enough to make you immortal," Saint-Germain said.

The big man grunted a bitter laugh. "My master does not

like me. He made me immortal and condemned me to wander the Shadowrealms as punishment for an old, old crime." He waved a hand in the air. "We will talk of it someday, but not today." Palamedes turned off the road onto a narrow track. There were no streetlights, but the headlights picked out the gnarled trunks of ancient trees lining the road.

The faintest smell of burnt leaves filled the air, and Saint-Germain's bright blue eyes briefly turned red. "You know we have met before, your master and I?"

"I know," Palamedes said miserably. "He remembers. He is old now—old, old, old—but there are certain things he never forgets. And unfortunately, you are one of those."

"Will I be able to bargain with him, do you think?" the Frenchman asked.

"You can try. Will Shakespeare and I will stand with you."

"You do not have to do that," Saint-Germain said quickly. "That could be dangerous. Possibly even deadly," he added grimly.

"We will stand by your side," the knight said. "You have stood with Will and me often enough, you have saved our lives on more than one occasion. What would we be if we abandoned you when you needed us?"

Saint-Germain leaned forward to squeeze Palamedes' shoulder. "I am lucky to count you as a friend," he said simply.

"You are more than a friend to me," Palamedes answered. "My blood family is long dead. And when I lost my sweetheart to another man, I never thought I would have a family again. Then, one day, I realized that almost by accident, I was drawing a family around me, a new family: first Will, then you and my fellow knights. You are my family now. Once, I fought for my faith and my country; later, I fought for Arthur out of a sense of duty to him and loyalty to his cause. In all my years of battle, I never fought for one of my family. But tonight, I will stand by your side because you are my brother."

The words took Saint-Germain's breath away, and he suddenly felt his throat burning and tears prickling his eyes. It took him several moments before he knew his voice would be steady enough to reply. "I was an only child," he said. "I always wanted a brother."

"Well, now you have two."

The cab swung into an empty car park, the sweeping headlights picking up a disheveled figure perched like a bird on a wooden picnic table. "Will," Saint-Germain said delightedly. He pushed the door open even before the car had fully stopped and hopped out. Shakespeare stepped off the table and the two men looked at one another for a moment; then each bowed deeply—though the Bard's bow was more restrained than Saint-Germain's dramatic flourish.

Shakespeare's pale eyes were troubled as he looked at his friend. "Welcome to Sherwood Forest." He shivered and added, "I hate this place."

CHAPTER THIRTY-FOUR

"Welcome to Point Reyes," Niten said.

Sophie and Josh looked out of the car windows. They could see nothing. Although there had been brilliant sunshine in Sausalito and for most of the journey up the 101 and the Sir Francis Drake Boulevard, tendrils of mist had started to appear shortly after they drove through Inverness. Then, with shocking suddenness, a thick opaque fog had rolled in off the sea, blanketing the landscape in salt-tinged clouds.

Josh hit the button that rolled down his window. The air that swept into the car was cold, but he put his head out and attempted to peer into the gloom.

"Close the window," Aoife snapped. "I'm freezing."

"You're a ten-thousand-year-old vampire," Sophie said with a grin, amused by the creature's reaction. "You're not supposed to feel the cold."

"I hate this damp," Aoife grumbled. "That's why I've always preferred warm climates."

Perenelle stirred. Nicholas was dozing with his head on her shoulder. "I thought your race were impervious to the weather."

"Some might be," Aoife said. "I'm not." She held up her arm and pushed back her sleeve. Her pale flesh was dappled with goose bumps. "Why do you think Scathach and I left Scotland and never went back? We couldn't stand the rain."

Josh pulled his head in and hit the switch that raised the window. Beads of cold moisture sparkled in his hair. Looking at Niten, he pointed to the thick fog billowing against the windshield. "Don't you think you should slow down?" he said nervously. "I can't even see the road—how can you tell where we're going?"

Niten's eyes didn't move, but a trace of a smile curled his lips. "I do not need my eyes to tell me where I'm going."

"I have no idea what that means," Josh said. "Is it like some sort of ninja trick?"

Niten shot Josh a warning look. "Whatever you do, don't mention—"

It was too late. In the backseat Aoife stirred. "Ninjas," she spat. "Why is everyone obsessed with ninjas? They were never that good. And they were cowards, sneaking around in their black pajamas, stabbing their victims with poisoned darts. I hate ninjas—they have no honor."

"Scathach said she tried training them, but they were never that good," Sophie added.

"She should have stayed well away from them," Aoife snapped. "They were her students until they thought they had learned all her secrets—then they tried to kill her." She grunted a laugh. "That was a mistake," she added grimly.

"What happened?" Josh asked, but Aoife had turned her face to the window, eyes blank and distant. He looked at the driver. "What happened?" he asked again. He was curious; he'd always thought ninjas were cool, and here was a chance to learn about them from someone who had actually seen and fought them.

"You do not want to know," Niten murmured. "When Scathach was finished with them, Aoife insisted on hunting down the few survivors." The small man pointed through the windshield, changing the subject. "What do you see?"

"Fog," Josh said.

"Look again," Niten urged.

Josh stared hard. Inches beyond the hood of the car, the road disappeared into a shifting wall of wet gray cloud. "There's nothing to see," he said finally, struggling to understand what the Japanese immortal was getting at.

"There is always something to see, if you only know how to look," Niten suggested. He raised his head slightly, pointing with his chin. "Look on either side of the road, see how the fog shifts and coils; now look directly ahead and see how it moves."

Josh squinted out through the glass and suddenly noticed something strange. "It seems to be moving quicker in front of us than it does on either side."

"The heat coming off the road keeps the fog in motion," Niten said. "There is no reflected heat coming off the soil and stones on our sides, so the fog is still."

"So that's how you keep the car on the road." He nodded, impressed.

Niten smiled. "Well, that and the white line running down the middle."

Perenelle leaned forward and breathed deeply. "But this is no ordinary fog is it?"

Aoife blinked and then she slowly and deliberately turned to look at the Sorceress. "No, it is not natural. *He* knows we're coming. Any moment now, we will shift . . ."

Even as she was speaking, the smooth hiss of tires on concrete changed to rattling grit.

". . . from this world into his Shadowrealm."

Josh frowned. Was it his imagination or was the fog clearing? He was turning to ask Sophie when, in the space of a single heartbeat, it vanished altogether, revealing a lush pastoral landscape that swept down to a distant blue sea. The road was now little more than a dirt track, lined on either side with fruit trees, only neither the trees nor the fruits they bore were at all familiar. He looked over the back of the seat at his sister and raised an eyebrow. *Where are we?* he mouthed.

She shook her head. *Safe.*

He was about to ask her how she knew, but he saw the way her eyes darted toward Aoife and understood instinctively that Sophie didn't want Scathach's twin to know the extent of her knowledge.

The landscape looked similar—very similar—to his own world, but there were subtle differences. The trees were just a little larger, the grass taller and all the colors sharper and brighter. He leaned forward and looked up into the sky. It was a bright eggshell blue streaked with white clouds, but he could see no sign of the sun. He ducked his head to get a better look out the windshield, then searched the sky. "There's no sun," he whispered in awe.

"That's because this is the realm of Prometheus," Nicholas answered from the backseat. "We're underground, in the Shadowrealm once known as Hades." He coughed, the sound wet in his chest, and sat back again.

"Everything you see around you is an illusion—remember that," Perenelle finished.

"Hades . . . ," Josh began, voice rising in alarm. A flicker of movement distracted him and he turned to look out his window. The car was now creeping along the dirt road, and he saw a figure step out from between the trees on one side. It was followed by a second and a third, and suddenly a long line of vaguely human-looking beings lined the narrow track. They appeared unformed, ill-shaped, with heads too large or one arm longer than the other, big feet on thin legs, hands with too many fingers. The faces were almost blank, with just slight impressions where a mouth or eyes would normally be, and they were all bald and had no ears or noses. As the car drew close, Josh saw that their deep brown skin was cracked and seamed with countless wrinkles . . . like dried mud. "They're Golems," Josh whispered in horror, remembering the mud men who had accompanied Dee when he'd attacked the shop.

"Not Golems . . . ," Sophie murmured. Memories were tumbling through her head; images had started to flicker, dark, terrifying thoughts of an ancient nameless city. "No, not Golems . . ."

"Not Golems," Aoife snapped, twisting in her seat to look at him. "Do not even mention them in the same breath. Golems are mere shadows of these creatures. These are the last remnants of the First People."

"The First People?" Josh shook his head. "I've never heard of them."

"You haven't?" Aoife asked incredulously. She looked at Nicholas, Perenelle and Sophie before turning back to Josh. "You *do* know that my uncle Prometheus created the original humani out of mud?"

The idea was so ridiculous that Josh started to laugh, and then he realized that no one else in the car was even smiling. He looked at his sister and saw her nod slightly. "The First People."

"He made humans out of mud? That . . . But that's just . . ."

"We've seen mud and wax people this week," Sophie quickly reminded him.

"I know, but they were artificial creations, animated by

174

the power of Dee's and Machiavelli's auras. I can—sort of—understand that." He looked at the misshapen figures lining the road and turned back to Aoife. "But you're saying that Prometheus created the human race!"

Aoife looked directly at Josh as she spoke. "My uncle appears in the mythology of many races. He has many names, but the story is the same: Prometheus created the first humani out of mud using an ancient technology that was so advanced it seemed magical. Some of the other Elders created beasts, but Prometheus went one step further. A step too far, for many. That was the reason the Elders hated him and banished him, and why he was sentenced to a long drawn-out death in the Hades Shadowrealm."

Josh twisted around to look at the humanlike figures standing unmoving by the sides of the road. A sudden thought struck him and he twisted in his seat to look at the four people in the back. "So if he helped create the first humani," he said hopefully, "then that means he'll help us?"

Aoife's laughter was ugly.

"What's so funny?" Sophie demanded.

The warrior's grin revealed her vampire teeth. "My uncle gave the humani life and taught them the Magic of Fire . . . but they abandoned him. They have always abandoned and betrayed him. Even your friend Saint-Germain," she said, and abruptly caught Sophie's arm, twisting it to expose the tattoo on her wrist. "First he befriended my uncle, and then he stole the secret of fire." She shook her head. "Prometheus has no time for the humani. He despises them."

Josh looked back out the window at the creatures, which

175

had begun to crowd ever closer to the car. "So what are these First People doing here?"

"They are the Shadowrealms' guardians." Aoife grinned. "And they are hungry. Always hungry."

The car suddenly jerked, then sputtered and died.

"I guess I don't want to know what they eat," Josh muttered.

"No, you don't," his sister said.

CHAPTER THIRTY-FIVE

"Niten?" Nicholas asked.

"Battery's dead." The immortal turned the key in the ignition, but it clicked uselessly.

Nicholas reached up to turn on the overhead light. Nothing happened. "The Shadowrealm has drained the power."

"What do we do?" Josh asked.

"We sit and wait," the Alchemyst said.

With a growing sense of unease, Sophie watched as the mud figures crowded in closer around the car. Wherever they touched it, they deposited streaks of what looked like dried and flaking earth on the shining metal. One flailing arm left a muddy smear across the windshield; another pressed against her door, completely coating the glass in sticky brown-gray mud. There was a thump as something fell onto the roof, and then the car rocked from side to side with the mass of heavy bodies pressing against it.

"What's happening?" Josh asked, a tremor in his voice. A figure started to crawl across the hot hood of the car, the heat drying out its soft flesh, leaving chunks stuck to the metal.

"Don't open the windows!" Sophie said suddenly, her voice cracking. She sounded different than usual—old and hoarse, her words heavy with an unidentifiable accent. "They must not touch us."

Aoife spun in the seat to look at her, green eyes narrowing suspiciously. "How do you know that?"

"The Witch told me," Sophie whispered. Her blue eyes flickered silver, then turned shockingly green for a single instant. She turned to look out the window. Directly in front of her, its unformed face inches from hers, was one of the muddy creatures. Sophie saw her own face reflected in the glass, superimposed over the blank mask, and she drew back in fright. She knew what had attracted the creatures and what they wanted. "They're drawn to our auras," she said very slowly, her voice still touched by the same accent. "Though they move, they are without the spark of true life. If they can but touch us, then they will be able to suck our auras away and wrap them around themselves, giving themselves the semblance of life."

Aoife's pale skin had turned ghastly white, her freckles looking like spots of blood across her cheeks and nose. "You sound like . . . like . . ." She shook her head. "But that's impossible."

Sophie turned to look at Aoife. She brushed strands of blond hair away from her face and looked directly at the warrior. She concentrated hard, and her blue eyes gradually paled, fading almost to white, then settling into a metallic silver. The faintest of glows touched them, and the car was filled with the scent of vanilla.

"Who are you?" Aoife demanded. "*What* are you?"

When Sophie didn't answer, Nicholas sat forward and said, "Sophie was Awakened by Hekate, and then your grandmother taught her the Magic of Air. At the same time, the Witch passed on her memories. Sophie knows all that the Witch knew."

Aoife pulled back from Sophie, her face suddenly blank. "I don't believe it."

"It's true," Josh said.

"Why are you frightened?" Sophie asked. Memories came flooding into her consciousness, and she nodded slowly as she answered her own question. "You fear what I know."

"I am afraid of nothing!" Aoife said quickly.

"I think you have been afraid all your life."

"This is some sort of trick," Aoife snapped, with the tiniest tremor in her voice. "Flamel or the Sorceress has schooled you." Wisps of her ugly gray aura coiled off her body like steam, leaking from her nose and ears. "If you truly know all that the Witch of Endor knew, then tell me her true name, her secret name."

"Zephaniah," Sophie breathed. And even as she said the name, her heart started to hammer as sudden vivid memories washed over her. Closing her eyes, she drew in a deep breath. . . .

CHAPTER THIRTY-SIX

Zephaniah drew in a deep breath and opened her eyes to look across the nameless Archon metropolis.

The city had been an ancient ruin before the Great Elders had stumbled across it and hacked it free of the primeval forest. There was even evidence to suggest that the mysterious Archons had not built the city, but had simply occupied the deserted glass-and-gold buildings, which dated from the Time Before Time. When the Great Elders relocated to the newly created Isle of Danu Talis, the unnamed city had been abandoned once again to the forest. Now the gleaming metal spires were wrapped around with thick vines, and the glass walls and glittering black stone streets were covered with creepers and trailing roots. It was deserted—no animals moved in the tumbled city, no birds flew overhead and the usual jungle noises were completely absent.

"This place frightens me," she said aloud.

Her huge red-haired, red-bearded companion remained silent. Shading his eyes from the sun, he slowly looked across the city, searching for any signs of life or movement.

Zephaniah unrolled a map etched onto a piece of skin from a long-extinct lizard and pressed it against a green glass wall. Tilting her head to one side, she tried to make sense of the squiggles and arcane script. "We're here," she said doubtfully, pointing at the map.

An enormous hand reached over her shoulder, flattened the map against the wall, then slowly turned it upside down. A blunt-nailed finger pointed. "We're here, sister!"

Zephaniah took hold of the coarse red hair that covered the back of the man's hand and tugged hard.

"Ouch! What did you do that for?" Prometheus demanded.

"Because."

"Because?"

"To remind you that not only are you my little brother, I'm in charge of this expedition."

The warrior in the rust-colored leather armor grinned. "That's only because Abraham likes you more than he likes me."

Zephaniah's smile faded. "To be honest, I don't think Abraham likes either of us," she said softly.

Prometheus rested his hand on his sister's shoulder and brought his head down close to hers, strands of his graying red hair mingling with hers. His solid green eyes were troubled. "I know you like him, but be careful, sister. I have heard rumors that he is mingling Archon technology and Elder magic in ways

181

that have never been used before." He saw something shift behind his sister's green eyes and cupped her small chin in his hand, tilting her face upward. "You knew this . . . ," he said accusingly.

"A little," she admitted. "He told me that he is creating an encyclopedia of the entire world's knowledge. He is calling it a Codex."

"That must be a big book," Prometheus said with a smile.

"He believes he can get it into twenty-one pages."

The red-haired warrior started to shake his head. "I was going to say impossible, and then I realized that for Abraham nothing is impossible. Did he tell you why?" Prometheus asked. But before his sister could answer, he spun around to look behind him, quickly scanning the edges of the encroaching forest. All morning he'd had the feeling that they were being followed. Although nothing moved in the city, the surrounding countryside teemed with life: he'd even spotted serpents that he'd thought had died out long ago. There were monstrous lizards in the rivers, and thunderbirds still soared high in the skies. But he didn't think it was a beast on their trail. On two separate occasions, he'd caught the smell of something rank and rotten, something long dead. He'd seen nothing, yet he knew this was not just his imagination: there was something in the forest, watching them.

"Abraham believes the world will end . . . ," the slight red-haired woman with the huge round green eyes said.

Prometheus laughed. "He's been promising that for centuries. If he says it long enough, then one day he'll be right."

Even though they were alone in the vast city, Zephaniah

182

lowered her voice. "He has entered into an alliance with Chronos. . . ."

Prometheus's face twisted in disgust.

"I believe the Master of Time has given him a date for the end of the world."

"I would not trust that old monster as far as I could throw him."

Zephaniah smiled at the sudden image. Her brother, Prometheus, was immensely strong, and Chronos was tiny. Rolling up the map, she stuck it into the metal tube she wore strapped across her back. "This way?" she asked.

Prometheus took a last glance over his shoulder before turning back to his sister. "No, it's this way. The library should be at the end of this street."

The two Elders had been traveling for ten days now and were both exhausted, but at last their goal was in sight.

The first part of their journey had been relatively straightforward. Leaving Danu Talis, they had traveled across the world, jumping from leygate to leygate, moving east to west, following the setting sun, until they reached the place where, legend had it, the Earthlords, Ancients and Archons had fought in the Time Before Time. Nothing grew in this devastated place, and intense heat had turned the earth to shining glass. The cataclysmic battle had upset the earth's magnetic forces so that even the ley lines no longer functioned properly. None of those who had jumped through the final leygate—a perfectly circular hole in a cliff face—had returned; their screams still echoed through the gates even though centuries had passed.

Zephaniah and Prometheus continued south on foot. The same forces that had upset the ley lines also sucked away at their auras, leaving them both weak and practically powerless. It had taken Prometheus—a Master of Fire—three attempts before he'd been able to raise a feeble flame to heat some water. Their auras had strengthened the farther they had moved away from the last leygate, but when they'd entered the forest that ringed the Nameless City, their auras had faded again.

Zephaniah was exhausted. It was an extraordinary feeling, one she had not experienced in hundreds of years. The bone-dry desert around the leygate quickly followed by the rank humidity of the jungle had destroyed her leather-and-metal clothes, and her indestructible boots had proven not so indestructible. Having no access to her aura had been a terrifying revelation. To have to rely on her unenhanced senses was like being deaf and blind, and even her sense of taste was limited, so that everything tasted the same—either sweet or salty. Now she could only smell the strongest—and usually the foulest—of odors. The sooner they got what they were looking for and left the Nameless City, the happier she would be. But Abraham's instructions had been clear: she was not to return without the records from the library. There was one particular book he needed to complete the creation of the Codex.

Initially, Zephaniah had contemplated making the journey on her own: she was both strong and fast, and her auric powers were incredible. However, her friend Hekate had begged her to bring someone with her, and surprisingly, Abraham had agreed to let her. She had been even more surprised when he had suggested her younger brother, the fearsome warrior-sage Prometheus.

"I'm glad you came with me," she said suddenly. "I'm not sure I would have liked to make this journey on my own."

"I have to look out for my sister," the warrior said with a grin. Then the smile faded. "But I do know what you mean. . . . There is something about this place . . . something wrong. No wonder our people abandoned it."

"I wonder why they never gave it a name," she said. "On the charts it is simply known as the City and Abraham called it the Nameless City." The pair continued down the middle of the broad street, following mysterious metal grooves cut into the primeval black stones. Although the age of the city could be measured in millennia, no metal had rusted, and while the glass walls were scratched and scored by the forest, not a single pane was broken.

"Here, I think . . . ," Prometheus said. He stopped outside an enormous stepped-glass pyramid. The entire front of the building was covered in intricate spirals and whorls. Just looking at them made him dizzy. Squeezing his eyes shut, he shook his head. "Check the map."

Zephaniah pulled the map from the metal tube; she held it up, comparing the symbols etched into the glass above the door with the pattern on the skin. They matched. "This is the library," she said, craning her neck to look at the top of the pyramid. It was topped with a cap of solid gold. "The proportions are wrong," she said suddenly, stepping back to look at the doors. "The handles are set too high and the doors are unusually tall."

Prometheus nodded. "And the steps are too shallow," he said.

"This city was not built for creatures like us," Zephaniah added.

"But for whom . . . or for what?" he wondered.

"The Ancients?" Zephaniah suggested.

"Not them: they resembled us to some degree. Legend has it that this city was created for the Earthlords."

"What did they look like?"

Prometheus shrugged. "No one knows. None survived the last battle, and all record of them was erased from history." Pulling two short double-headed axes from his belt, he stepped up to the door of opaque black glass and pushed hard, expecting it to be stiff with age.

It swung silently open.

Prometheus quickly stepped inside and put his back to the wall, waiting until his eyes had adjusted to the gloom. Zephaniah remained outside and pulled a coiled metal whip from around her waist. If there was anything inside, she didn't want to get in her brother's way, and it was her duty to protect him.

"I'm not sure this is the right place. . . ." Prometheus's voice echoed. "There are no books here, just statues. Hundreds—no, thousands of them."

A flicker of movement at the edge of the forest caught Zephaniah's attention. A branch had shifted slightly, moving against the wind rather than with it.

"I think we've got company," she said quietly. And then her nostrils flared as she caught the distinctive smell of anise, the odor of her brother's aura. "Prometheus?"

"Statues," he repeated, his voice growing fainter as he moved away from the door.

"Prometheus . . ."

"They look like they're made of clay. . . ."

The smell of anise was stronger now, and when she glanced over her shoulder, Zephaniah caught the dull red glow of her brother's aura from within the darkened building. But how was that possible? For the past few days neither of them had been able to bring their auras alight. Gripping the whip tightly in her right hand, she backed in through the open door, then turned . . . and stopped in horror.

Prometheus was standing in the middle of an enormous room. His axes had fallen to the ground and his arms were stretched straight out, his head thrown back. His aura was ablaze, streamers of fire coiling off his skin, his hair and beard crackling with static. Liquid fire puddled around his feet, and his outstretched fingers and thumbs spat tiny lightning bolts. His eyes burned like red-hot coals.

And he was surrounded by statues.

Intricately beautiful, delicately carved from clay, they ranged in color from deep black to palest white. And while their bodies were perfectly sculpted, their faces remained unfinished, little more than vague ovals, without eyes, ears, nose or mouth. Male and female stood side by side in identical positions, tall, elegant and otherworldly. They looked not unlike the Elders or even the legendary Archons, but were obviously different from those races.

And every inch of their carved clay bodies was covered in the same spiraling script that decorated the front of the building.

Prometheus's burning aura washed over the closest statues, red sparks running across the designs, crimson fire crawling along the archaic writing, bringing the lines of curling text to life.

"Prometheus . . . ," Zephaniah whispered.

Then the statue closest to Prometheus, a statuesque female, moved. A sliver of hardened clay fell away and shattered on the ground, revealing dark flesh beneath. Behind the Elder a second statue, a male, shifted slightly, and more clay fell away to expose rich golden skin.

"Little Brother . . ."

The Elder's fiery aura blazed higher, leaping from statue to statue, igniting the script with threads of fire. Crackling balls of it dripped off Prometheus's skin like sweat and rolled along the floor. When they reached a statue, they hissed and surged, and lines of flame crawled up the clay, igniting the writing. When all the writing was burning and the statue was bright with fire, the figure moved, hardened clay cascading off its body to shatter on the floor.

Zephaniah was suddenly aware that her brother's aura had changed color. It had become darker, almost ugly, and the bitter-sweet smell of anise had become sharp and sour.

"Prometheus!" she shouted in alarm, but he could not hear her. She knew what was happening: his aura had started to consume him.

The Elder's aura was an inferno now, a solid pillar of fire stretching up to the apex of the pyramid, and Prometheus was almost invisible in the middle of the flames. Fire bounced off the ceiling and fell onto the carvings like burning rain. The heat

188

was overwhelming, washing over the thousands of figures, burning away clay to reveal the flesh beneath.

Zephaniah knew she needed to distract her brother, to disrupt his aura before the fire destroyed him. She desperately pushed her way through the statues. Some toppled and fell, and where the clay shells had not been touched by Prometheus's aura, they shattered to dust when they hit the floor. When Zephaniah was close enough, she uncoiled the whip and lashed out at her brother, catching him around an outstretched arm. The metal and leather of the weapon instantly glowed bright red and started to burn. She pulled with all her might, and he staggered.

Prometheus's aura flickered, darkened, then blazed back even brighter. The smell of anise had turned unmistakably foul. Bitter.

Jerking the burning whip free, Zephaniah lashed out again, this time catching him around the throat. Gripping the whip with both hands, she jerked hard and managed to tug Prometheus off balance. He staggered, and then his aura flickered and died as he folded to his knees.

"Prometheus . . ." Zephaniah dropped to the ground, cradling her brother, ignoring the heat that burned her flesh and seared her clothes. He opened his green eyes and looked up at her.

"What happened?" he mumbled.

Zephaniah tore her gaze from her brother to look up. What had once been statues were now living beings. They crowded around, still and silent, and she realized to her horror that their once-formless faces had altered to take on a semblance of her brother's features.

"I think you've become a father," she said in awe. "Little Brother, they all look like you."

"Oh dear." He coughed. "Even the women?"

"Especially the women," Zephaniah said, closing her eyes.

Sophie Newman opened her eyes and instantly recognized the face glaring in through the window at them. "Prometheus," she breathed. "Little Brother."

CHAPTER THIRTY-SEVEN

$\mathcal{T}$he huge ravens Huginn and Muninn, each as big as a horse, fell toward Dee and Virginia Dare, razor-sharp talons splayed wide. Their instructions were clear: lift both of the immortals high into the air and, once they were over the Thames, drop the woman into the river as punishment for aiding the Magician.

Dr. John Dee shoved Virginia to one side, sending her sliding across the frozen pool, her flute spinning from her hand. The Magician tried to run but lost his footing, his feet shooting out from under him. The fall saved his life.

The two monstrous crows crashed into the ice, talons and beaks shattering the surface. Huginn disappeared under the water with a startled squawk, then reappeared a moment later in an explosion of glistening shards. Muninn slid across the slippery pool, scrambling to gain purchase.

Dee staggered to his feet and stood swaying as the ice shattered all around him. He felt water soak into his expensive shoes and, with a surge of annoyance, stamped his foot down hard. The surface froze again, trapping Huginn partially under water and immobilizing Muninn's feet.

The howling of the cucubuths was closer now.

Virginia Dare had clambered to her feet and retrieved her flute by the time Dee made his way across the frozen pool to her side. "Time to go," he snapped.

Muninn's huge head jerked toward them, jabbing its spearlike beak as the immortals tried to get past. Dee reached under his coat and pulled out the sword. The weapon crackled, red-blue fire running along the stone blade as he waved it in the air before the huge bird. The raven jerked its head back and then its beak opened and closed.

"Magician."

The voice that came from the bird was raw with disuse. It spoke in the ancient language of Danu Talis.

Virginia Dare stopped at this sound, shocked. "I've seen some strange things in my time . . ."

"Huginn and Muninn have the power of human speech," Dee reminded her. He lifted the sword. The blade brightened as he brought it close to the bird's head, the red-blue fire reflected in its huge eyes. "But I don't think it's the raven that is speaking to us now," he added, catching the bird's gaze, carefully inspecting the creature.

"Magiker . . ."

"No, this is something older, something foul," Dee said quietly. He suddenly swung the sword and the heavy lock barring the entrance to the Traitor's Gate pool fell away. "Odin, the ravens' master, speaks."

"You cannot escape me. There is nowhere in this Shadow-realm where you can hide from me."

"I am sorry if I destroyed your Shadowrealm, but you can create another," Dee began.

"You killed the woman I loved."

Dee was about to turn away, but he stopped to look at the trapped raven. "I am sorry about that too. She was a warrior; she died bravely in battle."

"You know what it is like to lose a loved one, Majiker?"

Surprised, Dee said honestly, "Yes, I know. I buried my wives and children. I watched them age, wither and die."

"I am going to destroy your world, Dee, before I destroy you. I will kill everything you hold dear."

"There is little I hold dear anymore."

"Not even this woman?"

Dee suddenly lashed out at the bird, the tip of his blade slicing through a single black feather on its neck. "Don't threaten me," Dee snarled. "I defeated you before. I will do it again." He held up the sword, moving it before the bird's eyes. "And last time, I did not have this!"

"It is as dangerous to you as it is to me," Odin said through the bird's mouth. Then there was a horrible coughing sound. It took Dee a few moments before he realized that Odin was laughing. *"That is the sword that killed Hekate; I think it will be your downfall too, Magiker."*

"Doctor, we need to go." Virginia grasped his hand in hers and pulled him through the open gate into the smaller

193

pool. "I hate to break up your chat, but we have company, lots of company, none of it friendly. And while they want you alive, the same rule does not apply to me."

The cucubuth howls were all around them, bouncing and echoing off the stones.

"What do we do now?" Dare demanded. "You do have a plan, don't you?"

"This," Dee said, taking the sword and plunging it point-first into the frozen pool. Ice shattered, water steamed and hissed, and then the couple fell into the inky black depths.

CHAPTER THIRTY-EIGHT

"Killing me," Billy the Kid said slowly, "or even *trying* to kill me, would be a mistake." There was no humor in his voice now, and his accent had turned hard and clipped. "Lots of men have tried, and lots have failed."

Kukulkan wheezed a laugh. "I am not a man."

The immortal edged away from the Elder.

"Billy," Machiavelli said softly, a note of warning in his voice.

Billy looked at the Italian and caught the hint of movement behind him. He turned to see the huge lynx standing in the doorway, its wide green eyes fixed on him.

"This one," Kukulkan said, pointing at the Italian, "I have chosen to keep alive. But why should I keep you alive?"

"Have you forgotten that I rescued you, saved your life?"

"And have you forgotten that I repaid that debt by making you immortal?"

"I've done your dirty work ever since," Billy said quickly.

"And now you have embarrassed me before my fellow Elders. I assured them you would be perfect for this small task," Kukulkan said. "And you failed me."

"Personally, I think *you* failed *me*," the American snapped, stepping away from the door. "You sent me out to perform a dangerous job without telling me what I was getting into." Still moving slowly around the room, he stabbed a finger at the Elder. "You underestimated the Sorceress."

"You are not the first," Machiavelli offered quickly. "Perenelle has chosen to live in her husband's shadow, and yet I have always believed she was the cleverer of the two. There is so much about her that is unknown."

Kukulkan came slowly to his feet and glared at the Italian. "Do not speak again," he hissed, "lest I change my mind and kill you too." He turned to focus again on Billy. "I gave you three simple tasks: escort this man to the island, kill the Sorceress and free the beasts. You failed."

"Well, one down, two to go. That ain't so bad!" Billy said. Then he suddenly lunged toward the shelf that held the Elder's collection of ancient artifacts and grabbed the jade club studded with volcanic glass. It was a Macuahuitl, an Aztec sword. As he lifted the club, the black obsidian shards sparkled in the afternoon light.

"How dare you raise a weapon in my presence." Kukulkan's head suddenly jutted forward and an unnaturally long black forked tongue flickered toward the outlaw.

But instead of pulling away, Billy took a step *toward* the Elder, slashing out with the Macuahuitl. The razor-sharp glass whistled as it cut through the air. Kukulkan immediately sucked his tongue back in and then coughed and gagged, choking on it. The Macuahuitl had missed it by inches.

"Do that again and I'll cut it off!" Billy yelled. "I know you'll grow a new one, but I bet it'll hurt."

The huge lynx padded silently toward the American, its jaws opening to reveal savage teeth.

"And you better tell your kitty cat to step outside," the American added, without looking away from the Elder. He tilted the Macuahuitl and sent sparkles of reflected light around the room, shining it into the cat's eyes.

The lynx stopped and fixed its narrow head on the Elder; then it turned and moved silently from the room.

"You have made an enemy of me," Kukulkan said.

"Well, I'm not feeling too friendly toward you right now either. You were talking about killing me," Billy reminded him. "That can upset a man."

"Am I the only adult here?" Machiavelli said suddenly. He had not moved from the chair and had watched the Elder with fascination: he was behaving like a spoiled child. "Enough of this nonsense; we are supposed to be on the same side."

"No humani threatens me . . . ," Kukulkan began.

"And no one—Elder, immortal, human or monster— threatens me," Billy said.

"OK, we've established that neither of you likes to be threatened," Machiavelli said mildly, "so let us now return to the business at hand. It seems to me," he continued quickly, looking at each of them in turn, forcing them to focus on him, "that we have all disappointed someone or other. How-ever, we have an opportunity to make amends." He looked at the Feathered Serpent evenly. "We are grateful—both of us—to still be alive. We know we've failed; now let us see how we can make amends."

"I didn't f—" Billy began, but a look from the Italian si-lenced him.

"We are aware that our failure reflects poorly on you," Machiavelli said, deliberately accepting blame in an attempt to calm Kukulkan. "But who else is aware that Billy and I have failed?" The Italian knew that if he could keep the Elder thinking and talking, then there was a chance he could re-solve this situation.

Kukulkan returned to his curved stone stool. "You mean other Elders?"

The Italian nodded.

"No one else; I am sure the news has not even percolated through to the Shadowrealms yet. Well, reasonably sure," he added, "though there may be spies in the city that I do not know about."

Billy the Kid returned to stand behind Machiavelli. "Do you people trust *anyone*?"

"No," Kukulkan said simply.

"So if Billy and I were to return to Alcatraz, awaken the army and set it loose on the city, then our mission would be considered a success. And no one would be the wiser."

Kukulkan thought about it for a moment and then nodded. "That is true."

Machiavelli spread his arms wide. "And no one would

need to know about our failure . . . and you would be spared any embarrassment."

"You were also tasked with killing Perenelle, and she has escaped," the Elder reminded him. "How do you intend to find her?"

"I will not need to." Machiavelli's smile turned icy. "I know the Flamels. I have spent centuries studying them—especially the woman." Almost unconsciously, he rubbed his left hand, which bore a faint pattern of white scars, the reminders of their last encounter. "I can almost guarantee you that they will return to the island to try to stop us. It is their nature, and all men and women are slaves to their nature."

Kukulkan's feathered tail beat a gentle tattoo on the floor as he considered the idea. "Are you confident that you can defeat the Alchemyst and the Sorceress if they come back to Alcatraz?"

Machiavelli bit the inside of his cheek to keep a straight face. He knew he'd won. "The Flamels are weak and aging fast. There is a sphinx on the island that will drain their powers, and I can use some of the creatures already there to help me." He leaned forward and lowered his voice, forcing the Elder to lean forward as well. It was a trick he had learned half a millennium previously. "Any help you could give us would, of course, be gratefully appreciated."

Kukulkan nodded. "Of course. Yes, I can help." His smile revealed his black forked tongue. Running his fingers through his white beard, he added, "there are some creatures I can call upon to assist you."

"And what about me?" Billy asked softly.

"Go with the Italian," Kukulkan snapped. "Maybe he can teach you some manners."

"So you're not going to try to kill me today . . . ," Billy teased.

"Billy!" Machiavelli glared at the American, who was in danger of irritating the Elder again.

"Not today," Kukulkan whispered, "but someday, yes. I have a long memory and I'll not forget what you did here." The Elder stood and padded to the door, then stopped and turned his head at an impossible angle to look back at the American. "You can put the Macuahuitl back where you found it. And be careful with it; it is older than the humani." With that he turned and strode out toward the field of tall grass. The lynx fell into step alongside.

Billy patted Machiavelli's shoulder. "Well, I think that went really well, don't you?"

The Italian stood and brushed off his ruined suit. "There is a lot I could teach you about negotiation."

"I never negotiate," Billy said firmly.

"A word of advice, my young friend: it is always a mistake to anger an Elder. All he said was that he was not going to kill you *today.*"

"Well, since we're in the advice business, let me trade you some," Billy said. He returned the Macuahuitl to its shelf, tilting it so the sunshine sparkled off the black glass and sent prismatic rainbows across the gloomy room. "An old gunslinger once told me that you never draw a gun unless you intend to use it, and you never—*ever*—tell someone you are going to draw your gun. You just do it." He smiled, revealing his prominent front teeth. "It's a big mistake to tell someone what you are going to do to them . . . they might decide to do it to you first." He turned to look at Kukulkan's retreating figure. "When all this is done and dusted, he and I will have a little conversation, a serious conversation . . ."

Machiavelli bowed. "I like how you think." He walked outside, blinking in the sunlight. "Now, how do we get back to the island?"

Billy held up his cell phone. "I'll call Black Hawk."

"I'm sure he'll be surprised to find us both still alive."

The American immortal shook his head. "Probably not. Black Hawk knows I'm impossible to kill. He's tried it often enough." He stopped as a sudden thought struck him. "What happens if your master dies? Do you lose your immortality?"

Machiavelli shook his head. "No, you remain immortal. There is no one to command you . . . and no one to revoke your immortality."

"That's interesting." Billy's cold blue eyes followed the Elder until he had disappeared into the grass. "Have you ever thought about killing your master?"

"Never," Machiavelli said.

"Why not?" Billy asked.

"In case there comes a day when I want my immortality removed, a day when I want to age and die."

CHAPTER THIRTY-NINE

"Didn't you set a couple of your plays in forests just like this?" Saint-Germain asked lightly.

"Only the comedies," William Shakespeare said in a hoarse whisper, "and my forests were populated by gentler creatures; this is an evil place."

Palamedes stopped suddenly and both Francis and William bumped into him. "Will you two be quiet?" he whispered. "You're making as much noise as a herd of elephants. And trust me, there are certain things in this forest that even I do not want to wake up."

"It makes no odds," Saint-Germain murmured. "I'm sure they know we're here. They knew from the moment we left the car."

"Oh, they know we're here. We're being followed," Shakespeare added.

The two immortals turned to look at him. Although the

forest was pitch black, their enhanced senses allowed them to see in surprising detail, though without color. Palamedes looked at Saint-Germain, who shook his head slightly; neither had been aware that they were being followed.

Shakespeare pushed his large glasses up his nose with his forefinger and smiled, quickly covering his teeth with his hand. "Right now, we are being observed by a forest spirit, female, short, dark-skinned, pretty, wearing an outfit which I presume is colored Lincoln green."

"Impressive," Palamedes said. "How do you know all this . . . ," he began, and then stopped. "She's standing behind us, isn't she?" he asked in Latin.

The Bard nodded.

"And she's not alone, is she?" Palamedes continued in the same language, still looking at Shakespeare.

"She's not," the Bard agreed.

Saint-Germain slowly turned to look over the knight's shoulder.

"I'll wager they're armed with bows," Palamedes continued.

"Bows and spears," Saint-Germain corrected.

The knight turned to face the welcoming committee. Their patterned clothing was the perfect camouflage, so it took a moment to pick out the dozen women scattered among the trees—he guessed that there were probably a dozen more he could not see. They were short and slender, with limbs a little too long, eyes wide and slanted, mouths thin horizontal lines across their faces. He recognized them as dryads, forest spirits.

One, a little taller than the rest, stepped forward. She was holding a short curved bow, a black-headed arrow already fitted to the string. "Identify yourselves." Her voice sounded like the whisper of leaves.

Palamedes bowed to the creature. "Merry meet," he said, using the traditional greeting. "I've not seen you before," he added.

"We're new."

The knight straightened. "And with a charming accent too. Naxos . . . no, Karpathos. So what are Greek dryads doing in an English forest?"

"He called us."

There was a flicker of movement behind the dryad, and she stepped aside as a tall, extraordinarily thin figure appeared. The face was that of a beautiful woman, but her body looked like it had been carved from the trunk of a tree. Arms that ended in twiglike fingers reached the ground, and knotted roots took the place of toes.

Palamedes turned, on the pretext of introducing the newcomer. "Don't look into her eyes," he whispered urgently. "Gentlemen, it is my honor to introduce you to Mistress Ptelea." He turned back to the creature and bowed deeply. "It is always a pleasure to meet you," he said, speaking in the language of his youth.

"Sir Knight." Ptelea came forward to stand before the immortal.

Palamedes kept his head bent, avoiding all eye contact. If he looked into her eyes, he would instantly fall under her spell. Ptelea was a hamadryad. The knight was unsure whether she was the spirit of an elm tree or an actual tree given life, and while she had always been courteous and polite to him, he knew how deadly hamadryads were. "I am here to see my master," Palamedes said, fixing his gaze on the point of her chin.

"The Green Man is expecting you," she said. She raised her head to look at Shakespeare and Saint-Germain and they both quickly bowed. "Does he know you are bringing company?"

The knight nodded. "I told him that I wish to petition a favor."

The hamadryad turned away and the knight fell into step behind her, taking care not to trip on the cloak of elm leaves that swept along the ground. "The dryads are new," he said lightly. "I've not seen them before."

"He has called together the forest and tree spirits from all across this Shadowrealm," the hamadryad said, leading them deeper into Sherwood Forest. "They have been gathering for months."

Palamedes nodded. "I wondered why I had not heard from him in such a long time. I had heard rumors that he was spending a lot of time in the Shadowrealms."

Ptelea bowed respectfully as they passed an ancient oak tree, and for an instant the hint of a beautiful female face appeared in the wood; then it sank back again, only the huge golden eyes remaining on the tree trunk, watching them.

Shakespeare and Saint-Germain looked at one another but said nothing. It took an enormous effort of will not to stare at the tree.

"A sister?" Palamedes asked.

"Balanos," she said.

Palamedes nodded. He knew Balanos was the hamadryad of the oak, but he'd never seen her in Sherwood Forest before.

"Are all the forest spirits here?" Shakespeare asked. "Dryads, hamadryads, wood nymphs . . . ? I would very much like to see them."

"They are all here," Ptelea whispered.

"Why?" Palamedes wondered. He understood that the forest spirits were solitary creatures, living in isolated forests and woods across the world.

When Ptelea spoke, the knight could hear a thread of excitement in her voice. "The Green Man has spent the last five centuries re-creating his favorite Shadowrealm, the Grove of Eridhu. It will be ready soon," she added, "and then he will lead us away from this foul and poisoned place and return us to a world of trees."

Looking at the Bard, the knight raised his eyebrows in a question.

"And what will happen to this world without the Green Man?" Shakespeare asked.

The hamadryad waved her long arms dismissively. "It is not our concern." Her head turned completely around, with the sound of cracking wood, and all three immortals quickly looked away from her face. "I have heard that this Shadowrealm will soon return to its Elder masters. We do not want to be here when that happens."

"Where did you hear that?" Palamedes demanded.

"I told them." The voice that spoke was male: slow and

deep, it vibrated up through the ground, shivering in the air, setting all the leaves trembling.

Ptelea pulled her leafy cloak around her and stepped aside. Pressing herself against an elm tree, she sank into it. For a moment her beautiful face lingered on the bark of the tree; then she closed her eyes and vanished.

The hamadryad had led the three immortals to a clearing in the very heart of the forest. The trees here were gnarled and twisted with age. Oak and chestnut, elm, ash, hawthorn and apple crowded together, all draped with ivy. Holly bushes with unseasonable ripe red berries clustered around the base of the trees, and white pearls of mistletoe speckled the boughs. From a mound in the center of the clearing rose a crude pillar of white stone, every inch of which was covered with a pattern of coiled spirals and intricate whorls.

"This world is coming to an end." For a moment it sounded as if the voice were coming from the stone. "And I do not want my creations here when that happens."

"You could stay and fight," Palamedes said, stepping into the circle of trees and approaching the stone. "You did that before."

"And we lost," the booming male voice said.

The figure that stepped out from behind the pillar was tall and slender, draped in a long white hooded robe patterned with metallic silver leaves. A fantastically ornate silver mask completely covered his face and head. It depicted the face of a young man peering out from a profusion of foliage that flared and extended behind the edges of the mask, making the figure's head seem enormous. Each leaf had been etched in incredible detail, right down to the veins and threads running through them.

Palamedes stepped forward and bowed deeply, going down on one knee before the figure. "Master Tammuz."

The hand that appeared from beneath the long sleeve to rest on the knight's right shoulder was covered in a silver glove embroidered with berries, leaves and twisting vines. "Your call was unexpected and unwelcome," the bass voice rumbled.

The Saracen Knight rose smoothly to his feet. He was a fraction of an inch shorter than his master, and he could see himself reflected countless times in the polished silver. Bright green eyes dappled with brown stared through the eyeholes in the mask. The pupils were flat narrow ovals. Not for the first time, Palamedes wondered what the Green Man really looked like.

"What do you want?" Tammuz asked, the leaves on the trees around him quivering with his words.

"A favor," Palamedes said simply. He had rehearsed this conversation countless times on the drive up from London, but he couldn't guess how his master would react. In the centuries he'd served his master, he'd come to recognize that Tammuz was that most dangerous of combinations: arrogant and unpredictable.

"It is not in my nature to do favors." Tammuz stepped away from the carved stone and looked across the clearing to where the other two immortals stood beside the tree that had swallowed the hamadryad. "And you have brought the Bard too." He leaned forward and added loudly. "I really do not like him."

William Shakespeare stepped toward the Elder and executed an exaggerated elegant bow. "We hate what we fear," he said sarcastically. He glanced at the knight. "Is that not so?"

"Then don't irritate the all-powerful Elder," the knight whispered.

"Do not anger me," Tammuz rumbled.

Shakespeare laughed. "You have no power over me, Green Man."

Tammuz turned to look at the third immortal and a profound silence fell over the grove. When he spoke again, the Elder's voice was soft, almost gentle, like the wind hissing through autumn leaves. "So we meet again, Saint-Germain."

The immortal stepped out of the shadows and bowed slightly. "Lord Tammuz," he said calmly.

"Ah, finally. I have waited centuries for this moment; I knew our paths would cross again. I have found that this world is very small indeed." The Elder's voice deepened, shivering the air with sound, sending leaves tumbling from their branches. "Francis, le Comte de Saint-Germain. The liar. The thief. The murderer!"

Scores of dryads suddenly appeared around the edge of the grove, bows and spears ready. Faces materialized in the tree trunks, and then, one by one, the hamadryads stepped out of the circle of trees. Tammuz raised a silver-gloved hand to point at the immortal. "Kill him!" he screamed. "Kill him now!"

CHAPTER FORTY

As night fell, the prehistoric landscape came alive with sound: howling and shrieking, screaming, calling and barking.

"I've suddenly realized why all of these animals died out," Scathach said. She was sitting cross-legged in the mouth of a cave with a pile of rocks beside her. "They probably died of exhaustion. None of them could get any sleep."

"I could get some sleep—if only you'd let me," Joan grumbled. The tiny Frenchwoman was in the cave behind the Shadow, lying on a bed of straw and covered with grass and branches they'd cut from trees and plaited together. Pulling the leafy blanket up to her chin, she closed her eyes. "I'm sleeping now," she announced, and almost immediately, her breathing settled into an easy rhythm.

Scathach reached over and fixed one of the branches on her friend's shoulders. In the pitch-darkness, she picked an enormous black beetle off a leaf and laid it on the ground outside the cave mouth. It slipped into the night, where it was immediately pounced upon by what looked like a small fox. Scathach shook her head: in this place and time, everything was either predator or prey.

Catching the hint of a musty odor, the Shadow picked up a rock and tossed it out into the night. Something yelped and scuttled off through the long grasses. "The Dire Wolves are back," she said quietly. Behind her, Joan started to snore very gently.

Scathach smiled. It gave her extraordinary pleasure to know that Joan had fallen asleep confident that she would be safe. Scatty guessed that this must be like the absolute trust a child had in a parent. Then her smile faded: she'd never had that trust in her own parents. The two figures had been almost strangers, aloof and distant, and although she had called them Mother and Father, these were empty titles; there had been no emotion behind the words. She'd been close to her grandmother and her uncle, but she'd always been closest to her sister.

Aoife of the Shadows: now, there was a name she'd avoided thinking about for years.

Something moved in the grass and she tossed another rock, sending the unseen creature crashing into the undergrowth.

Scathach rarely thought about her parents now. They were both alive—she would have been told if they were not—in a distant Shadowrealm that was supposedly patterned after the lost world of Danu Talis. She'd not been there in centuries. Not for the first time, it struck her that, unlikely as it

211

seemed, Nicholas and Perenelle Flamel had become the parents she'd never really had.

She frowned, trying to remember the first time she had encountered the Flamels. She was almost sure it was Paris in the middle of the fourteenth century, shortly after they had bought the Book of Abraham the Mage. She knew for certain that she had met up with them in Spain when they were trying to translate the Codex, and she had definitely been in Paris for Perenelle's funeral in 1402. Over the centuries she had crossed paths with them again and again. She had saved their lives—and they had saved hers on more than one occasion—and almost accidentally they had become her family. When she needed advice, she went to Perenelle, and when she needed money, she asked Nicholas.

Across the decades, there had been some others too who had become part of her new family—Joan was like a sister to her—but the problem with having humani friends was that they aged and died, and in the last few centuries she'd been careful not to cultivate them. The last time she'd had a circle of close friends was when she'd been in a Goth-punk band in Germany with three of her vampire clan. They'd had some wild times. Sleeping during the day, singing and partying all night, then hunting the savage water sprites Nix and Nixe in the twilight hours before dawn. Now that she taught martial arts in San Francisco, she had plenty of students, and on the last Friday of every month she met up with some of them for karaoke night in the local sushi bar, but that was just to keep up a normal appearance, and they were more acquaintances than actual friends.

And she wasn't lonely. Not really . . .

But these last few days had reminded her just how much she enjoyed the company of humani. She was thrilled to have been able to use her skills properly, rather than just in the dojo. She had millennia of martial arts training; she should be using it to protect her friends and keep them safe. It made her feel wanted and needed. The adventure in Paris had made her realize that it was time to take a more active role in the world again. She had promised herself that when all of this was over, she would do what she had always done for the humani: protect those who needed protection and punish those who deserved it.

Right now, however, she didn't think she was going to be able to keep that promise.

The Shadow had been in difficult situations before—trapped in Shadowrealms, facing fearsome odds, battling monsters, once even standing alone against an entire army—and yet she had never doubted that she would survive and make her way home. A Shadowrealm had both an entrance and an exit—all she had to do was to find that exit. Foes could be fought or tricked, defeated or won over.

But this was different.

There were enemies aplenty in this Pleistocene world—and none of them could be tricked or won over. Much of the flora was poisonous or inedible, and all of the fauna was hungry.

And there were just too many of them.

After their encounter with the saber-toothed tigers, Scathach and Joan had seen lions, huge bears and endless

213

herds of bison. Vast deafening flocks of condors flapped across the skies. As night had fallen, they had spotted the first of the wolves, tall, long-legged creatures keeping pace with them in the high grass.

"Wolves?" Joan asked

"Dire Wolves," Scathach corrected, "The ancestor of the modern wolf, and just as deadly. And for every one you see, there are at least a dozen that you don't."

"I can see four."

"Well, then there's a big pack out there watching us."

For the first time in her very long life, Scathach was beginning to consider that she might be in trouble. Real trouble. This was a situation in which not even her speed and special skills were useful. She tossed another rock into the darkness, heard it strike flesh and threw another in the direction she guessed the creature would run. A wolf barked in fright. "She shoots, she scores!" she whispered.

They had been in this landscape for only a few hours and already they were attracting the attention of the big predators. Scathach had no doubt she could fight them off, and Joan was almost her equal in battle, but sooner or later one of them would be injured. And while they were both immortal, they were not invulnerable—if the injury was devastating enough, they would die. The slash of a tiger's claw, a bite, even a scratch would quickly become infected. Her metabolism would help her heal . . . *if* she fed. The problem was, in this landscape, there was no one to feed off—except Joan . . . and she would never do that.

Scathach's vampire clan were not blood drinkers; they

had other needs. And while she rarely—very rarely—needed to feed, sooner or later the hunger would come upon her. Joan too would need food; she was vegetarian, but who knew what was safe to eat in this time and place?

The Shadow took a deep breath, drawing in the clean night air, and leaned back on outstretched arms to survey the landscape. Close by, a lion roared and something smaller squealed in alarm.

She had lived longer than she'd ever imagined, seeing civilizations rise and fall and rise again. She had lived through the best and worst of humani history. In the course of her long life, she had made mistakes, and while it was not in her nature to apologize for what she had done, there were things she would have done differently. Her biggest regret was that she had trained Cuchulain; she had taken a boy and turned him into a warrior, and that had ultimately killed him. Maybe she should have found an Elder master to make him immortal beforehand. Funny, she hadn't thought of Cuchulain in centuries; he was so inextricably entwined with memories of her sister, and those were painful memories.

If she'd had her life to live again, she would never—*ever*—have fought with her twin. When her parents and brother ignored her, Aoife had always been there for her; Aoife had always loved her unconditionally.

Drawing her knees up to her chest, Scathach wrapped her arms around her shins and rested her chin on her kneecaps. It had been a long time since she had thought about her sister. She wondered if Aoife was still on the earth. She thought so. Occasionally, she would hear rumors about a red-haired pale-skinned warrior, or she'd come across stories that confused her with Aoife, mingling and mixing their legends until sometimes even she could not tell them apart.

Gazing across the landscape, Scatty realized that there was a very good chance she could die here. Whenever she thought about dying, she imagined it would be in a dramatic battle, something huge and glorious that would ensure that her name would be remembered for generations. She didn't like the idea of dying in this lonely place, hunted down by prehistoric megafauna. A sudden thought made her sit up straight. She'd once been told that she would die in an exotic location. Well, it didn't get much more exotic than the Pleistocene era, did it?

Scathach tilted her face to the heavens. The sky was cloudless, the stars so bright and clear that they actually shed a little light on the ground. She started to look for the constellations. They had shifted in the heavens during the centuries she had lived on earth, but if she could find the polestar she should be able to find . . .

The huge gray wolf leapt out of the darkness, savage jaws gaping, saliva matting its fur.

Scatty dropped to her back and her legs shot out, catching the beast in the chest, lifting it high in the air and sending it sailing off into the night. There was a single yelp of surprise before it crashed into the grasses and then a snarl as it scrambled to its feet and trotted away.

The Shadow remained on her back, staring at the night sky.

There was something wrong with the stars.

Rising slowly to her feet, she stepped outside the cave

mouth to look across the arc of the heavens. An enormous swath of light that *almost* resembled the Milky Way washed across the sky, but there was something wrong with its over- all shape. It should have been an arch—but this looked too straight. And no matter in which direction she looked, she could not find the polestar.

"Where . . . ," she breathed.

And then the moon rose huge and yellow in the east and climbed steadily into the heavens, shedding milk-white light across the landscape. The sky was so clear that individual craters were visible on the surface.

A heartbeat later, the second moon rose.

Then a third.

And a fourth.

CHAPTER FORTY-ONE

"*H*e's big," Josh whispered in awe, glancing at Sophie. "I mean, really big."

She nodded, eyes fixed on the figure.

Prometheus was huge. The Elder stood close to seven feet tall and looked like he weighed at least three hundred pounds—all of it muscle. There was not an ounce of fat on his body. His jeans were ragged, worn through at both knees and frayed at the hems; the logo on his T-shirt was so faded it was almost invisible, and his work boots were thickly encrusted with dried mud. Although his hair was a mass of tight red curls, his beard was streaked with gray and silver.

"Uncle!" With a cry of delight, Aoife pushed open the car door and flung herself at the big man.

"Aoife!" He caught her as if she weighed nothing and threw her into the air, both of them laughing.

Josh suddenly felt himself smiling at the image of this

ferocious-looking man grinning as he tossed Aoife—who seemed like a child in his arms—into the air. He had a sudden vivid memory of his own father throwing him high just like that when he was younger. He'd loved that feeling of flying.

"My good girl." Prometheus flung Aoife into the air again, even higher, and she squealed once more.

"Don't let me fall," she gasped, beginning to hiccup.

"Have I ever let you fall?" the Elder demanded, and Josh suddenly realized that he spoke English with a surprisingly strong Southern drawl.

"Never," she said breathlessly.

"It's been so long. Too long." The big man caught Aoife, set her on the ground and stepped back, holding her at arm's length as he took her in. "You've grown. . . ."

"Not an inch since you last saw me," she said quickly.

"And when was that?" he wondered aloud.

"Oh, not too long ago. Just over a hundred and twenty years, I think." Aoife pushed her dark glasses onto her head and looked up into her uncle's broad face.

Josh immediately realized that their eyes were an identical shade of green.

"The last time I saw you," Aoife continued, "was when you and Niten came to my rescue when I got into trouble with the Nagas on Krakatoa."

Prometheus nodded and laughed. "Yes, yes, I remember!"

"Krakatoa," Josh breathed excitedly. "That's where Mom and Dad were five years ago. That's the island with the volcano . . ." He turned and looked into the back of the car, but no one was listening to him: Sophie, Nicholas and Perenelle were all staring at the Elder.

The twins' parents had spent an entire summer on the island when the twins were ten, and Josh had used the island and the photographs his mom and dad had taken as the basis for a school project two years ago. He knew that one of the biggest volcanic explosions ever recorded on earth had taken place on Krakatoa in the late nineteenth century . . . which was, he realized with a start, about one hundred and twenty years ago.

"And how is your boyfriend, the Swordsman?" Prometheus boomed.

"He's not my boyfriend," Aoife said quickly, bright spots of color appearing on her pale cheeks. "And he's fine."

"Have you seen him recently?"

"Very recently." Aoife turned as the driver's door opened and Niten stepped out. With his hands flat against his thighs, the Japanese immortal bowed to the huge red-haired Elder.

Prometheus matched his bow. "It is good to see you, old friend," he said warmly.

"And you, Firelord."

Josh looked around, suddenly realizing that the moment Prometheus had appeared by the side of the car, the mud figures had slipped away, disappearing back into the trees and tall grasses on either side of the narrow country road. He could see them between the leaves, blank faces toward the red-haired Elder like flowers turned toward the sun.

Prometheus ducked his head to look into the back of the

car. "So let's see what other surprises are in here," he said. "Is it a nice surprise . . ."

Perenelle helped Nicholas out of the car.

". . . or a not-so-nice surprise?" he finished. Then, straightening to his full height, he took the Sorceress's hand in his and bowed low over it. "I wish I could say that it is always a pleasure to see you, Mistress Flamel, but you and bad news travel hand in hand."

"I suppose that must make me the bad news." Nicholas stretched out his hand, but Prometheus ignored it, gently embracing the Alchemyst, actually lifting his feet off the ground.

"You are always bad news," the Elder said lightly, smiling to take the sting from his words. His green eyes were troubled as he looked over the immortal. "And today is no different, I see. You have aged, Alchemyst." He turned to look at the woman. "You are still as beautiful as ever."

"You always were a charming rogue, Prometheus, and no, you should never tell a woman she is looking old." Perenelle smiled.

"We are in trouble," Nicholas admitted. "I will explain all later. But first, there are two people I would like you to meet." Nicholas turned, and Josh suddenly realized that the Alchemyst was looking at him. Taking a deep breath, he pushed open the passenger door . . . and instantly felt a pressure in the air as if some unseen force was pushing him back.

He caught the impression of a faint red halo around the Elder, but the moment he stepped out of the car, he saw the glow intensify until it looked as if the Elder was wrapped in red mist rippling just above his skin. Behind Prometheus, Josh could see Aoife's gray aura rising like steam off her body. He took a step forward and his own aura bloomed around him. His head itched and he ran his fingers through his hair: crackling orange-scented sparks snapping under his flesh.

"Another Gold," Prometheus said sadly. Then his eyes hardened as he looked at the Flamels. "I thought we agreed after the last time—"

"Not just another Gold," Nicholas interrupted, "*the* Gold." He pointed at Josh. "Look at him closely, Prometheus. Look at this aura. He is the gold twin of legend. He is Awakened, and has learned Water magic from Gilgamesh. Now he needs to know Fire."

"And you expect me to train him?"

"Please. We don't have much time."

"Absolutely not," Prometheus snapped. "I told you after the last one that I would never train a humani again."

Shocked and puzzled, Josh was turning to Nicholas when he felt a cold chill run across his back. He turned around just as Sophie climbed out of the car.

The tingling had begun the moment she had seen Prometheus's huge head peering into the car. It was like a thousand pins and needles racing through her body, beginning in her fingers and toes, rushing up into her skull. And with the tingling came the surge of memories.

. . . *a red-haired boy on a cliff, a tentacled monster rising out of the raging sea* . . .

. . . the boy, now a young man in exotic silver armor, wielding a flaming red sword against a host of armored warriors . . .

. . . the same young man raining balls of fire down on a distant fleet of sparkling metal ships . . .

. . . the man, older now, walking away from the Nameless City, followed by thousands—tens of thousands—of newly created humani . . .

. . . the man, older still, terribly wounded and chained to a rock on a poisonous Shadowrealm, being attacked by savage birdlike creatures . . .

The moment her foot touched the ground, Sophie's aura blossomed around her, instantly hardening and solidifying into a suit of exotic-looking silver armor that encased her body. A smooth oval helmet completely covered her head, the eye openings protected with green glass, and although the gloves on her fingers were metal, they were as flexible as leather.

"Do you recognize this armor?" Sophie's voice echoed slightly inside the helmet, giving it an otherworldly quality. The armor was a perfect copy of the suit Prometheus had worn as a young man.

Prometheus took a step back, his skin now the color of chalk. Aoife reached for her uncle's hand.

"Do you remember when you made a suit like this for me out of your own aura? To keep me safe, you said." The smell of vanilla was strong in the air, and then it was touched by another odor: the crisp scent of burning leaves. A slender thread of brown now dappled the silver metal, making it resemble leopard skin.

Shaking his head, Prometheus backed away. Sparks had gathered in his red hair and beard. Shimmering crimson armor started to form over his chest and shoulders. "Who are you?" he asked in the lost language of Danu Talis.

"I am Sophie Newman," she replied in the same language before slipping back into English. "And I have a message from your sister."

Prometheus's aura blazed bloodred, and a suit of armor like the one Sophie wore shaped around his body. The two metal suits—one red, one silver—sparkled, leaking threads of colored aura into the air. "My sister is dead to me," Prometheus boomed, his voice amplified inside his helm. "She betrayed me . . . she betrayed all of us."

Sophie's armor paled, becoming transparent and crystalline, revealing the girl beneath. Her eyes were solid silver, like mirrors in her face. "She did what was necessary," she said. Suddenly her aura completely vanished, streaming up and away from her flesh in silver globules, and when she spoke, it was in the cracked and aged voice of the Witch of Endor. "Little Brother, I did what I had to do, and I did it for you. You spent your life protecting me and you paid a terrible price. And yes, I went with Chronos and I sacrificed my eyes to him, but I did it so that I could see the shifting threads of time, and so that I could always watch over you and keep you safe."

"Zephaniah . . . ," Prometheus whispered. His auric armor flowed down his body and puddled around his feet before sinking into the ground. Bright green grass speckled with tiny alpine flowers appeared all around him.

Sophie turned to the Elder. "The world will end," she continued in the Witch's voice. "This I have seen in every thread of time . . . all but one. In one there is a chance, a very slender chance, of survival. Do you remember when you and I fought for the newly created humani, Little Brother?"

Speechless with shock, Prometheus could only nod.

"Now it is time for another brother and sister to do the same. And they need your help, Little Brother."

Prometheus started to shake his head. His green eyes were huge with fiery tears. "Please, do not ask me . . ."

There was anger in the Witch's voice. "Your aura sparked the humani to life. You are their father, and like every father, you have a responsibility to your family. If you refuse, then you doom the humani to destruction." Sophie started to sway on her feet and Josh raced in to grab her. Threads of his gold aura wrapped around her, hissing, crackling and spitting when they touched her flesh. She shuddered, and when she opened her eyes, they were bright blue again. Her lids fluttered, and she blinked hard as she looked from Prometheus to Josh. "Do not disappoint me. I have always been so proud of my Little Brother," she breathed before she lapsed into unconsciousness.

CHAPTER FORTY-TWO

"I hate leygates!" Virginia Dare screamed as they plunged into the icy water.

"*Now* you tell me!" Dee shouted.

They fell, down, down, down . . . and then suddenly there was *no* water around them, only complete and utter darkness.

"And I particularly hate the falling ones. . . ." Virginia's voice sounded dull and muted, as if she was talking in a tiny space. "I'm not keen on the jumping ones either."

Dr. John Dee tried to orient himself, but in the blackness, he was unsure which way was up and which was down.

"What about a light?" Virginia said. "I think a light would be good right now."

"Has anyone ever told you," Dee began, "that you talk too much?"

"No." Virginia sounded genuinely surprised. "Do I? I guess I do." Her voice changed, turning savage. "But only when I'm plunging through a leygate in the pitch-dark! Then I suppose I might have a few things to say."

Their ears popped and a series of appalling scents wafted over them, as if they had just fallen through stinking clouds.

Suddenly all sense of movement stopped. They were still in a black void.

"Do you have a match?" Virginia asked.

"A match?" Dee asked, confused.

"I thought you magicians always carried matches with you. To light your candles. Aren't magicians always lighting candles?"

"I've used electric light for the past century," Dee muttered. "I don't carry matches."

"It's very dark," Virginia said, stating the obvious. "Scary."

"Don't tell me you're afraid of the dark."

"Not the dark, Doctor, but what lives in it."

With a sigh, Dee reached under his coat and pulled out the stone sword. The moment his flesh touched the blade, it started to glow, gray first, then blue, and then blooming bright and white before it suddenly flamed red, filling their surroundings with a cold, stark light. Streamers of fire blazed off the sword, but it was a chilly fire that left speckles of ice spinning in the air.

"Hmm . . . not much to see," Dee said, looking around.

Virginia Dare stood beside him, face ghastly in the light of the cold red flames. Then she slowly turned. "I think I preferred it when we could not see."

A flat barren landscape stretched gray and unbroken in

every direction. Beneath their feet, the only marks in the powdery dust were their footprints.

"Where are we?" Virginia asked.

Holding the sword high, Dee turned in a complete circle. "I've heard about these . . . though I've never seen one first-hand. It looks like an unmade Shadowrealm."

"Unmade?"

"Started, but never finished." He lowered the sword and the shadows clustered closer. "Elders create Shadowrealms using their auras, imaginations and memories. Sometimes a powerful individual can create an entire realm, but often groups will come together to shape their own world." He gestured with the sword. "This one was never finished."

"Why?" Dare wondered out loud.

"I have no idea . . . ," the Magician began, then caught Virginia by the arm, dragging her away. "Run!" he yelled.

She turned and looked up . . . and saw four cucubuths dropping out of the black sky.

"They must have fallen through before the leygate closed," Dee said.

The four creatures settled lightly onto the ground, turned, obviously disoriented, then focused on the glowing light from the sword. With triumphant howls, the creatures raced toward Dee and Virginia.

Once they started to run, they changed. The transition from human to beast was instantaneous. One moment they looked like shaven-headed young men; the next they were enormous wolflike creatures with human faces. They ran upright on two feet, but hunched over, their claws sending up whorls of dust.

"Doctor?" Virginia said calmly.

"Send them to sleep," Dee called out. "Can you play and run at the same time?"

Dare pulled her flute from its leather cover, put it to her lips and blew gently.

And yet no sound came out.

"Oh," she gasped, "that's not good."

The four cucubuths were closer now, their handsome faces marred by the ragged teeth that filled their mouths. Hairless tails thrashed the ground.

There was a flicker of movement in the air behind the cucubuths, and Huginn and Muninn appeared. The huge ravens tumbled from the sky, crashing to the ground in a cloud of dust. They flapped their wings, but only rose a few feet off the ground before they settled down again. Then, spotting the blazing sword, they screamed Dee's name in unison. The giant birds darted toward the only light in the landscape, moving in a running hop that quickly ate up distance.

"Doctor, if you have a genius plan, now is the time to use it," Virginia panted, shoving her flute back into its cover and pulling a flat-headed tomahawk from under her coat. When Dee didn't immediately reply, Dare risked a quick sidelong glance at him. "John?"

Dee stopped.

"John?" she said again. She had actually run past him, but returned now to stand by his side. The Magician's face was completely expressionless. His cold gray eyes turned red and blue in the reflected light from the burning sword. And then Virginia realized that the grit of this unmade Shadowrealm was coiling and twisting around his feet, creating patterns—intricate spirals and snaking ripples. She moved her hand past his eyes, but they did not blink, and she knew then that he wasn't seeing her, nor could he hear her. "You always were trouble, Dr. John Dee. No wonder everyone around you died." Then she turned to face the cucubuths and the crows alone.

Fire that was cold.

Ice that was hot.

The sensations rolled off the sword and flowed through his wrists up his arms and settled into his chest.

And with the warmth and the chill came the memories, terrible, terrifying memories of a time before the humani, of a time when the Elders ruled the earth, and then beyond, to the world of the Archons; and before them, to the Ancients; and back further, to the Time Before Time, when the Earthlords ruled.

Memories of the four great swords of power . . .

. . . of their creation . . .

. . . and their powers . . .

. . . and why they had been separated . . .

. . . and why they must never be brought together . . .

And the shocking realization that these were not weapons, these were more; much, much more.

❖　❖　❖

"John!"

The Magician slowly turned his head to look at Dare, and whatever she saw in his face left her speechless. Something ancient and alien peered out through his eyes. She watched, frozen, as his hand rose, bringing the weapon up before his face.

Fire.

The stone sword blazed with white-hot fire.

Ice.

Ice crackled and formed on the blade and hilt.

Suddenly the sword shifted and separated, leaving him holding Clarent burning red-black in his left hand and Excalibur cracking with blue fire in his right.

"Where do you want to be, Virginia?" Dee's voice was a hoarse whisper.

"Anywhere but here."

The cucubuths were almost on top of them now, circling warily around the two swords. The ravens were laughing in Odin's voice.

"Do you know where I want to be?" Dee asked. His arms described two enormous perfect circles—blazing red, crackling blue—in the air. The circles overlapped in the middle to create a long oval that shimmered like melting ice.

"John, you're scaring me."

"I want to go home," Dee said. He stepped *into* the oval and vanished. Immediately, the fire started to die, the ice began to melt. The cucubuths howled and darted forward; the ravens screamed.

Closing her eyes, Virginia Dare threw herself into the burning melting oval . . .

231

✧ ✧ ✧

. . . and opened them to the sun on her face. She breathed in warm salt-scented air and discovered that she was lying on grass, listening to the sound of traffic. Car horns blared, and it suddenly occurred to her that it was the most musical sound in the world. She sat up and looked around. Dee was sitting beside her. Excalibur and Clarent lay on the grass alongside him, a puddle of ice around one, scorched earth around its twin. "John, your hands . . . ," Virginia said in horror.

Dee lifted his hands. They were both burned black, the flesh raw and ugly, blisters already beginning to form. "A small price to pay." He grimaced.

Virginia stood up and looked around. She could hear voices close by. There were trees all around her, and she could see the tops of nearby buildings. One, a tower, seemed familiar—very, very familiar. "John, what did you do? Where are we? Tell me this isn't another Shadowrealm."

"I suddenly realized what the swords could do," Dee said quietly. "No, *realized* is the wrong word. I was *told* what the swords were capable of." When he turned to look at Virginia, she noticed the tiny speckles of blue and red, like chips of ice and cinders, in his gray eyes. "The Elders created the Shadowrealms with the swords . . . but the Archons used them to fashion the leygates."

"You created a leygate!" Virginia looked down at him, shocked. "Even for you, John, that is very impressive. And what about the cucubuths and the crows?"

"Trapped forever . . . unless Odin goes after his pets."

"How did you get us here?" Virginia asked.

Dee's smile grew pained. "I just *saw* where I wanted us to be—" He stopped suddenly and looked at his hands again. "You know, these are really starting to hurt. . . ."

"Put some aloe vera on them," Dare said automatically. "And where, exactly, are we?"

"Pioneer Park, San Francisco." He turned his head to where Coit Tower rose above the treetops. "Five minutes from my home."

CHAPTER FORTY-THREE

"So there are four moons, and this is *good* news?" Joan of Arc stood at the cave mouth and looked at the four moons—one huge and yellow, another smaller and tinged sepia; the third was a bright green emerald, while the fourth was colorless. The slender Frenchwoman ran her fingers over her short boyish hair, flattening it. "There is so much that I do not know, and astronomy is not one of my strongest subjects, but even I know that the earth does not have four moons, has *never* had four moons."

The moonlight turned Scatty's red hair black and made her skin even paler than usual. Her eyes were silver mirrors. "Don't you see what this means?" she said excitedly.

Joan shook her head.

"It means we're in a Shadowrealm."

Joan continued to look at her blankly, four pinpricks of

moonlight reflected in her gray eyes. "So we're not in the past."

"No," Scatty said, taking her friend's hands in hers and squeezing tightly. "We're not."

"And that's good?"

"If we were in the past, then we'd be stuck, with no way out. Or at least, I couldn't think of any way out, other than someone coming through time to find us, and the chances of pinpointing us in time would have been astronomically small. The only way for us to get back to our own time would be by living maybe a million years."

"Is that even possible?"

"Theoretically, yes. Elders and Next Generation can live incredibly long lives, but I'm not sure about the humani. Look at what happened to poor Gilgamesh after ten thousand years. I think the body can live on, but the mind breaks down under the weight of all the memories and experiences."

"So if this is a Shadowrealm . . . ," Joan began.

". . . then there must be a leygate," Scatty finished delightedly.

"And how do we find it?" Joan asked.

Scathach's smile faded. "I haven't quite worked out that bit yet. But there's got to be one around here somewhere."

The Dire Wolves attacked at dawn.

Scathach and Joan beat them off easily, sending them howling into the thick mist lying heavily across the landscape.

A single lion prowled around the foot of the cave shortly

afterward, but Scatty pelted it with rocks until it scrambled out of range.

The giant short-faced bear appeared next.

The two women watched it approach, loping on all fours, its head thrown back to sniff the air. The creature was huge.

"It has to weigh at least twenty-five hundred pounds," Scatty said, loosening her short swords and checking her nunchaku, "and I'll wager it probably stands close to eleven feet tall when it's up on two legs."

"I don't want to have to kill it," Joan said.

"Trust me, it's not going to share your reservations about killing." She pointed with her folded nunchaku. "It's looking at us now and thinking: breakfast."

Joan shook her head firmly and pushed her sword into its sheath, then slung it across her shoulders.

Scatty sighed. "If we don't kill it, it will kill us."

Joan shook her head firmly. "I'll not kill it."

"Can I remind you that you once led an army?"

"That was a long time ago. I will defend myself, but I will not kill an innocent creature."

"Is that why you became a vegetarian?"

Joan shook her head. "No," she laughed. "Shortly after Nicholas gave me your blood, I discovered that I really hated the taste of meat."

The bear paused at the bottom of the incline and looked up at them. Then it reared up on its hind legs, threw its head back and growled.

Scatty revised her original assessment of the beast's

height. "Twelve feet tall." She examined the creature critically. "I could take him."

"Look at those claws," Joan said. "One swipe will take your head off. And I know you can do many things, but growing a new head is not one of them."

They ran for most of the morning, moving easily across lush waving grassland. Now that they knew this was a Shadowrealm, the tiny inconsistencies in the world became obvious. The breeze only blew from the south and always smelled of lemons, there were no insects in the air and although the sun rose in the east and climbed into the heavens, it seemed to remain at its highest point for far too long.

"It's as if someone created—or re-created—the Pleistocene era from memory," Scatty said.

"Well, they got the animals right," Joan said, in French. Although she kept herself fit and in condition, she thought they'd run the equivalent of a marathon so far, and there was no end in sight. She had a stitch in her side and her calves were beginning to cramp. She was also conscious of the blisters starting to form inside her boots. "I'm going to need to rest soon," she said. "I need some water."

Scatty pointed to the right. "There's a stream down there."

Joan could see nothing. "How can you tell?"

"Look down," the Shadow said, pointing. The earth at their feet was impressed with scores of hoof and claw tracks, all leading off to the right.

"If there's a watering hole down there, then we're sure to find something drinking there . . . ," Joan began.

"How thirsty are you?"

"Very."

Scathach slipped both nunchaku out of their sheaths and turned to the right, following the animal trail. "Let's get you that drink. And I promise not to kill anything that doesn't try to kill me first."

The trail dipped down into a hollow, and the grass, which had been waist high, now grew to their shoulders. It hissed and rasped together noisily. The air was filled with the rich cloying odor of life and growth. Without the cool lemon-scented wind on their faces, the temperature immediately rose.

Scathach held up her hand and Joan stopped and immediately turned to look behind them. The Shadow stood with the back of her head against her friend's. "Be careful," she said, using the French language of Joan's youth. "Something's wrong here."

Joan nodded. "We cannot see through the grass, our sense of smell has been overwhelmed, even our hearing is impaired. Coincidence?" she wondered.

"I don't believe in coincidences," Scatty answered. Pushing her nunchaku back into their holders, she pulled out her matched short swords. "Something is wrong here," she repeated, "very, very wrong."

They moved forward carefully, conscious that with limited vision, hearing and even smell, they were at a disadvantage. Anything could be hiding in the tall grasses.

"Snakes," Joan said suddenly.

Scatty jumped and spun around. "Where?"

"Nowhere. I've just realized we haven't seen any since we arrived. Yet this place should be filled with them. Especially here, in this grassland; it's the ideal environment."

They took another half-dozen steps and the grass suddenly ended. Directly ahead of them lay a sparkling blue pool, the perfectly still water reflecting streaks of unmoving white clouds in the sky above.

And sitting on the boulder by the side of the river was a man wrapped in a long hooded leather cloak. He turned his head to look at them, and they saw that the bottom half of his face was concealed by a scarf, leaving visible only a pair of bright blue eyes.

"Scathach the Shadow and Joan of Arc. Where have you been? I have been waiting for you for such a long time. Welcome to my world." The hooded man stood, and as he spread his arms wide, they saw the curved metal hook that took the place of his left hand.

CHAPTER FORTY-FOUR

Sophie opened her eyes and Josh's face swam into view. She watched the relief wash over his features. His blue eyes were suddenly magnified by tears.

"Hi, sis," he whispered, but there was a tremble in his voice, and he coughed and tried again. "Hi, sis. How do you feel?"

Sophie drew in a slow deep breath as she thought about his question. She felt . . . actually, she felt fine. More than fine; she felt *great*—alert, strong and clearheaded. Sitting up, she looked around. She'd been lying on a narrow couch in a tiny cramped room that looked like it had been decorated sometime in the 1960s. The walls were covered in a hideous brown wallpaper inscribed with black and red circles that matched the curtains and the brown linoleum on the floor. A bright red plastic cloth covered a small kitchen table, and only two of the four chairs matched. The room was gloomy and smelled stale and unused, and the only light came from a cob-webbed lamp on a table in the corner. "I'm good," she said, standing up and turning to look out the windows. She was surprised to discover that night had fallen and automatically looked at her wrist, but her watch was missing. "How long have I been asleep?"

"Over four hours . . ."

"Four hours! What time it is?" she wondered. The last thing she remembered was looking at Prometheus. . . .

Josh handed Sophie her watch, which he'd been holding in his hand. "I was using yours. The battery in mine is dead," he explained. "It's just after eight now." He looked closely at his sister. "Are you *sure* you're OK? When I heard the Witch's voice coming out of your mouth, I thought she'd finally taken you over completely."

"Don't worry, Josh. That's not going to happen," Sophie said gently. She laughed at his astonished expression. "Nicholas was wrong. Perenelle told me that the Witch's memories can *never* take over mine."

"And you believe her?" Josh said cautiously. He was watching his sister closely. If he half closed his eyes, he thought he could see the faintest hint of her silver aura—and was it his imagination, or was it tinged with just the faintest hint of brown . . . the color of the Witch of Endor's?

"Yes. I believe her," Sophie said.

Josh shook his head. "Soph, be careful. I don't think we should trust either of them. And the more I learn about Mrs. Flamel, the less I trust her."

Sophie felt a vague twinge of annoyance at her brother's

caution. Yes, Nicholas was not to be trusted; they'd discovered that he'd kept information from them. But with the Witch of Endor's memories and knowledge swirling inside her, surely she'd know if Perenelle was lying to her. "Perry was apprenticed to Dora for something like ten years. She said that if the Witch had wanted to take over my thoughts, she could have just done it when she Awakened me." Sophie smiled at her brother again. "So we were worried about nothing: Nicholas was wrong. I'm fine. Really. I'm fine."

Josh blinked, confused. That didn't sound right; when Nicholas had been talking to them in London about the power of the Witch's memories, he'd sounded so sure that he'd even sounded a little frightened himself. "So . . . tell me, what *exactly* did Perenelle say?" he asked.

"She told me . . ." Sophie frowned, trying to remember the exact words. "She said that Nicholas had told us what he believed to be true, and then she added that he was often wrong. She said he makes mistakes. Her exact words were 'Nicholas is often wrong.' "

"Often wrong?" Josh repeated. "Wow . . . that's something—especially coming from his wife." He sat back in the couch his sister had vacated and tried to absorb this new piece of information. "Can we believe her?"

Sophie shrugged. "I do," she said simply, then looked quickly at her brother, reading the expression in his eyes. "But you don't."

"Why should I?" he asked. "I know you like Perenelle, but don't let that influence you. I liked Nicholas—really, I did—but once I discovered that he'd been lying to us and that he'd put us in danger, I knew I could never trust him again."

"That was Nicholas . . . not Perenelle. She was a prisoner on Alcatraz."

Josh shook his head in frustration. "Sis, remember, it's the Flamels—both of them—who've been collecting twins for centuries. And we both saw that Perenelle seems to be in charge. I think she's as guilty as he is. I just don't trust her."

"Were you always this suspicious?" Sophie asked.

"This last week has made me think twice about everything and everyone," Josh said. "What was it Scatty said to us on the very first day: follow your hearts, trust no one . . ."

". . . except each other," Sophie finished. "I remember."

"And I'm right to be suspicious. I was right about Nicholas from the very beginning."

"Yes, you were. But we know so much more now. And I know all that the Witch knows, so that has to give us an advantage. And I know that the Witch trusted Perenelle, so I do too. But Josh, listen to me—if we're going to survive, we have to learn to trust people."

"But which people?" he asked, watching her closely, trying to keep his temper in check. Why couldn't she see that the Flamels were dangerous? "Who do we trust? Nicholas and Perenelle? They've both lied to us. Scathach? Even her own sister told us that she's a liar. Saint-Germain? We know he's a thief. And Soph, these are supposed to be the *good* guys. Then there's Dee, who everyone says is insane, and Machiavelli, who is . . . well, I don't know what he is, but I sort of liked him. He was the only one who was straight with me."

"And don't forget Gilgamesh," Sophie added with a small sad smile.

"Well, I liked him, too, but he was crazy," he reminded her.

"I'm not so sure about that." Sophie wandered around the room, running her fingertips over the plastic chairs, the Formica tabletop and the squat rectangular box that was the radio. She turned the dial and the radio hissed static that was touched with just the hint of voices. She clicked it off, leaned back against a bulky cream-colored Prestcold fridge and looked at her brother. "Now that I know the Witch's memories are safe and can't hurt me, I've been trying to remember everything she knew about Gilgamesh . . . but there are big blanks."

"Blanks? What sort of blanks?"

"You know when you're trying to remember the words of a song? You sort of know what it sounds like, you can hum the tune, but the whole thing just won't come out. It's like that."

Josh nodded. "Happens to me all the time during finals. I know that I know the answer, I just can't get at it."

Sophie took a deep breath. "I'm concentrating on Gilgamesh now, for example. I can almost remember what he looks like, I can even picture him as a young man—I can see black curly hair and eyes the color of the ocean—but I can't remember anything else." She shook her head, frustrated. "It'll come, I'm sure."

"Can you remember anything about the Flamels?" Josh asked.

"Only bits and pieces. The Witch didn't know a lot about them. She'd heard of them, of course. All the Elders and Dark Elders knew about the Flamels, but the Witch hasn't had much contact with them . . . or with anyone, for that matter. For generations, she's lived a very reclusive life. She's wandered alone through the Middle East and the Russian steppes, and she lived in Transylvania, Greece, Switzerland and France before she came over to America sometime toward the end of the nineteenth century."

"And Perenelle was apprenticed to the Witch?" Josh asked. "Where?"

"In France. But apparently Perenelle didn't tell the Witch that she was married to Nicholas. She went by her maiden name. It was only later, much, much later, that the Witch discovered the truth."

"That seems odd. Why did she do that?" Josh asked.

Sophie shook her head. "The Witch didn't know."

Josh stood up and ran his hands through his hair, pulling it back off his forehead; then he rubbed his palms against his jeans. His hair felt greasy and he realized how badly he needed a shower. "Look, it's clear that Nicholas isn't in charge anymore—"

"Josh," Sophie interrupted with a laugh. "I don't think he's ever been in charge! Perenelle admitted that she was the one who convinced Nicholas to hire you. Apparently your interview wasn't great," she added. Before her brother could respond, she continued, "And she was the one who suggested to Bernice that she hire me at the Coffee Cup."

"So who is Perenelle Flamel?" Josh asked. He walked to

his sister and looked into her eyes. "What does the Witch remember about the Sorceress?" Even as he was asking the question, he had a feeling he knew the answer.

Sophie grimaced in frustration. "I've been trying to remember . . . but that's one of the blanks."

Josh nodded. He wasn't surprised. "But the Witch *must* remember Perenelle."

Sophie nodded. "She must. She spent ten years with her."

"And you can't remember anything from that time?" Josh asked incredulously.

"Nothing." She frowned. "The memories are there—I can almost grasp them, but they just slip away when I try to focus on them."

"I wonder why," Josh murmured, pacing the room.

"I'm not worried. It'll come to me. It's been less than a week since Hekate Awakened me and the Witch gave me her memories. I think they're just settling down."

Josh stopped in front of the old-fashioned fridge, pulled it open and peered inside. Flickering yellow light washed into the room. "Could someone be stopping you from remembering?" he asked, trying to pretend it was just a casual question.

"Like the Sorceress?" Sophie asked, the tiniest thread of doubt in her voice.

"Like the Sorceress," Josh echoed. He straightened and turned to face his sister. "Nicholas tells us the Witch's memories can take you over. Perenelle says they can't. But you can't remember what the Witch knew about the Sorceress. That's really odd, don't you think?"

"Really odd," Sophie agreed uncomfortably. "You think Perenelle is lying to me?"

"Sophie, I think *everyone* is lying to us. Remember what Scatty said—trust no one . . ." His sister nodded and they finished the sentence together. ". . . except each other."

Josh closed the fridge door. "Completely empty. I wonder what an Elder eats."

"Most don't," Sophie said immediately. She frowned as the knowledge popped into her head. Why could she remember this and not something more important? "They've got a different metabolism than the humani. . . ."

Josh turned to look at his twin before she could finish explaining. "That's interesting."

Sophie jumped, surprised by the anger in her brother's voice. "What is?"

"You called the human race humani," he said quietly. "I've never heard you call them—*us*—that before."

"That's what the Witch called them," she said.

"Exactly. Maybe it's not Nicholas who's wrong—maybe it's Perenelle."

Sophie shook her head. "I believe the Sorceress," she said firmly, and before her brother could respond, she folded her arms and turned away, looking around the room. "Where are we, anyway?" she asked, deliberately changing the subject.

Josh took a deep breath and thought about trying to continue the conversation, but he knew from experience that once Sophie folded her arms and turned her back on him, she'd made a decision. If he pushed, they'd fight, and that was the last thing he wanted right now. All he could hope was that she'd think a little more carefully about everything the Sorceress told her.

"Prometheus's house in Point Reyes. I caught a glimpse of it earlier. We're really isolated. There's a main house and about a dozen small cabins scattered around it. We're in one of the cabins, and I have to tell you—it's a dump." He started looking through drawers. One held a mismatched assortment of knives, forks and spoons, but they were all dull and tarnished, as if they hadn't been touched in years. Another drawer was stuffed with linen tea towels. Josh pulled out a handful: they were all gray and stiff with age, and showed tourist scenes from cities across Europe: Buckingham Palace in London, the Eiffel Tower in Paris, the Brandenburg Gate in Berlin, the Royal Palace in Madrid, the Acropolis in Greece and finally, at the bottom of the pile, the pyramids in Egypt. Josh opened one and a fine cloud of dust filled the air. "I wonder when the last time anyone actually stayed here was," he said. A blast of chill air made him turn. Sophie had pushed open the kitchen door and stepped out into the damp night. The lights of San Francisco filled the sky to the south with an orange glow.

"Where is the Elder?" she asked quietly, without looking around.

"I don't know. I haven't seen him—I haven't seen anyone—since you fainted or collapsed, or whatever you did earlier. The car was dead, so Prometheus carried you up here. Then, when we got here, all he said was 'Let her sleep. She'll be fine when she wakes,' and he left." Josh shrugged. "I've been sitting here for the past four hours waiting for you to wake up." He paused and added, "I'm starving."

"You're always hungry."

"Well, aren't you?"

Sophie took a moment to consider. "No," she said, "not really." She knew she should be hungrier—the only food she'd had all day was the fruit she'd eaten with Aoife on the houseboat—but for some reason she felt fine. "We don't have to stay here," she said. "We could go looking for them."

"This is a Shadowrealm," Josh reminded her. "And the mud people are out there. I'll bet there are other guardians too."

"So where is everyone?" she asked, but even as she was speaking, two figures materialized out of the night. As they approached, Sophie could see it was Nicholas and Perenelle Flamel, arm in arm, walking slowly toward the house. "We've got company," she said softly.

Josh stepped outside and stood beside his sister on the wooden deck. "He looks older," he said quietly. "Older than Perenelle for sure."

"And she's ten years older than him," Sophie reminded her brother.

"So why isn't she aging as fast?"

"Maybe she hasn't used her aura as much as he has," Sophie suggested.

Josh shook his head. "That doesn't make sense—she must have used her powers on Alcatraz."

Almost as if she felt his gaze, Perenelle raised her head to look at Josh, her eyes dark smudges against the pale oval of her face. She smiled, but it looked forced, artificial. "You're awake," she called to Sophie, and then turned to Josh. "And you must be hungry."

"Famished," he said lightly. "I don't suppose you brought any food?"

"There's food aplenty, but you cannot eat just yet," Perenelle answered. She was close enough now that the wan light from the table lamp in the room behind the twins washed her face in a yellow glow, turning the whites of her eyes the color of lemons.

"Prometheus has agreed to train you in the Magic of Fire."

Josh blinked in surprise. "I'm going to learn Fire magic now?"

"Right now." Nicholas nodded. "It will nicely complement your Water magic."

"Could we do it after dinner?" he asked, feeling his stomach grumble.

Nicholas looked at Josh closely. "It's never a good idea to learn an Elemental Magic on a full stomach."

"But Saint-Germain taught Sophie Fire magic after dinner," Josh pointed out, almost petulantly. His sister might not need food, but he hadn't eaten all day.

Perenelle's smile vanished from her face, turning it hard. "You are not your sister; she is infinitely more powerful than you will ever be, Josh. She can do things that would be impossible for you."

"And of course, you have your own skills," Nicholas said to Josh hastily, glaring at his wife.

Josh looked at the couple, confused and surprised about what they'd just said. "I thought we were equal," he said eventually.

Perenelle looked as if she was about to reply, but Josh saw Nicholas catch her hand, squeezing it and silencing her. "You are twins," he said, "but you have never been equals— you each have your strengths and weaknesses. It is the combination of your strengths, one canceling out the other's weakness, which makes you special."

"The two that are one, the one that is all," Perenelle finished.

Nicholas squinted at Josh, his pale eyes looking somewhat unfocused. "You could eat now if you wish, but by the time you've finished, Prometheus might have changed his mind." He smiled and asked lightly. "So, Josh, Fire magic or food?"

"What's it to be?" Perenelle demanded, but there was no humor in her voice.

Josh looked from the Sorceress to the Alchemyst. Something had happened between them. He'd seen his parents like this on occasion when they were arguing. They would be polite but brittle with one another and would lash out at anyone who irritated them. He wondered what the immortals had been arguing about. And at the back of his mind, he kept remembering that when Perenelle had trained with the Witch of Endor, she'd used her maiden name. She hadn't admitted she was the Alchemyst's wife. "Fire magic," he said quietly.

The Alchemyst nodded in agreement. "Fire magic it is."

"I thought Prometheus said he would never train anyone again," Sophie said.

"The Elder had a change of heart," Perenelle answered, looking at the girl as she spoke.

"Prometheus will always do the right thing," Sophie said quietly, and Josh was startled to hear just a hint of the Witch's accent in her voice. Then she turned to look at Josh. "Are you ready?"

He nodded. "I think so. . . ."

"Come on, then, let's go."

The Alchemyst shook his head. "The Elder just wants Josh," he said, his voice barely above a whisper. "He said that he doesn't want to see you again."

Sophie looked surprised. A feeling of extraordinary sadness washed over her.

"I think you frighten him," Perenelle added.

Nicholas looked at Josh. "The Elder has agreed to train you. This is quite an honor; it's been a long time since Prometheus had a student."

"I thought Saint-Germain learned Fire magic from him," Josh said.

Nicholas shook his head and laughed. His chuckle came from deep in his chest and sounded wet and wheezy. "Saint-Germain stole fire from the Elder. Whatever you do, try not to mention his name. Prometheus hates him. In fact, I think most of the Elders hate Saint-Germain. He has a gift for irritating people."

CHAPTER FORTY-FIVE

Saint-Germain raised both hands and spread his fingers wide. Each fingertip popped alight, flickering with varicolored flames. In the dancing firelight, the immortal's face was savage. "Don't threaten me, Green Man," he snarled, his accent pronounced. "I will burn this forest to the ground without a second thought."

Tammuz drew back, reflected light running liquid across the silver mask, making it look as if the carved leaves were trembling in a breeze.

The dryads, their drawn bows nocked with black-tipped arrows, looked at the Green Man, awaiting his instructions.

Tammuz hesitated and Saint-Germain immediately stepped forward. He had pushed up his sleeves, exposing his butterfly tattoos. The flames from his fingertips made their wings appear to beat softly. "I came here to bargain with you, Lord Tammuz, maybe even plead with you. Most certainly not to threaten you. But you know what I am capable of, so don't push me." He paused and added with an icy smile, "Remember what happened to your precious forest in Russia in 1908."

"Go—go now." The Green Man waved his arm and the dryads disappeared back into the forest, the hamadryads melting back into the trees.

Ptelea was the last to leave. "My lord, I am sorry, I did not—"

"This has nothing to do with you," Tammuz boomed. "I blame these two," he said, pointing to Shakespeare and Palamedes, "and especially you, Sir Knight."

Palamedes straightened and a shimmer of his green aura flickered briefly in the air. "We came to talk," he said, "to support our brother's petition, nothing more. And," he added slowly, "I was expecting to be listened to, not treated in this shabby manner and threatened. Saint-Germain is my friend—more than my friend, he is my brother-in-arms—and he is under my protection. Threaten him and you threaten me."

Even through the silver mask, the Green Man's shock was clear. His voice gave his surprise away. "How dare you speak to me like that! Have you gone mad, Palamedes? Has this magician ensorceled you? Have you any idea just who your *friend* is? Do you know what he has done?"

"I do not. Nor do I care. We're not here to talk about that."

"Perhaps you should be. Look at him now. . . ." The Elder waved his hands toward Saint-Germain. "Threatening me. Threatening my forest, my creatures. Bringing cursed fire into the heart of my realm." He stretched out a silver-gloved hand. "He may be beyond my reach, but you are not. All I have to do is lay my hand upon you. I gave you immortality; I can remove it with but a single touch."

William Shakespeare stepped out from behind Palamedes to stand between the knight and the Elder. "But you are not *my* master; you have no power over me." Shakespeare's glasses slipped down his nose and he looked over the top of the black frames. His smile was ugly. "And I doubt you have any idea what I can do to you." The Bard leaned forward. "Anger me and I will teach you the true magic of words . . . and believe me, sirrah, when I am through with you, you will wish that Saint-Germain had burned down your precious forest."

For a long moment the only sound in the night was the soft crackling of the flames at Saint-Germain's fingertips. A globule of fire dripped from his thumb and splashed to the ground. Leaves crisped and curled and the air suddenly filled with the odor of burning. "Whoops." The French immortal smiled as he stubbed out the sparks with the toe of his boot.

The Green Man had retreated almost to the center of the glade. He stopped when his back hit the white pillar, the edges of his metal mask singing off the stone. Raising his head, he looked beyond the Bard at the French immortal. "If I give you what you want, will you go and leave me in peace?" he asked.

Saint-Germain grinned triumphantly. "Nothing would give me greater pleasure." He closed his hands into fists and extinguished the flames to colored smoke.

"Tell me, then. What do you want?"

"My wife, Joan, and Scathach have become trapped in the past. If it is beyond your powers to draw them forward to this time, then I would like you to send me back to my wife." Reaching into his jacket pocket, he pulled out a white envelope and handed it to Will Shakespeare, who was standing closest to him. The Bard passed it over to Palamedes, who approached the Elder. Tammuz stretched out his hand and the knight carefully held the envelope over the silver glove, taking care not to touch the Elder. He let it drop into the Green Man's hand and stepped back.

"Joan and Scathach activated the ancient leygate outside Lutetia," Saint-Germain continued. "It should have taken them across the world, to the West Coast of America, but they never arrived. When I investigated, I found a curious substance on the Point Zero stone."

The Elder tilted his head down and peered into the envelope. It was half filled with gray powder.

"I did some alchemical tests," Saint-Germain said. "I found traces of ground-up mammoth bones from the Pleistocene era and the remnants of an Attraction spell. It stinks of that serpent, Machiavelli."

"And you believe your wife and the Shadow have been pulled back into the past?"

"Into the Pleistocene era," the immortal specified.

"I have no power over the time lines; I cannot call them back to the present."

Saint-Germain nodded quickly. "I suspected that. But you *do* have a little control over time. I know time runs differently in the Shadowrealms. A day there could be a week, a month, a year here. I know you have sent your immortal humani knights into the Shadowrealms and ensured that they are not affected by the time differences. So you must know something about time?"

"I learned a little from Chronos," Tammuz admitted.

"Could you send me back?" Saint-Germain asked eagerly.

The Green Man raised his head, light running off his silver mask. "I could. That is certainly within my powers." Tilting the envelope, he poured some of the powder into his left hand. It hissed, then sizzled where it touched the silver glove, and gauzy gray smoke gathered in the Elder's palm, slowly forming into a ball. "But if I send you to the past, it is a one-way journey: there is no return. Only Chronos, the Master of Time, could bring you back again." The Green Man chuckled. "And he's not going to do that; he hates you even more than I do."

Shakespeare turned to look at Saint-Germain and winked. "Bold, bad man. Does everyone hate you?"

"Just about." The immortal sounded almost pleased. "It's a gift."

The ball of smoke continued to gather in Tammuz's silver glove. "Once you go back, you will be trapped there for all eternity." The Elder looked closely at the Frenchman. "Why do you want to do this?" he asked curiously. "Why is this woman so important to you?"

Saint-Germain blinked in surprise. "Have you ever loved anyone?" he asked.

"Yes," Tammuz said cautiously, "I had a consort once, Inanna. . . ."

"But did you love her? Truly love her?"

The Green Man remained silent.

"Did she mean more to you than life itself?" Saint-Germain persisted.

"They do not love that do not show their love," Shakespeare murmured very softly.

The French immortal stepped closer to the Elder. "I love my Jeanne," he said simply. "I must go to her."

"Even though it will cost you everything?" Tammuz persisted, as if the idea was incomprehensible.

"Yes. Without Joan, everything I have is worthless."

"Even your immortality?"

"Especially my immortality." Gone were the banter and the jokes. This was a Saint-Germain whom neither Shakespeare nor Palamedes had ever seen before. "I love her," he said.

The Green Man stared at the sphere of smoke in the palm of his hand. The globe had turned pale, almost transparent in places. He added a little more of the gray powder from the envelope and watched as it swirled through the ball like snowflakes.

"I was never sure that the humani were the rightful inheritors of this planet," Tammuz said suddenly. "When Danu Talis sank, some of my race choose to create Shadowrealms; others decided to live on this earth. We became kings and princes. Some were even worshipped as gods, and a few took on the role of teachers, claiming that the humani possessed attributes that would make them great. And love and loyalty were counted among the greatest of those attributes. Love and loyalty." He shook his head slightly. "Perhaps if my race had possessed a little more of both, we would still rule this earth," he said with a sigh. "Now, you say your wife is lost in the Pleistocene era . . ."

The globe cradled in his palm turned clear.

And suddenly the three immortals could see Joan of Arc and Scathach within it. The two women were standing at the bank of a river, swords drawn, facing off against an unseen opponent.

Saint-Germain gasped. "Jeanne . . ."

"But something is amiss. . . ." The Green Man's voice echoed and his eyes blazed, illuminating his silver helmet with emerald light. His voice rose as the image within the orb spun . . . and revealed that the women were facing a hooded man. The figure moved and the Elder and the immortals saw the semicircle of metal that took the place of his left hand. "No! Not him. That is not possible . . . ," Tammuz breathed in horror.

Saint-Germain was also shocked by what he was seeing. "The hook-handed man." His voice was thick with emotion. "But that is impossible," he said, echoing the Elder's words.

"You both know this creature?" Palamedes demanded, looking from Saint-Germain to the Elder.

"I know him." The Green Man's voice was shaking. "I saw him ten thousand years ago. He was there when Danu Talis fell." His voice cracked. "He destroyed my world. I was sure he had perished with the island. If I had known he was still alive," he added savagely, "I would have hunted him down and slain him."

"Saint-Germain—who is this?" Palamedes demanded, peering into the globe.

"I stole fire from Prometheus," he whispered, "but this is the creature who taught me its secrets."

"What is he—Elder, Next Generation, immortal or humani?" Palamedes demanded.

"I am not sure. I believe he is neither Elder nor Next Generation. Nor do I think he is fully human. I have no idea what he is. Nicholas met him also, long before I did. He taught the Alchemyst how to translate the Codex, showed him the immortality formula."

"What is he doing in the past?" Will Shakespeare asked.

"He is not in the past," Tammuz said, surprising them all. "You're looking at a Shadowrealm which has been modeled after a prehistoric world."

And then, clear and distinct on the air, they heard a thin voice. "Scathach the Shadow and Joan of Arc. Where have you been? I have been waiting for you for such a long time. Welcome to my world."

Clustered around the globe in Tammuz's hand, the three immortals saw the figure stand and spread his arms wide—and then, suddenly, the hooded man looked up and seemed to stare out of the ball of smoke. They saw his blue eyes blaze and shimmer with silver light. "And Saint-Germain, too. I told you this day would come. It is time to pay your debts. Why don't you join us? Tammuz," the figure commanded, "send him here to me now."

Without a word, the Green Man reached out and caught the front of Saint-Germain's coat with his left hand; then he jammed the smoking globe into the center of the immortal's chest.

Saint-Germain instantly turned to gray vapor and vanished.

CHAPTER FORTY-SIX

$\mathcal{T}$he intercom on Dee's desk buzzed softly. "Ms. Dare has returned, sir."

"Send her in." Dr. John Dee swung his leather chair away from the view of the streets of San Francisco. A slender red-haired male secretary held the door open and allowed Virginia Dare, laden down with bags, to stride into the enormous glass and chrome office, boot heels clicking on the marble floor.

"I love shopping," she announced.

Dee looked at the secretary. "Thank you, Edward, that will be all. You can go now, and thank you for staying late."

The man nodded. "Will you be in tomorrow? There are some papers that need signing."

"I'm not sure at the moment. And if anyone is looking for me, I am still away."

"Yes. I issued a press release earlier saying that you were

in Hong Kong," the man said, backing from the room and closing the door.

"You look stunning," the doctor said, turning his attention back to Virginia. He sat forward, carefully placing his burnt hands on the desk. Although he'd coated them in aloe vera and a numbing cream, they were still stinging, and blisters were starting to form.

"Why, thank you," Virginia said with a smile. "I want you to know that you paid for everything, and it was all very expensive."

"You always did have expensive tastes," Dee said.

Beneath a heavily fringed waist-length black boar-suede coat, Virginia was wearing powder blue jeans, a red Western-style shirt and a black lizard-skin belt that matched her black cowboy boots. Sinking into a chair facing the English Magician, she propped her boots up on the edge of his desk and stared at him across the slab of black marble. "I had forgotten what great boutiques there are in San Francisco."

"When was the last time you were here?" he asked.

"Not too long ago," she said vaguely, "but you know I do not like to spend much time in the Americas—there are too many sad memories for me here."

Dee nodded. He avoided England for the same reason.

"How are your hands?" she asked, changing the subject.

"Sore," Dee said, holding them up. "What's frustrating me is that if I could use my aura for just a single instant, I could heal them."

"Yes, and alert everything in this city to your presence."

The Magician nodded. "Exactly."

"I presume you have a plan?" Dare asked.

Dee sat back in his chair and swiveled around to look out across the city again. "I always have a plan," he said. "I was just thinking about it when you came in. Almost everything is in place." He pointed into the night. "Alcatraz is out there. My company owns the island now, and access is restricted. All the cells are filled with monsters and there is a sphinx wandering free."

Virginia Dare shuddered. "I hate those creatures."

"They are useful. We thought it would be able to control Perenelle Flamel. We were wrong."

"We?"

"My masters and I," Dee clarified.

Virginia went around the desk to stand beside the English Magician. "Pretty," Dare said.

"My favorite view," Dee murmured. Unlike his offices in London or New York, where he was so high he could barely see the streets, here he could look across Pioneer Park and see San Francisco spread out below him, close enough to touch. Almost directly opposite was the triangular shape of the Transamerica Building picked out in lights against the night sky.

"You know your masters will never rest until they have hunted you down," Virginia said quietly.

"Yes. I know that."

"Every moment you remain free and unpunished offends them. Your masters will lose status with the other Elders. They must make an example of you."

Dee nodded again. He could see himself and Virginia

reflected in the dark glass. They looked as if they were floating over the city. "You killed your master . . . and yet no one
came after you," he said.

Virginia laughed, but the sound was brittle and false. "I
did not kill my master. The fool became both arrogant and
careless in his old age. He made the mistake of challenging
the authority of a Deer Woman and then insulted her and her
tribe of Shapeshifters."

"What happened?"

Virginia laughed again. "What do you think happened?
There were Deer Women on this land long before the Elders
fled Danu Talis. They know every hidden trail, secret path-
way and leygate, and how and where they all connect. One
moment my Elder was in Oklahoma, threatening the
woman . . . the next he was in Badwater, in the heart of Death
Valley at the height of summer. I believe he used his aura to
keep himself cool for the first few days . . . until he had no
aura left." She clapped her hands together suddenly and the
Magician jumped. "His own aura finally consumed him in a
ball of flame. There wasn't even dust left."

"How do you know all this?" Dee wondered.

"Because I was there," Dare said lightly. "Who do you
think led the Deer Woman to him?" She patted Dee's shoulder. "I was tired of him: he had lied to me once too often,
made me promises he had no intention of keeping." Her
voice dropped to a whisper and her fingers curled slightly.
"Don't make the same mistake."

"I won't," Dee answered, watching Dare's reflection the
whole time.

"So tell me, what you are going to do, Doctor?" Virginia demanded.

Dee came stiffly to his feet. Without saying a word, he crossed the room and stepped into a small private elevator. Dare hesitated a moment, then followed him. The elevator was uncomfortably small, obviously designed for only one person. With great care, the Magician pushed his burnt thumb against a button marked Emergency Stop. The button glowed a dull blue and then the doors hissed closed.

"The latest in fingerprint recognition," Dee explained. "If anyone else pushed the button, the lift would fill with gas."

"Very clever," the woman said sarcastically.

Although there had been no sense of movement, the lift door suddenly opened. Virginia stepped out, followed by Dee. "Where are we?" she asked, looking around.

They had stepped out into a vast open-plan living room. All four walls were glass and featured panoramic views of the city. Various configurations of leather couches and chairs were scattered around the room, and four enormous flat-screen television sets arranged in a square hung from the ceiling. They were all tuned to the History Channel. At the far end of the space was a kitchen, and at the other end, behind a series of ornate painted screens, was a sleeping area centered around a Japanese futon.

"We're on the thirteenth floor."

"Your building does not have a thirteenth floor," Dare snapped.

"Not on the floor plans," Dee agreed, "but there is a thirteenth floor, accessible via this lift and a narrow maintenance stairway. Welcome to my home," he said with a broad sweep of his arms. "It is built between the twelfth and fourteenth floors and steals square footage from both. The windows are one way and the entire floor is completely soundproofed."

Virginia looked around. "It needs a woman's touch," she said, unimpressed. "You do know that couches come upholstered in material other than leather, and metal and glass tables haven't been chic since the nineteen eighties." She turned and stopped, suddenly speechless. "Artificial flowers? John, you can't be serious."

"The real ones kept dying," Dee said. "And when did you become an interior decorator? The last time I met you, you lived in a tent."

"Still do," she said. "You're never homeless in a tent."

Dee crossed the floor to the area that served as a kitchen and pulled open the fridge door.

"If you ate, I'd wager you'd have paper plates," Virginia said, following him. "I suppose it would be pointless asking you for milk?" she asked as he reached into the fridge.

"Pointless," he agreed. "You can have water, flat or sparkling," Dee pulled out two bottles and then, from the back of the fridge, a short narrow object wrapped in a rag. He laid it on the table before Dare, and then reached back into the fridge to pull out two more similarly shaped objects. One was wrapped in red silk, the other in green leather.

Virginia Dare felt the tickling crawl of ancient power

across her skin and stepped back, automatically brushing her tingling hands along the length of her jacket. She felt as if ants were crawling across her skin.

Dee then pulled open the oven and extracted a rectangular wooden box, which he also laid on the table.

"I'm not going to even ask you why you store things in the fridge and the oven," Dare muttered. "Are these what I think they are?" she asked.

"What do you think they are?" he asked.

"Dangerous. Powerful. Deadly."

"That they are." The Magician carefully unwrapped the object in red silk, slowly peeling back the wafer-thin cloth. "I was thinking earlier that I've been a fool."

Virginia Dare squeezed her lips tightly shut and resisted the temptation to comment.

"Why did I spend centuries working for the Elders, doing their errands like a servant or a trained dog?"

"Because they made you immortal?" Virginia reminded him.

"Others have become immortal without an Elder," Dee pointed out. "The Flamels, Saint-Germain and Shakespeare, too. Maybe if I had searched for the secret of immortality, I would have found it myself."

"Maybe you would have died before you'd found it," Virginia suggested.

"I gave the Elders centuries of service. . . ."

"I know, I know, I know. I'm becoming bored with this self-pitying nonsense," Dare snapped, deliberately goading him. She knew the Magician well enough to know that he hated to be interrupted. If Dee had a failing, it was that he loved the sound of his own voice. "Tell me what you intend to do."

"First, I am going to summon Coatlicue from her prison and set her loose into the Shadowrealms," he said, burnt fingers fumbling with the red silk.

Dare watched him closely but made no attempt to help him.

"The Elders will be forced to draw most of their forces on earth back into the Shadowrealms to battle the Mother of All the Gods. They will not care what happens here. In the meantime, Machiavelli should have released the monsters on Alcatraz into the city."

Dare blinked in surprise but knew better than to interrupt him now.

The red silk fell away, revealing a simple stone sword. The hilt was unadorned and the gray blade polished so that it looked like metal. Dee looked over at Virginia, his eyes sparkling. "Do you recognize it?" he asked.

"One of the swords of power," she breathed. "Which one?"

"Durendal," he whispered.

"The indestructible." Dare stepped closer to look at the ancient weapon. "You've always been fascinated with these toys, haven't you, Doctor?"

"A one-handed man once read my fortune; he told me that my destiny lay entwined with the swords."

"I thought it would look more impressive," Virginia said.

The Magician pulled at the thick string knotted tightly

around the green-leather-wrapped object. "San Francisco will quickly fall to the beasts," he continued, ignoring her comment. "The humani armies will not be able to stand against the monsters. The fear factor alone gives us a tremendous advantage. And there are similar caches of creatures in all the major cities around the globe. The world will dissolve into chaos in a matter of days."

"And what about those Elders who refuse to leave the earth to fight Coatlicue in the Shadowrealms?" Virginia asked. "And the immortals who are not allied to the Dark Elders? They will fight the monsters."

"Oh, I'm counting on it," Dee muttered. Two of the cords fell away from the object he was fumbling with, but he could not undo the third knot. He looked at the woman. "Would you . . . ?"

"I'm going nowhere near it," Virginia said. She slipped a short flat-bladed knife from a hidden sheath in her sleeve and tossed it to the Magician. He deftly caught it and sliced open the last knot.

"I know the locations of most of the Elders, Next Generation and immortals here on earth. Once they come out of hiding, I can pick them off one by one. When I'm finished, you and I will be the last two immortals on this planet. My Elder masters once promised me this planet: now I'm taking it on my terms."

"And sharing it with me," Virginia reminded him.

"And sharing it with you," he agreed.

"You still haven't told me what you want me for," Dare said.

"Why, my dear, you are central to my plan." He stopped and looked up, smiling slyly. "I always knew we would end up together."

"Did you, now?"

"We are alike, you and I."

"I'm sure we are," Virginia Dare muttered. She dipped her head and said nothing. Dee had known her for most of his life and still had no idea just what she was, or what she was capable of. He had grown up in the Elizabethan Age and his opinions of women had been shaped by that age. Dare was convinced it was one of the many reasons he—and Machiavelli, too—had consistently underestimated Perenelle Flamel.

Dee carefully unfolded the green leather to reveal a twin of the first sword.

"A twin blade," Virginia Dare said, surprised. "It must be Joyeuse, Charlemagne's sword."

"The first sword I ever owned," the Magician said. "And now I have the complete set." Dee laid Excalibur and Clarent alongside the first two swords.

Now that the swords lay together on the glass-topped table, the similarities between them were obvious—they were all about twenty inches long and carved from a single piece of stone. Of the four swords, only Clarent was dull and ugly—the rest were polished to a high shine. Virginia noticed subtle differences in the patterns of their hilts, but had she not watched Dee lay them out, she doubted she would have been able to tell them apart—except for Clarent, of course.

"Once I have located and killed any remaining Elders, Next Generation and immortals on this world, I am going to use the swords to destroy the entrances to the Shadowrealms here on earth. Then this will truly become our world."

"Very clever, I'm sure," Dare said. "I have just one question. . . ."

"Just one?"

"Why me?"

Dee looked at her blankly.

"You have this so neatly planned out: what do you need me for?" The Magician opened his mouth, but Dare held up her hand to stop him. "And don't even think about lying," she whispered. "Not when there are four swords on the table in front of me." Although the smile did not leave her lips, the threat was plain.

The Englishman nodded. "I came to you because . . . well, I told you: you are central to my plan. I need your flute."

"My flute?" Virginia was completely taken aback.

Dee looked vaguely embarrassed. "Well, yes. When the monsters have been released into the city, I should be able to control them for a few days. But once they've fed and become feral, I will lose control. . . ." His voice trailed off as he watched for Dare's reaction.

"And you believe my flute will be able to enchant and control them."

"I'm sure of it. Remember, I was with you when you stood on the banks of the Red River and turned back a herd of three thousand stampeding buffalo. I have some inkling of the flute's powers."

"There is a difference between buffalo and whatever menagerie of nightmares you've collected."

Dee shook his head. "They are all beasts. And earlier, I watched you fell both cucubuths and humani. I have absolute confidence in you."

"Thank you," Virginia said sarcastically. "So once I render the creatures unconscious what do you intend to do with them when they wake up?"

Dee shrugged dismissively. "Kill them, or return them to Alcatraz and let them fend for themselves." He reached for the rectangular wooden box on the table, opened the lid and lifted out a small copper-bound book.

The air in the room immediately crackled with static electricity, green sparks running across all the metal surfaces.

Virginia felt as if all the breath had been sucked from her body. "Is that what I think it is?"

Dee placed the book on the table in the center of the swords. Bound in tarnished green copper, the book was about six inches across by nine inches long, the pages within thick and yellow with ragged edges.

"The Codex—the Book of Abraham the Mage," Dee said, almost reverentially. "I devoted my entire life to finding this book. . . ." Wrapping a corner of the red silk around his fingers, he carefully opened the cover. "And when I finally acquired it, the last two pages were ripped out." He turned to the back of the book, where the torn edges of two thick leaves jutted from the binding. The Magician giggled, the sound high-pitched and unnerving. "And do you know something, Virginia: the last two pages contain the Final Summoning, the formula needed to bring the Elders from their Shadow-realms into this world. My masters were very upset that I'd lost it." His giggling turned to laughter, which quickly grew louder and more hysterical, shaking his entire body. "But now it turns out that we don't need the Final Summoning, because the Elders will not be coming back."

"Doctor!" Virginia snapped, suddenly growing fright-ened of Dee. She'd never seen him like this. "Control your-self."

John Dee drew in a deep shaky breath. "Of course. I apol-ogize." He closed the Codex and ran his silk-covered hand across the metal surface. "We will let the monsters ravage the earth for a week, we'll allow the armies, navies and air forces to exhaust themselves battling the creatures, and then, just when all seems lost, you and I will announce ourselves as the saviors of mankind. We'll draw away the creatures and take control of the planet. We will become the immortal rulers of the world. You have no master, and mine will either be dead or trapped in a Shadowrealm with no access to this world, so I am safe. I can use this book to remake and reshape the earth in any way that we wish." He smiled. "The only limits are our imaginations."

"I've got a very vivid imagination," Virginia murmured. "However, haven't you forgotten one tiny thing?" she added calmly.

Dee looked at her in surprise. "What?"

"All of this depends on Coatlicue's doing your bidding."

"She will," he said confidently. "The real moment of danger is when she first awakens: she will be ravenous. I just have to make sure to feed her."

"Coatlicue is not a vegetarian," Virginia reminded him.

The Magician's smile turned feral. "Yes, I know. And I've got such a tasty feast lined up for her."

CHAPTER FORTY-SEVEN

Josh leaned against the door of the study and peered inside. Two of the walls were lined with books, a third with DVDs, while an enormous projection TV took up the fourth wall.

The red-haired Elder was stretched out in a lounger, idly flicking through cable channels at high speed. He hesitated when he came to CNN, watched it for a moment, then clicked to another channel.

Josh rapped on the doorframe. "You wanted to see me," he said quietly. He was surprised by how calm he felt. There were no nerves, but he wasn't feeling much excitement, either.

"Come in," Prometheus said without turning around. He pointed to a matching lounger with the remote control. "Sit for a minute, let us talk."

Josh climbed onto the lounger and hit the button that

brought the footstool up. "My dad has one just like this," he explained. "He has the model with the massage and heat functions."

"I had that one, but every time I used the massage, I thought there was an earthquake, so I sent it back."

They sat in silence while Prometheus continued to surf the channels. The Elder only slowed at news and black-and-white movies. "Hundreds of channels and never anything worth watching," he muttered.

Josh took the opportunity to look at the Elder: the only light in the study came from the flickering TV, which made it seem as if his face was constantly in motion. Now that he was close, Josh could see that Prometheus's cheeks and chin were crisscrossed with tiny scars that were partially hidden by his beard. There were more scars on his forehead.

"They're little keepsakes of my time in prison," the Elder said, his deep rumbling voice making Josh jump.

"I'm sorry. I didn't mean to stare." Josh had no idea how the Elder had known he was looking at him.

Prometheus rubbed the back of his hand against his forehead. "I rarely think of them now. I could heal myself and make them disappear, but I like to keep them as reminders."

"Of what?" Josh wondered.

"That some things are worth fighting for . . . and that everything has a cost."

"Why were you in prison?" Josh asked. "If you don't mind me asking," he added quickly.

The huge man waved his hand dismissively. "An old, old

story, too long and too complicated to tell you now." He paused and added, "You should ask your sister about it sometime. She will know."

"Because the Witch knew?"

"How long has she known my sister?" the Elder asked. He turned his huge green eyes on the boy.

"Would you believe, we met her once, very briefly, last Friday. . . ." Josh's voice trailed away. It was hard to even try to think back to earlier that week, when all of this had begun. It seemed like a lifetime ago. "She taught Sophie the Magic of Air, and passed on all her knowledge at the same time. I don't know how. I wasn't in the room when it happened."

"And you've no idea why my sister did that?"

"None. You'd have to ask Sophie," he said, "though I doubt she knows."

"You don't look much like any of the other Golds I've seen," the Elder said finally, breaking the long silence that followed Josh's statement.

"Have you seen many other Golds?"

"Too many."

"And what does a Gold look like?" Josh asked.

"Frightened."

"Oh, I'm not frightened anymore," Josh said simply. "I've gone beyond frightened, past terrified. Now I'm into petrified."

Prometheus stared intently at Josh. "What frightens you?"

Josh picked up the remote control and started flipping through the channels. "Everything. This place. You. The

Flamels. Dee. Machiavelli. The Shadowrealms, the leygates. The magic." His voice rose with each sentence. "The thought that everything we were taught—every single thing we've ever learned, at home and in school, from books, from TV—is wrong. And Sophie," he finished in a hoarse whisper, finally admitting his deepest fear. "I don't think I know her anymore. And it's all your sister's fault." He glared at the Elder, his anger making him reckless. "She changed her when she gave her those memories."

Surprisingly, Prometheus nodded in agreement. "Sisters are a trial," he said. "And it doesn't matter if they're Elder or humani. Sometimes I think they exist solely to upset and annoy their brothers. I was once as close to mine as you are to yours." He paused and added, "I've not spoken to her in millennia."

"What happened?"

Prometheus shifted uncomfortably in his seat. "I thought I knew. Now I am beginning to think that I might have been wrong. For ages I thought she had betrayed me to Chronos. Now . . . now I am not so sure. I made the mistake of not speaking directly to her." His green eyes glowed in the dark. "Whatever happens between you and your sister, make sure you talk to her before making any decisions. Don't allow anyone to tell you what she said, or what she did—make sure she tells you herself."

"Is that, like, a warning?"

Prometheus grunted a laugh. "No, I just don't want you making the same mistake I did."

They sat in silence while Josh continued to flip through

the channels. "You get a lot of foreign stations," he said, eventually stopping at a soccer game. The commentary was in a language he couldn't identify, Korean maybe. They watched that together until one team scored a goal and then Josh said casually, "You've trained some of the other Golds in the Magic of Fire."

"Some," Prometheus admitted.

Still concentrating fiercely on the television, Josh continued, "And do you know what happened to them? Where they are now?"

"I believe most are dead, Josh," Prometheus said very softly.

"Most of them?"

"All the ones I trained. I cannot speak for the others."

Stopping at the Weather Channel, Josh swiveled in the chair to face the Elder. "That doesn't sound like good news for me, then, does it?"

"Probably not," Prometheus agreed.

"I know the process is dangerous. . . ."

Prometheus shook his big head. "No, the Awakening is the most dangerous process of all." Tilting his head back, he breathed deeply. "And I can tell by the stink that clings to you that you were Awakened by Mars Ultor himself."

Josh nodded, surprised by the vehemence in the Elder's voice. "In the Catacombs of Paris."

"Ah, so that's where she hid him," Prometheus said enigmatically. "When all this is over I must go and pay my respects."

"You don't like him?" Josh asked, curious.

"He was my friend, my closest friend, closer than a brother. He married my sister and I was thrilled. . . ." The Elder's voice faded away.

"Something happened?"

"The swords happened. Mars found Excalibur in an abandoned temple on a deserted island. And it led him to Clarent. Zephaniah claimed it was the swords that corrupted him, but I was never sure about that. All I know is that he betrayed the people he had sworn to protect. I hunted him across the world and through the Shadowrealms, and just when I was closing in on him, he disappeared. Later, centuries later, I discovered that my sister had secreted him away to keep him safe from my vengeance, but I never knew where." He bared his teeth in a grimace that might have passed for a smile. "Until now. Thank you."

"Leave him alone," Josh said fiercely. "He's in terrible pain, trapped in a shell of molten lava. He's been that way for thousands of years."

"Good," Prometheus said cruelly. "It is a small price to pay for what he did to my people."

"Your people?"

"My people. The humani. I created them, Josh. It was my aura that brought them to life. Every humani on this planet— including you—has a spark of my aura within them. Do you know why Mars Ultor enslaved the humans and sacrificed them on the ancient pyramids?"

Josh shook his head, but he suddenly remembered the flickering images he'd caught while he'd been carrying Clarent. They started to make sense now.

"For that spark of life. Mars Ultor was harvesting my aura."

"Why?"

Prometheus shook his head. "That is also another tale for another day. You are here to learn the Magic of Fire," he said suddenly, changing the subject.

"Yes. If you will teach me."

"I will. But I want you to know that I am doing this against my better judgment," Prometheus continued. "I am doing this because my sister said I should, and as you know, saying no to your older sister is practically impossible. And also because I don't think she has ever been wrong."

Josh sighed. "That sounds just like Sophie."

Prometheus flicked his thumb and a flat gray disc spun in the air.

Startled, Josh caught it in his right hand and leaned forward so that he could examine it in the light from the TV. It was a small stone circle about the size of his palm. The stone was polished smooth, and there were traces of gold and bronze paint on the surface. In the center was a round-eyed open-mouthed face with a series of rings around it. Etched and carved into each ring were countless blocky symbols. Josh frowned. He'd seen something like this before. "It's an Aztec calendar," he said finally. "My mom has one just like it in her study."

"It's called a sunstone," Prometheus said quietly.

Josh turned the smooth stone disc over in his hands. It felt warm.

"I know your sister was taught Fire magic by Saint-Germain."

Josh squirmed uncomfortably. "Nicholas told me not to mention his name in front of you."

The Elder waved a huge hand. "Saint-Germain is a rogue, a liar and a thief, but I forgave him. He was my student for a long time; then he either got lazy or greedy. He stole the secret of fire from me, but"—the Elder shrugged—"it was hard for me to remain mad at him, because I'd originally stolen fire myself. Someone—not me—taught Saint-Germain how to use the Magic of Fire, but they did not know all my secrets. I will teach you more about the Magic of Fire than your sister will ever know. Look at the sunstone."

Josh looked down into the palm of his hand, and his breath caught in his chest. The disc had started to throb and pulse with a dull golden light, and for a moment, he thought the eyes on the carved face had blinked and the tongue had flickered.

"I swore I would never teach another humani the Magic of Fire, but there are some promises which should be broken."

Wisps of yellow smoke steamed off the stone and the scent of oranges filled the room.

"You are the sun, Josh; fire is your natural element. Your sister is the moon, and her primary element is water. Yes, your sister knows fire, but you, Josh, you will know it a hundred times better!"

And the disc burst into flame.

CHAPTER FORTY-EIGHT

Sophie screamed.

She leapt up from the kitchen table clutching her hand.

Perenelle and Aoife surged to their feet on either side of her. Only Flamel and Niten remained seated.

"What's wrong?" Perenelle demanded.

Sophie held up her right hand. Her palm was bright red. "I thought . . . It felt like something burned me," she said, blinking away tears.

Perenelle crossed to the sink and ran cold water onto a tea towel, then pressed it against Sophie's palm. "So, it's begun," she said, looking into the girl's eyes. "Prometheus is teaching your brother the Magic of Fire."

"But it didn't hurt when Saint-Germain taught me."

"There are as many ways to teach magic as there are teachers," Perenelle said.

"I should go to him . . . ," Sophie began.

"You cannot. This is something he has to do alone."
Perenelle drew Sophie back to the table. "Sit; there is something *we* must do."

Perenelle sat down across from Nicholas at the small kitchen table. Aoife had taken the third seat, facing Sophie. Niten sat on the couch where Sophie had slept earlier. He was slowly and methodically running a cloth along the length of his katana.

In the center of the table sat a carved wooden box.

Sophie looked closely at it. She was aware of a hint of exotic spices in the air, and she recognized one of the smells as jasmine, Aunt Agnes's favorite perfume. And when she looked at the box, she realized she'd seen the triple spiral carved into the sides and the top of the box before. She had a sudden flash of Zephaniah seeing the same triple spiral carved into the glass walls of the Nameless City.

Sophie watched as Nicholas carefully lifted the lid and reached into the box to remove an object wrapped in a bag of finely woven grass and wicker.

One by one all of their auras started to spark and crackle, darting cinders of light around the room—green and white, silver and gray, and speckles of royal blue from Niten. Perenelle's hair rose slightly off her shoulders, static snapping through it.

Perenelle picked up the box and the lid and set them on the ground, and the Alchemyst placed the grass-wrapped object in the center of the table. He began to tug at the twisted strands of grass, crackling threads of power crawling across his fingers.

"You might have seen this before," Perenelle said to Aoife, and then she looked at Sophie. "Maybe you, too. Well, not you, but the Witch. In fact," she added lightly, "you may know more about it than we do."

Nicholas peeled apart the grass knots and the covering fell away to reveal an intricately beautiful crystal skull that was almost—but not quite—human. When the Alchemyst laid his hand on it, a slow wave of mint green light pulsed through the translucent crystal. Perenelle put her hand on top of his and the skull started to glow.

"Now you," Nicholas said, looking at Aoife.

She looked at him with an expression of absolute disgust on her face. "I am not touching that abominable thing," she said hoarsely.

"As you wish." He looked at Sophie. "We need the strength of your aura. . . ."

Numb with shock, Sophie felt as if all the air had been sucked from the room. She had seen this before. . . .

Zephaniah was in the Nameless City again.

She was trying to protect her unconscious brother from the hordes of monsters that were gathering outside. Yet it was just as dangerous inside the library; all around her, the animated clay people moved and shuffled, threatening to crush her.

She was dragging Prometheus deep into the heart of the building. Night had fallen outside, and unseen creatures roamed the deserted streets, claws clicking, flesh slithering and rasping. She could make out their rancid odor: they smelled like crocodiles.

286

Zephaniah discovered a room deep in the heart of the library. The unusually tall doors were locked, but a section of the glass wall close to the floor was missing. In ages past, an earthquake must have rocked the city and a section of the floor given way; the wall's glass blocks had shifted and pulled apart, creating a wide gap.

She crawled through the opening and pulled her brother into the safety of the room just as the monsters surged into the building above. She could hear them hissing and snapping, could hear the sound of clay shattering.

When she straightened, the room instantly lit up with a soft milky glow. The walls were empty—though they must have once held countless books—and all that remained in the center of the room was a crystal skull on a plinth of polished metal.

Zephaniah watched as light flickered through the skull and it started to pulse, and she discovered that it was beating in time with her heart.

And then it spoke to her. . . .

And its revelations were terrifying.

Sophie knew what the skull was, knew its origins and its powers.

This was Archon technology, and they had created the skulls based on even older knowledge. The Witch had spent centuries searching for artifacts just like it, and when she'd found them, she had destroyed them utterly. She had erased countless millennia of knowledge, burning vast caches of metal books; melting into slag the ancient objects and artifacts that looked like swords, spears and knives; shattering crystal balls and grinding fabulous jewels to powder. Zepha-niah had spent fortunes—several fortunes—in search of the Archon skulls. They were impossible to break, impervious to blade or tool, but she had finally discovered that she could destroy them by tossing them into the mouths of active vol-canoes, where they were swallowed by the molten lava. Once she had rid the world of as many magical objects as she could find, the Witch had set about killing the storytellers who kept alive the memories of the Archons and the Earthlords who had come before them.

But all that had come later.

Much later.

After the Fall of Danu Talis.

After she had realized just how dangerous the skulls truly were.

"Sophie?" Perenelle leaned forward, eyes fixed on the girl's face. "We need your aura. Put your hand on the skull."

Sophie shook her head, a tiny, almost imperceptible movement.

The Sorceress blinked in surprise. "Do you—or rather, does the Witch—know anything about the crystal skull?"

Sophie looked into the Sorceress's eyes and slowly and deliberately shook her head. Instinct—or was it the Witch's knowledge?—made her lie: "No," she said.

Even as she was speaking, there was a pop as the lightbulb shattered and the room plunged into darkness . . . except for the glowing skull.

CHAPTER FORTY-NINE

The disc burned red-hot, then white-hot, in waves of shimmering heat. Each square pictograph throbbed and pulsed, red, orange and black, forming patterns, making shapes. The concentric rings turned left and right, the inner circle moving clockwise, the next ring counterclockwise, to create new designs. Josh realized to his horror that the etched designs were like snakes swallowing their own tails. And he hated snakes.

And then the face in the center of the stone moved.

The eyes opened, and they were fire red, flecked with glittering black cinders. The mouth moved, and it spoke in the voice of Prometheus.

"It is said that the Magic of Air or Water or even Earth is the most powerful of all. But that is wrong. The Magic of Fire far surpasses all others, for fire is both the life-giver and the death-bringer."

Abruptly the fire vanished, leaving Josh in utter darkness.

He couldn't tell if his eyes were open or even where he was. He'd lost all sensation and was conscious only of the weight of the warm stone in his palm. He clutched it with both hands now, holding it tightly, concentrating on it. He realized that he wasn't afraid, yet wasn't excited, either . . . he was simply curious.

"In the beginning . . ."

A spot of light, a pinprick, appeared in the darkness.

". . . there was fire."

The tiny dot suddenly expanded, growing, growing, growing, amber, orange, red, before detonating into a brilliant white-hot globe. The left and right edges of the fireball peeled off into broad horizontal lines speckled with points and streaks of multicolored light. And as the light rolled toward him in a huge slow wave, Josh suddenly recognized it: he was looking at a galaxy . . . no, he was seeing the universe.

"Before air, there was fire. . . ."

The wave of blazing light flowed over him—or had he fallen into it? Flames and curling threads of plasma washed around him, bathed him. He could see himself now. He was standing, floating, flying, and his skin was the same color as the golden flames. On one level he knew he should be terrified, but he still felt no fear, only a peculiar sense of sadness that his sister was not here to share this with him.

"Before water . . ."

His skin became translucent. Looking down, he could see the thin twisting veins and arteries, the knots and strands of muscles, the darker masses of organs and the lines and curves of bones beneath his flesh.

"Before earth . . ."

Fire was streaming off his skin in long ropes, thickening, hardening into a shell, trapping him inside a burning sphere.

"Fire is the creator of worlds . . ."

Suddenly Josh was back in darkness again, but this time the darkness was not complete. On all sides he could see the finest traces of light, wriggling hair-thin cracks of red fire. It was like looking at an eggshell, he realized. The cracks widened and broke apart, and then the fire cascaded downward. He realized then that he was in a cave, standing on the edge of a lava pool, while molten rock flowed past him.

"And at the center of every world is its fiery heart."

Josh was unsure whether he was moving past the images or standing still while the images raced past him. He felt as if he was rising up through bubbling rock and blazing stones, glutinous boulders and dripping globules of fire. He rose faster, faster, faster, the burning walls streaking by him . . . and abruptly there was sky above, shockingly, spectacularly blue, though smudged with filthy smoke and boiling clouds.

"Fire created this world . . . shaped it. . . ."

Josh soared high into the air, shot up in a plume of lava and smoke from the maw of an enormous volcano, one of a line that erupted in sequence, tearing away huge chunks of landscape, forming and re-forming the barren world, giving it shape before ripping it apart again.

"It was fire which ignited the spark of life on this primitive planet. . . ."

Thick gritty clouds swirled around Josh, then suddenly cleared, and he discovered he was walking along the edge of a lake, though it was not a lake of water. The thick souplike substance steamed and boiled with enormous noxious popping bubbles. And floating on the surface of the boiling mud was a sludge of gray algae.

"Heat brings life . . ."

Even as Prometheus was speaking, the landscape before Josh's eyes was changing impossibly quickly: vast swaths of grasslands appeared, and died away, replaced by trees that rose spectacularly high only to crumble and be replaced by smaller trees, ferns and bushes.

". . . in all its myriad forms."

And now the animals appeared. Small at first, then morphing into huge hideous beasts, pelycosaurs and archosaurs. Josh knew these were the creatures that had predated the dinosaurs. Fascinated, he tried to look around this primeval world, but the images flickered past, leaving little more than an impression of scales and fur, claws and teeth.

"And fire destroys. . . ."

The sky darkened; lightning flashed, and then fire ravaged the forest, and in a single instant the world was blackened, the trees scarred with the evidence of a terrible conflagration.

"Fire destroys, but it also creates. A forest needs fire to thrive; certain seeds depend on it to germinate."

And at the base of the trees, brilliant green shoots poked through the cinders, twisting and writhing up to the light. . . .

"And it was fire which warmed the first of my people, the humani, allowing them to thrive in harsh climates."

The forest died, and was replaced by a desolate ice-locked

landscape, rocky and snow-covered. But on a cave-dotted cliff face, tiny fires burned brightly.

"Fire allowed the first humani to cook their kills, and made it easier for them to digest the nutrients from the meat they hunted. It kept them warm and safe in their caves, and the same fire hardened their tools and weapons, turned soft clay into pots, even sealed their wounds. Fire has driven every great civilization from the ancient world right up to the present day."

A modern city grew before Josh's eyes, glass and steel and concrete, highways and bridges, skyscrapers and suburbs, rail lines and airports.

"And the fire which created this planet can also destroy it."

A huge mushroom cloud blossomed in the center of the city directly in front of Josh, the light at its heart brighter than any sun, burning everything in its path . . . and a heartbeat later, all that remained was an incinerated wasteland.

"This is the power of fire," Prometheus said.

And suddenly Josh was back in the study, sitting in the lounger. He looked at the Elder and tried to speak, but his mouth was dry, his lips cracked, and his tongue felt thick and heavy.

"Every living thing on this planet—and in the Shadowrealms, too—exists because of fire," Prometheus said quietly. In the gloom, his eyes were bright, burning red. "We carry its spark deep within." Reaching over, he tapped Josh in the center of the chest with his index finger. The young man shuddered as a wash of heat tingled through his body. "Josh, the Magic of Fire is linked to your aura, and yours is one of the most powerful I have ever encountered. But you need to know that your aura is inextricably bound to your emotions. You must be careful, so very, very careful. Never call upon the Magic of Fire when you are angry. Fire is the one magic that must be called upon only when you are calm; otherwise, it can rage out of control and consume everything—including you."

Josh managed to gather enough saliva to croak out, "But when do I learn the magic?"

Prometheus chuckled. "You already have. Open your hands."

Josh looked down. He was still holding the Aztec sunstone in his right hand, but he'd covered it with his left. When he lifted his left hand, the stone came with it. It was stuck to his skin. Puzzled, he looked at the Elder.

"Wait," Prometheus whispered.

Suddenly Josh's left hand glowed gold and an agonizing pain shot up the length of his arm. He gasped; then he smelled oranges and the pain vanished.

The sunstone dropped to the ground.

And when he turned his hand over, he discovered that the Aztec face had seared into the flesh of his palm. It resembled a black tattoo. "A trigger?" he whispered.

"A trigger," Prometheus said. "When you wish to call upon the Magic of Fire, visualize the type of flame you would like to create and press the thumb of your right hand to the face."

Josh looked at the barbaric image burned into his palm

and grinned. This was way cooler than Sophie's boring circle tattoo.

"Leave me now," Prometheus said. "Get some rest. Tomorrow is going to be a busy day." The Elder sat back into his chair and reached for his remote control. He watched the boy climb unsteadily to his feet.

"Thank . . . thank you," Josh mumbled.

"You're welcome. . . . Oh, and Josh—try not to burn yourself too often."

CHAPTER FIFTY

*I*n the heart of the Catacombs beneath Paris, the Elder Mars Ultor awoke. For a single instant his eyes were a brilliant blue, but they quickly turned an ugly burning red.

The boy, the twin, the one he had Awakened, the one he was connected to, had mastered his second magic, the Magic of Fire.

Closing his eyes, forcing himself to ignore the pain that ate away at his entire body, he looked through the boy's eyes and found he was staring into the face of his wife's brother: Prometheus. He broke the connection instantly, afraid that the Elder would sense his presence. Mars Ultor, the Avenger, who feared nothing and no one, was terrified of the Firelord.

Then, almost reluctantly, he concentrated on visualizing the English Magician's face, and when Dee turned his head to look up with wide gray eyes, the Elder said: "It is done."

"It is done." John Dee jerked awake with such force that he fell out of the chair and sprawled on his burnt hands. The pain was excruciating, but he ignored it: his dreamless sleep had been interrupted by the image of the Sleeping God, Mars Ultor, trapped in his bone prison deep beneath Paris. In his dream the Elder's eyes had opened and looked at him, and Dee heard him speak behind the mask.

"It is done. The boy has mastered fire."

Climbing to his feet, Dee cradled his arms across his chest and pressed his forehead against the cool glass wall. Focusing, he visualized Mars Ultor's prison in precise detail, until he could actually *see* the imprisoned Elder. "I want the boy," he said aloud.

And on the other side of the world, bloodred smoke curled from the Sleeping God's eyes. "Josh," Mars whispered. "Josh."

Exhausted and sore, Josh Newman lay back on the hard uncomfortable bed and closed his eyes. A single heartbeat later, he was asleep.

And then his eyes snapped open.

No longer blue, they were the same color as Mars Ultor's.

CHAPTER FIFTY-ONE

Scathach caught the hint of movement above them and jerked Joan to one side . . . in the instant before Saint-Germain tumbled out of the air to land in a heap at their feet.

The immortal sat up and fastidiously dusted himself off as the two women looked at him in astonishment. He was just standing up when there was a crash in the undergrowth behind them. The two women turned, weapons ready . . . as Palamedes and William Shakespeare strolled out of the long grass.

"When shall we three meet again!" Shakespeare said with a smile that exposed his bad teeth.

Joan squealed with delight and launched herself at Saint-Germain, wrapping her arms and legs around him, sending him staggering backward. Catching her in his arms, he swung her around and around. "I knew you would come for me," Joan whispered in French.

"I said I would follow you to the ends of the earth," he murmured in the same language, "and now you know I really mean it." Returning Joan to the ground, he bowed to the Shadow. "You are unharmed and in good health, I see."

"We are." Scatty returned his bow. "I thought I'd lost the capacity for surprise a long time ago," she said, "but I guess I was mistaken. And I really do hate surprises," she added.

Saint-Germain turned to Palamedes and the Bard and raised his eyebrows in silent shock. The knight grinned, teeth white against his dark skin. "What, did you think we would let you have all the fun?"

"But how . . . ?" Saint-Germain wondered.

Palamedes turned to Shakespeare. "Tell him."

The Bard shrugged modestly. "I suggested to the Green Man that he send us after you." Will smiled. He stopped and bowed to Scatty and Joan. "Ladies."

"And Tammuz did it?" Saint-Germain sounded surprised.

"He raised a few minor objections," Palamedes rumbled, "until Will threatened him with some horrible fungus disease." The Saracen Knight bowed. "Ladies: it is good to see you both."

"And you, Sir Knight," Joan said.

"Been a long time, Pally," Scathach added with a smile.

The knight made a pained face. "Please, don't call me Pally. I hate that."

"I know."

The hooded man had remained seated on the rock, bright blue eyes watching each immortal in turn, absently running his index finger along the length of the hook that took the place of his left hand.

William Shakespeare stepped forward, took off his black-framed glasses and wiped them on his sleeve. "I believe, sir, that we are due an explanation."

Although his mouth and nose were hidden by a scarf, the hooded man's eyes crinkled with amusement. "And I believe I will tell you only what I think you need to know, and no more."

Palamedes' hand moved and the broadsword strapped to his back appeared in his grip. "An explanation, and then you send us back to our own time."

The hooded man laughed. "Why, Sir Knight, you—none of you—can return home just yet."

Palamedes raised his sword and took a step forward.

"Oh, don't be stupid," the man said almost impatiently. Palamedes' sword suddenly turned into a length of wood, which quickly sprouted leaves. Vines immediately started to coil around the knight's wrist and arm. He dropped the sword to the ground, where it was swallowed into the earth, leaving nothing more than a darkened patch in the dirt by his feet.

"That was my favorite sword," the Saracen Knight muttered.

"This is my world," the hooded man said. "I created it. I control it and everything in it." He stretched his hook out over the water and moved it clockwise, and the pool instantly froze into a crackling sheet of ice. When he moved it counter-clockwise, the ice transformed into foul-smelling bubbling lava. "And right now," the man said, "you are here . . . which means that I control you." His hand moved again and the lava turned back into crystal-clear water.

Will Shakespeare stepped closer to the water's edge, then stooped to scoop up a handful of the liquid. He paused before he brought it to his lips. "I take it that it is safe to drink."

"I can make it any flavor you like."

The Bard sipped the water. "You're not going to kill us, are you?"

"I am not."

Shakespeare straightened slowly and looked closely at the hooded man. He frowned: there was something almost familiar about him. "Have we met before?"

The figure held up his left arm, tilting the hook so that it caught the sunlight. "If we had, I am sure you would have remembered this."

"Still, there is something about you . . . ," Shakespeare said, squinting hard at the man. "I feel I should know you."

The hooded man turned to Saint-Germain. "However, *we* have met before. It is good to see you again. You have prospered in the centuries since our last encounter."

"All thanks to you." Saint-Germain stepped forward and bowed. "It has just occurred to me that this is all your doing. You planned this. In fact, I think you've been planning this for a long time, haven't you?"

"Yes," the man said, surprising the others. "For a very long time."

"Flamel said he met you when he was traveling across Europe looking for someone to translate the Codex."

The hooded man bowed. "I met him and Mistress Perenelle briefly."

"And you taught me how to master the Magic of Fire."

"It was necessary. If I had not taught you what I knew, then sooner or later your own Fire magic would have consumed you. I needed to keep you alive."

"I'm grateful," Saint-Germain said.

The hooded man looked at each of them in turn. "I have worked hard to keep all of you alive and in good health— even you, Scathach," he added. "I have been waiting ten thousand years for this day to come."

"Ten thousand years?" Shakespeare asked.

"Since the Fall of Danu Talis."

"You were on the island?" Scathach breathed.

"Yes, I was. And so were you, Scathach, and you too, Palamedes, and you, Shakespeare and Saint-Germain and Joan. You were all there. You went to stand and fight with the original twins."

There was a long silence, when even the sounds of the landscape faded to stillness.

Finally, Scathach shook her head. "That's impossible. If I was on Danu Talis in the past, why don't I remember?"

"Because you've not been there yet," he said simply. He slid off the rock and stood before them. He was slightly taller than Saint-Germain, though not as tall as Palamedes. "I've gathered you here to take you back to Danu Talis with me. The twins need warriors they can trust. Come now, there is little time to waste."

"Just like that?" Palamedes demanded. "You cannot

expect us to travel into the past and fight just because you say so. Why should we fight for you?"

"You are not fighting for me," the hooded man said impatiently. "You are fighting for the continued existence of the human race. If you choose not to come, then Danu Talis will not sink and the creatures you know as humani will never rise to civilization. You have all in your differing ways been champions of the humani. It is time to champion their cause again."

"But we cannot go with you, not now," Saint-Germain said. "We've got to get back to our own time."

Joan nodded. "What about Nicholas and Perenelle and the creatures on Alcatraz that Dee and Machiavelli are about to release into the city? We need to fight with the Flamels."

The hooded man shook his head. "If we fail and Danu Talis is not destroyed, then nothing else matters."

"A moment," Shakespeare said. "You said Danu Talis *has* to fall."

"Of course. If the island is not destroyed, then there is no human history. The Elders will remain and the world you know will never have existed."

"But Nicholas and Perenelle . . . ," Joan began.

"I am afraid that the Flamels and the twins are on their own. You cannot help them. But you can help fight for an entire species. If you do not, there really is no reason to worry about the Flamels—for they will not exist."

The group was silent for a moment, trying to piece together what the man was saying. Danu Talis hadn't fallen yet because there had been no battle yet. And they themselves were the warriors who would fight the battle. A group brought together from the future to shape the events of the past.

"What if we refuse?" Saint-Germain asked. "Can you send us back to our own world? To Paris, Sherwood Forest or San Francisco?"

"No. It took an enormous expenditure of power to create this Pleistocene Shadowrealm; I have neither the power nor the ability to send you back to your own worlds. As soon as I leave the world, it will start to decay and die."

"So we really do not have much choice, then, do we," Saint-Germain said.

"There are always choices," the hooded man said quietly. "Some are just harder to make than others. You can come with me and live, or stay here and die."

"Those are not great choices," Palamedes said.

"They are the only choices you have."

"And on Danu Talis, we must fight?" the knight asked.

"Yes. You will fight—in the biggest battle you've ever fought."

Palamedes looked over at the Bard, and Shakespeare smiled and nodded. "I've always wanted to see a mythical land. I've got this idea for a play—all it needs is a setting. . . ."

"And I think I would like to see my birthplace before it sank," Scatty said, a strange note of urgency in her voice. She looked even paler than usual.

The hooded man's eyes crinkled again. "Yes. And you might get to see your parents."

The Shadow took a step back, suddenly looking startled. That was exactly the thought that had been in her head.

"I have a question," Joan said quietly, and everyone turned to look at her. "What is your name? You know us—indeed, you seem very familiar with us—but we've no idea who you are."

The hooded man nodded. "I have had many names through the centuries, but the one I prefer is the one I was first called on Danu Talis: Marethyu."

Scathach gasped and the immortal humans turned to her. Joan laid a hand on her friend's arm. "What does it mean?" She glanced over her shoulder at the hooded man.

"Tell them," he said to the Shadow.

"In the language of Danu Talis, it means 'death.' "

WEDNESDAY, *6th June*

CHAPTER FIFTY-TWO

$\mathcal{S}$ophie Newman knew the moment she awoke in the tiny cramped bedroom that something was wrong. There was a vague fluttering in the pit of her stomach and a dull ache at the back of her head, and she was painfully aware that her heart was pounding. Wrapping her arms tightly around her chest, she attempted to control her suddenly frantic breathing. What was happening to her: was this a panic attack? She'd never had one before, but her friend Elle in New York has them all the time. Sophie felt light-headed and just a little sick, and when she rolled out of bed and came to her feet, a wave of dizziness washed over her.

Stepping out into the hallway, she stopped and listened carefully. The little guesthouse was quiet. And it *felt* empty. With her left hand brushing the wall, she walked down the corridor into the kitchen. The night outside had started to pale toward dawn. Perry had told her that Prometheus kept his Shadowrealm in synch with earth time and it had a regular cycle of day and night.

The crystal skull sat in the center of the kitchen table.

Last night, she'd watched the Flamels put their hands on it, allowing their auras to sink into it. The crystal had glowed dully, the hint of ice-white, the merest suggestion of pale green winking deep within its core, but nothing else had happened, and the effort had exhausted Nicholas.

Sophie hurried past it. She didn't see the crystal as it pulsed silver and the eye sockets darkened, filling with shadow. The light faded as she moved away from the table and walked to the couch, where Josh had spent the night.

But the couch was empty.

"Josh?" she said, her voice barely above a whisper. Maybe he was in the bathroom, or he'd probably gone up to the main house looking for food. Yet even as she was making excuses, she knew they weren't true. When Josh had returned after learning the Magic of Fire from Prometheus, he had been ashen-faced, staggering with exhaustion. He'd fallen sound asleep the moment he'd crawled onto the couch.

"Josh?" she called again. "Josh?"

The fluttering in her stomach was worse now, like really bad indigestion, and her heart was racing so fast she was feeling breathless.

"Josh!" Louder now. "Where are you?" If this was a joke, it wasn't funny. "Josh Newman, you come here right this minute!"

She heard movement at the door and the handle turned.

Spinning toward it, Sophie put her hands on her hips. "Just where have you—"

The door swung open and Aoife stepped into the room, followed by Niten. The Japanese immortal carried two swords, one much longer than the other, while Aoife clutched a long ugly leaf-bladed knife.

"It's Josh," Sophie began breathlessly. "He's missing."

They split up without a word, Niten moving to the right, Aoife to the left. The guest cottage was tiny and they were back in the kitchen within moments. "No sign of a struggle," Niten said calmly. "Looks like he just walked out." He turned and disappeared back into the night, leaving Sophie alone with Aoife.

"He's gone," Sophie whispered. "He's gone." It was all she could say as waves of panic began to wash over her.

Aoife returned the knife to the sheath strapped to her leg. "Talk to me," she said. "What happened?"

Sophie shook her head. "When I woke up, I felt . . ." She pressed both hands to her stomach as she searched for the words.

"Empty," Aoife suggested.

Sophie looked at the red-haired warrior. "Yes," she breathed, suddenly able to identify the feeling. "I feel empty. I've never felt that way before."

Aoife nodded, her pale face expressionless.

Niten opened the door and spoke quickly to the warrior in Japanese, then turned and raced away.

"What's wrong? What's happening?" Sophie was starting

311

to feel breathless with terror again. "What's happened to my brother?" she asked. Static curled through her hair, and tendrils of her silver aura smoked off her skin. She began to shake, and Aoife stepped forward and wrapped her arms around her, holding her tightly. When Aoife spoke, her voice echoed inside Sophie's head, and even though she used the ancient Irish tongue of her youth, Sophie understood every word. "Breathe deeply, calm yourself. . . . You need to be in control now. For your sake. For Josh's sake."

Sophie shook her head. "I can't. You don't know what it feels like. . . ."

"Yes," Aoife said in a fierce whisper. "Yes. I do."

And when Sophie looked up, she found the warrior's green eyes sparkling and bright with tears. "I lost my own twin," Aoife said. "I know exactly how you're feeling."

Sophie nodded. She drew in a deep shuddering breath. "What did Niten tell you just now?" she asked.

"He said the car is missing."

Before Sophie could ask anything else, the door opened and Perenelle stepped into the cottage, followed by Nicholas and Prometheus, making the small room seem even tinier. Niten came last, but he remained in the open doorway, facing out into the night.

"Gone?" Nicholas snapped in French.

"Missing," Aoife agreed.

"Was he taken?" Perenelle asked.

"Nothing can get into this Shadowrealm without my knowledge," Prometheus said.

Perenelle went to Sophie and opened her arms, but the

girl made no move to close the distance. She remained with the warrior. The Sorceress took a step back and allowed her arms to drop to her sides. "So he went of his own accord?" she asked.

"There are no signs of a struggle," Niten said from the doorway. "And only one set of footprints heading down the valley toward the car."

"But the car was dead," Nicholas answered, "the battery drained."

Prometheus folded his arms across his massive chest. "Yes, but the boy has learned the Magic of Fire. All that raw energy is coursing through his aura right now. He could easily have sparked the car to life."

"Where did he go?" Sophie asked. "I don't understand. He wouldn't have just left without telling me." She looked at Prometheus. "Maybe something here took him? Maybe those mud people?"

Prometheus shook his head. "The First People will not approach the house. I agree with Perenelle: he went of his own accord."

"But where has he gone?" Sophie asked again. "Home?" She shook her head. She had never, in all her life, been so confused or felt so lost. "He wouldn't have left me."

"*Why* is he gone, is the better question," Aoife said.

But Perenelle shook her head. "No, the real question is, who called him? I wonder . . . ," she began, then stopped. The Sorceress turned and made her way to the kitchen table. Sitting down, she held her hands on either side of the crystal skull, not touching it, and looked over at Sophie. Her lips were drawn into a thin, almost bitter smile. "Perhaps you will lend us your aura now."

"Why?" Sophie whispered, completely confused.

"So we can try to see your brother. See if he's gone of his own accord or if he's been kidnapped."

Aoife rested her hand on the girl's shoulder. "If you possess my grandmother's memories, then you know just how dangerous the skull is, Sophie." She lowered her voice. "While you're looking into the skull, it is looking into you. Stare too long into its crystal depths and you can—quite literally—lose your mind. You don't have to do this."

"Yes I do," Sophie said simply. She looked into the vampire's eyes. "You said yourself that you would do everything in your power to get Scathach back. . . ."

Aoife started to nod.

"I'll do the same for Josh."

The warrior stared at her, and then she pulled out a chair. "That I truly understand. Sit. I will stand guard over you." For an instant the hard lines of her face softened, and she was the image of her sister.

"Go raibh maith agat," Sophie whispered in Irish, a language she had never learned. "Thank you." She looked into the warrior's face.

Aoife nodded. "Scathach would have done the same," she murmured.

"Put your hands on the crystal skull," Perenelle commanded.

CHAPTER FIFTY-THREE

*J*osh knew it was a dream, nothing more than a particularly vivid dream.

He dreamt that he was driving Niten's black limousine north along Sir Francis Drake Boulevard. It was still night overhead, though the sky to his right was already starting to lighten.

It was one of those dreams that were perfect in every detail. Sometimes he dreamt in black-and-white and without sound, but this was in color, and he could even smell the polished leather interior of the car and the vaguely floral scent from some hidden air conditioner. He sniffed. There was another odor too: the smell of burning plastic. A curl of gray smoke drifted past his eyes and he looked down. At first he thought he was wearing red-gold gloves; then he realized that his hands were glowing hot and actually melting into the steering wheel. As he pulled them away, threads of sticky rubber and plastic, like chewing gum, stretched from the wheel.

It wasn't a scary dream. It was just . . . odd.

He wondered where he was going.

"Think of your brother," Perenelle commanded.

Sophie took a deep breath and rested both hands on the skull. Instantly the crystal turned a rich metallic silver, making it appear as if it had been carved out of metal.

"Think of Josh," Nicholas said.

Sophie concentrated on visualizing her brother, determined to see him in every detail. The skull's empty eye sockets turned dark, then mirror bright, and abruptly an image formed in the air above the crystal, but it was vague and fragmented, little more than a smear of colors.

Sophie felt Aoife's fingers tighten on her shoulders, and a cool strength soaked into her flesh. She realized that the warrior was giving her some of the strength of her gray aura, and then she felt the woman's breath warm against her right ear. "Think of your twin," Aoife commanded.

Her twin brother: the same blond hair, the same blue eyes. Twenty-eight seconds her junior. Until they were three, no one had been able to tell them apart.

And suddenly the shifting colors floating above the skull whirled and settled, taking on shape and definition. They were looking at the image of a melting steering wheel. They were seeing through Josh's eyes.

316

After a while, the dream became boring.

Josh wished he could wake himself up.

He drove for a long time on Sir Francis Drake Boulevard, then turned right onto Highway 1 and then Shoreline Highway. It was a narrow two-lane road, wreathed in early-morning mist that bounced off his headlights, but he wasn't concerned. Nothing could happen to him in a dream. If he crashed, he'd wake up. Still, it was a shame it was a driving dream; it would have been much better if it had been a flying dream. He loved those.

"How is he doing this?" Sophie whispered. "Is he awake or asleep?"

Nicholas leaned forward, put his elbows on the table and rested his chin in his cupped hands. He stared hard at the images hovering in the air over the skull. "He is probably aware on some level, but something has taken control of him. I believe that something—someone—has called to him."

Prometheus eyed the skull with an expression of profound disgust. "If I'd known you had that abominable thing, I would not have allowed you to bring it into this Shadowrealm. My sister spent most of her life and squandered the family fortune destroying these Archon toys."

Nicholas glanced sidelong at Perenelle before looking up at Prometheus. "Archon? I thought these were Elder."

Prometheus ignored the question, concentrating his attention on the perfect three-dimensional image floating above the skull. "We could possibly shock him awake."

317

"No!" Sophie said immediately, instinct warning her that it would be the wrong thing to do.

"No," Aoife agreed. "He could lose control of the car."

"So we sit and wait for him to reach his destination?" Prometheus asked.

"Well." Perenelle spoke without removing her gaze from the image above the skull. "I believe our first duty is to try to ensure that he reach his destination safely. If he crashes, he could be badly injured or killed. Sophie"—the tone of the Sorceress's voice softened—"concentrate on your brother, make him focus on his driving."

"How?" she asked desperately. She was having a hard time controlling the panic that threatened to overwhelm her. "How do I do that?"

Perenelle looked blank. She turned to Nicholas, but he shook his head. "I don't know," she admitted. "Just don't let him do anything stupid."

"This is Josh we're talking about," Sophie muttered. "He does stupid things all the time." And always when she wasn't there.

He was thinking about driving really fast.

This section of Shoreline Highway was relatively straight, and the fog wasn't too thick. He could put his foot to the floor and just roar down the road.

Sophie wouldn't like that.

The thought popped into his head even as his foot was pressing on the accelerator.

This was a dream.

Sophie wouldn't like that.

His foot eased off the accelerator. He shook his head. Even in his dreams, she still tried to be the boss.

The group had been sitting around the table for more than ninety minutes, and Sophie was shaking with fatigue.

Aoife stood over her, both hands on her shoulders, pouring strength into her, but Sophie's silver aura was now almost entirely the same pewter gray as the warrior's, and the images hovering over the skull had faded and become almost transparent. "I'm not sure . . . how much longer . . . I can keep this up," Sophie whispered. Her head was thumping and there were solid bars of pain across her taut shoulders and down her spine.

"Where is he now?" Flamel rasped, trying to make sense of the images, the snatched glimpses of streets and landmarks.

Niten leaned over Aoife's shoulder, squinting at the flickering color image. "Turning off Van Ness Avenue onto Bay Street."

Perenelle looked up at Prometheus. "Who is he going to? There must be some Dark Elders in San Francisco."

"Several," he said matter-of-factly. "Quetzalcoatl, the Feathered Serpent, keeps a house here, but this is too subtle for him. Eris is here; she used to hang out in Haight-Ashbury and still keeps an apartment there, but her glory days are over. She hasn't got this sort of power." The Elder suddenly leaned forward. "Sophie, have you any control over your twin?"

She looked at him, her eyes dull with fatigue.

"Can you make him turn or look in a certain direction?"

"I don't know. Why?"

"See if you can get him to adjust the mirror. I want to see his eyes."

Josh fiddled with the heater.

He turned on the radio but there was only static, so he rooted through the collection of CDs, but they were all by people he'd never heard of: Isao Tomita, Kodo and Kitaro. He adjusted the seat back and forth, up and down, checked the glove compartment, found a tin of mints that were two years past the expiration but ate them anyway, fiddled with the air conditioner, adjusted the electric side mirrors and then, finally, reached for the rearview mirror. . . .

His eyes were bloodred.

Reflected in the mirror, they hung in the air over the crystal skull, unblinking, unmoving, without a trace of pupil.

The wave of horror that struck Sophie was palpable. She was looking at her brother's face, but these were the eyes of . . .

"Mars Ultor," Prometheus said firmly. "The boy is in thrall to the Sleeping God."

"Mars Awakened Josh," Nicholas whispered, aghast.

"And so he controls him," the Elder said.

"But where is he taking him?" the Alchemyst said.

"They've just turned onto Lombard Street," Niten announced. "He's going to Telegraph Hill."

"Dee's company, Enoch Enterprises has offices just below

Coit Tower," Perenelle said quickly, then added, as if she was thinking out loud, "but Dee is trapped in England. There is no way he could have gotten here. . . ."

"Are you sure?" Prometheus asked. "This is Dee we're talking about now."

Nicholas nodded. "Even if he booked a flight this morning, he'd still be in the air. He's not in the city."

"What about a leygate?" Aoife asked.

"There are only a few that could bring him here. And he hasn't got the power to charge up the Stonehenge gate. Also, using his power would betray his location to his Dark Elder masters. And I'm not sure he'd want to do that."

"He's turned up Telegraph Hill," Niten said. "That's a dead end."

In his dream state, Josh really had no idea where he was.

He'd driven through San Francisco, turning left and right, only vaguely aware of the street names—Van Ness Avenue, Bay Street, Columbus and Lombard. Some were almost familiar, but when he finally turned the car onto Telegraph Hill, he suddenly realized where he was: close to Coit Tower. Although the tower was within walking distance of Aunt Agnes's house, he and Sophie had never managed to find the time to visit it. To his left, he could see the Bay Bridge, while on his right he saw expensive-looking houses and apartments. He drove on, and as the road rose, he could see the city, which was beginning to appear out of the fog.

The view was stunning, but he was completely bored with this dream. He wanted it to end so he could wake up. He was half tempted to drive the car off the road just to see what would happen.

Sophie wouldn't like that.

Josh shook the thought from his head. When he looked back to the road, however, a woman had appeared. The instant he saw her, Josh knew she was there to meet him, and he was already slowing and turning into the curb as she raised a hand and smiled. He stopped and hit the switch that rolled down the window. She was young and pretty and was dressed in jeans and a fringed black suede jacket. A thick mane of jet-black hair flowed to the small of her back. And when the woman leaned in the window and smiled at him, Josh noticed that her eyes were the same color as his aunt Agnes's, the same color as Dr. John Dee's. He took a deep breath and was overwhelmed by the distinctive odor of sage.

And because this was a dream, the woman knew his name. "Hello, Josh Newman. We've been waiting for you."

"Virginia Dare," Prometheus said grimly. "The killer."

Sophie was the only one not to turn to look at the Elder. She focused on the woman's face, seeing it through Josh's eyes.

"Her master was a friend of mine," Prometheus continued. "Because of her, he is dead."

Nicholas looked at his wife. "Wasn't Dare once associated with Dee?" he asked.

"A long time ago, but I don't believe they've seen one

322

another in centuries. Still, it cannot be a coincidence that she is here."

"I agree," the Alchemyst answered grimly. "There are no such things as coincidences."

The images were flickering wildly now, fading in and out like a badly tuned television set. "I'm losing the connection," Sophie whispered. She turned her head to look up at Aoife. "Help me. Please."

The warrior's strong hands tightened on the girl's shoulders, holding her upright, pouring strength into her.

Josh followed the woman up to a smoked-glass door with the words *Enoch Enterprises* in fancy gold script on the glass. He saw her reach for the intercom button, but the door swung open wide before she had a chance to press it. And because this was still a dream, he was unsurprised to find a smiling Dr. John Dee waiting for him.

"Josh Newman, it is good to see you again. You're looking well, and I understand you're a Master of Fire now." Dee stepped back. "Enter freely and of your own will."

Without hesitation, Josh stepped through the door.

Nearly seventy miles away, in the last flickering ghostlike images, the silent watchers heard Dee ask, "So, Josh, how would you like to learn one of the most powerful of all the magics—something not even the legendary Nicholas Flamel could teach you?"

"That would be cool," Josh said.

And then the door clicked shut and the image died.

Sophie drew in a deep shuddering breath and peeled her hands off the now-warm crystal skull. She slumped forward and would have fallen if Aoife had not been holding her. She looked at the Alchemyst. "What can Dee teach him that you can't?" she rasped hoarsely, sick with worry.

Nicholas shook his head. "I've no idea. We studied very similar disciplines: alchemy, mathematics, astronomy, astrology, biology, medicine—" He stopped suddenly.

"Except?" Sophie asked.

"There is one." All the color had drained from Nicholas's face, and the dark rings under his eyes were pronounced. "There was one art I refused to learn—but one which Dee mastered and excelled in."

"No!" Perenelle drew in a quick shocked breath.

"Necromancy," the Alchemyst said. "The art of raising the dead."

CHAPTER FIFTY-FOUR

Standing at the prow of a speedboat bouncing across the icy waters of San Francisco Bay, Niccolò Machiavelli closed his eyes and allowed the salt spray to hide the sudden tears on his face.

When Machiavelli had still been mortal, his wife, Marietta, had once accused him of being an uncaring inhuman monster. "You will die lonely and alone, because you don't care for anyone," she'd screamed at him, and thrown an antique Roman plate at his head. He'd long since forgotten what the argument was about, but he'd never forgotten the words. And whenever he thought of them, he remembered Marietta, whom he had loved dearly and still missed, and he wept for her. He never minded the tears: they reminded him that he was still human.

He'd once thought that being immortal was an extraordinary gift.

And in the beginning it was. He had all the time in the world to plot and scheme, to lay plans that would take generations to complete. Working behind the scenes, he had shaped the destinies of a dozen European and Russian nations, had organized wars and revolutions and arranged peace treaties. He had backed leaders, funded inventors, invested in artists and designers. Then he had sat back and watched his grand plans unfold. But somewhere amid all the scheming and plotting, he had stopped thinking about the individuals he was manipulating. He thought of the humani—the humans—merely as objects to be pushed about like pieces on a chessboard.

He had served his Elder master devotedly, doing as he was told even when he disagreed with his orders. Initially, he had believed—because it was the logical conclusion—that the earth would be a better place if the Dark Elders returned.

Now he was not so sure.

He hadn't been sure for the past two hundred years.

And today . . . today everything had changed. The turning point had come when he had sat facing Quetzalcoatl the Feathered Serpent and listened while the arrogant Elder almost casually determined whether Machiavelli should live or die. Shockingly, the only reason he had been allowed to live was because Quetzalcoatl felt that he owed Machiavelli's master a favor. No consideration was given to the centuries of loyal service Machiavelli had performed for the Elders. His skills, his knowledge, his experience, were all dismissed.

His life had been spared by nothing more than chance.

And sitting in that chair, arguing for his life, it had struck him that on far too many occasions he had acted just like Quetzalcoatl. He had passed judgment on the lives of countless men, women and children he had never met and would never know. He had made decisions that would shape their lives and the lives of their descendants for generations to come.

Marietta was right: he didn't care for anyone.

But she was also wrong. He had always cared for her and adored his children, especially his son Guido, who had been born a few short years before Machiavelli's "death."

What had happened? What had changed him?

It all came back to the same answer: *immortality*.

Immortality had transformed him utterly, had warped his thinking, had made him the uncaring inhuman monster Marietta had accused him of being long before he actually was. He had stopped thinking of humans as individuals—he thought of them as masses of people, as either enemies or friends.

He had become blinded by his own ambition. In his arrogance he had thought that he was different from the humans, that he was, in some way, like the Elders. But today, he had realized that the Elders thought as much of him as he thought of the rest of the human population.

And now he was on another mission for the Elders, one that would affect the lives of millions of people all across the globe. He had tinkered with the destiny of nations; now he was about to reshape the future of the world.

"I'm not liking what I'm seeing," Billy the Kid drawled, taking up a position alongside the Italian.

Machiavelli looked toward the fast-approaching island. "Is something wrong?"

"Not over there. Here," Billy said. He shoved his hands into the back pockets of his jeans and pitched his voice just above the hum of the engine and the splashing of the waves so that only Machiavelli could hear it. "You've got a look on your face that I don't like."

Machiavelli composed himself. "A look?"

"Yep. The look of someone who is thinking deep thoughts. Dark thoughts. Stupid thoughts."

"And you would be an expert on facial expressions?" Machiavelli said sarcastically.

"Sure am," Billy said, blue eyes twinkling. "Kept me alive long enough."

"And what do you think my face reveals?" Machiavelli asked. He'd always been able to keep his face expressionless and was irritated that this uneducated young immortal had managed to read him so easily. Perhaps he had underestimated the American.

Billy took a hand out of his back pocket and rubbed it across his chin, stubble rasping. "You've never been in a gunfight?" he asked.

Machiavelli blinked in surprise. "Don't be ridiculous. Of course not."

"What about a duel? Didn't you have duels in Europe—swords and pistols at dawn, that sort of thing?"

The Italian nodded. "I've attended some."

"I bet you always knew who was going to lose."

Machiavelli considered, then nodded. "Yes. I suppose I did."

"How could you tell?" Billy asked.

"From the expression on their face, the way they stood, the set of their shoulders . . ."

"Exactly. They expected to lose. And therefore, they lost. Now, I was never a great shot, and never very fast. All that quick-draw nonsense comes from books written about me, and most of those are lies. But I always expected to win. *Always.* And I made sure to associate with others who expected to win." He paused and added, "People who start thinking deep dark thoughts in the middle of a war start expecting to lose. And they end up dead because they're not thinking straight, they're not focused."

Machiavelli's head tilted in a slight bow. "That is a very astute observation. And do you have a suggestion?"

Billy nodded toward the island. "Let's stay focused on the task at hand. Let's do what our Elder masters have commanded and awaken these sleeping beasts, before we start thinking deep dark thoughts."

"We?"

"We." Billy smiled. "I bet you could teach me a lot."

Machiavelli nodded, surprised. "And I believe I could learn a lot from you."

The boat bumped against the dock and Black Hawk pulled them in against the wooden pilings. "All ashore," he called.

Billy the Kid leapt onto the wooden gangway and then

stooped to offer his hand to the Italian. Machiavelli hesitated a moment, then took it, and Billy hauled him up. Black Hawk immediately revved the engine, water churning white as he backed away.

"Are you not joining us?" Billy asked.

"You must be joking! I wouldn't set foot on this island. It is a cursed place." Even as he was speaking, dozens of women's faces appeared just below the surface of the water. Iridescent fishtails flickered. "Call me when you're done. Will you be long?"

Billy looked at Machiavelli and raised his eyebrows.

"A couple of hours."

Billy the Kid grinned. "Time enough to change the world."

CHAPTER FIFTY-FIVE

Sitting alone at the kitchen table with the crystal skull between them, Nicholas and Perenelle Flamel looked at one another. The Alchemyst's shoulders slumped, exhaustion clear on his face and in his sunken eyes. Taking a deep breath, he looked at his wife and said, "So what do we do now?"

Perenelle absently reached out to stroke the skull. She could actually feel the vague tingling residue of Sophie's and Aoife's auras on the crystal. "This changes nothing," she said finally. "We fight."

Nicholas wheezed a laugh. "Look at us . . . well, look at *me*. I can't help you."

"Between us we have more than a millennium of knowledge," Perenelle reminded him gently. "We use our brains; that's all we need."

The door opened and Prometheus stepped back into the room. "Niten and Aoife have gone with Sophie. I've given them a car," he said. "But it'll take them two and a half, maybe three hours to get into the city."

"Three hours?" Perenelle looked at Nicholas. "Could Dee teach Josh anything about necromancy in that time?"

"Last night, Josh learned Fire magic in a couple of hours. . . ."

"He learned the basics. But it will take him a lifetime to master it," Prometheus said.

"And who knows what Dee can do," Nicholas added. "How he got here from London is beyond me."

"He's been declared *utlaga*," the Elder said. "The message rippled through the Shadowrealms yesterday. His own masters have put an enormous price on his head."

"They want him dead?" Nicholas was shocked.

There was only pity in Prometheus's laugh. "They want him alive first."

The Alchemyst sat back into the creaking kitchen chair and rubbed his face with his hands. "But this changes everything," he said. "If Dee is no longer working for the Dark Elders, why does he need Josh? Why would he want to teach him necromancy?"

Prometheus moved away from the door. "Dee obviously has his own plans," he said.

"Dee and Dare," Perenelle reminded them. "A dangerous combination."

"And now Josh, too," Nicholas whispered. "A gold twin, trained in Water and Fire magics."

Prometheus pulled out a chair and spun it around so that he could straddle it. It creaked ominously under his weight.

Nicholas squinted into the Elder's face. "What happens if a pure gold twin, knowledgeable in the Magics of Water and Fire, is trained in necromancy?"

Prometheus shook his head. "It has never happened before, to the best of my knowledge. It is a powerful combination, but the real potential lies in the strength of his aura. The boy is extraordinarily powerful . . . he simply does not realize that yet."

"Dee does," Nicholas muttered.

"So Josh is more powerful than Dee?" Perenelle asked.

"Yes, I believe so. Much more powerful," Prometheus agreed. "Just untrained."

"And necromancy raises the dead, and with Josh's power . . ." Perenelle began slowly.

Nicholas finished the thought. "So whom—or what—does Dee want to raise from the dead?" He placed his hand flat on top of the crystal skull. "If we could only see what's happening . . ." A pale green light pulsed once deep within the skull and then faded. Perenelle placed her hand on top of her husband's. Speckles of white crawled along her fingertips, sank through Flamel's wrinkled flesh and seeped into the crystal. A white light tinted with the hint of green throbbed in the eye sockets. Then it faded. "We're not strong enough." Nicholas slumped back into the chair, though Perenelle kept his hand pressed to the crystal.

"Why did you bring this evil thing?" Prometheus asked.

"We were going to use it to try to control the monsters on Alcatraz," Perenelle explained. "Areop-Enap is still on the island. I thought if we could see through the Old Spider's eyes, we would be able to turn the creatures against one another. Many of them are natural enemies. I thought it might buy us a little time until Sophie and Josh were fully trained."

"A good plan," Prometheus agreed. "But you need to fuel the skull with your auras."

"We were rather counting on Sophie and Josh to help us."

The Elder looked at each of them in turn. "You do realize that when you are feeding the skull, it is feeding off you, drinking your auras, your memories, your emotions," he said slowly. "The skulls are true vampires. The twins are young; the process would have taken a few years off their lives, but they would have survived. In your present state, you would not."

"We have spent our entire lives fighting for the survival of the human race," Perenelle said quietly. "We cannot stop now. We will fight to our last breaths to protect it from the Dark Elders."

"You would have paid a heavy price."

"Everything has a price," Nicholas said simply. "And some prices are worth paying." He drew in a deep breath and looked at the Elder. "You paid a heavy price for bringing the humani to life."

Prometheus nodded.

"Have you ever regretted it?"

"Not for a moment." Prometheus stared at the skull. "Not for a single moment," he said softly, and then grunted a bitter laugh. "Crystal libraries, my sister called these. She suspected that they might even have been partially responsible for the annihilation of the Archon race, and she destroyed as many as she could. Some knowledge should not be passed on, she said. And there was one piece of advice she gave me time and again: an Elder must never, *ever*, touch the skulls."

"Why not?" Nicholas asked.

Prometheus ignored the question. He reached out and placed his hand on top of the Flamels'. Instantly, the room was flooded with the smell of aniseed and the skull turned a deep ruby color. "I can link to the boy, but you will need to focus on the Magician," he said almost apologetically. "Are you sure you want to do this? It will age you."

"Do it," Perenelle said, and the Alchemyst nodded.

"Then let us see what the Magician has in store for the boy," the Elder said through gritted teeth as images formed over the skull: crystal-clear pictures in vivid color.

And suddenly they were looking through Josh Newman's eyes at Virginia Dare's face.

CHAPTER FIFTY-SIX

"*C*an't you drive any faster?" Aoife snapped. "I could push this heap quicker."

"My foot is flat to the floor," Niten said calmly, "but the vehicle is forty years old and it's only got a fifty-horsepower engine."

"Piece of junk," Aoife muttered. She looked at Sophie stretched out on the long backseat behind them. Reaching over, she pulled a blanket across the girl's shoulders. "You'd think an Elder would have a better car than this antiquated minivan," she said, turning back to Niten.

"I'm surprised Prometheus even had a car. And it's not a minivan, it's a microbus. I like it," the Japanese immortal said. "This is a 1964 Volkswagen Microbus. And it still has its original red and white paint job. Usually they're painted all the colors of the rainbow."

"Listen to you. Since when did you become such a car expert?" Aoife asked sarcastically.

The tiniest of smiles moved Niten's lips. "You *do* know that I collect classic cars, don't you?"

Aoife looked at him in surprise. "No," she said finally. "I never knew that."

"How long have you known me, Aoife?" he asked in formal Japanese.

She frowned and replied in the same language. "There was a battle, I seem to recall."

"We met at the Battle of Sekigahara in 1600."

She nodded slowly. "Yes, I remember."

"I thought you were Scathach," he reminded her.

Aoife smiled and nodded again.

"But the moment we started to fight, I knew you were not the girl I had fought before. You had a different style."

"And I defeated you," she reminded him.

"You did," he agreed. "Just the once." He turned the big steering wheel, maneuvering the van onto the narrow two-lane highway. "So you've known me—what?—for more than four hundred years . . . and yet, what do you really know about me?"

Aoife stared at the slender black-suited man and shook her head. "Not a lot," she admitted.

"And why is that?" he asked.

She shrugged.

"Because you were never interested," Niten said gently. "You are the most self-obsessed, selfish person I know."

The warrior blinked in surprise. "You say that like it's a bad thing."

"This is not a criticism," he continued, "merely an observation."

They drove in silence for a long time before Aoife said, "So, after four hundred years, why are you telling me this now?"

"I am just curious," Niten said. His dark brown eyes drifted to the rearview mirror, and he tilted it so that he could look at Sophie. "You don't know this girl. You only met her yesterday, and I got the impression that you either did not like her or were afraid of her."

"I am afraid of no one," Aoife said automatically.

Niten bowed. "You are fearless in battle," Niten agreed diplomatically. "So why are we now driving her toward a confrontation with a dangerous and powerful adversary?"

Aoife stared straight ahead, and when she finally answered, her voice sounded lost and distant. "She is looking for her twin," she whispered.

"And is that the only reason?" he probed gently.

"She asked for my help, Niten," Aoife said quietly. "Do you know who the last person was to ask me for help?"

Niten shook his head, though he suspected he knew the answer.

"My twin, Scathach," she murmured. "And I refused." She turned to look at Sophie again. "I don't want to make that mistake twice."

"Aoife, this girl is not your twin."

"But she asked for my help, old friend. It's been a long

time since anyone asked me for anything. I have a . . ." She paused, hunting for the right word. "I have a duty."

"Ah, duty. That I understand." The Japanese immortal turned right onto Shoreline Highway, heading for San Francisco. "It is duty and responsibility that separates humankind from the beasts . . . and the Elders," he added. "No offense."

"None taken."

They continued in silence for many miles, and then, much later, Aoife said, "So, tell me about this car collection of yours. I mean, are we talking real cars or just models?"

CHAPTER FIFTY-SEVEN

"*H*e looks so young," Virginia Dare said, staring into Josh's unblinking red eyes.

"He's fifteen and a half," Dee said absently. "You *could* help me here," he added. He was standing in the middle of his living room, attempting to push the heavy sofas out of the way to clear a space in the center of the floor.

"I don't push furniture," Virginia said, still staring at Josh. "These red eyes are creepy. I've only seen them a couple of times before."

"The boy was Awakened by Mars Ultor. . . ."

Virginia Dare's head snapped up. "The Avenger is still alive?" she gasped.

Dee's smile was cruel. "Sort of. As you know, there is always a connection between an Elder and the humani he or she Awakens. Sometimes—though not always—the same Elder will offer the humani immortality."

Virginia nodded. "That's what happened to me. My Elder Awakened me when I was a child and then, fifteen years later, made me immortal."

"One day you're going to tell me who that Elder was," Dee grunted, trying to move an enormous black leather lounger. "Why did I buy this?" he muttered.

"Is he asleep?" she asked, waving her hand in front of Josh's eyes. They remained open and unblinking.

"He's in a dream state. He's aware enough to walk and talk and drive, but he's only semiconscious. No doubt he believes all of this is a dream."

"Like hypnosis?"

"Just like hypnosis," Dee agreed. He finally managed to get the chair up against a wall and collapsed into it. "I'm getting too old for this," he wheezed.

"Doctor," Virginia said quietly, "you need to see this."

The tone in the woman's voice brought Dee quickly across the room. Josh was sitting on a stool at the kitchen table. The four swords and the Codex were on the glass tabletop before him, where Dee had left them. When the boy had rested his hands on the table, all of the swords had immediately started to glow, throbbing gently like beating hearts. There was the sudden odor of oranges, and abruptly the glass surface turned into a sheet of solid gold.

Virginia tapped the gold with her fingernail. "Now, that's impressive."

"The boy is powerful indeed," Dee said. "I've never seen a pure Gold before."

Gossamer threads of Josh's gold aura drifted across the

341

table like smoke, curling around the stone swords. Crackling sparks leapt from blade to blade. Particles of ice sparkled across Excalibur and red-black smoke drifted off Clarent; gritty brown sand formed on Joyeuse's blade, and Durendal's surface rippled as if a chill breeze were blowing across it. Then the heavy copper cover of the Codex flapped open and the pages began to riffle as if blown by a strong breeze. Dee carefully reached out and lifted the book off the table. "He is so strong," the Magician said, "it seems almost a shame to have to kill him."

CHAPTER FIFTY-EIGHT

Josh.
    Wake up.
    Josh. Wake up.
    Josh.

And Josh woke up, hearing Nicholas and Perenelle Flamel's voices ringing in his head.

He remembered lying down on the uncomfortable couch in Prometheus's guesthouse; then there was a dream . . . a long, boring dream.

Or was it a dream?

He was sitting on a high stool in a modern-looking apartment, with Dr. John Dee and the almost-familiar-looking young woman from his dream watching him.

"You're awake!" Dee said, sounding surprised.

Confusion gave way to fear, which quickly turned to

anger. "What have you done to me?" Instinctively, Josh snatched Clarent from the table and slid off the stool, holding the sword in both hands. Instantly, he felt its familiar heat flow up his body, and his aura started to harden into gold-plated armor around his flesh. He looked around quickly, trying to get his bearings. "Where am I? Where's my sister? What have you done with Sophie?"

Keeping the Codex pressed close to his chest, Dee stepped right up to the tip of the outstretched blade. "Do you remember the dream, Josh? The dream of the long drive?"

Josh took a step backward and nodded.

Dee stepped forward. "That was no dream."

"What did you do—put a spell on me?" he said, horrified by the thought.

Dee shrugged. "I don't like the word *spell*—it's so old-fashioned. Technically, I asked Mars Ultor to call you. You are connected to him; you will remain connected to him for the rest of your life."

"Where am I?" Josh asked, though he already had an inkling of the answer.

"You know where you are: in San Francisco, just below Coit Tower, in the offices of Enoch Enterprises, my company."

Clarent was shivering in Josh's grip. Golden gloves had formed around his hands and forearms, but the metal around his palms and fingertips where he held the sword was stained rust-red.

"So thank you for coming," Dee continued, smiling as if

nothing were out of the ordinary. He half turned. "This is my associate, Miss Virginia Dare."

The woman nodded but didn't smile. Josh noticed that she had a wooden stick—a flute?—in her hand.

"Miss Dare is, like myself, an immortal." Dee turned quickly to Josh. "Would you like that, do you think? Would you want to become immortal?"

Josh blinked in surprise. Listening to Nicholas, then Scathach and Aoife talking about it, he'd vaguely wondered what it would be like to live forever, but he'd never actually thought about it seriously. "I'm not sure," he said.

"I can't make you immortal, nor can Virginia, but we know Elders who could grant you that gift," Dee continued. "In fact, Mars would probably make you immortal if you asked."

Completely confused now by the bizarre situation, Josh looked from the Magician to the woman. "I'm not sure I . . ."

"He's too young to become immortal," Virginia said abruptly. "He's still a boy. He would be trapped as a boy forever. Ask him again in five years' time."

Dee smiled, gray eyes sparkling. "In five years. Yes, what a good idea. We'll put that question to you then. Think about it," he said lightly. "To be twenty-one forever."

"I want to go," Josh said, looking around for a way out.

"Of course." The Magician pointed with the hand holding the Codex. "There is a lift over there, and a staircase in the corner."

Josh blinked in surprise. "I can just leave?" he asked.

"Of course." Dee laughed. "Josh, I am not your enemy. I have never been your enemy. I told you the last time we met who the Flamels were—*what* they were. Didn't I?"

Josh nodded and he slowly lowered the sword.

"You've been with them—what?—a week. I daresay you've discovered some unpleasant things about them yourself."

Josh nodded again.

"And the question is, of course: what else have they lied to you about?"

"We learned about the other twins," Josh admitted. He was reminded again of the great difference between Dee and Flamel. The Alchemyst always seemed to be talking down to him; the Magician spoke to him as an equal.

"Did they tell you how many?"

Josh shook his head. "I got the impression that there had been a dozen, something like that."

Dee shook his head. "Hundreds," he said. "Well, hundreds that we know of. When they could not find twins, they went hunting individuals with gold and silver auras—and when they could not find gold, they took any shades they could find: bronze, orange, even reds, and when there was no silver to be found, they used gray, alabaster, even white. Some children went willingly with them, others they bought, some they even kidnapped."

"What happened to them?" Josh asked in a horrified whisper. "Flamel said some survived."

"Flamel lies."

"Tell me what happened to them!" Josh demanded this time, his voice rising to a shout.

Dee turned away, shaking his head. "It is too horrible to even think about. Did you ask the Alchemyst?"

"He didn't give us a real answer."

"Well, that tells you all you need to know," Dee said. "Josh, let me say this to you again: I am not your enemy. I have always dealt fairly and truthfully with you. And, you'll admit, I have always answered your questions. Can you say that about the Alchemyst and his wife?"

Josh shook his head. He was frightened now—terrified—because his sister was still with Flamel and the others. He had to get her away from them. A sudden thought struck him. "What about the army of monsters on Alcatraz?"

"There are beasts on the island, that is true. But Alcatraz is, as it has always been, a prison, Josh. When someone like me comes across a monster on this earth, we capture it and imprison it on the island. That is why Perenelle—who is as monstrous as any beast—was there."

Clarent was now pointing toward the floor, and the gold had gone from most of Josh's hands. Only his fingertips remained metallic and bloodred where they touched the stone.

"Why did you call me?"

"First to get you away from the Alchemyst and the Sorceress's influence so you could think for yourself and make your own decisions. And second, to make you an offer." Dee laid the Codex on the table and crossed the room to slump on a couch. Still holding Clarent, Josh followed and sat

347

directly opposite him. Virginia moved around to stand in the shadows behind Dee.

"You are Gold, Josh. Pure Gold. There have been perhaps a dozen people in the history of the world to have a pure gold aura: Tutankhamen, Moctezuma, Askia, Osei Tutu, Midas, Jason and even the creator of the Codex, Abraham himself. In less than a week, you have been Awakened and trained in Water and Fire." Dee shook his head. "That is astonishing. But you need to make a decision now. You need to know which side you are fighting for."

Josh placed the sword on the floor and buried his head in his hands. "I don't know what to think," he said, confused and miserable. "I just don't know. When I'm talking to Flamel . . . he makes it sound as if you're the villain . . . and yet, when I'm talking to you, you sound so reasonable. I think I sort of believe you. Not completely, though," he added quickly.

"I understand," Dee said gently. "Truly, I do." He paused and then leaned forward, elbows on his knees. "There is something I can do for you, a gift I can give you that will allow you to discern the truth for yourself."

Josh looked up, frowning, suddenly remembering. "When I got here—you said something about being able to teach me one of the most powerful of all the magics, something that not even Nicholas could teach me." He stopped, cautious about continuing. "Or did I dream that?"

"No, you did not dream it." Dee stood and dusted off his hands. "There is one art that the legendary Alchemyst never learned."

Josh stood. "Why not?" he asked.

"Because your friend Nicholas is neither as powerful nor as clever as he likes to appear." Dee's eyes sparkled. "Josh, I can give you the power to raise the dead, to talk to them, to command them."

Josh blinked. "The dead . . . ," he began, not quite sure how he felt about that. It didn't sound like a particularly powerful gift.

"Think about it." Dee grabbed Josh's arms, and threads of his yellow aura coiled like tiny serpents around the boy's wrists. "You will be able to question any dead people, from any age, about the Flamels. Ask them whatever you wish— and they can only tell you the truth. While you animate them, you are their master and they must obey you. Find people who knew the Flamels—who knew me, even—and question them. You will be able to determine the truth for yourself. *Then* decide whom you want to fight for."

The possibilities shocked Josh into silence. Finally, incredulously, he asked, "Anyone?"

"Anyone." Dee nodded. "All you need is the smallest fragment of bone."

"Or a piece of clothing or jewelry," Virginia Dare said quietly from the shadows. "Or a sword they carried," she added, indicating the sword lying at his feet.

"Is that how you raised the creatures in Ojai?" Josh asked Dee.

"Yes."

"You animated animals. Could I bring back dinosaurs?"

"Yes. Anything dead you can bring back to life. It is an awesome power," Dee said. "Do you want to learn it?"

"Yes," Josh said eagerly, "what do I have to do?"

"Well, first you can help me push this furniture out of the way. Apparently Miss Dare does not move furniture."

Josh helped Dee shove a heavy sofa up against the wall. "What's this magic called, and why are we clearing the floor?"

"I am going to make you a necromancer, Josh." Dee smiled. "Normally, it would take decades to train you, but there is someone who can grant you this gift instantaneously. All you have to do is summon her." He indicated the cleared floor. "She's traveling through a distant Shadowrealm, but we can call her back here."

"An Elder?"

"Better than an Elder: an Archon. We are going to call Coatlicue, the Mother of All the Gods."

350

CHAPTER FIFTY-NINE

"*Coatlicue!* What madness is this?" Prometheus cried. He pulled his hand away from the pulsing red skull and pressed it close to his chest. The skin was pale and wrinkled, veins and bones prominent.

Nicholas was ashen-faced. "What is Dee doing? Coatlicue cannot train Josh in necromancy."

"Coatlicue hates the Elders," Prometheus whispered. "In ages past she gathered an army of Archons and their creations and rampaged through the Shadowrealms, destroying all in her path. She cannot be killed, so she was banished to the most distant and inhospitable Shadowrealm ever created— little more than a flat disc of rock. She has been there for tens of millennia."

"Dee is no fool," Nicholas said. "He knows he cannot bring Coatlicue into this world. He would not be able to control her."

"I don't think he intends to loose Coatlicue on the earth," Perenelle said quietly, looking at Prometheus. "You told us Dee had been declared *utlaga*. I think Dee has declared war on the Dark Elders," she whispered. "He's going to set her on *them:* if they are fighting her, they will have no time for him."

"But this Archon, she is like no other," Prometheus said. He tapped the crystal skull. "I have seen the records of the battles she fought with the Great Elders." He tried to laugh, but it came out as a croak. "If Dee calls her and manages to bring her through to this world, she will be ravenously hungry. She will eat him."

"Of course!" Flamel whispered urgently. "That's why he'll not call the Archon himself. He'll get Josh to do it!"

Prometheus turned to the Alchemyst, mouth set in a grim line. "No, Dee wouldn't . . ."

Nicholas Flamel nodded, and huge ice-white tears welled up in Perenelle's eyes. "Yes, he would. He's going to sacrifice the boy to the Mother of All the Gods."

CHAPTER SIXTY

*N*iten fit a Bluetooth earpiece into his left ear and pressed a button. "Yes." He listened intently while Aoife watched him closely. In the backseat, Sophie stirred.

"We're stuck in morning traffic," Niten said quietly. He looked out the window. "Route 101 isn't moving. I'd say we could be at least an hour away from our destination. Maybe ninety minutes. It depends what traffic is like over the bridge."

Sophie stretched and leaned forward over the front seat. She looked at Aoife, who mouthed, *Flamel, I think.*

"That's not good . . . ," Niten said into the tiny microphone. "Not good at all."

Sophie and Aoife looked at one another. The immortal's tone was grim.

"Do you have any control over the boy? Any influence at

all?" He listened, nodding. "I'll tell her," he said finally, and hung up.

Aoife and Sophie sat in silence, waiting for the immortal to gather his thoughts, and when he finally spoke, it was in the formal language of his youth. "There is no easy way to say this, and I would be doing you a disservice if I tried to disguise the seriousness of the situation: the English Magician intends to sacrifice Josh to an Archon. Nicholas, Perenelle and Prometheus are using the skull to see through Josh's eyes. They can hear everything he hears, but they have no way of warning him . . . and even if they could, they are not sure he would believe them. Dee has been working on him, poisoning his mind. And the Magician can be very persuasive. Apparently, he has told Josh that an Archon called Coatlicue will make him a necromancer."

"Coatlicue," Sophie breathed. The name brought on a flood of the Witch's memories.

And they were terrifying.

"Coatlicue!" The girl felt as if she had been struck in the chest. For a moment she couldn't breathe; black spots danced before her eyes. She pressed both hands to her mouth to prevent herself from screaming.

"Who is this Archon?" Niten asked. He looked to Aoife for an answer.

But the warrior shook her head. "I've heard the name, but only vaguely. It's long before my time. I think there was a war and she was banished. . . ."

"She is called the Mother of All the Gods," Sophie said, her voice shaking. "She was an Archon scientist and a great beauty. But she experimented on herself and her experiments turned her hideous and insane. Now she's like a ravenous beast." Sophie turned to look at Aoife. "Out of her own DNA she created the original blood drinkers who eventually became your race. Coatlicue was the first vampire."

CHAPTER SIXTY-ONE

"Did I ever tell you," Billy the Kid began, "that I was afraid of nothing?"

"No, I don't believe you did," Machiavelli said tiredly. He didn't think he'd ever met anyone who talked as much as the American immortal.

"Good. Because that would have been a lie, and I really don't like to lie." The American pointed with his chin at the creature standing outside the building with the American eagle and the words *Administration Building* over the doors. "There's no shame in admitting that I'm afraid of this . . . *thing*. What is it?"

"It is a sphinx," Machiavelli said quietly. "Body of a lion, wings of an eagle, head of a beautiful young woman. And try not to irritate her, Billy. This creature would have you for a snack."

"She is one ugly lion. . . ."

"Billy," Machiavelli began.

"And she's got mangy wings. . . ."

"Billy!"

"And she stinks like she's just stepped in something."

"I also have excellent hearing," the sphinx said. Her tiny female head moved from Billy to Machiavelli and then back to Billy again. A forked black tongue flickered between her thin lips, dancing in the air between them. The American immortal's eyes crossed, trying to focus on it.

"And your breath smells," Billy muttered.

The creature's long flat pupils dilated. "Once you've done what you came to do, immortal, you should not linger here," she rasped.

"Why not?" Billy asked defiantly.

"I'm hungry," the sphinx whispered, tongue flickering.

"Shall we begin?" Machiavelli said quickly, before Billy could reply. Reaching under his coat, he pulled out a single sheet of paper and waved it in the air. "I've got my instructions here."

The creature's small head turned to Machiavelli and then looked back at Billy again. "Are you sure you need this one?" The tongue flickered through the American's greasy hair. "Tasty."

"Yes," Machiavelli said. "I need him."

"And afterward? Maybe you could leave him for me," she suggested in a wheedling tone. "A little treat."

"I'll see," Machiavelli said. Billy opened his mouth, but Machiavelli dropped his hand onto the back of his neck and squeezed hard, and whatever the American had been about

357

to say came out as a strangled squawk. "Come now," Machiavelli continued. "Take us to the cells. My instructions are to start with the amphibious creatures. I have to remove the sleeping spell and release them into the bay. Nereus and his daughters will guide them toward the city. Once they reach San Francisco and move into the streets, Quetzalcoatl's agents will hijack one of the tourist boats and bring it over here. We'll load up the rest of the creatures and sail them back to the mainland."

"Will this take long?" the sphinx asked.

"Why, you in a hurry to go somewhere?" Billy asked.

The creature's mouth opened to reveal a maw of needle-sharp teeth. "I've not had breakfast yet." The sphinx looked at Machiavelli. "Arrogance always tastes sweet, like chicken. If you will not give him to me, then let me buy him from you. I will give you a fortune for this humani."

"How much of a fortune?" Machiavelli asked with a smile.

"Hey!" Billy said indignantly.

"How much do you want?" the sphinx asked seriously.

"I'm not for sale!" Billy snapped.

"We'll talk about it later," Machiavelli said to the sphinx. "We must hurry; time is moving on. Our masters want these creatures loose in the city by noon."

The sphinx turned and padded away. "Go through these doors. I will meet you downstairs," she said, and then Billy realized that the creature was too big to fit through the double doors. Her head turned at an unnatural angle and she flicked her long black tongue at Billy. He stuck out his tongue in return. "Like chicken . . ." She padded away, claws clicking on the stones.

"That wasn't funny," Billy hissed to the Italian. "You know these Elders and Next Generation have no sense of humor. She thought you were serious."

"How do you know I wasn't?" the Italian asked.

"I knew you were going to say that," Billy said. He watched as Machiavelli stopped in the doorway and turned to look at the city across the bay. "Having second thoughts?" he asked.

Machiavelli shook his head. "Just taking a last look." He turned to Billy. "Once we do this, nothing will ever be the same again. We will be outlaws."

Billy the Kid grinned. "I've been an outlaw all my life. It's not so bad."

CHAPTER SIXTY-TWO

"*C*oatlicue . . ."

The word rippled through the spaces between the Shadow-realms.

"Coatlicue . . ."

The word vibrated and trembled, pulsed and throbbed.

"Coatlicue . . ."

A single voice, calling, calling, calling.

All she had left were dreams.
Dreams of a golden age.
Dreams of a golden time.
Of a time when she was beautiful.
Of a time when she was young.
Of a time when she ruled the world.
And now those dreams were disturbed.

"Coatlicue . . ."

Josh Newman took a deep breath and focused on the four swords, which Dee had arranged in a square on the floor. They were each glowing softly, steaming red and white, green and brown smoke into the air.

"Coatlicue . . ."

"All you have to do is to call her," Dee had said. "There is a magic in names, a power in them. She will hear you and she will come. The unique combination of the swords and your powerful aura will draw her here."

"And she will teach me necromancy?" Josh asked.

"Yes," Dee had said, and for a single instant, Josh had thought he'd heard Nicholas and Perenelle screaming *"No!"* Then he realized that that was what they probably would say. If he could learn necromancy, he would be able to find out the truth about the Flamels and the Elders and more, much, much more. He'd be able to talk to all the great men and women of history, ask them questions, discover their secrets, find out where they had hidden their treasures. He could resurrect dinosaurs from single bones, even—and the thought was shocking—re-create primitive men so that his parents could study them firsthand. And somewhere, at the back of his mind, he wondered why, if Dee was a necromancer, he had not used the power in the same way. Just what had the Magician used necromancy for?

"Coatlicue . . ." Josh focused on the swords. Clarent was at the bottom of the square, the blade pointing to the left. Durendal was on the left-hand side, its blade pointing up; Ex-calibur was on top, its blade pointing right, toward Joyeuse, whose blade was pointing down. The stone swords were trailing fire into the air, and the colors had started to weave and entwine in the middle of the square.

She slept.

And her sleep lasted eons.

She dreamt.

And her dreams lasted centuries.

But the nightmares lasted millennia.

And in this place without light, without sound, without sensation, she did not know whether she woke or slept. She simply existed.

Red. A spot of color.

But in this foul prison, there was no light.

Another speck: white. Tiny, distant.

The Elders had bound her in utter darkness. There had never been light. Until now.

A third spot: brown.

And now a fourth light, and it was green.

She turned toward the lights.

The smoke from the blades wavered, twisted, as if blown by a breeze.

Virginia's fingers bit deeply into Dee's arm. "Something's happening."

"When she comes we'll have to be quick," the Magician said. "As soon as she appears in the square, we shove the boy in with her. So long as the square is not broken, she'll be trapped within."

"And if it is broken?" Virginia asked.

"That would not be good," he said.

"Is she not hideous?"

"In the Nahuatl language, she is called the One with the Skirts of Serpents."

"Nice!" Virginia said. "How's he going to react to that?"

"When I touched him a moment ago, I implanted a simple spell. He will see only a beautiful young woman. I'm not sure how long the spell will last, but even if he hesitates, I want you to push him in with her. Once she feeds, we'll be able to deal with her."

"And if she refuses?" Virginia asked quietly.

"You lull her to sleep with your flute and we send her back to her prison," he said calmly.

"You've thought of everything, haven't you, Doctor?" she asked sarcastically.

"Yes."

Vague, frightening thoughts had started to crowd at the back of Josh's head. Images of a snake-headed monster wearing a skirt of writhing serpents, leading a monstrous army across the muddy battlefield.

And facing her: the figure of a hooded man who had a hook in place of his left hand, and alongside him, a red-haired pale-skinned female warrior.

"Coat—" he began, but his voice faltered.

Dee stepped forward out of the shadows. "Josh, is everything all right?"

"I'm . . . I'm not sure," he said, pressing his hand to his

forehead. "I suddenly have a splitting headache. This Coatlicue . . ." He licked his lips. "What is she like?"

"When she was an Archon, she was considered extraordinarily beautiful," Dee said carefully. "Why do you ask?"

"I keep thinking about snakes, and I hate snakes, I really do." Josh pressed both hands to his throbbing head and squeezed his eyes shut. He'd never experienced agony like it before. It felt as if his head were about to explode. Was this a migraine? Even doing something as simple as moving his eyes sent daggers of pain into his skull.

"How bad is the headache?" Dee asked, glancing at Virginia. "Have you any painkillers?"

"I am an Awakened immortal, don't be ridiculous," she said with a roll of her eyes. "I'll wager that headache is not natural."

"Migraine," Josh whispered. "I'll have to stop. Can you take over?" he gasped.

"Coatlicue will only deal with whoever calls her," Dee muttered. He put his hand under Josh's chin and tilted it up so that he could look into the boy's eyes. "You can trust me. I am a doctor." The boy's eye color had started to change, the red beginning to fade, traces of white and the original blue returning. "Do you suffer from migraines normally?"

"No. Never had one before in my life. Aunt Agnes gets them all the time. But these aren't normal times, are they?" Josh said through gritted teeth. His stomach had started to turn and he thought he might throw up.

"No, they're certainly not," Dee said very softly, looking deep into Josh's eyes. . . .

364

✧　✧　✧

Seventy miles away, in Point Reyes, Nicholas and Perenelle reared back as Dee looked directly at them.

Prometheus had pressed both hands onto the crystal skull, which was now pulsing like a giant beating heart. The Elder's eyes were squeezed tightly shut; his lips moved, and they heard him whisper in a dozen languages, "I can see wonders . . . and horrors . . . wonders and horrors."

Nicholas and Perenelle looked at Dee and watched his lips move. Half a second later, they heard him speak as if he were standing in the same room.

"Josh," Dee said. "I think I have a cure for your headache. Say goodbye, Nicholas; goodbye, Perenelle," he directed.

The Alchemyst and the Sorceress heard Josh numbly repeat the words. "Goodbye, Nicholas; goodbye, Perenelle."

And abruptly the image vanished.

The skull went black and Prometheus shuddered and slid off his chair to lie in a heap on the floor. Perenelle looked at her husband. They were both haggard and exhausted. "What happened?"

"Dee knew we were watching. He must have thrown up a Warding spell. Josh is on his own now. Let's hope he can hold out until the others get there."

CHAPTER SIXTY-THREE

A uniformed guard came to the door and looked at the odd trio standing outside. A slender, impeccably dressed Japanese man in a black suit, a red-haired woman, also in a tailored black suit, and a wild-haired teenager. Behind them, an antique Volkswagen van was haphazardly parked at the curb.

The blond teenager had her finger on the intercom, and the incessant chiming was starting to get on the guard's nerves. He jabbed a stubby finger at the sign pasted to the door.

NO ADMITTANCE WITHOUT APPOINTMENT.

The girl took her finger off the bell and rummaged through her pockets. She produced a tube of lip balm and wrote in greasy letters across the glass:

YCNEGREME

The guard shook his head, turned his back and stepped over to his desk in the foyer of Enoch Enterprises. Tourists. Every day, people knocked on the door, looking for directions, wondering if they could get onto the roof to take photos. No one got in. Ever.

Before he was able to sit, however, a blast of heat seared all the small hairs on the back of his neck, and he caught the fleeting impression of the heavy door sailing across the lobby and smashing into the wall before something struck him at the base of the skull and the world turned black.

"You could have just opened the door," Aoife suggested, looking at the smoldering ruin of metal and glass. "Or even melted the lock."

Sophie shook her hands to cool them. "Sometimes I don't know my own strength."

Niten shrugged out of his black suit coat and strapped two swords, a katana and the shorter wakizashi, around his waist, so that they hung over his left hip.

Aoife settled two matched short swords over her shoulders on her back, and a pair of nunchaku dangled from each hand. She wore her broad-bladed knife strapped to her leg.

And Sophie uncoiled the silver and black leather whip Perenelle had given her before they had left Prometheus's Shadowrealm. "This is woven from snakes pulled from the Medusa's hair," the Sorceress had explained. "It will slice through stone and cut metal. Be careful with it."

Two guards raced into the foyer, drawn by the noise, and stopped abruptly at the sight of the ruined door and their colleague lying in a crumpled heap on the floor. One went for his weapon, the other for his radio . . . and a heartbeat later they were both unconscious on the floor as well. Aoife rubbed her hands together as she slipped her nunchaku back into her belt. "This could be fun."

There was an explosion of sparks as Niten drove his short sword through the computer server and the cables in the small office behind the front desk. "Phones and Internet are down," he announced.

Aoife laughed delightedly. "Good. We've got a few minutes before someone notices the door is missing and calls the police. Let's find your brother."

"If he's still here," Niten said quietly.

"Oh, he's here," Sophie said. She pressed her hand to her stomach. "I can feel him. He's . . ." She jabbed her finger upward. "Upstairs."

The smoke rising off the Swords of Power had turned foul, mixing into a dark miasma that hung in the air.

"Coatlicue is coming," Dee said quietly, standing behind Josh. "Stay focused. Stay strong. You have been Awakened. You have learned the Magic of Water and the Magic of Fire. But these are not entirely practical magics. Soon you will know the rarest magic of all, the dark art of necromancy—and then there is nothing you cannot achieve. You will learn wonders. I did."

The column of filthy smoke almost reached the ceiling. It was the color of mud streaked with rusty red. A rancid smell seeped into the room: the distinctive stink of serpents.

"Coatlicue . . ."

Josh tried to concentrate, but the serpent odor sickened him and the images of the snake-headed creature had returned. He wasn't sure where the images were coming from—from the Flamels, maybe? Were they trying to distract him? They knew he was terrified of snakes. Dee had told him that Nicholas and Perenelle had caused his migraine and had probably been trying to control his thoughts. The doctor had protected him with what he called a Warding spell, and the moment he'd activated it, all traces of the terrible headache and the stomach-churning nausea had vanished, so he'd obviously been right about the Flamels attacking Josh. But what Josh didn't understand was *why*? The only reason he could come up with was that they didn't want him to become a necromancer, and he was beginning to suspect that it was because they were afraid of what he might discover—about them, about the Elders.

Light.
And heat.
And flesh.
The mouthwatering scent of life.
The tingle of a powerful aura.
Calling to her. Calling, calling, calling.
Running and falling, crawling and walking, on limbs that had not been used in millennia, Coatlicue moved toward the light, toward freedom.

369

"Coatlicue . . . ," Josh rasped, his voice hoarse.

The smoke from the blades on the floor before him had solidified into a thick brown sheet. He thought he saw something move behind it.

He was still trying to work out what he'd do with the Magic of Necromancy . . . but wait, hadn't Dee called it an art rather than a magic? What was the difference? And were there rules to necromancy? It had to be fueled by his aura, which meant that it probably followed some of the basic rules of the magics he'd already learned. So he'd have to choose very carefully before he decided to bring someone back from the dead. And how long could he keep them alive? Was there a time limit . . . ?

"Coatlicue . . ."

Josh squinted. There was a definite shape moving behind the gauzy smoke.

He'd bring back Leonardo da Vinci, who was supposed to be buried in Amboise, France. And he'd love to talk to Mark Twain and Einstein and . . .

The brown smoke rippled; then two hands appeared and pulled it apart like a curtain.

Coatlicue emerged.

And she was beautiful.

"Where is he?" Sophie screamed, frustration and panic churning inside her.

They had fought their way up the stairs. There were no staff in the offices, only a scattering of uniformed guards, and they fell quickly to Aoife's nunchaku and Niten's lightning-fast fists and feet.

"We're on the top floor," Niten announced as he drove a foot through the plate-glass door. The lock snapped and he stepped into what was obviously Dee's private office. He moved swiftly around the room, checking the small side corridors. "Nothing. A bathroom, a kitchen, a small private elevator. No sign that Josh has even been here."

Aoife spun around to look at Sophie. "You said he was here. You felt him."

The girl nodded. Her head was starting to thump with a sick headache.

"You said he was upstairs. *Think*. Where is he now?"

Sophie breathed deeply and concentrated on her brother. Then she frowned in confusion. "Downstairs."

With Niten in the lead, they raced down the stairs, leaping over the bodies of the unconscious guards. "Twelfth floor," the Japanese immortal called. Standing in the middle of the stairwell, Aoife turned to Sophie. "Where is he now?"

Sophie visualized her brother's face . . . and then blinked. She raised a tentative finger and pointed to the ceiling. "But that can't be right. It feels like he's upstairs now."

Niten grinned and looked at Aoife. "Secret floor," they said in unison.

CHAPTER SIXTY-FOUR

*J*osh stared at Coatlicue. She was the most elegant and beautiful creature he had ever seen in his life. She was tall—seven, maybe eight feet—and looked like she'd stepped out of a painting on the wall of an Egyptian tomb. Jet-black hair cut in a straight line across her forehead hung in a silky curtain to her shoulders, and her eyes were outlined in kohl. Her skin was copper and her eyes were a deep lustrous brown. She was wearing a simple white robe and was barefoot. When she looked down at Josh, she smiled warmly, and although her lips did not move, Josh clearly heard her voice in his head. *You called me and I came. I am Coatlicue. . . .* When she stretched out her hand, he noticed that her fingernails had been painted in a snakeskin pattern.

Without even thinking, Josh took a step toward the creature and raised his right hand.

A solid sheet of flame blossomed in front of Josh, crisping his hair, searing his eyebrows and sending him staggering back. He shouted as he slipped and fell to the floor, voice high-pitched with terror, and he heard Dee roar and Virginia scream. He rolled over, and through the dancing flames he saw his sister standing at an open door on the opposite side of the room, fire still curling off her fingers.

"Sis?" Confused, disoriented, he climbed to his feet and then grunted as someone hit him from behind, sending him staggering forward, into the flame, toward Coatlicue. He threw up his hand to protect himself from the fire—and the flame instantly winked out, and he fell on his hands and knees at Coatlicue's bare feet.

"Josh!" Sophie screamed.

Your name is Josh? Take my hand, Josh.

Immediately, Josh slipped his hand into Coatlicue's.

Sophie watched in horror as Josh stepped toward the creature trapped within the square of swords. Coatlicue had a body that was vaguely female, but with the claws of a crocodile and two serpents' heads coiling from a thick neck. A long robe composed entirely of writhing snakes covered her body. Dee's companion, the woman who had to be Virginia Dare, stood behind Josh and shoved him forward—toward the fire and into the sword square on the floor.

Instinctively, Sophie uncurled Perenelle's whip and lashed out with it. It keened through the air and laid open a long stripe across Coatlicue's back. One hissing snake head darted toward Sophie and spat a shower of white liquid at her. It fell short, bubbling and burning into the floor, giving her an inkling of what it could do to her skin.

Niten drew both swords and leapt toward Dee. A blade of smoking sulfurous yellow appeared in the Magician's hand and struck at the Japanese immortal. Niten easily countered the blows, sparks exploding where his metal swords clashed against Dee's burning blade. The Japanese immortal closed in on Dee, swords whirling, while the Magician desperately backpedaled, flailing wildly with the blazing longsword.

Sophie's silver armor bloomed around her body as she strode toward Coatlicue, whip cracking and whistling as she lashed the creature again and again. "Let my brother go!"

Aoife was darting toward Josh when Dare reared up in front of her, a wooden flute in one hand, a tomahawk in the other.

"You think that can hurt me?" The warrior sneered at the crude tomahawk.

"No, but this can," Dare said, and brought the flute to her lips and blew a single note. The warrior instantly dropped to the ground, writhing in agony, hands pressed to her ears. Virginia stood over Aoife and twirled the tomahawk loosely above her. "I've never killed one of the Next Generation before," she said lightly. "First time for everything, I suppose," she added, then raised the axe.

Josh watched in horror as his sister lashed out at the beautiful young woman with a long screaming whip. Coatlicue opened her mouth and shrieked, and the sound was heartbreaking. She turned her huge eyes on Josh and her fingers tugged him forward, toward the swords, toward her. *"Why?"* she moaned in pain.

Josh didn't know the answer. He shook his head. This was wrong, so, so wrong. Sophie shouldn't be whipping Coatlicue. He turned and watched Niten savagely attack Dee, his swords blurs of light as he slashed and cut, driving the Magician back against the wall. Only Virginia seemed to be holding her own. The red-haired warrior was lying at her feet. He grinned: maybe the great Aoife was not so great after all.

Josh turned to look at his sister. Her armor had fully formed around her, giving her an almost alien appearance, and she was lashing out mercilessly at the defenseless Archon.

"No!" he whispered, then shouted, "No!" He tried to raise his own armor, but he was drained from calling Coatlicue. "Stop," he croaked uselessly.

Sophie ignored him.

And then Josh's toe touched the stone blade at his feet and Clarent pulsed, throbbed, called to him. Of course! It would renew his aura, give him the strength he needed to protect Coatlicue. Kneeling, Josh closed his hand around the hilt of the warm stone sword.

From the corner of his eye, Dee saw Josh stoop and reach for the sword and his heart stopped. If the square was broken, then Coatlicue would be free . . . and all would be lost.

Niten, realizing that Dee was distracted, attacked again. Both swords hammered into Dee's chest. And shattered. Niten blinked in surprise. "You forget who I am," the Magician snarled. He wrapped a burning fist in Niten's shirt, lifted him high and flung him across the room. The immortal hit a leather sofa and bounced off.

Sophie saw Dare raise the tomahawk over the fallen Aoife and sent a curl of leather whip at Dee's cohort. It seared Dare's flesh as it wrapped around the weapon, jerking it out of her hand.

Virginia snarled in rage, a cry that was cut short as Aoife's hand shot up and clutched her throat.

And Josh lifted Clarent off the floor and broke the square.

The wash of energy picked the boy up off the ground, jerked him free of Coatlicue's grip and flung him back against Dee, slamming them both against the wall. It ripped Virginia from Aoife's grasp, sending the immortal tumbling over and over across the floor. It buffeted Sophie to the ground, stripping away her armor, completely draining her aura in an instant.

With a hiss of triumph, Coatlicue stepped into the world.

"Oh, but I have waited a long time for this. A new world to conquer. Fresh meat. Fresh blood." The twin snake heads turned, fixed on Sophie. "You first. Your little toy stung me." All the snakes in her dress raised their tiny heads, and thousands of forked tongues flickered, tasting the air. "A silver aura. It will be an appetizer before I devour the gold." Coatlicue took a step toward Sophie.

And staggered.

And stopped.

"I don't think so," Aoife said very quietly. She had leapt up onto the Archon's back and wrapped her arms around the two snake heads. Coatlicue struggled, trying to pry Aoife's fingers free, but the warrior's grip tightened. All the snakes in the Archon's dress struck out at Aoife, biting her again and again and the warrior grimaced in pain. "Let's see who dies first," she said, mouth opening to reveal her savage teeth. "You created my race. We are from your DNA. So you know how strong the Clan Vampire are." She jerked the Archon back, away from Sophie, jerked her again, pulling her toward the three swords and the ragged smoking curtain. Then her bright green eyes locked on Sophie's face. "You saved my life."

Sophie staggered to her feet. "Aoife?"

"Aoife. One of the Next Generation. It seems I will devour *you* first. You are weakening." Coatlicue's voice was triumphant. More and more of the serpents bit into the warrior, and her skin was wet with their pale venom.

Sophie realized what was happening and lifted the whip, but she didn't dare crack it toward Coatlicue in case she hit the warrior. "Aoife, let her go, step away from her. . . ."

The warrior jerked the Archon again, pulling her back, and the creature's claws left deep scratches in the floor.

Sophie saw an opening and lashed out at Coatlicue, but her arms were leaden with exhaustion and the whip only scratched the Archon's foot.

Coatlicue lifted her foot and Aoife took the opportunity to pull her back once more. Off balance, Coatlicue staggered and fell, but the warrior never released her hold on the two snapping snake heads. The snakes went into a frenzy of biting and spitting. Aoife's eyes locked on Sophie's. "When you find my twin," she whispered, "tell her . . . tell Scathach that I did this . . . for her." And then, with a final massive effort, Aoife hauled Coatlicue back into the broken square of swords and through the torn curtain of dirty smoke.

The curtain winked out of existence in a detonation that shattered every piece of glass in the building. The hanging television sets crashed to the floor; pipes burst, spraying water into the room; and a huge crack ran up one wall, raced across the ceiling and brought part of the floor above thundering down into the room. A dozen fires started as broken wires rained sparks everywhere.

Shocked and numb, deaf and unable to move, Sophie Newman watched as Dee clambered to his feet. She saw him haul Virginia Dare from the floor, then pick up Josh.

Josh stood and stared at her . . . but all she could see were his bloodred eyes . . . and the look of absolute loathing on his pale face.

Dee darted forward to gather the three swords. He tossed Josh a second sword and picked his way across the devastated floor to lift the Codex off the table.

Sophie tried to say her brother's name, but her mouth was full of grit and she couldn't shape the word. And when she stretched out her hand to him, he slowly and deliberately turned his back on her and followed John Dee and Virginia Dare out of the burning building.

He did not look back.

CHAPTER SIXTY-FIVE

"It's a henge," William Shakespeare said, looking at two tall standing stones topped with a massive slab. "Just like Stonehenge."

"I modeled it on Stonehenge," Marethyu agreed. "Every Shadowrealm is connected to another by at least one gate. Some have two, and the bigger realms, the huge planet-sized worlds, have multiple gates. When I created this world, I needed just two gates. One to connect to the leygate in Paris—"

"So you knew we were going to use that gate?" Scathach interrupted.

"I knew."

"One day you're going to tell me how you knew that," Scathach said seriously.

"Maybe I will. One day."

"This is the second gate?" Joan asked, looking at the standing stones. "Where does it lead?"

"To the Crossroads of the Shadowrealms," Marethyu said, then stepped between the two uprights . . . and vanished.

"I hate leygates," Scatty muttered. "Just let me make sure there are no nasty surprises waiting for us on the other side." Drawing her swords, she darted through. A second later, her slightly green-looking disembodied face appeared in midair. "All clear."

Shakespeare went next, followed by Joan and Saint-Germain, hand in hand. Palamedes was the last to step from the Pleistocene Shadowrealm. He turned to look back and realized that the world was beginning to fade and die. Colors were leaching away, paling to grays, and the edge of the horizon was drifting off into a fine sparkling dust. As he watched, it swirled away into the cloudless sky and then the sky itself dissolved into utter darkness. One by one, the moons winked out. Palamedes shivered. The world and all it contained—all the extraordinary flora and diverse fauna—was dying because the hook-handed man had no further use for it. This realm had been created for one purpose, and one purpose only: to ensnare—or was it to save?—Scathach and Joan. Marethyu must have known that Saint-Germain would come after his wife. The big knight frowned: had he also known that Palamedes and Will would come after their friend? Marethyu said he was from the past . . . how, then, did he know so much about the future?

Who was the hook-handed man?

The Saracen Knight leapt through the henge in the last moments before the gates themselves dissolved to dust.

The hook-handed man waited until Palamedes had appeared. "Glad you could join us," he said. "I was hoping you would not linger too long." Then he turned to the small group and lifted his left arm. The hook glowed with warm golden light, partially illuminating the massive cave. "Welcome to Xibalba," Marethyu said. "Thankfully, there is no time for sightseeing. We need to get out of here right now," he added, and set off at a run. "Our body heat and auras will attract some spectacularly foul guardians. Follow in my footsteps. And do not, whatever you do, step off the path."

"I hate this place," Scathach grumbled, holding her nose shut in an attempt to block out the stink of sulfur.

"You've been here before?" Marethyu asked, surprised.

"So you don't know everything," she said with a quick grin.

"Not everything," he said. "I just know enough."

"Where are we going?" Saint-Germain called.

"I'm going to take you through a series of gates . . . ," Marethyu said.

"Not more leygates," Scathach groaned.

"I am afraid so. Though these are not your normal leygates. I did a favor for Chronos, and in return he sequenced these gates for me. But you will all have to stick close behind me. We're going into Shadowrealms which each have thirteen gates—we must go through the correct ones in the proper order."

"Otherwise . . . ?" Will demanded.

Marethyu shook his head. "Trust me: you do not want to know."

"I do, actually," the Bard muttered.

They raced along a narrow path that snaked across an enormous pool of black-crusted lava. Bubbles gathered and burst on the surface, sometimes spitting firework-like streamers of liquid rock high into the air. Occasionally, the ribbons would fly high enough to touch the ceiling far above, and then the molten threads would stick and dangle for a moment, swaying, before crashing to the ground below like fiery hailstones.

"This way!" Marethyu shouted, pointing to the narrowest of nine openings in the huge circular cave. "These are the Nine Gates to the Shadowrealms. From here, you can travel throughout the myriad realms." Although all the gates were decorated with archaic glyphs, Shakespeare noticed that the designs over the gate they were running toward looked older, cruder than the rest. "The zero gate," Marethyu said before he plunged through.

They followed him . . .

Into a crystal world, where even the sun was glass, and the ground was made of shards of broken crystal. Thirteen translucent gates stood on a mirrored lake.

"Through the first gate," Marethyu said, pointing to a delicate tracery of spun glass. They raced through . . .

Into a realm of green sand that rippled and shifted in hypnotic patterns. A giant red sun dominated the sky, close enough that they could see the flares curling off it. The solar flares matched the pattern in the sands. Here the thirteen gates were shaped from sparkling silica.

"Again, the first gate," Marethyu said, darting between two squat pillars.

And now the world was ice and stank of sour milk, and the thirteen gates were like curdled cream.

"Through the second gate . . ."

Into a world of metal, where the ground was steel and the sky the color of lead, and the thirteen gates were slabs of rusty iron.

"The third gate . . ."

A world of noxious yellow fog filled with what sounded like the piteous crying of babies. The thirteen gates were amorphous shifting pillars of smoke, barely distinguishable from the fog.

"The fifth gate . . ."

Into a world of black oil and sticky tar, where metallic insects ate the oil and the thirteen gates were intricately carved from single blocks of coal.

"The eighth gate . . ."

A world devastated by a cataclysm, an empty shell of a city, and rain that tasted of ashes. A building that might once have been a hotel had thirteen gaping doorways.

Marethyu pointed. "The final gate, the thirteenth . . ."

They came out onto a gently sloping hillside covered in tiny yellow and white flowers. The sky overhead was the palest blue, streaked with white clouds, and the air was warm and tasted of salt.

They all breathed deeply, clearing their lungs of the noxious odors and tastes of the Shadowrealms. Marethyu walked up the side of the hill and stopped at the top, looking into the distance. One by one, the immortals climbed the hill to stand beside him.

They were looking down over an island paradise.

Below them, as far as the eye could see, spread a golden city. From this great height it looked like a maze, sparkling blue waterways encircling and weaving through the city. Countless multicolored flags and pennants waved over the buildings, and the sound of music and laughter drifted faintly on the perfumed air.

Dominating the center of the island was a huge stepped pyramid. The top of the pyramid was flat and filled with hundreds of flagpoles, and the tiny dots moving up and down its sides gave some indication of its incredible size.

"You are looking at the legendary Pyramid of the Sun," Marethyu said, pointing with his hook. "Welcome to the Isle of Danu Talis."

CHAPTER SIXTY-SIX

*P*rometheus folded the cell phone and looked at Nicholas and Perenelle. The Elder had visibly aged in the past hour. His red hair was streaked with white, and he looked tired and ill.

"That was Niten," he said very quietly, and the Flamels knew it was not good news. "Josh called Coatlicue. Sophie, Niten and Aoife arrived just as she stepped out from her Shadowrealm, but she was still trapped by some spell of Dee's. Josh accidentally released her into this world." His voice thickened, and the tears that rolled down his face were touched with white smoke. "Aoife sacrificed herself to drag Coatlicue back to her Shadowrealm prison. The warrior is gone. Gone forever."

"And the twins?" Perenelle breathed.

"Sophie is safe with Niten. But when the Magician and Dare fled, Josh left with them. He went by choice. We've lost him to the Dark Elders."

AUTHOR'S NOTE
ALCATRAZ

"I named this island Isla de los Alcatraces [Island of the Pelicans] because of their being so plentiful there."—Spanish lieutenant Juan Manuel de Ayala, 1775

The locations used in The Secrets of the Immortal Nicholas Flamel are all real. In the four books published so far, it is possible to trace the twins' journey across San Francisco to Mill Valley; through the streets of Paris; from St. Pancras Station in Euston Road, England, to Stonehenge; and from Sausalito to Point Reyes and back into the heart of the city of San Francisco. There is one place that has played an important role in all four books, one location around which the rest of the story revolves: Alcatraz.

The Rock is central to this series.

Although it was officially "discovered" and named by Juan Manuel de Ayala in 1775, the indigenous Ohlone or Costanoan Indians had been gathering eggs and fishing off the island for generations. There is no evidence that there was ever a permanent settlement there, though nearby Angel Island was inhabited.

In 1853, Alcatraz became home to the first lighthouse on the West Coast. Because fog often rendered the light ineffective, the lighthouse originally had a fog bell, which would have been rung by hand. One hundred and ten years later, in 1963, the light was automated. The Fog Bell House survives to this day; the light is still operational.

Nowadays we think of Alcatraz as a former federal prison, but there are records dating to around 1861 showing that it held Civil War prisoners. The first official jailhouse was built there in 1867. It was originally a military prison, but in the aftermath of the great earthquake in 1906, it temporarily housed inmates from the mainland. Alcatraz remained a military prison until 1933, when it became a federal prison. Most of the legends surrounding the Rock and its notorious inhabitants—including Al Capone, who was incarcerated there from 1932 to 1939—date from this time. Alcatraz was a federal prison for only thirty years, before it finally closed in 1963.

Six years later, a party of eighty Native Americans representing more than twenty different tribes landed on the abandoned and decaying island and attempted to reclaim it for the native peoples. In a political statement, the group, who called themselves Indians of All Tribes, offered to purchase the island from the American government for "$24 in glass beads and red cloth." The ironic offer was meant to convey the tribes' conviction that the island had been stolen from them. They wanted to take back what they saw as Indian land and to establish a Center for Native American Studies and a Great Indian Training School. The Native American occupation of Alcatraz lasted nineteen months, and while it ultimately failed and the occupiers were removed, it successfully drew attention to the plight of Native Americans across the United States. Graffiti evidence of this period can be found around the buildings on the island today, most noticeably on the wall behind the large sign on the dock. Around the official United States Penitentiary sign, the words *Indians Welcome* and *Indian Land* have been daubed in red paint.

In 1972, Alcatraz became part of the Golden Gate National Recreation Area, and every year more than a million people visit the island.

When I began to develop the idea that became the series The Secrets of the Immortal Nicholas Flamel, I needed a location that fulfilled several requirements. It had to be close to a major city and yet relatively inaccessible. It had to be big enough to hold a vast army of creatures, and, of course, it had to be firmly rooted in history. Over a number of years, I looked at abandoned mining towns in California, particularly Bodie; ghost towns in the Old West; deserted homesteads along the Boston Post Road; and some of the forts on the Sante Fe Trail. Each one offered interesting possibilities, but none was quite right.

Then, finally, eight or nine years ago, I visited Alcatraz. I knew, almost from the moment I stepped off the boat, that it was perfect. And that single decision shaped everything else. Choosing the island meant that the series had to be set in San Francisco, and from that flowed all the other West Coast locations. Not only did Alcatraz become a key location, it became almost another character in the series. Here was a tiny island—only twenty-two acres—that was also rich in history. Juan Manuel de Ayala became its "voice."

I have been back to Alcatraz countless times over the years, and every time, I discover something new. If you get a chance to visit the Rock, go at night: that's when you'll hear the whispers of the ghosts of Alcatraz. . . .

A special preview of

THE
WARLOCK

The Secrets of the Immortal
Nicholas Flamel

BOOK 5

WEDNESDAY, 6th June

CHAPTER ONE

The anpu appeared first, tall jackal-headed warriors with solid red eyes and saber-teeth, wearing highly polished black glass armor. They poured out of a smoking cave mouth and spread around Xibalba, some taking up positions in front of each of the nine gates that opened into the enormous cave, others sweeping through the primitive Shadowrealm, ensuring that it was empty. As always, they moved in complete silence; they were mute until the final moments before they charged into battle, and then their screams were terrifying.

Only when the anpu were satisfied that Xibalba was deserted did the couple appear.

Like the anpu, they were wearing glass and ceramic armor, though theirs was ornate rather than practical, and in a style that had last been seen in the Old Kingdom of ancient Egypt.

Minutes earlier, the couple had left an almost perfect facsimile of Danu Talis to travel across a dozen linked Shadowrealms, some remarkably similar to earth, some completely alien. And although the couple were both by nature intensely curious about the myriad worlds they ruled, they did not linger. They raced through a complex network of leygates that would lead them to the place known as the Crossroads.

There was so little time left.

Nine gates opened out into Xibalba, each one little more than a roughly carved opening in the black rock wall. Avoiding the bubbling pits of lava that spat sticky strings of molten rock across their path, the couple traversed the width of the Shadowrealm from the ninth gate to the third, the Gate of Tears. Even the anpu, which were by nature fearless, refused to approach this cave. Ancient memories rooted deep in their DNA warned them that this was the place where their race had almost been exterminated after they'd fled the world of the humani.

As the couple neared the circular cave mouth, the crude and blocky glyphs carved over the opening began to glow with a faint white light. It reflected off their mirrored armor, illuminating the interior of the cave, painting the couple in stark black and white and, in that instant—briefly—they were beautiful.

Without a backward glance, the couple stepped into the dark cave mouth . . .

. . . and less than a heartbeat later, a couple dressed identically in white jeans and T-shirts winked into existence on the circular stone known as Point Zero before Notre Dame Cathedral in Paris, France. The man took the woman's hand in his and together they set off at a brisk pace, picking their way through the debris of stones and broken statues that still littered the square where Sophie and Josh Newman had used Elemental Magic to defeat the cathedral's animated stone gargoyles.

And because this was Paris, no one looked twice at a couple wearing sunglasses at night.

Have you read them all?

BOOK 1 – THE ALCHEMYST

The truth: Nicholas Flamel was born in Paris on September 28, 1330. Nearly 700 years later, he is acknowledged as the greatest Alchemyst of his day. It is said that he discovered the secret of eternal life. The records show that he died in 1418. But his tomb is empty.

The legend: Nicholas Flamel lives. But only because he has been making the elixir of life for centuries. The secret of eternal life is hidden within the book he protects – the Book of Abraham the Mage. It's the most powerful book that has ever existed. In the wrong hands, it will destroy the world. That's exactly what Dr. John Dee plans to do when he steals it. Humankind won't know what's happening until it's too late. And if the prophecy is right, Sophie and Josh Newman are the only ones with the power to save the world as we know it.

BOOK 2 – THE MAGICIAN

In the second book in the *New York Times* bestselling series, Nicholas, Sophie, Josh and Scatty emerge in Paris, the City of Light, home to Nicholas Flamel. Only this homecoming is anything but sweet. Niccolò Machiavelli, immortal author and celebrated art collector, lives in Paris and is working for Dr. John Dee. He's in hot pursuit, and time is running out for Nicholas and Perenelle. Josh and Sophie Newman are the world's only hope . . . If they don't turn on each other first.

BOOK 3 – THE SORCERESS

Without the Codex, Nicholas Flamel has lost the means to create the Elixir of Life, which makes him immortal, and he grows weaker with each passing day. Perenelle is trapped in Alcatraz and Scatty has gone missing, leaving the group without protection. Josh and Sophie have fled to London with Nicholas, looking for help. The twins need to learn the Magic of Water. That means they need to find Gilgamesh the King and he is said to be quite, quite insane . . .

BOOK 5 – THE WARLOCK

Josh and Sophie Newman, the twins of prophecy, have been divided and the end is finally beginning. With most of their allies – Scatty, Joan of Arc, Saint-Germain, and others – all occupied elsewhere, Sophie is on her own with the ever-weakening Nicholas and Perenelle Flamel. She must find an immortal to teach her Earth Magic. The surprise is that she will find her teacher in the most ordinary of places . . .

BOOK 6 – THE ENCHANTRESS

The twins of prophecy have been split. Nicholas Flamel is near death. John Dee has the swords of power. And Danu Talis has yet to fall. The future of the human race lies in the balance – how will the legend end?

Acknowledgments

Once again I am indebted to all of those people who make this series happen. The list grows bigger with each book, but some names remain:

I will always be indebted to Beverly Horowitz and Krista Marino at Delacorte Press, who allow me the time and space and offer continued and indeed continuous support, as well as to Colleen Fellingham.

To Barry Krost and Richard Thompson, who attempt (usually successfully) to keep me on the straight and narrow.

To Sherrod Turner and Jim Di Bella, who provided the getaway.

To Jill Gascoine and Alfred Molina for the retreat and safe haven.

And to the many others who, in their various ways, made this book happen, especially Colette Freedman and Robert and Sharon Freedman. With sincere thanks to: Melanie Rose, Julie Blewett Grant, Michael Carroll, Patrick Kavanagh and Garth Nichols.

And, of course, to Claudette Sutherland.